NATE

BY
DELORES FOSSEN

MILLS & BOON

First published in Great Britain 2013
by Mills & Boon, an imprint of Harlequin (UK) Limited,
Eton House, 18-24 Paradise Road, Richmond, Surrey TW9 1SR

© Delores Fossen 2012

ISBN: 978 0 263 90344 7
ebook ISBN: 978 1 472 00692 9

46-0213

Printed and bound in Spain
by Blackprint CPI, Barcelona

Imagine a family tree that includes Texas cowboys, Choctaw and Cherokee Indians, a Louisiana pirate and a Scottish rebel who battled side by side with William Wallace. With ancestors like that, it's easy to understand why *USA TODAY* bestselling author and former air force captain **Delores Fossen** feels as if she were genetically predisposed to writing romances. Along the way to fulfilling her DNA destiny, Delores married an air force top gun who just happens to be of Viking descent. With all those romantic bases covered, she doesn't have to look too far for inspiration.

Chapter One

Lieutenant Nate Ryland took one look at the preschool building and knew something was wrong.

He eased his hand over his Glock. After ten years of being a San Antonio cop, it was an automatic response. But there was nothing rote or automatic about the iron-hard knot that tightened in his stomach.

"Kimmie," he said under his breath. His fifteen-month-old daughter, Kimberly Ellen, was inside.

The side door to the Silver Creek Preschool and Day Care was wide open. But not *just* open. It was dangling in place, the warm April breeze battering it against the sunshine-yellow frame. It looked as if it'd been partially torn off the hinges.

Nate elbowed his car door shut and walked closer. He kept his hand positioned over his gun and tried to rein in the fear that had started to crawl through him. He recognized the feeling. The sickening dread. The last time he'd felt like this he'd found his wife bleeding and dying in an alleyway.

Cursing under his breath, he hurried now, racing across the manicured lawn that was dotted with kiddie cars and other riding toys.

"What's wrong?" someone called out.

He snapped toward the voice and the petite brunette whom he recognized immediately. It wasn't a good recognition, either.

Darcy Burkhart.

A defense attorney who had recently moved to Silver Creek. But Nate had known Darcy before her move. Simply put, she had been and continued to be a thorn in his side. He'd already butted heads with her once today and didn't have time for round two.

Nate automatically scowled. So did she. She was apparently there to pick up her child. A son about Kimmie's age if Nate recalled correctly. He remembered Kimmie's nanny, Grace Borden, mentioning something about Darcy having enrolled the little boy in the two-hour-long Tuesday-Thursday play sessions held at the day-care center.

"I asked, what's wrong?" Darcy repeated. It was the same tone she used in court when representing the scum she favored defending.

Nate ignored both her scowl and her question, and continued toward the single-story building. The preschool was at the end of Main Street, nestled in a sleepy, parklike section with little noise or traffic. He reminded himself that it was a safe place for children.

Usually.

He had no idea what was wrong, but Nate knew that something was—the door was proof of that. He prayed there was a simple explanation for the damage. Like an ill-timed gust of wind. Or a preschool employee who'd given it too hard a push.

But it didn't feel like anything *simple*.

Without stopping, he glanced at the side parking lot. No activity there, though there were three cars, all belonging to the employees, no doubt. He also glanced behind him at the sidewalk and street where he and Darcy had left their own vehicles. If someone with criminal intentions had damaged the door, then the person wasn't outside.

That left the inside.

"Why is your hand on your gun?" Darcy asked, catching up with him. Not easily. She was literally running across the grassy lawn in high heels and a crisp ice-blue business suit, and the slim skirt made it nearly impossible for her to keep up with him.

"Shhhh," he growled.

Nate reached the front porch, which stretched across the entire front of the building. There were four windows, spaced far apart, and the nearest was still a few feet away from the door. He tested the doorknob.

It was locked.

Another sign that something was wrong. It was never locked this time of day because, like he had, other parents would arrive soon to pick up their children from the play session.

He drew his gun.

Behind him, Darcy gasped, and he shot her a get-quiet glare that he hoped she would obey. While he was hoping, he added that maybe she would stay out of the way.

She didn't.

Continuing to be a thorn in his side, she trailed along right behind him with those blasted heels battering like bullets on the wooden planks. Of course, he couldn't blame her. Her son was inside, and if she had any intuition whatsoever, she knew something wasn't right.

Nate moved to the window and peered around the

edge of the frame. He tried to brace himself for any-thing and everything but instead saw nothing. The room was empty.

Another bad sign.

It should literally be crawling with toddlers, the teacher and other staff members. This should be the last fifteen minutes of the play session, and the staff was expecting him. Nate had called an hour earlier to let them know that he would be arriving a little early so he could watch Kimmie play with the other kids. Maybe Darcy had had the same idea.

He lifted his head, listening, and it didn't take him long to hear the faint sound. Someone was crying. A baby. And it sounded like Kimmie.

Nothing could have held him back at that point. Nate raced across the porch and jumped over the waist-high railing so he could get to that door with the broken hinge. He landed on the ground, soggy from the morn-ing's hard rain, and the mud squeezed over the toes of his cowboy boots. It seemed to take hours to go those few yards, but he finally made it. Unfortunately, the sound of the crying got louder and louder.

Nate threw open the broken door and faced yet an-other empty playroom. His heart went to his knees. Be-cause the room wasn't just empty.

There were signs of a struggle.

Toys and furniture had been knocked over. There was a diaper bag discarded in the middle of the floor, and it looked as if someone had rifled through it. The phone, once mounted onto the wall, had been ripped off and now lay crushed and broken on the counter.

He didn't call out for his daughter, though he had to fight the nearly overwhelming urge to do just that and therefore alert a possible intruder. Kimmie had to be all right. She just had to be. Because the alternative was unthinkable. He'd already lost her mother, and he couldn't lose her.

Trying to keep his footsteps light so he would hopefully have the element of surprise, Nate made his way across the room and looked around the corner. No one was in the kitchen, but the crying was coming from the other side. It was one of the nap rooms, filled with beds and cribs, and normally it wasn't in use on Tuesday afternoons for the play group.

He heard the movement behind him, and with his Glock aimed and ready, he reeled around. It was Darcy, again. She gasped, and her cocoa-brown eyes widened at the gun pointed directly at her.

"Stay put," Nate whispered, using the hardest cop's expression he could manage. "Call nine-one-one and tell my brother to get out here."

Even though Darcy was new in town, she no doubt knew Sheriff Grayson Ryland was his brother. If she hadn't realized before there was something wrong, then she certainly knew it now.

"My son!" she said on a gasp.

She would have torn right past him if Nate hadn't snagged her arm. "Make the call," he ordered.

Her breath was gusting now, but she stopped struggling and gave a shaky nod. She rammed her hand into her purse and pulled out her cell phone.

Nate didn't wait for her to call the sheriff's office. She would do it, and soon Grayson and probably one of his other brothers would arrive. Two were deputies. And a nine-one-one call to respond to the preschool would get everyone in the sheriff's office moving fast.

Nate took aim again and hurried across the kitchen toward the nap room. The baby was still crying. Maybe it was Kimmie. But he heard something else, too. An adult's voice.

He stopped at the side of the door and glanced inside. At first, Nate didn't see the children. They weren't on the beds or in the cribs. But he looked down and spotted them.

Six toddlers.

They were huddled together in the corner with the teacher, Tara Hillman, and another woman Nate didn't recognize, but she no doubt worked there since both women wore name tags decorated with crayons. The babies were clinging to the adults, who were using hushed voices to try to comfort them.

"Lieutenant Ryland," Tara blurted out. Her eyes, like the other woman's, were red with tears, and they looked terrified.

With a baby clutched in each arm, Tara struggled to get to her feet. "Did you see them?"

"See who? What happened here?" Nate threaded his way through the maze of beds to make it to the other side of the room. He frantically looked through the huddle so he could find Kimmie.

"Two men," the other woman said. "They were wearing ski masks, and they had guns."

"They barged in before we could do anything to stop them," Tara explained.

"What happened here?" Nate repeated. He moved one of the babies aside. The one who was crying.

But it wasn't Kimmie.

"They took her," Tara said, though her voice hardly had any sound.

The words landed like fists against Nate and robbed him of his breath, maybe his sanity, too. "Took who?" He knew he was frantic now, but he couldn't stop himself.

"Kimmie." She made a hoarse sound. "They took Kimmie. Marlene, the other helper who works here, was holding her, and they made Marlene go with them. I couldn't stop them. I tried. I swear, I tried."

Everything inside Nate was on the verge of spinning out of control. That knot in his stomach moved to his throat and was choking him.

"What did they want? Where did they go?" he somehow managed to ask.

Tara swallowed hard and shook her head. "They drove away in a black van about ten minutes ago."

"Which direction?" Nate couldn't get out the question fast enough.

But Tara shook her head again. "They made us get on the floor, and I can't see the windows from there. They said if we went after them or if we called the sheriff that they'd come back and kill us all."

Nate turned to run. He had to get to his car *now*. He had to go in pursuit. He also had to get at least one of the deputies out to protect Tara and the babies just in case the gunmen followed through on their threat and returned. But he only made it a few steps before he smacked right into Darcy.

"They took Kimmie," he heard himself say.

But Darcy didn't seem to hear him. She was searching through the cluster of children. "Noah?" she called out. She repeated her son's name, louder this time.

Nate couldn't take the time to help her look. He had to find that van. He snatched his phone from his pocket and pressed the number for his brother. Grayson answered on the first ring.

"We're on the way," Grayson assured him without waiting for Nate to say a word. His brother had obviously gotten Darcy's call.

"According to the teacher, two armed men took Kimmie," Nate got out. "They kidnapped her and one of the workers, and they left in a black van. Close off the streets. Shut down the whole damn town before they have a chance to get out with her."

Nate didn't hear his brother's response because of the bloodcurdling scream that came from the preschool. That stopped him, and it wasn't more than a second or two before Darcy came tearing out of the building.

"They took Noah!" she yelled to Nate.

Hell. Not just one kidnapped child but two. "Did you hear?" Nate asked Grayson. He ran toward his car.

"I heard. So did Dade. He's listening in and already working to get someone out to look for that van. He'll get there in just a few minutes."

Dade, his twin brother and a Silver Creek deputy. Nate had no doubts that Dade would do everything he could to find Kimmie, but Nate wasn't going to just stand there and wait. He had to locate that van. He had to get Kimmie back.

"I'm going east," Nate let his brother know, and he ended the call so he could drive out of there fast.

Nate grappled to get the keys from his pocket, but his hands wouldn't cooperate. He tried to push the panic aside. He tried to think like a cop. But he wasn't just a cop. He was a father, and those armed SOBs had taken his baby girl.

He finally managed to extract his keys, somehow,

and he jerked open his car door. Nate jumped inside. But so did Darcy. She threw herself onto the passenger seat.

"I'm going with you," she insisted. "I have to get Noah."

"We don't even know who has them," Nate said. He dropped his cell phone onto the console between the seats so he could easily reach it. He needed it to stay in touch with Grayson.

"No, we don't know who has them, but they left this." She thrust a wrinkled piece of notebook paper at him. "It was taped to the side of the fridge."

Nate looked at her, trying to read her expression, but he only saw the fear and worry that was no doubt on his own face. He took the paper and read the scrawled writing.

This was his worst nightmare come true.

Nate Ryland and Darcy Burkhart, we have them. Cooperate or you'll never see your babies again.

Chapter Two

Cooperate or you'll never see your babies again.

The words raced through Darcy's head. She wanted to believe this wasn't really happening, that any second now she would wake up and see her son's smiling face. But the crumpled letter in Nate Ryland's hand seemed very real. And so was the fear that bubbled up in her throat.

"Cooperate?" she repeated. "How?"

There were a dozen more questions she could have added to those, but Nate didn't seem to have any more answers than she did. The only thing that appeared certain right now was that two gunmen had taken Nate's daughter, her son and a preschool employee, and they had driven off in a black van.

Nate's breath was gusting as much as hers, and he had a wild look in his metal-gray eyes. Even though his hands were shaking and he had a death grip on his gun, he managed to start his car, and he sped off, heading east, away from the center of town.

"This is the way the kidnappers went?" Darcy asked, praying that he knew something she didn't.

He dropped the letter next to his cell phone. "We have a fifty-fifty chance they did."

Oh, God. That wasn't nearly good enough odds when it came to rescuing Noah. "I should get in my car and go in the opposite direction. That way we can cover both ends of town."

"Grayson will do that," Nate snarled. He aimed a glare at her. "Besides, what good would you do going up against two armed men?"

"What good could I do?" Darcy practically yelled. "They have my son, and I'll get him back." Even though she didn't have a gun or any training in how to fight off bad guys. Still, she had a mother's love for her child, and that could overcome anything.

She hoped.

"You'll get yourself killed and maybe the children hurt," Nate fired back. "I'm not going to let you do that." And it wasn't exactly a suggestion.

He was right, of course. She hated that, but it was true. Even if she managed to find the van, she stood little chance of getting past two armed men, especially since she didn't want to give them any reason to fire shots. Not with her baby in that vehicle.

Nate flew past the last of the buildings but then slammed on the brakes. For a moment she thought he'd spotted the van. But no such luck. He was stopping for the dark blue truck that was coming from the opposition direction.

"My brother Dade," Nate told her. "He might have some news that'll help us narrow the search."

Good. She was aware that Nate had a slew of brothers, all in law enforcement. And she was also aware that Dade was a deputy sheriff since only two months earlier he'd been involved in the investigation

of one of her former clients. A client killed in a shoot-
out with Nate.

The two vehicles screeched to a stop side by side,
and both men put down the windows. Darcy ducked
down a little so she could see the man in the driver's
seat of the truck.

Yes, definitely Nate's brother.

He had the same midnight-black hair. The same icy
eyes. But Dade looked like a rougher version of his
brother, who had obviously just come from his job in
SAPD. Nate wore jeans but with a crisp gray shirt and
black jacket. Dade looked as if he'd just climbed out of
the saddle, with his denim shirt and battered Stetson.

The brothers exchanged glances. Brief ones. But
it felt as if a thousand things passed silently between
them. "Anything?" Nate asked.

Dade's troubled eyes conveyed his answer before he
even spoke. "Not yet."

"There was a note," Nate said, handing it through the
window to his brother. He immediately started to slap
the fingers of his left hand on the steering wheel. He
was obviously eager to leave and so was Darcy. "Later
I need it bagged and checked for prints."

Later. After they'd rescued the children. Darcy didn't
want to think beyond that.

"Once one of the other deputies arrives at the preschool, I'll be out to help you look," Dade offered. "Was
anyone in the building hurt?"

Nate shook his head. "It looked like a smash and
grab. Entry through the side door. No signs of…blood."

Dade returned the nod. "Good. Hang in there. We'll
find these goons, and we'll find Kimmie."

Nate gave Dade one last brief look, maybe to thank

him, and he hit the accelerator again. He sped off in the opposite direction of his brother while he fired glances all around. He wasn't just checking Main Street but all of the side roads and parking lots.

Silver Creek wasn't a large town, but there was a solid quarter mile of shops and houses on Main Street. And there were no assurances that the kidnappers would stay on the main road. Most of the side streets wound their way back to the highway, and that terrified her. Because if the kidnappers made it to the highway, it was just a few miles to the interstate.

"I have to do something," she mumbled. Darcy couldn't stop the panic. Nor the fear. It was building like a pressure cooker inside her as Nate sped past each building.

"You can do something." Nate's voice was strained, like the muscles in his face. "You can keep watch for that van and try to figure out why those men did this."

That didn't settle the panic, but it did cause her to freeze. Why had those men done this? Why had they specifically taken Nate's daughter and her son?

"You're a cop," she blurted out. "This could be connected to something you've done. Maybe someone has a grudge because you arrested him." It was a possible motive. And that caused anger to replace some of the panic. "This could be your fault."

It wasn't reasonable, but by God she wasn't in a reasonable kind of mood. She wanted her son back.

Nate kept his attention nailed to the road, but he also scowled. He clearly wasn't pleased with her accusation. Or with her. But then he always scowled when she was around.

"If this is my fault, then why did they take your son?" Nate asked.

She opened her mouth to explain that away, but she couldn't. Darcy could only sit there and let that sink in. It didn't sink in well.

"If I counted right, there were eight toddlers in that play group today. Eight," he spat out with his teeth semi-clenched. "And they only took ours. They said cooperate or we'd never see our babies again. *Our babies,*" he emphasized. "So what the devil did you do to bring this down on us? You're the one who likes to muck around with slime."

She shook her head, trying to get out the denial. Yes, she was a defense attorney. She'd even successfully defended the man who'd originally been arrested for masterminding the murder of Nate's wife. But that was resolved. His wife's killer was now dead, and so was her former client Charles Brennan.

But he hadn't been her only client.

In the past she had indeed defended people with shady reputations, and in some cases she hadn't been successful. Maybe one of those less-than-stellar clients was holding a grudge.

Oh, mercy. Nate was right. This could all be her fault.

The tears came. She'd been fighting them from the moment she realized something was wrong in the pre-school, but she lost that fight now.

"I need you to keep watch," Nate growled. "You can't do that if you're crying, so dry your eyes and help me look for that van."

"But this is my fault." She tried to choke back a sob but failed at that, too.

"Stop thinking like a mother for just a second. They took both children so it's connected to both of us. Not just me. Not just you. *Both*."

Her gaze flew to his, and she met his frosty-metal eyes. The raw emotions of the moment were still there, deep in those shades of gray, but she could also see the cop now. Here was the formidable opponent she'd come up against in the past.

"The man who killed your wife is dead," she reminded him. "And so is the person who hired him."

"Wesley Dent isn't in jail," Nate provided. He took his attention off her and put it back on the road.

Yes. Wesley Dent was her client. A San Antonio man under investigation for poisoning his wife. Dent had retained her a few days after his wife's death because he was concerned about the accusatory tone the police were taking with him. She'd accompanied him to several interviews and had successfully argued to put limits on the search warrant that was being issued for his house and vehicles.

And the lead investigator in the case was none other than Nate.

Darcy gave that some thought and shook her head. "I don't think Wesley Dent would do this. I'm not even sure he's capable of poisoning anyone."

"He's guilty," Nate said with the complete confidence that only a cop could have.

Darcy was far from convinced of that, but to the best of her knowledge, Dent was the only thing that connected Nate and her. Still, it didn't matter at this point if Dent was the one responsible. They needed to find the van.

Nate's cell phone rang, and without picking it up, he jabbed the button to answer the call on speaker.

"It's Grayson," the caller said.

The sheriff, and from what she'd heard, a very capable lawman. Darcy held her breath, praying that he had good news.

"Anything?" Nate immediately asked.

"No. But we're putting everything in place." He paused just a second. "Dade said you have Ms. Burkhart in the vehicle with you."

"Yeah. She jumped in as I was driving away."

The sheriff mumbled something she didn't catch, but it sounded like profanity. "I shouldn't have to remind you that if you find this van, you should wait for backup. You two shouldn't try to do this alone."

Nate paused, too. "No, we shouldn't. But if I see that van, nothing is going to stop me. Just make sure you have a noose around the area. I don't want them getting away."

"They won't. Now, tell me about this note you gave Dade."

"It said, 'Nate Ryland and Darcy Burkhart, we have them. Cooperate or you'll never see your babies again.' And yes, I know what that means." Nate tightened his grip on the steering wheel. "They won't harm the children because they want them for leverage. I think this is connected to a man named Wesley Dent. Call my captain and have Dent brought in for questioning. Beat the truth out of him if necessary."

Darcy knew she should object to that. She believed in the law with her whole heart. But her son's safety suddenly seemed above the law.

"I don't suppose it'd do any good to ask you to come

back to the station," Grayson said. "We have plenty of people out looking for the van."

"I'm not coming back. Not until—" Nate's eyes widened, and she followed his gaze to what had grabbed his attention.

Oh, mercy. There was a black van on the side street. It was moving but not at a high speed.

Noah could be in there.

"I just spotted the possible escape vehicle on Elmore Road," Nate relayed to his brother. "It's on the move, and I'm in pursuit."

Nate turned his car on what had to be two wheels at most, and with the tires squealing, he maneuvered onto the narrow road. There were houses here, spaced far apart, but thankfully there didn't seem to be any other traffic. Good thing, too, because Nate floored the accelerator and tore through the normally quiet neighborhood.

So did the driver of the van.

He sped up, which meant he had no doubt seen them. Not that she'd expected them to be able to sneak up on the vehicle, but Darcy had hoped they would be able to get closer so she could look inside the windows.

Nate read off the license-plate number to his brother, who was still on the line, though she could hear the sheriff making other calls. Grayson was assembling backup for Nate. She only prayed they wouldn't need it, that they could resolve this here and now.

"Can you try to shoot out the tires or something?" she asked.

"Not with the kids inside. Too risky."

Of course, it was. She obviously wasn't thinking

clearly and wouldn't until she had her baby safely in her arms. "How will we get it to stop?"

"Grayson will have someone at the other end of this road. Once the guy realizes he can't escape, he'll stop."

Maybe. And maybe that shoot-out would happen, after all. Darcy tried not to give in to the fear, but she got a double dose of it when the van sped over a hill and disappeared out of sight.

"Are there side roads?" she asked. She'd never been on Elmore or in this particular part of Silver Creek.

"Yeah. Side roads and old ranch trails."

That didn't help with the fear, and she held her breath until Nate's car barreled over the hill. There, about a quarter of a mile in front of them, she could see the van. But not for long. The driver went around a deep curve and disappeared again.

It seemed to take hours for Nate to reach that same curve, and he was going so fast that he had to grapple with the steering wheel to remain in control. The tires on her side scraped against the gravel shoulder and sent a spray of rocks pelting into the car's undercarriage. It sounded like gunshots, and that made her terror worse.

They came out of the curve, only to go right into another one. Nate seemed to realize it was coming because he was already steering in that direction.

Darcy prayed that it wouldn't be much longer before Grayson or someone else approached from the other side of the road so they could stop this chase. She didn't want to risk the van crashing into one of the trees that dotted the sides of the road.

She could hear the chatter on Nate's cell, which was still on speaker. People were responding. Everything was in motion, but the truth was Nate and she were the ones who were closest to the van. They were their children's best bet for rescue.

"Hold on," Nate warned as he took another turn. "And put on your seat belt."

Her hands were shaking, but she managed to get the belt pulled across her. She was still fumbling with the latch when their car came out of yet another curve followed by a hill.

The moment they reached the top of the hill, she saw the van.

And Darcy's heart went to her knees.

"Stop!" she yelled.

Nate was already trying to do just that. He slammed on the brakes. But they were going too fast. And the van was sideways, right in the middle of the road. The vehicle wasn't moving, and there was no way for Nate to avoid it.

Darcy screamed.

Just as they crashed head-on into the black van.

Chapter Three

Nate heard the screech of his brakes as the asphalt ripped away at the tires. There was nothing he could do.

Nothing.

Except pray and try to brace himself for the impact.

He didn't have to wait long.

The car slammed into the van, tossing Darcy and him around like rag dolls. The air bags deployed, slapping into them and sending a cloud of the powdery dust all through the car's interior.

It was all over in a split second. The whiplashing impact. The sounds of metal colliding with metal.

Nate was aware of the pain in his body from having his muscles wrenched around. The mix of talc and cornstarch powder from the air bag robbed him of what little breath he had. But now that he realized he had survived the crash, he had one goal.

To get to the children.

Nate prayed they hadn't been hurt.

He lifted his head, trying to listen. He didn't hear anyone crying or anyone moaning in pain. That could be good.

Or very bad.

Next to him, Darcy began to punch at the air bag that

had pinned her to the seat. He glanced at her, just to make sure she wasn't seriously injured. She had a few nicks on her face from the air bag, and her shoulder-length dark brown hair was now frosted with the talc mixture, but she was fighting as hard as he was to get out of the vehicle. No doubt to check on her son.

"When we get out, stay behind me and let me do the talking," Nate warned her.

Though he doubted his warning would do any good. If the kidnappers hadn't been injured or, better yet, incapacitated, then this was going to get ugly fast.

Nate got a better grip on his gun and opened his door. Or rather, that's what he tried to do. The door was jammed, and he had to throw his weight against it to force it open. He got out, his boots sinking into the soggy shoulder of the road, and got a good look at the damage. The front end of his car was a mangled heap, and it had crumpled the side of the van, creating a deep V in the exterior.

Still no sounds of crying. In fact, there were no sounds at all coming from the van.

"I'm Lieutenant Nate Ryland," he called out. "Release the hostages *now!*"

He waited, praying that his demand wouldn't be answered with a hail of bullets. Anything he did right now was a risk and could make it more dangerous for the children, but he couldn't just stand there. He had to try something to get Kimmie and Noah away from their kidnappers.

In the distance he could hear a siren from one of the sheriff department's cruisers. The sound was coming from the opposite direction so that meant Grayson or one of the other deputies would soon be there. But Nate didn't intend to wait for backup to arrive. His daughter could be hurt inside that van, and he had to check on her.

Darcy finally managed to fight her way out of the wrecked car, and she hit the ground running. Or rather, limping. However, the limping didn't stop her. She went straight for the van. Nate would have preferred for her to wait until he'd had time to assess things, but he knew there was no stopping her, not with her son inside.

"Noah?" she shouted.

Still no answer.

That didn't stop Darcy, either, and she would have thrown open the back doors of the van if Nate hadn't stepped in front of her and muscled her aside. This could be an ambush with the kidnappers waiting inside to gun them down, but these SOBs obviously wanted Darcy and him for something. Maybe that *something* meant they would keep them alive.

"Kimmie?" Nate called out, and he cautiously opened the van doors while he kept his gun aimed and ready.

It took him a moment to pick through the debris and the caved-in side, but what he saw had him cursing.

No one was there. Not in the seats, not in the back cargo area. Not even behind the wheel.

A sob tore from Darcy's mouth, and if Nate hadn't caught her, she likely would have collapsed onto the ground.

"Where are they?" she begged. And she just kept repeating it.

Nate glanced all around them. There were thick woods on one side of the road and an open meadow on the other. The grass didn't look beaten down on the meadow side so that left the woods. He shoved his hand over Darcy's mouth so he could hear any sounds. After all, two gunmen and three hostages should be making lots of sounds.

But he heard nothing other than Darcy's frantic mumbles and the approaching siren.

"They were here," Nate said more to himself than Darcy, but she stopped and listened. He took the hand from her mouth. "That's Kimmie's diaper bag." It was lying right against the point of impact.

"And that's Noah's bear," Darcy said, reaching for the toy.

Nate pulled her back. Yes, the children had likely been here, but so had the kidnappers. The diaper bag and the toy bear might have to be analyzed. Unless Nate found the children and kidnappers first.

And that's exactly what he intended to do.

"Wait here," he told Darcy. "I need to figure out where they went." He tried not to think of his terrified baby being hauled through the woods by armed kidnappers, but he knew it was possible.

By God when he caught up to these men, they were going to pay, and pay hard.

"Look!" Darcy shouted.

Nate followed the direction of her pointing index finger and spotted the name tag. It was identical to the ones he'd seen Tara and the other woman wearing in the preschool. This one had the name Marlene Lambert, a woman he'd known his whole life. Her father's ranch was just one property over from his family's.

"The name tag looks as if it was ripped off her," Darcy mumbled.

Maybe. It wasn't just damaged—one of the four crayons had been removed. He glanced around the name tag and spotted the missing yellow crayon. It was right at the base of the rear doors.

"She wrote something." Darcy pointed to the left door at the same moment Nate's attention landed on it.

There was a single word, three letters, scrawled on the metal, but Nate couldn't make out what it said. Later, he would try to figure it out, but for now he raced away from the van and to the edge of the road that fronted the woods.

Nate didn't see any footprints or any signs of activity so he began to run, looking for anything that would give them a clue where the children had been taken. Darcy soon began to do the same and went in the opposite direction.

He glanced up when Dade's truck squealed to a stop. His brother had put the portable siren on top of his truck, but thankfully now he turned it off. Unlike Darcy and Nate, Dade was coming from a straight part of the road and had no doubt seen the collision in time. That was why Nate hadn't bothered to go back to his car and try to retrieve his cell phone so he could alert whoever would be coming from that direction.

"They're not inside," Nate relayed to his brother, and he kept looking.

Dade cursed. "There's a helicopter on the way," he let Nate know. "And I'll call the Rangers and get a tracker out here. Mason, too," Dade added the same moment that Nate said their brother's name.

Mason was an expert horseman, and he was their best bet at finding the children in these thick woods. First, though, Nate needed to find the point at which they'd left the road. That would get him started in the right direction.

And he finally found it.

Footprints in the soft shoulder of the road.

"Here!" he called out to his brother. But Nate didn't wait for Dade to reach him. Nor did he follow directly in the footsteps. He hurried to the side in case the prints were needed for evidence, and there were certainly a lot of them if castings were needed.

But something was wrong.

Hell.

"There's only one set of footprints," Nate relayed to Dade.

Dade cursed too and fanned out to Nate's left, probably looking for more prints. There should be at least three sets since the adults would be carrying the babies.

"The person who made this set of prints could be a diversion," Nate concluded, and he hurried to the other side of the road, hoping to find the real trail there.

Darcy quickly joined him. She was still limping, and blood was trickling down the side of her head. He hoped like the devil she wasn't in need of immediate medical attention or on the verge of a panic attack. He needed her help, her eyes, because these first few minutes were critical.

"Go that way," Nate instructed, pointing in the opposite direction where he intended to look.

He ran, checking each section of the pasture for any sign that anyone had been there. He knew the kidnappers weren't on the road itself because Darcy and he had come from one end and Dade the other. If two kidnappers and three hostages had been anywhere near the road, they would have seen them.

Nate made it about a hundred yards from the collision site when he heard Dade's cell ring. He didn't stop looking, but he tried to listen, hoping that his brother was about to get good news. Judging from the profanity Dade used, he hadn't.

"This van's a decoy," Dade shouted.

Nate stopped and whirled around. Darcy did the same and began to run back toward Dade. "What do you mean?"

"I mean two other eyewitnesses spotted black vans identical to this one."

Darcy made it to Dade, and she latched on to his arm. "But there's proof the children were inside. Noah's bear and Kimmie's diaper bag. Marlene's name tag is there, too."

Dade looked at Nate when he answered. "This was probably the van initially used in the kidnapping, but the children and Marlene were transferred to another vehicle. Maybe they were even split up since at least two other vans were seen around town."

Nate had already come to that conclusion, and it made him sick to his stomach. He couldn't choke back the groan. Nor could he fight back the overwhelming sense of fear.

"If they split up, then there are probably more than two of them," Nate mumbled.

That meant things had gone from bad to worse. The kidnappers could have an entire team of people helping them, and heaven knows what kind of vehicle they had used to transfer the children.

Nate was betting it wasn't a black van.

It could have been any kind of vehicle. Darcy and

he could have driven right past the damn thing and wouldn't have even noticed it.

"We have people out on the roads," Dade reminded them. "More are coming in. And there's an Amber Alert and an APB out on the van. SAPD and all other law-enforcement officers in the area will stop any van matching the description. We'll find them, Nate. I swear, we'll find them."

Nate checked his watch. About twenty minutes had passed. That was a lifetime in a situation like this. The kidnappers could already have reached the interstate.

"I'll take you back to the sheriff's office," Dade insisted. He glanced down at Darcy. In addition to the nicks on her face, her jacket was torn, and there were signs of a bruise on her knee. "You need to see a medic."

"No!" she practically shouted. "I need to find my baby."

But the emotional outburst apparently drained her because the tears came, and Nate hooked his arm around her waist. He didn't feel much like comforting her, or anyone else, for that matter, but the sad truth was there was only one person who knew exactly how he felt.

And that was Darcy.

She sagged against him and dropped her head on his shoulder. "We have to keep looking," she begged.

"We will." Nate looked at his brother. "We need another vehicle. And I need to call the San Antonio crime lab so they can come out and collect this van." Silver Creek didn't have the CSI capabilities that SAPD did, and Nate wanted as many people on this as possible.

Nate adjusted Darcy's position so he could get her

moving to Dade's truck, but he stopped when he took another look at the scrawled letters written in yellow crayon. He eased away from Darcy and walked closer.

"You think Marlene wrote that?" Dade asked.

Nate nodded. "She might have tried to leave us a message." He studied those three letters. *"L-A-R,"* he read aloud.

"Lar?" Dade shook his head, obviously trying to figure it out, too.

"Maybe it's someone's initials," Darcy suggested. She moved between Dade and Nate, and leaned in. "Maybe she's trying to tell us the identity of the person who took her."

It was possible. Of course, that would mean it wasn't Wesley Dent, and it would also mean Marlene had known her kidnapper. That possibility tightened the knot in Nate's stomach. But there was something more here.

Something familiar.

Dade rattled off names of people who might fit those initials. He only managed two—an elderly couple with the last name of Reeves. Nate figured neither was capable of this. But his own surname began with an *R*.

Did that mean anything?

"A street name, then," Darcy pressed.

Dade lifted his phone and snapped a picture. "Come on. Let's go. We'll try to work it out on the drive back to the sheriff's office."

It was a good plan, but Nate couldn't take his attention off those three letters. They were familiar, something right on the tip of his tongue.

"Let's go," Darcy urged. She tugged on Nate's arm to get him moving.

They only made it a few steps before Nate heard a phone ring. Not Dade's. The sound was coming from his wrecked car, and it was his phone. He hurried toward it, but it stopped ringing just as he got there. He located his cell in the rubble and saw the missed call.

The number and caller's identity had been blocked.

Hell. It had probably been the kidnappers. "It could have been the ransom call."

"Try to call them back," Darcy insisted. But the words had hardly left her mouth when another phone rang. "That's my cell." She frantically tore through the debris to locate her purse. She jerked out the phone and jabbed the button to answer it.

She pressed the phone to her ear, obviously listening, but she didn't say a word. When the color drained from her face, Nate moved closer.

"But—" That was all she managed to say.

Nate wanted the call on speaker so he could hear, but he couldn't risk trying to press any buttons on her phone. He darn sure didn't want to disconnect the call. All he could do was wait.

"I want my son. Give me back my son!" she shouted. The tears welled up in her eyes and quickly began to spill down her cheeks. Several seconds later, Darcy's hand went limp, the phone dropping away from her ear.

Nate snatched the phone from her, but the call had already ended.

"Who was it and what did they say?" Nate demanded. He caught her by the shoulders and positioned her so that it forced eye contact.

She groaned and shook her head. "The person had a mechanical voice, like he was speaking through some kind of machine, but I think it was a man. He said he had the children and Marlene and that if we wanted them back, he would soon be in touch. Then he hung up."

"That's it? That's all he said?" Nate tried to calm down but couldn't. "He didn't say if the kids were safe?"

"No," she insisted.

Nate took her phone. He tried the return-call function on his cell first. It didn't go through. Instead he got a recording about the number no longer being in service. The same thing happened when he tried to retrieve the call from Darcy's phone.

A dead end.

But maybe it was just a temporary one.

Dade gathered both cells. "I'll see if we can get anything about the caller from these. Darcy, you need to write down everything you can remember from that conversation because each word could be important."

She nodded and smeared the tears from her cheeks. "Let's get that other vehicle so we can look for them."

Nate agreed, but he stopped and stared at the three letters written on the door of the van.

LAR.

"I already have a picture of it," Dade reminded him. "You can study it later."

Nate cursed. "I don't need to study it." He started to run toward Nate's truck. "I know what Marlene is trying to tell us. I know where we can find the children."

Chapter Four

"LAR," Darcy said under her breath.

Lost Appaloosa Ranch.

Well, maybe that's what the initials meant. Of course, Nate could be wrong, and it could turn out to be a wild-goose chase. A chase that could cost them critical time because it tied up manpower that could be directed somewhere other than the remote abandoned ranch. According to Nate, the owner had died nearly a year ago, and his mortgage lender was still trying to contact his next of kin.

"Hurry," Darcy told the medic again. And yes, she glared at him. She'd spent nearly fifteen minutes in the Silver Creek sheriff's office, and that was fifteen minutes too long.

Darcy didn't want to be here. She wanted to be out looking for Noah, but instead here she was, sitting at the sheriff's desk while a medic stitched her up. God knows how she'd gotten the cut right on her hairline, and she didn't care.

She didn't care about anything but her son.

"I'm trying to hurry," the medic assured her.

She knew from his name tag that he was Tommy Watters, and while she hated being rude to him, she couldn't stop herself. She had to do something. *Anything*.

Like Nate and his four brothers were doing.

Just a few yards away from her, Nate was on the phone, his tone and motions frantic, while he talked with the helicopter pilot, who was trying to narrow down the search zone.

"No," Nate instructed. "Don't do a direct fly over the Lost Appaloosa. I already have someone en route, and if the kidnappers are there, I don't want to alert them. I want you to focus on the roads that lead to the interstate."

Nate had a map spread out on the desk, and every line on the desk phone was blinking. Next door, Deputy Melissa Garza was barking out orders to a citizens' patrol group that was apparently being formed to assist in the hunt for the kidnappers and the babies. The dispatcher was helping her.

Grayson, Dade and Mason were all out searching various parts of Silver Creek, interviewing witnesses and running down leads on the other black vans that had been spotted. The other deputy, Luis Lopez, was at the day care in case the kidnappers returned.

Darcy was the only one not doing anything to save Noah and Kimmie.

"I can't just sit here." The panic was starting to whirl around inside her, and despite the AC spilling over her, sweat popped out on her face. She would scream if she couldn't get out of there and find Noah.

Darcy pushed aside the medic and would have run out of the room if Nate hadn't caught her shoulder.

He got right in her face, and his glare told her this wasn't going to be a pep talk. "You have to keep yourself together. Because I don't have time to babysit you. Got that?"

She flinched. That stung worse than the fresh stitches. But Darcy still shook her head. "Noah is my life." Which, of course, went without saying. Kimmie was no doubt Nate's life, too.

Nate nodded, and eased up on the bruising grip he had on her shoulder. The breath he blew out was long and weary. He looked up at the medic as he put Darcy back in the chair. "Finish the stitches *now*," he ordered.

Actual fear went through the medic's eyes, and he clipped off the thread. "It'll hold for now, but she should see a doctor because she might have a concussion."

Before the last word left the medic's mouth, Darcy was out of the chair. "Let's go," she insisted.

Thank God, Nate didn't argue with her. "We're headed to the Lost Appaloosa, Mel," he shouted to Deputy Garza, and in the same motion Nate grabbed a set of keys from a hook on the wall.

Finally! They were getting out there and doing something. She hoped it was the *right* something.

"You have to keep yourself together," Nate repeated. But this time, there was no razor edge to his tone. No glare. Just speed. He practically ran down the hall. "My brother Kade should arrive at the Lost Appaloosa in about ten minutes, and then we'll have answers."

"Answers *if* the babies are really there," Darcy corrected.

Nate spared her a glance, threw open the back door and hurried into the parking lot. "Marlene probably risked her life to write those initials. They mean something, and if it turns out to be the Lost Appaloosa, then Kade will know how to approach the situation."

"Because he's FBI," she said more to herself than Nate.

Darcy prayed Nate's FBI brother truly knew what he was doing. It gave her some comfort to know that Kade would likely be willing to risk his life to save his niece. And maybe Noah, too.

Nate jumped into a dark blue SUV, started the engine and barely waited long enough for Darcy to get inside before he tore out of the parking lot.

"I need to know if you're okay," he said, tipping his head to her new stitches.

"Don't worry about me," Darcy said. "Focus on the kids."

"I can't have you keeling over or anything." The muscles in his jaw stirred. Maybe because he didn't like that he had to be concerned about her in any way.

"I'm fine," she assured him, and even though it was a lie, it was the end of the discussion as far as Darcy was concerned. "How far is the Lost Appaloosa?"

"Thirty miles. It's within the San Antonio city limits, but there's not much else out there." His phone buzzed, and he shoved it between his shoulder and ear when he answered it.

She listened but couldn't tell anything from Nate's monosyllabic responses. He certainly wasn't whooping for joy because the babies had possibly been found.

Darcy leaned over to check the odometer so she would know when they were close to that thirty miles, and her hair accidently brushed against Nate's arm. He glanced at it, at her, and Darcy quickly pulled away.

"Thirty miles," she repeated, focusing on the drive and not on the driver. Nate put his attention back on the call.

That was too many miles between her and her baby, and the panic surged through her again. Nate was already going as fast as he could, but at this speed and because of the narrow country roads, it would take them at least twenty, maybe twenty-five, minutes to get there.

An eternity.

Nate cursed, causing her attention to snap back to him. She waited, breath held, until he slapped the phone shut. "Grayson just found another empty black van on a dirt road near the creek. Only one set of footprints was around the vehicle."

So, not a call from Kade. Just news of another decoy van. Or else the team of kidnappers had split up. Did that mean they'd split up the children and Marlene, as well? Darcy hoped not.

"Shouldn't you have heard from Kade by now?" she asked.

He scrubbed his hand over his face. "My brother will call when he can."

Nate looked at her again, and his eyes were now a dangerous stormy-gray. "The person behind this has a big motive and a lot of money," he tossed out there. He was all cop again. Here was the lieutenant she'd butted heads with in the past. And the present.

"You mean Wesley Dent," she supplied.

Darcy didn't even try to put on her lawyer face. Her head was pounding. Her breath, ragged. And her heart was beating so hard, she was afraid her ribs might crack. She didn't have the energy for her usual power-attorney facade.

"Wesley Dent," Nate verified, making her client's name sound like profanity. "He's a gold digger, and I believe he murdered his wife."

Darcy shook her head and continued to keep watch in case she spotted another black van. She also glanced at the odometer, remembering to keep her hair away from Nate's arm. Twenty-five miles to go.

"I won't deny the gold-digging part," she admitted, "but I'm not sure he killed his wife."

Though it did look bad for Dent.

A starving artist, Dent had married Sandra Frasier, who wasn't just a multimillionaire heiress but was twenty-five years his senior. And apparently she often resorted to public humiliation when it came to her boy-toy husband, who was still two years shy of his thirtieth birthday. Just days before what would have been their first wedding anniversary, Sandra had humiliated Dent in public at Dent's art show.

A day after that, she had received a lethal dose of insulin.

"Sandra was diabetic," Darcy continued, though she really didn't want to have this conversation. Twenty-four miles to go. "So, it's possible this was a suicide. Her husband even said she wrote about suicide in her diary." But her death certainly hadn't been accidental because the amount of insulin was quadruple what she would have normally taken.

"There was no suicide note," Nate challenged. "No sign of this so-called diary, either."

But that didn't mean the diary didn't exist. Dent had told her that his wife kept it under lock and key, so maybe she'd moved it so that no one would be able to read her intimate thoughts.

"The husband is often guilty in situations like this," Nate went on. He had such a hard grip on the steering wheel that his knuckles were white. "And I think Dent could have orchestrated this kidnapping to force me to stop the investigation. I'm within days of arresting his sorry butt for murder."

Darcy wished the pain in her head would ease up a little so she could think straighter. "There are other suspects," she reminded him.

"Yeah, the dead woman's ex-husband and her son, but neither has as strong a motive as Dent."

"Maybe," Darcy conceded. Another glance at the odometer. Twenty-three miles between the ranch and them. "But if Dent masterminded this kidnapping to stop the investigation, then why take Noah? I'm his lawyer, the one person who could possibly prevent him from being arrested."

Nate shook his head, cursed again. "Maybe he thinks if he has your son that you'll put pressure on me to cooperate."

She opened her mouth to argue, but that kind of fight just wasn't in her. Besides, there was a chance that Nate could be right.

In some ways it would be better if he was.

After all, if Dent took the children, then he would keep them safe because he would use them to make a deal. Darcy was good at deals. And she would bargain with the devil himself if it meant getting her son back.

Nate didn't tack anything else on to his specula- tions about Dent, and the silence closed in around them. Except it wasn't just an ordinary silence. It was the calm before the storm because Darcy knew what was coming next.

"Charles Brennan," she tossed out there since she knew Nate had already thought of the man. Over a year ago Brennan had hired the triggerman who'd murdered Nate's wife.

"Yeah," Nate mumbled. "Any chance he's behind this?"

Well, Brennan was dead, but she didn't have to remind Nate of that. Because Nate had been the one to kill Brennan in a shoot-out after the man had taken a deputy hostage.

"Brennan made me executor of his estate," Darcy volunteered. "I've gone through his files and financials, and there is no proof he left any postmortem instructions that had anything to do with you. Or me, for that matter."

"You're sure?" Nate pressed.

"Yes." As sure as she could be, anyway, when it came to a monster like Brennan.

Nate made a sharp sound that clipped from his throat. It was the sound of pure disapproval. "Brennan was a cold-blooded killer, and you defended him."

She had. And two months ago she would have argued that it was her duty to provide representation, but that was before her client had nearly killed a deputy sheriff, Nate and heaven knows how many others.

Darcy kept watch out the window. She didn't want to look at Nate because she didn't want him to see the hurt that was in her eyes. "There's nothing you can say that will make me feel worse than I already do," she let him know.

Silence again from Nate, and Darcy risked touching him so she could lean in and see the mileage. Just under twenty miles to go. Still an eternity.

Nate's cell buzzed. "It's Kade," he said and flipped open the phone.

Just like that, both the dread and the hope grabbed her by the throat. She moved closer, until she was shoulder to shoulder with Nate. Darcy no longer cared about the touching risk. She had to know what Kade was saying.

"I'm on the side of the hill with a good binocular view of the Lost Appaloosa," Kade explained. "And I have good news and bad."

Oh, mercy. She wasn't sure she could handle it if something had happened to the children. Nate's deep breath let her know he felt the same.

"The good news—there's a black van parked on the side of the main house," Kade continued. "Something tells me this one isn't a decoy."

"How do you know?" Darcy asked before Nate could. She wanted to believe that was good news, but she wasn't sure. "Do you see the children?"

"No sign of the children," Kade told them. His voice was practically a whisper, but even the low volume couldn't conceal his concern.

Kade paused. "Nate, call Grayson and the others and tell them to get out here right away. Because the bad news is—there are at least a half-dozen armed guards surrounding the place."

Chapter Five

Nate parked the SUV near Kade's truck—a good quarter mile from the Lost Appaloosa ranch house.

This had to work.

He'd already set his phone to vibrate and had Darcy do the same. Now, he slid his gun from his shoulder holster, eased his SUV door shut and started down the exact path his brother had instructed him to take. A path that would hopefully keep them out of sight from those guards patrolling the place.

Nate glanced back at Darcy and put his index finger to his mouth, even though he had already made it clear that they had to make a silent approach. Not easy to do considering Darcy was wearing those blasted high heels. Still, she'd have to adjust. The last thing he wanted was to give anyone a reason to fire in case the babies were nearby.

Part of him prayed this wasn't another decoy—even though, according to Kade, the half dozen or more guards were armed to the hilt. At least if Noah and Kimmie were here, then Nate would finally know where the children were. Of course, that was just the first step.

He had to get them out—safe, sound and unharmed.

Even though it was late afternoon, it was still hot, and sweat began to trickle down his back. So did the fear. He'd never had this much at stake. Yes, he'd lost Ellie, but that had been different. His wife had been a cop, capable of defending herself in most situations.

Kimmie was his little girl.

Nate choked back the fear and followed the beaten-down path until he spotted Kade on the side of a grassy hill. His brother was on his stomach, head lifted so he could peer over the top. Kade also had his gun drawn.

Kade glanced at him, but his brother's eyes narrowed when he looked at Darcy.

Yeah.

Nate wasn't pleased about her being there, either, but he hadn't had a choice. If he'd left her at the sheriff's office, she would have just tried to follow them. And he couldn't have blamed her. If their situations had been reversed, he would have done the same.

"The others are on their way," Nate whispered. He dropped down next to Kade.

Darcy did the same, her left arm landing against Nate's right one. Close contact yet again. Contact Nate decided to ignore. Instead, he took Kade's binoculars and looked at their situation.

It wasn't good.

Nate didn't need but a glimpse to determine that. All the windows had newspaper taped to the glass. No way to see inside.

Outside was a different set of problems.

There were armed gunmen milling around the ranch house. All carried assault rifles and were dressed in black. Nate counted three, including the one standing guard at the front door, but then he saw one more when the man peered out from around the back of the house. There was yet another on the roof and one on the road near the cattle gate that closed off the property.

The gunmen had an ideal position because they controlled the only road that led to the ranch, and they obviously had good visibility with their comrade perched on the roof. Plus, there was a lot of open space around the ranch house itself. There were barns and a few other outbuildings that could be used for cover, but it wouldn't be easy to get to the house without being spotted by one of those armed goons.

"Are the children there?" Darcy whispered.

"Can't tell." Nate handed her the binoculars so Darcy could see for herself.

"Grayson and the others should be here soon," Nate relayed to Kade. "I called him just a few minutes before we got here, and he's bringing an infrared device so we can get an idea of who's inside."

And how many. That was critical information so they would know the full scope of what they were up against.

"How many will be with Grayson?" Kade asked.

Nate mentally made a count. Grayson, Dade, Mason and Mel. "Six total with you and me."

Even odds. Well, even odds for the gunmen outside the house, but Nate was betting there was some firepower inside, as well.

"The FBI should have a choke hold on the surrounding area in place in about an hour," Kade let him know.

A choke hold. In other words, the agents would be coming from the outside and moving in to make sure no one got away if the gunmen scattered. Nate was thankful for the extra help, but an hour was a lifetime.

Besides, he didn't want the gunmen spotting the agents and opening fire.

"This is San Antonio P.D.'s jurisdiction," Nate reminded his brother.

Kade nodded. "I want family calling the shots on this."

Yeah. Because for Nate and the rest of the Rylands, this was as personal as it got. Nate trusted the FBI, had worked well with them on many occasions, but he didn't want anyone thinking with their trigger fingers or their federal rules. But he also didn't want emotions to create a deadly scenario.

That included Darcy.

Beside him, her breath was still racing, and she had the binoculars pressed to her eyes. "How do we get in there?" she asked.

"*We* don't," Nate quickly corrected her. He took the binoculars from her and had another look. "You'll stay here."

"And what will you be doing?" she challenged.

That would be a complicated answer so he turned to Kade. "I need a closer look at the house. A different angle so I can try to see in one of the windows."

Kade gave him a flat look. "Grayson is bringing infrared," he reminded Nate.

Yes, but Nate didn't think he could just lie there waiting for his brother and the equipment to arrive. "I have to know if Kimmie is all right," he mouthed, hoping that Darcy wouldn't hear him and echo the same about Noah.

Kade huffed, glanced around and then grabbed the binoculars. "You stay here with Ms. Burkhart."

Nate caught his arm. "It's my daughter. I should take the risk."

No flat look this time. This one was cocky. "Won't be a risk if I do it," Kade assured him. "Stay put, big brother. My head is a lot more level than yours right now."

Nate couldn't argue with that, but man, he wanted to. He wanted just a glimpse of his baby to make sure she was okay.

Kade hooked the binoculars around his neck, shot a stay-put glance at them and began to crawl to the left side of the hill. He went about twenty feet, ducking behind some underbrush and then behind an oak.

Nate kept his eyes on Kade until he disappeared from sight, and he turned his attention back to the gunmen. He wouldn't be able to see as well without the binoculars, but at least he could detect any movement that might indicate if one of them had spotted Kade.

"They have to be all right," Darcy mumbled. She, too, had her attention nailed to the patrolling gunmen.

Nate heard the sniffle that she was trying to suppress. This was obviously ripping her apart, and he wanted to comfort her.

Okay, he didn't.

He didn't want to be pulled into this strange bond that was developing between them. He couldn't. But then Darcy sniffed again, and Nate saw the tear slide down her cheek.

Hell.

So much for cooling down this bond.

He couldn't slip his arm around her because he

wanted to keep his gun ready, but he did give her a nudge, causing her to look at him.

"I'm a good cop," he reminded her. "So are my brothers. We *will* get the children out of there."

Darcy blinked back fresh tears. Nodded. And squeezed her eyes shut a moment. She also eased her head against his shoulder. It wasn't a hug, but it might as well have been. Nate felt it go through him. A warmth that was both familiar and unfamiliar at the same time. He recognized the emotions, the comfort, that only a parent in Darcy's position could give.

But there was also some heat mixed with that warmth.

Even though she was still the enemy on some levels, she was also a woman. An attractive one. And his body wasn't going to let him forget that.

She opened her eyes, met his gaze. Until Nate turned his attention back where it belonged—on the gunmen.

"I could go out there," Darcy whispered. "I could offer myself in exchange for the children. Hear me out," she added when he opened his mouth to object. "If they kill me, then you'd still be here to save Kimmie and Noah."

"Admirable," Nate mumbled. "But stupid. We don't need a sacrificial lamb. We just need some equipment and a plan."

And apparently both had arrived.

He heard movement—footsteps—and Nate took aim in that direction just in case. But it wasn't necessary because he spotted Grayson, Dade, Mason and Mel inching their way through the grass toward them.

Nate eased away from Darcy, putting a little space between them, but it was too late. He knew from Grayson's slightly raised eyebrow that he'd taken note of the contact and was wondering what the devil was going on.

"Kade's trying to get a look inside the windows," Nate said, ignoring Grayson's raised eyebrow. He tipped his head in the direction where he'd last seen Kade.

"This should help." Grayson handed Nate the hand-held infrared scanner, and all four crouched down on the hill next to Darcy and him.

Nate didn't waste any time. He put his gun aside, turned on the device and aimed it at the house. The human images formed as red blobs on the screen, and the first thing he saw was an adult figure.

And then two smaller ones.

"The babies," Darcy said on a rise of breath. She probably would have bolted off the hill if Nate hadn't latched on to her and pulled her back to the ground.

Yes, the smaller figures were almost certainly the children, and the person who appeared to be holding them was probably Marlene. Judging from the position of the blobs, Marlene was sitting with the babies on her lap. They were in a room at the back of the ranch.

Mason mumbled some profanity, and Nate didn't have to guess why. Marlene and the babies were alone in the room, but they weren't *alone*. There were two larger figures at the front part of the house. Men. And judging from the placement of their arms, they were holding weapons.

"At least eight of them," Nate supplied. That meant whoever was behind this had some big bucks and a very deep motive.

Dade took the infrared and aimed it at other out-buildings, no doubt to see if there were guards inside.

The movement to their left sent them all aiming their weapons in that direction, but it was only Kade.

"The windows of the house are all covered," he re-layed to them. "But I do have some good news. No cam-eras or surveillance equipment that I can see mounted on the house or anywhere near it. Plus, four FBI agents are in place on the outside perimeter of the property, and more are on the way. The ones here are waiting for orders."

Grayson pulled in a long breath and looked at Nate. "We should wait here for another call from the kidnap-pers. It's clear they want something, and eventually they'll have to say what so we can negotiate release of the hostages."

It was standard procedure. The most logical option. And Grayson had spelled it out like the true cop he was.

"Wait?" Darcy challenged. Nate kept her anchored to the ground by grabbing her arm.

Grayson nodded. "I've already alerted the bank in case we need a large sum of cash, and every road lead-ing away from the area is being watched."

"But our babies are in there," Darcy sobbed. She was close to hysterical now, and Nate knew he had to do something to keep both her and himself calm.

"I vote for having a closer look," Mason said. With just those few words, he had everyone's attention.

"We don't need a warrant because we've seen proof that the children are inside with armed kidnappers. That makes it an immediate-threat situation."

Nate couldn't argue with that.

"I brought a tranquilizer gun rigged with a silencer,

and I can get on the roof and take out the guard there. That would give us some breathing room. Plus, I'm wearing all black, just like them, so I can blend in."

Nate took that all in and saw an immediate problem. "The guy on the road—"

"Would have to be taken out, too," Kade supplied, finishing what Nate had started to say. "I can do that hand-to-hand. I can sneak up on him using those trees to the right. I'll knock him unconscious before he can take a shot and neutralize the threat." He looked back at Mason. "And how the devil do you plan on getting up on the roof?"

"Black van," Mason growled. "It's parked right by the side of the house."

It was, and if Mason could make it that far undetected, he might be able to crawl on top of the van and tranquilize the guard on the roof. The key to this kind of approach was to go in as quietly as possible.

"And then what?" Grayson pressed, staring at Mason.

Mason shrugged. "I'll see if I can quietly take out some of the others with the tranquilizer gun."

Grayson stayed silent a moment and then tapped the infrared screen. "Someone would have to be positioned to go in through the back to get to Marlene and the children while someone else is occupying the two in the front of the house—especially the one on the porch."

"I'll take the front," Dade volunteered. "Once Kade's finished playing hand-to-hand with the guy on the road, he'll be close enough to move in so he can help me out if I need it."

"That leaves the back of the house for me," Grayson spelled out.

"Or me," Nate piped up.

"Bad idea," Grayson let him know.

Kade echoed the same, and it was Kade who continued. "If you're down there and the kidnappers call, then you could get us all killed just trying to answer your phone."

"Best if Darcy and you wait here," Grayson finished.

Darcy looked at Nate and shook her head. "I have to do something to help."

Oh, this was going to be hard. Nate understood Darcy's need because it was his need, too, but Grayson was right. A call from the kidnappers could be deadly if Darcy and he were near the ranch house.

"We have to stay here," Nate told her. And like before, he got at face level with her so he could force eye contact. He kept his voice as calm and gentle as he could manage. "We'll be able to help. We can keep watch and alert them if anything changes or goes wrong."

There was no debate in her eyes. Just the inevitable surrender. "I'll watch the infrared," she finally said. Darcy took the device and focused on it.

Nate looked up at Grayson. "You'll need backup."

"Yeah. I'll have Mel positioned with a rifle somewhere down there." Grayson pointed to a heavily treed area that was still on high ground but much closer to the ranch than they were now.

"And then there's you," Grayson added. He handed Nate another rifle, which he'd taken from the equipment bag that Mel had with her.

His brother didn't mention that if Nate had to fire, it would be dire circumstances. But it would be.

"Kade, call your agents and tell them the plan. I want

them positioned and ready as backup." Grayson paused a moment. "And if anything goes wrong, then we all pull out. No shots are to be fired into the house." He glanced at each of them. "Questions?"

No one said a thing. Grayson gave Nate one last glance, and his brothers and Mel started to move. They were already out of sight before Nate admitted to himself that the plan could be a really bad idea. But staying put could, too. Without a working crystal ball, he had no idea what approach was best, but he did know he had to do everything to get the babies out of there.

The sooner, the better.

"It'll be okay, right?" Darcy asked without taking her attention from the infrared.

"It will be." Nate tried to sound as convinced as he wanted to be, and he put his handgun in his holster so he could get the rifle into position.

"I think they're sleeping," she added, staring at the screen. "And it looks as if Marlene is rocking them."

It did. The babies certainly weren't squirming around, but that made him wonder—had they been drugged?

That tore right at Nate, and he had to take a deep breath just to loosen the knot that put in his throat.

"Noah will want his dinner soon," Darcy whispered.

Nate knew where she was going with this, and he figured it had to stop. They would drive themselves mad considering all the things that could go wrong. He glanced at her. But stopped when he heard a sound.

A snap, as if someone had stepped on a twig.

Not to the side, where the others had walked. This sound came from behind them.

Nate turned, trying to get the rifle into position. But it was already too late.

The man stepped through the wall of thick shrubs, and aimed the gun right at Nate.

Chapter Six

From the corner of her eye, Darcy saw the alarm register on Nate's face.

She whirled around, praying it was one of Nate's siblings but no such luck. Dressed head to toe in black, the man also had black-and-dark-green camouflage paint smeared on his face. He had on some kind of headset with a marble-size transmitter positioned in front of his mouth.

But it was the gun that grabbed her attention.

It was big and equipped with a silencer similar to Mason's weapon.

Oh, mercy.

This was *not* part of the plan.

"Don't," the man warned when Nate tried to shift his rifle toward him. "If you want to live long enough to see your kids, then put the gun down. Slowly. No sudden moves."

Darcy hung on every word. She didn't want to do anything to cause him to fire. But she also studied what she could see of his face.

Did she know him?

It certainly wasn't Wesley Dent or anyone associated

with his case. In fact, she was reasonably sure she'd never seen this man before.

"Boss," the gunman said into the transmitter of his headset, "we got visitors. The kids' parents are up here in the woods. They got guns and infrared. They're looking at you right now."

Darcy glanced at the infrared screen and saw one of the men move from the front of the house to the back, where Marlene and the children were.

"Will do," the man said to his boss. He kept his cold, hard stare and his gun on Nate. "Stand up," he demanded. "We're going for a little walk."

That nearly took the rest of Darcy's breath away, but then it occurred to her, if he'd wanted them dead, he could have just shot them while he was in the bushes.

Nate started to move, but the man growled, "Wait!" in a rough whisper. His eyes narrowed, and he adjusted the transmitter portion of his headset. "Boss, there's a uniform with a rifle at your eight o'clock. About three hundred yards from where I'm standing. She's in firing range of the house."

Oh, no. He'd spotted Mel, and the deputy wasn't looking back at them. Mel had no idea she'd been detected.

Darcy couldn't hear what the person on the other end of the line was saying, but she figured it wasn't good.

"How many are here with you?" the gunman demanded, his attention still fixed on Nate.

"Just the three of us," Nate lied.

The gunman didn't respond to that, but his eyes narrowed. "Boss, I'll take out the uniform and then bring these two down for a chat."

Darcy watched in horror as the gunman took aim at

Mel. She reacted completely out of instinct. She drew back her foot and rammed the thin heel of her right shoe into his shin. Nate reacted, too. He dived at the man, slamming right into him, and they both went to the ground. So did the man's headset.

"Run!" Nate told her.

Darcy turned to do just that, but she stopped. Nate was literally in a life-and-death struggle with a much larger, hulking man, and she had to do something to help.

But what?

She glanced over her shoulder to see if Mel had noticed what was going on. The deputy hadn't. Darcy started to yell out a warning to her, but again she stopped. If she yelled, heaven knew how many gunmen she'd alert, and the men inside the house might try to get away with the children.

Or they might do something worse.

Besides, Mason and the others were probably close to approaching the house now, and if she sounded the alarm, it could get one of them killed.

Darcy looked around and spotted the rifle. She couldn't risk firing a shot, but maybe she could use it. She grabbed the barrel and tried to use the rifle butt to hit the gunman.

She failed.

Nate and the man were rolling around, their bodies locked in the struggle, and if she were to hit Nate accidentally, then it could cost them the fight. And this was a fight they couldn't lose.

"What's going on?" she heard someone ask over the headset.

Her heart dropped again. It wouldn't take long before

the person on the other end of that transmitter realized something was wrong, and that might cause the boss to take some drastic measures.

Nate must have realized that, as well, because she heard him curse, and he revved up his attempt to control the man's gun. Both had fierce grips on the weapon, and the gunman was trying to aim it at Nate.

Darcy kicked the guy again when she could reach his leg. And again. While Nate head-butted the man.

The sound somehow tore through the noise of the struggle.

It was a loud swish. As if someone had blown out a candle. But Darcy instinctively knew what it was. The gun had been fired, the sound of the bullet muffled through the silencer.

"Nate!" she managed to say.

Oh, mercy. Had he been hit?

She dropped to her knees and latched on to Nate's shoulder, to pull him away. There was blood. Lots of it. And a hoarse sob tore from her throat.

"I'm okay," Nate assured her. But he didn't say it aloud. He mouthed it so that no one on the other end of that transmitter could hear him.

But Darcy shook her head. He couldn't be okay, not with that much blood on the front of his shirt.

He repeated, "I'm okay." Again, it was mouthed, not spoken. And he scrambled off the gunman, who was now lying limp and lifeless on the ground.

Nate wrenched the gun from the man's hands and put his mouth right against Darcy's ear. "He pulled the trigger," he let her know. "And missed me. He hit himself instead."

Her sob was replaced by relief, and she threw her

arms around him. Nate was alive and unharmed. She couldn't say a prayer of thanks fast enough.

"We can't stay here," Nate insisted, his mouth still against her ear. He glanced at the headset next to the dead man.

Darcy nodded. He was right. They couldn't stay there because it wouldn't be long before someone came to check on him. Nate and she had to be long gone by then.

Nate kept the gun with the silencer in his right hand, and caught her arm with his left. He started to run, hauling her right along with him, and he headed in the direction that his brothers had taken.

Darcy's heart was already pounding from the fight, and her heels didn't make it easy to race over the uneven terrain. But she couldn't stop or give up. Not with her baby's life at stake.

She wanted to know where Nate was taking her, but she didn't dare ask. The woods were thick, without much sunlight here, and she didn't know if there were other armed guards hiding in the shadows, waiting to strike.

They ran, zigzagging their way through the trees and underbrush. No sign of his brother or Mel, even though Darcy thought they were heading in the deputy's direction.

Nate glanced down at his hip, and for one horrifying moment, she thought maybe he'd been hurt, after all. But she realized his phone was vibrating. He mumbled some profanity and ducked behind a tree.

"It's Grayson," he whispered. Nate didn't answer it. Instead, he fired off a text: Position compromised. Am on the run.

Nate shoved his phone back in his pocket and took her by the arm again. He jerked her forward as if ready to run but then stopped.

"Hell," he mumbled. His grip melted off her arm.

Nate lifted his hands in the air. Darcy did, too, though it took her a moment to realize what was going on. She finally saw the gun. Not a handgun, either, but some kind of assault rifle.

And, just like earlier, it was aimed right at them.

"DROP YOUR GUN," the man ordered Nate. "Take the other one from your holster and drop it, too."

Nate couldn't believe this. He still had blood on his hands from the last attack, and here he was looking down another gun barrel.

"Now!" the man snarled.

Nate glanced at Darcy, to let her know he regretted what he had to do, and he dropped the guns. First, the one he'd taken from the dead guard and then his own Glock.

"Start walking," the gunman demanded the moment the weapons were on the ground. He used the assault rifle to point the way.

This guy was even bigger than the other, and he kept several yards between them so it would be next to impossible for Nate to attack him.

"What do we do?" Darcy whispered. She stumbled, and Nate caught her arm to stop her from falling.

"We look for an opportunity to escape," he whispered back. But he knew that wouldn't be easy.

The guard was leading them straight to the ranch.

Darcy's suddenly rapid breathing let him know that she realized that, as well.

Nate kept walking and glanced around, hoping he'd see one of his brothers or Mel. But he saw no one, other than the guard who was patrolling the road. Once Darcy and he were out of the trees and into the open, the guard on the porch would spot them, as well.

But where were Mason and Kade?

They should have made it to this point now. Nate prayed nothing had gone wrong.

And then there was Mel to consider.

If she was still perched on the side of that hill, she might try to take out one or two of the guards when she saw that Darcy and he had been taken captive. That would mean bullets being fired much too close to the house. Nate knew Mel was a good cop with good aim, but he was uneasy enough with Mason's plan. Nate didn't want bullets added to this already dangerous mix.

Darcy stumbled again right as they reached the dirt road that separated the woods from the ranch. Again, Nate caught her.

"Should I pretend to faint or something?" she whispered.

"Keep moving!" the guard demanded, and this time he didn't whisper.

"Do as he says," Nate instructed. It appeared the guy had plans to take them inside the house.

When they stepped out onto the road, the guard moved closer to them. Probably to protect himself. Did he know Grayson and the others were out there? Maybe. Or maybe he was just being cautious.

The guard by the cattle gate came closer, as well, and he kept his rifle aimed at Darcy and Nate. The man fired glances all around, and his message was clear—if anyone took a shot at him, he would shoot back, and at this range, he wasn't likely to miss.

"They're taking us to the children," Darcy mumbled. She quickened her pace, hurrying across the yard and to the porch.

The door swung open, and the two guards forced them inside, following right behind them. They shut the door and immediately started watching out the gaps in the newspapers that covered the two front windows.

Other than a tattered sofa and some boxes, the room was empty, and Nate couldn't hear the babies or Marlene.

"Welcome," a bulky man said from the doorway of the kitchen. Like the others, he was dressed all in black and had camo paint on his face. And he was armed.

"Are you the boss?" Nate asked.

"Yeah," he readily admitted.

Nate tried to commit every detail of this man's appearance and demeanor because when this was over, the boss was going down.

"Where are the children?" Darcy demanded. Her voice was shaking. So was she. But she managed to sound as if she was ready to tear them limb from limb.

"I'll let you see for yourself." The boss stepped to the side and motioned for them to go toward the back of the house.

Was this some kind of trick?

Maybe.

Nate certainly didn't trust them, but several of the guards had had more than ample opportunity to kill them.

"This way," the boss instructed. He led them through a dining room and then to a hall.

That's when Nate saw the open door. And the room.

"Noah!" Darcy practically shoved the boss aside and hurried toward Marlene and the babies. They'd been right about the rocking chair. Marlene was seated in it with Kimmie in the crook of one arm and Noah in the other.

Marlene's eyes widened, but that was her only reaction. Maybe because she was in shock. No telling what these goons had put her through.

"Noah," Darcy repeated.

She scooped up her sleeping son into her arms. Nate did the same to Kimmie, but neither baby stayed asleep for long. Noah immediately started to fuss, and Kimmie slowly opened her eyes.

Nate felt the rush of panic as he tried to check his daughter to make sure she hadn't been hurt. She was still wearing her pink overalls, and there were no signs of bruises or trauma.

"Da Da," Kimmie babbled, and she smiled at him.

That nearly broke his heart and filled it in the same beat. His baby had been through so much—too much—and yet here she managed a smile. Nate didn't even attempt one. He just pulled Kimmie deep into his arms and held her as close as he could while he kept an eye on the goon standing behind them.

Beside him, Darcy was doing the same to Noah, and there were tears streaming down her face.

"I tried to stop them," Marlene said, shaking her head. She backed away from them as if she might try to bolt through the window.

"She did," the boss verified. "And she might have a few bruises because of it."

Nate had to stop his hands from clenching into fists.

He wanted to break this guy's neck for hurting Marlene and putting them through this nightmare. But he had to hold on to his composure. He would do battle with him, but it wouldn't happen now. First, he had to figure out how to get Kimmie, Noah, Marlene and Darcy out of there.

"Why did you do this?" Nate demanded. He tried to keep the rage out of his voice for Kimmie's sake.

The boss met Nate's glare. "I've been instructed to offer you and Ms. Burkhart a deal."

"What kind of deal?" Darcy snapped. Noah was still fussing so she began patting his back.

Nate waited for what seemed an eternity for the boss to respond, and the dangerous thoughts kept going through his head. All the things that could go wrong. His brothers might not know Darcy and he were inside, and if they didn't, they could be about to put their plan in motion.

A plan that might cause these SOBs to fire shots.

Nate brushed a kiss on Kimmie's forehead and prayed nothing would go wrong.

"It's a simple request." The boss didn't continue until he leaned against the doorjamb. What he didn't do was lower his gun. "You're to transfer two million into an offshore account."

This was about money?

Of course, Nate had considered it, but then why had they taken Noah? Darcy was doing okay financially, but he was pretty sure she wasn't rich.

"Two million?" Nate verified. He could transfer that amount with a phone call.

"Yeah," the boss said. "For starters. Part two of the deal is slightly more…complicated. You're to make sure

Wesley Dent is not only arrested for his wife's murder.
He's also to be convicted."

Nate heard Darcy pull in her breath. He had a similar reaction, including disgust. Yeah, he thought that
Dent might be guilty, but he wasn't a dirty cop, and he
didn't fix investigations.

So, why did this bozo want him to fix this one?

His first guess was that these gunmen worked for
either Sandra Dent's son, Adam, or her ex-husband,
Edwin. Both had motives for wanting Dent behind bars.

Which meant Dent might be innocent, after all.

"Wesley Dent is my client," Darcy clarified. "I'm
supposed to defend him to the best of my abilities."

"Admirable," the man snarled. "But being admirable
won't get your son back."

"What do you mean by that?" Nate demanded.

"I mean we're holding your children until we have
the results we want for Dent. If you want to speed
things up, I suggest you get Dent to confess. Or create
a confession for him."

"That can't happen." Nate turned, adjusting his position so that Kimmie wouldn't see the anger on his face.
"And you can't keep our children for what could turn
out to be months."

Another shrug. "Well, we can't keep them here, of
course. We have to move them as soon as you leave."
He checked his watch. "And your time is up. You have
to go now."

"No!" Darcy tightened her grip on Noah.

"This could all be over by tomorrow," the boss
calmly explained. "Talk Dent into confessing and then
arrange for his suicide because he feels so guilty for
killing his wife."

"No," Darcy repeated, and she looked at Nate and shook her head. "I can't leave Noah here."

Nate was about to assure her that they weren't leaving, but the sound stopped him cold. Not a shot.

But a thud.

The boss's expression changed immediately. He was no longer calm. "See what's wrong," he barked to the young gunman behind him. The boss reached out, latched on to Marlene's hair and pulled her in front of him.

And he put the gun to her head.

Hell.

They didn't need that. Nate had figured he could give Kimmie to Marlene so his hands would be free, but that option was out now. Instead, he handed her to Darcy, and he was thankful that his baby seemed to enjoy being in the arms of this stranger, who cuddled her as protectively as she was cuddling her own son.

"Don't do anything stupid," the boss warned Nate.

There was another sound. Not a thud. But the noise of a tranquilizer gun.

Mason.

His brother was out there. The Ryland plan was in motion.

Nate moved closer to Darcy and the babies, positioning himself between them and the gunman. It wasn't much, but it was the best he could do for now. He braced himself in case he had to lunge for the guy. What he didn't brace himself for was the crash that came through the window behind him.

Darcy tried to move away from the breaking glass. And the boss let go of Marlene. The man took aim at the window and probably would have fired, but Nate dived at him, knocking both the man and his weapon to the floor. His body was still stinging from the fight with the last guard, but he had adrenaline and need on his side. His baby's life was at stake.

"Mason?" Darcy called out. There was relief in her voice, which hopefully meant his brother hadn't been hurt.

Nate continued the struggle, trying to pin the boss to the ground. But the guy just wasn't giving up, and he was fighting hard.

"Stay back," he heard Mason say, and a moment later, his brother was there. The tranquilizer gun was in the waist of his pants, and he'd drawn his sidearm.

Mason reached into the scuffle, and he grabbed the boss by the throat. He dragged him away from Nate and put his gun directly under the man's chin.

"Move and I'll kill you now," Mason warned. "Less paperwork for me to do."

Nate thought that was a bluff. But then, maybe not.

"Get Darcy and the babies out of here," Mason told Nate. He hauled the boss to his feet and muscled him toward the front. "Marlene, too. And hurry."

Nate took Kimmie from Darcy. "Is the outside secured?" Because he didn't want to bring the children out of the house if the gunmen were still out there.

"Kade's people found some explosives," Mason informed him. "They disarmed the ones they found, but they might not have gotten them all."

"Explosives?" Darcy asked. There was no relief in her voice now.

"Yeah," Mason verified. "We must have tripped a master wire or something because they're all set to detonate in about five minutes. Get out of here *now*."

Chapter Seven

Run!

The word kept racing through Darcy's head as she, Nate and Marlene rushed out of the house with the babies cradled in their arms.

Mason was behind them, dragging the boss along, but Darcy concentrated only on her own steps. Running in high heels put her at a huge disadvantage, but she couldn't fall. Couldn't stop. Even though her lungs were already burning.

She had to get her baby away from a possible explosion.

"This way!" someone shouted.

It was Dade, and he was motioning for them to follow him onto the road. Beside him, on the ground, was one of the gunmen, and he was either unconscious or dead because he wasn't moving. There was no sign of Grayson or Kade.

Nate dropped behind her and used his free hand to latch on to her arm. Good thing, too. Because she stumbled, and if it hadn't been for Nate she would have fallen.

"I'm taking genius, here, this way," Mason let them know.

And he started in another direction through the

woods where Darcy had last seen Mel. Maybe because Mason didn't want the boss anywhere near the children. Darcy was thankful for that, but she also hoped the gunmen wouldn't attack again and help their boss escape.

The sound that came from behind them was deafening, a thick blast. Darcy just held her son closer and didn't look back, but it was clear that something had blown up. She prayed Nate's brothers, Mel and the FBI agent hadn't been hurt or killed.

Both Noah and Kimmie were crying now, and their sobs tore at her heart the way nothing else could.

Mercy, what they'd been put through.

And for what?

To rig the investigation so that her client would be arrested and convicted of his wife's murder. Once they were safely away from this place, Darcy wanted answers about who had orchestrated everything. No one was going to get away with endangering these children.

Dade led them back toward the start of the path, where they'd left the vehicles. It seemed to take forever, and each step was a challenge.

"Get in the SUV," Nate ordered, and he jerked open the door and shoved Darcy into the backseat. He pushed Kimmie into her arms and looked behind him.

"Where's Marlene?" Nate asked.

Dade, who was breathing hard, looked behind them, as well. He only shook his head and cursed.

Marlene was nowhere in sight. God, no. Had she fallen? Darcy certainly hadn't heard her, but then she hadn't been able to hear much over the roaring in her ears.

"Go ahead," Dade insisted. "Get them away from here. I'll look for her."

Nate didn't argue. He ripped the keys from his pocket, jumped into the driver's seat and started the engine. He gave Dade one last glance before he hit the accelerator and sped away.

Darcy held a crying baby in each arm, and she pulled them to her and tried to soothe them. "Shhh," she whispered, brushing kisses on each of their heads. "It's okay. Mommy and Daddy are here."

Kimmie looked up at her, the tears spilling down her cheeks, and she glanced at Nate, whose attention was fastened to the road. For a moment Darcy thought the little girl might sob again, but Kimmie rubbed her eyes, smearing the tears on her little hands, and she settled her head against Darcy's shoulder.

All right.

That required a deep breath. Darcy hadn't expected to feel this, well, attachment to Nate's daughter. But Kimmie felt as right in her arms as Noah did. Strange. It had to be a reaction to the fear.

Darcy didn't have time to think about it because there was another blast. It was so loud, so strong, that it shook the SUV.

"Hell," Nate mumbled.

Terrified of what she might see, she looked back and saw more of the nightmare that had started when she'd first learned someone had kidnapped her son.

The house was a fireball. The barn, too.

And so were the woods where she'd last seen Mason.

"CALL ME THE MINUTE you know anything," Nate said to Grayson.

Nate pushed the end-call button on his cell and released the breath he'd been holding. Finally, he had some good news to go with the not so good. Of course, the best news was in his arms.

Kimmie was asleep, her head resting right against his heart, and they were safely back at the Ryland ranch.

Nate had already said prayers of thanks, but he intended to add a lot more. Having Kimmie safe was the most important thing in his life, but his brothers were a close second.

He looked across the foyer and saw Kimmie's nanny, Grace Borden. The petite woman with graying red hair was studying his face. "Well?" she asked in a whisper.

"My brothers are okay," he relayed. Grayson had just let him know that. "And they found Marlene hiding in some bushes. She's shaken up but all right."

Grace nodded and walked to him. "Why don't you let me take Kimmie and put her in her crib for the night?"

Nate wanted to hold her. Heck, he didn't want to let go, but his baby would sleep much better in her own bed than in his arms. Besides, he had to check on Darcy and Noah. He didn't want to wake Kimmie doing that.

Grace eased Kimmie from his arms. "I'll take good care of her," she assured him. It wasn't necessary. Nate trusted her completely, but it still tugged at him to see his daughter being whisked away. It might be a lifetime or two before he started to forget that she'd been stolen from him.

Someone would pay for that.

He felt the anger boil inside him. A lethal mix, but he pushed that powder keg of emotion deep inside him. Soon, he would get the men responsible for what had happened.

Nate went to the bar in the living room and poured himself a shot of whiskey. He took it in one gulp, even though he preferred beer to the fireball of heat that slid down his throat. Still, he needed something to settle his nerves.

He made his way to the family room, where he'd left Darcy as soon as they'd gotten back from the Lost Appaloosa. He had to tell her that Bessie, the house-keeper, had fixed a room for Noah and her.

Before he even got there, he heard the voices coming from the family room. Not Darcy's voice. But Kayla Brennan's, Dade's fiancée, who had already moved into the ranch. Good. Maybe talking with Kayla had managed to calm Darcy down because Nate didn't want to tackle that job.

"Yes, that was an obstacle," Kayla said. "Dade's family hated me."

Nate groaned silently and stopped. This didn't sound like a calming-down kind of conversation. He peered around the corner and saw both women seated on the leather sofa. Darcy held a sleeping Noah in her lap. Kayla had her sleeping son in her arms.

"I was Charles Brennan's daughter-in-law," Kayla continued. "The man who ordered Nate's wife to be killed."

"But Dade and his brothers obviously got past that," Darcy pointed out.

Yeah. But it hadn't been easy. Just a short time ago, Kayla had been the enemy.

Much as Darcy was now.

And that gave Nate a jolt. A nasty feeling in the pit of his stomach.

"That's true." Kayla shrugged. "I fell in love with

Dade, and everything else fell into place. The Rylands and my son are my family now." Her gaze flew to the doorway, where he was standing. "Nate," she greeted. She stood, slowly. "You have news?"

"They're all okay," Nate said as quickly as he could. "Dade doesn't have a scratch on him, and he'll be home soon."

Kayla made a sound of relief and blinked back tears. "Thank you."

Darcy mumbled a thank-you under her breath, and she closed her eyes for a moment.

Kayla glanced down at her son. Then, at Darcy, before her gaze went back to Nate. "It's time I put Robbie to bed." There was an inflection in her voice, an implied *so you two can talk*.

Yeah, they needed to do that. And Darcy probably wasn't going to like what he had to say. Nate waited until Kayla was out of the room before he started what was essentially a briefing.

One with a bad twist.

"Are your brothers really okay?" she asked.

"They are. Kade has a few cuts and scratches because he was close to one of the blasts, but his injuries are minor." He took a deep breath and rested his hands on his hips. "And they found Marlene. She said she got separated from us when we were running, and she hid in some bushes."

"That's good." Darcy stared at him, waiting.

"Come on." Nate motioned for her to stand. It might be better to finish this if he didn't have to see her face. There was concern, and fear, written all over it. "Bessie made up a bed for you. Noah, too."

She stood, not easily. Her legs were wobbly, but Nate

didn't move to help her. He'd been doing too much of that lately. Instead, he led her out of the family room, across the foyer and into the hall that fed into the west wing of the house.

"Okay, what's wrong?" Darcy asked.

Well, the woman was perceptive. "Only one of the kidnappers survived. The boss, aka Willis Ramirez. And he's not talking. Plus, I'm not sure how long we can even hold him."

"What?" It wasn't a whisper, either. Noah jolted, and Darcy frantically started rocking him. She also stared at Nate. "The man kidnapped our children."

"Yes, but Mexico has an extradition order for him. He worked for one of the drug lords and gunned down six people, including a high-ranking police officer."

The color blanched from her face, and he got her moving again so she could put Noah down. She looked too shaky to be holding anything right now, especially a baby.

"How much time do we have to interrogate him?" Darcy wanted to know.

"Not much. A day or two at most. Grayson is with him now and will keep pressing until the federal marshals arrive and take custody."

Darcy shook her head, mumbled something. "Grayson has to get a confession. We have to find out who hired him to kidnap the children."

"We will," Nate promised.

He opened the door to the guest suite and took her through the sitting area and into the bedroom where Bessie had prepared the crib. Bessie had also left Darcy a loaner gown, a robe and some toiletries.

Darcy laid the baby down, kissed one cheek and then

the other. She lingered for several moments, and Nate didn't rush her. He understood her reluctance to leave her baby.

Finally, she stepped away, keeping her eyes on Noah until she was in the sitting room. She groaned softly and leaned against the wall. "I don't know how I made it through this day," she whispered.

Nate was right there with her on that. He'd faced down armed criminals before, had even been wounded in the line of duty. But only Ellie's death came close to this.

"Tomorrow I'll have someone drop by your house and get some things," he told her. "If you need anything specific, make a list."

The weariness didn't fade from her eyes, but they did widen a bit. "I'm not going home?"

"No." Nate thought about how to say it and decided to just toss the truth out there. "The danger isn't over. If Ramirez doesn't give up the person who hired him, then one way or another I'll have to find out who he is. That might take some time."

She didn't argue. Didn't look as if she had the strength to put up even a token resistance. "And in the meantime?"

"Noah and you will stay here." That was the logical solution. The ranch had a security system. Plus, there were at least a dozen ranch hands on the grounds at any given moment. It also didn't hurt that five lawmen lived there.

And four of those lawmen might be a problem.

"Your brothers?" she said, getting right to the heart of the matter.

"There'll be tension," he admitted. "But no one here

will turn you out. The kidnappers went after our children. They might try again."

She shivered, and closed her eyes. Did she see the same nightmarish images that he did? The gunmen, the children huddled on the floor of the preschool? The explosions that tore apart the Lost Appaloosa only minutes after they'd rescued Noah and Kimmie?

Her eyelids fluttered open, and she met his gaze. "If Ramirez doesn't talk, I think we know where your investigation starts. Sandra Dent's son, Adam, or her ex-husband, Edwin Frasier."

Yeah. That ball was already rolling. Mason was arranging for both men to be brought to Silver Creek for questioning. Too bad they couldn't find the dead woman's missing diary. Then maybe they would know who was behind this. Nate knew from accounts from Sandra's friends that the diary existed, but it hadn't turned up in any of the searches of her estate. Of course, her killer could have destroyed it, and with it any possible evidence.

"I can't rule out Dent himself," Nate added. "He could have orchestrated this to make himself look innocent." He braced himself for the lawyer to kick in.

But she only nodded. "About how much would it have cost to put this kidnapping together?"

"Three vans, seven men, weapons, explosives. We're probably looking at a minimum of a hundred thousand." He hesitated. "Unless Ramirez's drug-lord connections are behind this. Then the men could have been coerced into helping with the kidnapping."

A heavy sigh left her mouth, and she plowed her hands through her hair to push it away from her face.

But then she winced when her fingers raked over her stitches.

Nate moved her hand so he could have a look, which required him to push aside a few strands. Her hair was as soft as silk. And despite their ordeal in the woods, she didn't smell of sweat and blood but rather the faint aroma of the fragrant cedars. Her own scent was there, too. Something warm and musky.

Something that stirred feelings best left alone.

"Well?" she prompted.

"The stitches held." But there was an angry bruise around the edges. He made a mental note to call the doctor and ask him to come out to the ranch to examine Darcy. He also made a mental note not to let her scent get to him.

"How does it look?" she asked. But she waved him off. "Never mind. I know I look bad."

That was the problem. She didn't. Even with the fatigue, the stitches and the bruise, Darcy managed to look amazing.

Beautiful.

And that was not a good thing for him to notice.

Nor was her body. It was pretty amazing, too. She was a good eight inches shorter than he was. On the petite side. But she still had interesting curves. Curves that reminded him it'd been too long since he'd held a woman.

Or had one in his bed.

His own body responded to that reminder. His blood started to race. His heart, too. And his jeans were no longer comfortable.

Nate stepped back, or rather, tried, but she caught his arm. "I'm sorry."

Of all the things he'd expected her to say, that wasn't one of them.

He studied her eyes. Also beautiful. And he shook his head, not understanding her apology. He was the one with the bad reaction here.

"I'm sorry for everything," Darcy clarified. Her voice was mostly breath now. "Especially for defending the man whose hired gun killed your wife. I'm sorry I managed to keep him out of jail so that he could go after Dade and Kayla."

Oh, hell, no. Nate didn't want to go there. He didn't want to talk about Ellie. So he shook off her grip and turned to leave.

"For what it's worth," Darcy continued, "I've applied to be the assistant district attorney here in Silver Creek."

That froze him in his tracks, and Nate eased back around to stare at her. As the A.D.A, she'd have to work with Grayson, Dade and Mason. Work *closely* with them, on the same side of the law.

"I'm not a bad person." Her voice trembled again. So did her bottom lip, and her eyes began to water. "I just got wrapped up in doing…what I thought I needed to do. Old baggage," she added in a mumble. "Something you might know a little about."

Oh, yeah. His old baggage had baggage.

"When did yours start?" she asked.

Nate didn't have to think about that. He also didn't have to think about it to know this was a conversation he didn't want to have. But he answered her, anyway. "Twenty years ago when I was fifteen, my grandfather was murdered, and it was never solved."

"Yes. Sheriff Chet McLaurin. Kayla asked me about him."

Nate was sure he blinked. "Why would she ask you that?"

"She called me a few weeks ago and wanted to know if I'd come across a photo of your grandfather in any of Charles Brennan's things. She faxed me a copy of the picture and said it was taken on the day the new sheriff's office opened."

Now, he understood. Kayla had asked because Darcy was the executor for Brennan's will, and the picture was definitely in question. Kayla had seen a copy, and now the family wanted to know why a man like Brennan had held on to a photo seemingly unrelated to him.

"Did you find the picture in Brennan's things?" Nate asked.

Darcy shook her head. "I looked but didn't find anything. It might turn up, though, because I'm still going through his estate." She paused. "Is it important?"

"Could be. Maybe there's something in Brennan's files that will tell us who killed our grandfather."

"I see." And a moment later, she repeated it. "When this is over, I'll look again." Another pause. "His death is the reason you became a cop?"

"Yeah." And this was another wound Nate didn't want reopened tonight so he turned the tables on her. "What baggage made you become a defense attorney?"

A pained look flashed across her face, and Darcy opened her mouth. Closed it. And that pained look got significantly worse.

"It's okay," he quickly assured. "The conversation's over." And he was probably as thankful for that as she was.

They didn't need to be delving into baggage or what had brought them to this point. Didn't need to be discussing anything personal.

He especially didn't need to be thinking of her as an attractive, troubled woman he should haul off to his bed.

Besides, he had a mountain of stuff to do—stuff that didn't require getting Darcy naked and in his bed. Phone calls to make. An investigation to start. He also needed to see if Grayson had made any progress with Ramirez.

"If you need anything, my room is just across the hall," he let her know. "The security system is on, and all the ranch hands are on watch to make sure no one suspicious enters the property."

There. He'd doled out all the info she needed for the night, and he could go. Good thing, too, because he was exhausted.

But he didn't move.

His feet seemed glued to the floor.

Her eyes widened, as if she knew a fierce storm was already upon them. And it was. The storm inside him. Nate cursed. Because he saw the alarm on Darcy's face.

Followed by the heat.

Oh, man.

One-sided lust was bad enough, but two-sided was a disaster in the making.

His feet finally moved. In the wrong direction. Nate went to her, catching her hands and pinning them against the wall. Hell, he pinned her, too. Pressing his body against hers as he lowered his head.

And kissed her.

He captured her breath and the sound of her surprise

all at once. Nate might as well have had sex with her because the slam of pleasure was that intense. The instant awareness that he was about to lose it. And that taste.

Yeah.

Like something forbidden.

"Nate," she managed to say, the heat burning her voice.

He didn't attempt to say anything for fear that the sound of his voice would bring him back to his senses. For just this moment he wanted to be pulled deep into the fire.

He wanted to feel.

And he did. For those scalding-hot moments, Nate felt it all. The desire for a woman. The need to take her. The ache that he'd suppressed for way too long.

But he forced himself to remember that even with all those aches and burning needs, he shouldn't be kissing Darcy. Nate pushed himself away from her. Not easily. He had to force his body to move, and then he had to force it not to go right back after her again.

Their gazes collided.

In her eyes, he saw all that fire still raging. Heard it in her thin breath. Felt it pulsing in her wrist.

He let go of her, and her hands dropped to her sides. Nate watched her recover, hoping that he could do the same.

"What was that?" she asked, breathless.

"A mistake." He was breathless, too.

She stared at him, the pulse hammering in her throat. Since looking at her throat made him want to kiss her there, Nate took another step back. And another for good measure.

Her gaze slid over his face, his chest, which was pumping as though starved for air. In a way, it was. Then, her eyes lowered to the front of his jeans.

Where she no doubt—*no doubt*—saw the proof of just how much that kiss had aroused him.

"We can blame it on the adrenaline," she whispered.

For some reason, a stupid one, probably, that made him smile. For a split second, anyway. And then reality crashed down on his head. He shouldn't be kissing her and he shouldn't be smiling.

"Good night, Darcy," Nate told her.

"Wait. There's something bothering you. Something other than *that*," she clarified, her attention dropping to the front of his jeans again.

Oh, man. This brain connection they had was almost as bad as the fire she'd started in his body. Darcy was right—something was bothering him. He'd intended to keep it to himself. Because it could alarm her. But heck, he'd already opened a big box of alarm just by kissing her.

"Did you think there was anything strange about Ramirez when the gunman took us into the ranch house?" he asked.

She stayed quiet for a moment. "You mean stranger than the fact he had kidnapped our children?"

"Yeah. He didn't ask us how we'd found them."

"You're right." Darcy pulled in her breath. "Neither did the gunmen in the woods."

Nate made a sound of agreement. "They seemed ready for us. As if they'd been expecting us all along. But why would that be? The only reason we went to the Lost Appaloosa was because Marlene wrote the initials on the van door."

She pressed her fingers to her forehead. "And from what we know, Marlene might not have even been in that particular van. It could have been just a decoy."

"So who wrote the initials?" Nate finished for her. "And why did Ramirez want us to find him?"

"I don't know." She shook her head. "Do you?"

"No. But first thing in the morning, I intend to find out."

Chapter Eight

"I'm fine, really," Darcy told the Stetson-wearing
doctor again, but Dr. Doug Mickelson continued to slide
his penlight in front of her eyes. He'd already examined
her stitches and a small cut she'd gotten on her elbow.

She wanted this exam to end so she could go back to
her son. Darcy could feel the anxiety creeping through
her, again, and she wondered how long it would take
before she could get past the ordeal of the kidnapping.

Never was a distinct possibility.

"You're sure the children are okay?" Darcy asked
when the doctor plugged the stethoscope into his ears
so he could listen to her heart.

"They're right as rain," he assured her. "They were
lucky."

Yes, and she hated that something as fragile as luck
had played into keeping Noah and Kimmie safe.

"All done," the doctor finally said. He hooked the
stethoscope around the collar of his cowboy-style light
blue shirt. "No concussion, but I'll need to see you early
next week so I can take out those stitches."

She nodded but couldn't think beyond the next hour,
much less next week. Darcy hurried off the foot of the
bed, then out of the guest room and into the hall, leav-

ing the doctor as he was putting his gear back into his medical bag. She got to the nursery, where she'd left Noah with Kimmie and the nanny, Grace Borden.

But the nursery was empty.

Just like that, the panic grabbed her by the throat. *No!* Had her son been taken again? She knew that wasn't a logical conclusion, but her mind wasn't logical right now. The pain was still too fresh.

"Noah?" she called out. She didn't even wait for an answer before she shouted out his name again.

"In here," Nate answered.

Darcy practically rammed into the doctor coming out of the guest suite, but she followed the sound of Nate's voice. And the sound of laughter. She found him in the last room at the end of the hall. A massive sun-washed playroom. Bright. With lots of windows and shelves loaded to the brim with books and stuffed animals.

It took her a moment to pick through the toys and the brightly colored furniture, but she finally spotted Nate. Not in danger. Not trying to stop another kidnapping. He was on his hands and knees on the floor.

Both Kimmie and Noah were on his back.

And Nate was giving them a pseudo horsey ride. He was even making the neighing sounds while holding on to them.

Kimmie's auburn curls were bouncing all around her face. Noah was doing some bouncing, too. Clearly her brain had overreacted because the children were in no kind of danger.

"Grace is in the kitchen having some breakfast, and Bessie brought you some of that cinnamon tea you said you liked," Nate let her know, tipping his head toward the tray on a corner table. But he must have noticed her expression. "What's wrong?"

"Nothing," she managed to say. "I panicked when I couldn't find Noah."

"Sorry. I thought it would be okay to bring him down here while you were with Doc Mickelson." He reached behind him and gently moved the children off his back and to the thick play mat.

"It's okay." Her son had obviously been having fun, and her panic had ended that fun.

Well, sort of.

Even though Noah was no longer on Nate's back, her son giggled and crawled into Nate's lap the moment he sat up. Noah babbled something and threw his arms around Nate's neck for a hug.

"He's not usually this comfortable with strangers," Darcy remarked. To give her hands something to do, and to settle her nerves, she went to the table and poured herself a cup of tea.

Nate shrugged. Or rather, he tried to, but Kimmie toddled right into him and he had to catch her to keep her from falling. Noah giggled again. Kimmie did, too.

"I guess Noah knows I like kids," Nate remarked.

And he did. There was no mistaking that. Nate started a gentle wrestling game that ended up with both babies landing on him in a tumbled heap.

Now, Nate was the one to laugh.

The sound was rich, thick and totally male. It went through her much as his kiss had the night before, and suddenly the panic was gone. In its place was that spark. Okay, it was more of a jolt that touched every part of her body.

Every part.

His looks didn't help ease that jolt. Nate was drop-dead hot—that was a given—but this morning he was rumpled hot with his dark stubble, jeans and charcoal gray shirt. It was only partially buttoned, and she got a great look at the perfectly toned chest that he'd used to pin her against the wall for that kiss.

Suddenly, Darcy wanted to be pinned and kissed again.

"What?" Nate asked, snapping her attention back to him. "You're smiling. I've never seen you smile before." His gaze slid down her body. "And I've never seen you wear jeans."

She glanced down at her jeans and rose-colored top because for a moment she forgot she was wearing anything at all.

Get ahold of yourself.

"Someone picked up clothes from my house for Noah and me," she told him, but he obviously already knew that.

"Kade," he supplied. "He also brought your cosmetics and meds that he found in your bathroom."

Oh.

Meds, as in birth-control pills.

She almost blurted out that the pills were to control her periods and not because she was having sex, but that seemed way too personal to tell Nate.

"I'll make sure to thank Kade. And all your brothers. Bessie and Grace, too." She added some milk to the tea so she could cool it down for a quick drink. "Your family really pitched in when we needed them."

"They always do," Nate mumbled, and it sounded like a personal confession that he hadn't intended to reveal to her.

Darcy understood. Other than Noah, she hadn't had any family for a very long time, and she missed the closeness. The blind acceptance.

The love.

And that was a personal confession she wasn't ready to make, either.

Since it seemed the wrestling play might go on for a while, Darcy finished her tea, put the cup aside and sank down on the floor next to them. Nate didn't look at her. He kept his attention on the children.

"Do I need to apologize?" he asked.

For a moment Darcy had no idea what he meant, but then Nate glanced at her. And she knew. This was about that scalding-hot kiss. "No apology needed. We just got caught up in the moment."

And that moment was still causing some heat to flow through her body.

"Yeah." He sounded as if he wanted to believe that. Did that mean he was still thinking about the effects of that kiss, too?

Darcy decided it was a good time to change the subject, especially since they had plenty of non-kissing things to discuss. "Any news about Ramirez?"

Nate shook his head. "He's still not talking, and the extradition is moving at lightning speed."

So, time was ticking away. Darcy hoped the man would spill something before he was flown back to Mexico.

"Grayson's bringing in both Adam and Edwin for questioning." He glanced at the cartoon clock on the wall. "He'll let us know when they arrive."

Good. Sandra Dent's son and ex-husband were keys to unraveling all of this. Darcy just hoped she could hang on to her temper and composure if one of them confessed to taking the children.

"The rangers have their CSIs at the Lost Appaloosa. Or rather, what's left of it. The explosions destroyed a lot of potential evidence." Nate paused. Definitely no smile or laughter now, though he continued to play with the children. "Two of the gunmen have been identified, and they both belonged to a drug cartel linked to Ramirez. One of them is Ramirez's kid brother."

"His brother?" she questioned.

"Yeah, his name was David Ramirez. He was just nineteen, and he was the one I got in a wrestling match in the woods. The one I shot." Another pause. "We believe the brother and all the gunmen belonged to the cartel because they each had a coiled rattlesnake tattoo on their left shoulders. That's the cartel's symbol."

That erased the warm, jolting memories of the kiss and chilled her to the bone. Drug dealers had kidnapped her son. The doctor had been right—they were lucky. Things could have gotten a lot worse than they had.

"It's okay," she heard Nate say. And she felt his hand on her arm. Touching her. Rubbing gently with his fingertips. Darcy figured she must have looked on the verge of fainting or something for him to do that.

"I've run financial reports on Adam and Edwin Frasier," he explained. His voice wasn't exactly all cop now. Or maybe that was her interpretation because he was still touching her. "Both father and son have the ready cash to set up an operation like the kidnapping."

"But why would they have risked something like this?" she asked.

"More money, maybe. Sandra Dent died without a will. That means her husband will inherit everything."

"Unless he's convicted of her murder," Darcy supplied. "Then Adam would inherit everything. And that makes him the top suspect."

"Yes, it does. But it's possible Adam and his father worked out this deal together. Or if Edwin is working alone, he could have figured it'd be easier to continue to get an allowance from his son than Dent. As it stands now, Edwin is paid an allowance for managing Sandra's charity foundations. You can bet if Dent inherits everything, he'll cut off Edwin without a penny."

Yes. But Darcy was having a hard time wrapping her mind around anyone risking children's lives for money. Even the fifty million dollars that was in Sandra Dent's estate.

She jumped when she heard a sudden sound in the doorway. It was Mason. With his shoulder propped against the frame, he was holding a cup of coffee and had his attention fastened to Nate's hand, which was still touching her.

Darcy quickly got to her feet.

She didn't want to cause trouble between Nate and his brothers, and judging from Mason's semi-glare, he didn't approve of her or little arm rubs.

"Ma Ma Ma," Kimmie babbled, and with her wispy curls haloing around her face, she toddled toward her dark, brooding uncle.

Mason put his cup on a shelf and scooped her up. "We gotta work on that vocabulary, curly locks. It's Uncle Mason, not Ma Ma."

Kimmie smiled a big toothy smile, dropped a kiss on his cheek and babbled some more. "Ma Ma Ma."

"Don't give her any candy," Nate warned when both

Kimmie and Mason started to reach in his denim shirt pocket.

"Later," Mason whispered to the little girl. He placed his hand over hers. "When Daddy's not watching. I'll leave one for your pint-size boyfriend, too."

Darcy was more than a little surprised that this particular Ryland also had a way with children. Mason always made her want to take a step back, and until now she'd never suspected there was a fatherly bone in his body. Noah, however, didn't move. He stayed right by Nate.

"A problem?" Nate asked his brother. He stayed on the floor and accepted some plastic blocks that Noah began to dump in his lap.

"Not with the investigation. A ranching situation. Another cutter quit this morning."

"Again?" Nate mumbled something indistinguishable under his breath. He was clearly upset, and this conversation was a reminder that the Rylands had more going on in their lives than law enforcement.

"Yeah," Mason snarled. "What can I say? I'm not into arm touching to keep folks happy."

Mason had noticed, after all. She felt herself blush.

"What's a cutter?" Darcy asked to fill in the very uncomfortable silence that followed. "I was born and raised a city girl," she clarified when Mason gave her a flat look.

"A person who trains cutting horses. They're used to cull out or cut individual livestock from a herd," Mason finally explained. "But folks use them for competitions and shows."

"People pay a lot of money for a well-trained cutting horse," Nate went on. "And despite going through a trainer every six months, Mason produces some of the best cutting horses in the state."

If Mason was flattered by that, he didn't show it. Instead, he gave Kimmie one of those flat looks. "You impressed, curly locks? Didn't think so."

Mason kissed Kimmie on top of her head and set her back on the floor. "Cause some trouble today, okay?" He eased two foil-wrapped pieces of candy on the shelf, grabbed his coffee cup and strolled away.

"Bye-bye." Kimmie added a backward wave and then reached up toward the shelf where she'd no doubt seen her uncle leave the candy.

"Later, baby," Nate insisted.

But Kimmie didn't give up. The little girl went to Darcy, caught her hand and babbled something.

"Maybe I can distract her," Darcy said, smiling, and she lifted Kimmie into her arms.

Kimmie waggled her fingers in the direction of the shelf with the candy, but Darcy took her in the opposite direction. To another shelf.

One Darcy hadn't noticed when she walked into the room.

There were more pictures here. Dozens of them, all in gleaming silver frames. Some were candid shots of Nate and his brothers, including one Ryland she'd never seen. That had to be his late brother, Gage, who resembled Mason except he had a cocky grin. There was also a copy of the picture of Nate's grandfather, the one that Kayla had faxed her.

"I called my assistant this morning," Darcy told Nate, "and asked her to look into the matter of your grandfather's photo. If Charles Brennan had something

to do with Chet McLaurin, then we might find it in
his files."

Files that she and her assistant had total access to.
If she could give Nate and his family this information,
then she would. Of course, Darcy hoped it wouldn't be
another round of bad news because her former client,
Brennan, was now dead, but when alive he'd no doubt
committed murder and a litany of other crimes.

"There's Daddy." Darcy pointed to one of Nate holding Kimmie. Behind them were several horses.

"Da Da Da," Kimmie babbled, and then she switched
to "Ma Ma."

Darcy expected to see a photo of Mason, but it
wasn't. She recognized the beautiful smiling woman
from articles in the newspaper. This was Nate's late
wife, Ellie, and she was wearing a wedding dress.

"Ma Ma," Kimmie repeated, and she clapped her
hands.

"Ellie died when Kimmie was six weeks old," Nate
said softly. "I thought the picture might help her know
who her mother is."

Well, it was obviously working because Kimmie was
reaching for the photo now and had forgotten all about
the candy. Darcy carefully lifted the picture from the
shelf and brought it closer to Kimmie.

"Ma Ma." And the little girl kissed it. Darcy saw
then that there were dozens of smudges on the glass.
No doubt from Kimmie's kisses.

It put a lump in Darcy's throat, and she eased the
picture back onto the shelf. She saw it then. The little
silver disk. When Kimmie reached for it, Darcy picked
it up so the little girl couldn't get to it. She didn't want
to risk Kimmie choking on it.

"A concho," Nate provided.

Darcy turned it over and saw the double *R*s on the back. "For your ranch?"

"Yeah." And that was all he said for several seconds. His mood darkened a bit. "My father gave me and each of my five brothers a concho. A family keepsake, he said. And then a few weeks later, he walked out and never came back."

She turned, stared at him. "What happened?"

But judging from the pain that went through his eyes, she was sorry she'd asked. "I'm not sure why he left. My mother wasn't sure, either, and his leaving destroyed her. She killed herself, and in her suicide note she begged Grayson to keep the family together." Nate lifted his shoulder. "And he did. End of story."

No. Not the end. The pain was still too raw for that. It didn't help with that lump in her throat, and it gave her added respect for the Ryland brothers. They'd raised themselves, kept their family together, and they'd done that under the worst of circumstances.

"Do you hate your father for abandoning you?" Darcy asked, holding her breath.

"Yeah. All of us do. Well, except for Kade. He was only ten when our father walked out." Nate tipped his head to the concho. "Mason put a bullet through his. Dade threw his away."

"But you kept yours," she pointed out. And he'd polished it. Or someone had. Because it had a gleaming shine.

"Only so I could remember how much it hurts when people do irresponsible, selfish things." He shook his head. "I don't want to be anything like my father because I would never put Kimmie through that. *Never.*"

It was the answer she'd feared. "Noah's father, Jake Denton, abandoned him. Jake's never seen Noah and swore he never would." And Darcy could see firsthand the pain that abandonment could cause.

Would Noah have the same bitterness that Nate had?

Darcy hated Jake for that. Hated that Noah would have this wound.

"It's my fault, of course," she added. "I should have chosen a better partner." Even though her pregnancy had been an accident. One she certainly didn't regret.

"Sometimes, even when you choose the right partner, it's not enough," Nate said. She followed his gaze, and he was staring at Ellie's picture.

Kimmie looked at her dad. Then, at Darcy, and even though she was just a baby, she seemed to realize something wasn't right. Kimmie hooked her arms around Darcy's neck and kissed her cheek.

Darcy smiled in spite of the sad moment.

Children were indeed magical, and Nate's daughter was no exception. Noah, however, disagreed. He must have objected to Darcy giving this little girl so much attention because he toddled toward them and tugged on her jeans. Darcy treated herself to holding both of them, even though they were a double armful.

She glanced at Nate, who was smiling again. After the hellish day they'd had, this seemed like a moment to savor.

What would it be like to have moments like this all the time?

Darcy hadn't let herself consider a relationship, not after Jake had burned her so badly. But what would it be like to be with Nate? Thinking about that caused the heat to trickle through her body again.

Nate made a *hmm* sound.

Did he know what she was thinking? Probably not. But that didn't erase the little fantasy in her head.

Then Nate's phone buzzed, and the moment vanished. Darcy snapped back to reality. Especially when she heard Nate greet the caller.

"Grayson," he answered. "You have news?"

She stepped closer, watching Nate's face.

"What?" Nate asked several second later, and he paused. Darcy couldn't hear anything his brother was saying, but Nate finally snapped his phone shut.

"Edwin and Adam Frasier just arrived at the sheriff's office," Nate relayed to her after dragging in a long breath. He was the cop again. All business. And he got to his feet.

"What's wrong?" she asked, afraid to hear the answer.

Nate looked her straight in the eyes. "Edwin and Adam both claim Dent and *you* were behind the kidnapping plot, and they say they can prove it."

Chapter Nine

Darcy wasn't denying anything that Edwin and Adam Frasier had claimed. In fact, she hadn't said more than two words on the drive from the ranch to the sheriff's office. She just sat in the passenger's side of his SUV and stared out the window.

That caused Nate to do some mental cursing.

He didn't need this now. He needed clear answers that would lead him to the person responsible for kidnapping Kimmie and Noah, and with this latest allegation, Nate was afraid these interviews wouldn't give him anything useful.

The moment Nate parked the SUV, Darcy got out, and she didn't wait for him. She stormed toward the back entrance, threw open the door and hurried inside.

"Where are they?" Darcy asked Mel, and the deputy hitched her thumb toward the interview room at the front of the building.

"Grayson's in there with them now," Mel let her know. "How are the kiddos?"

"Fine," Darcy mumbled. "Kade and Mason are staying with them while I straighten out this mess."

Okay. She clearly wasn't pleased, and Nate couldn't blame her since they'd accused her of being involved with the kidnapping. Still, he hoped she wouldn't try to attack one of them. He'd faced Darcy in court and legal hearings and had never once seen her lose her composure. But now her fuse seemed short and already lit. Just in case her temper was about to explode, Nate hurried to catch up with her.

She marched into the room and shot past Grayson, who was standing. Edwin and Adam were seated, and Darcy planted her fists on the metal table that separated them. She leaned in and got right in their faces.

"Explain to me what *proof* you think you have that would implicate me in this crime," she demanded.

The men exchanged glances but didn't exactly seem unnerved. Nate decided to do something about that. He, too, moved closer.

"Ms. Burkhart asked you a question," Nate clarified. He shut the door, locked it, pretended to turn off the interview camera and then slid his hand over his gun in his shoulder holster.

That got their eyes widening.

Nate knew both men. Had interviewed them extensively about Sandra's death. Edwin was fifty-three and looked pampered and polished in his blue suit. To the best of Nate's knowledge, the man had never had a job in his life, even though he did get an allowance for managing one of his late wife's charity foundations.

Adam was a younger version of his father. There were no threads of gray in his brown hair. No tiny lines around his blue eyes. But there was no mistaking he was his father's son. Like his father, he also lived off an allowance from his mother's estate.

"You're going to shoot us?" Edwin challenged, eyeing the stance Nate had taken with his gun.

"Depends," Nate tossed back. Normally, he didn't play cop games, but he was almost as pissed off as Darcy was. "Right now, I consider you two my top suspects. I think one or both of you is responsible for endangering my daughter and Ms. Burkhart's son."

Nate adjusted his position and leaned in so that Darcy and he were shoulder to shoulder. "And I'm also thinking you're both dangerous enough to try to run out of here now that you know you're suspects. If you do that, I'll stop you."

Adam practically snapped to attention, but the threat didn't seem to faze Edwin. Except for the slight stirring in his jaw muscles. Because Nate had interviewed him and because he'd cataloged the man's responses, Nate was guessing that Edwin was also riled to the core. The man was just better at hiding his emotions than his son.

"Why would you say I had a part in this?" Darcy demanded again.

Edwin lifted his shoulder, but it was Adam who answered. "Because you stole seventy-five thousand dollars from my mother."

Darcy looked at Nate and shook her head. "When, where and how did this supposedly happen?" Nate asked.

"A week ago at my mother's estate," Adam continued. "The money was taken from a safe while Darcy was in the house."

Darcy huffed. "I was there," she admitted. "With two San Antonio police officers who work for Nate. I wanted to see where Sandra had died in case it came up at the trial. But I didn't go anywhere near a safe, and I didn't take any money."

"Well, it was there before you arrived, and it wasn't

there after you left." Adam folded his arms over his chest. "We think you used the money to orchestrate this kidnapping."

"And why would I do that?" Darcy spaced out each word and glared at Adam.

"Simple. This makes your client look innocent. He's not. But the truth doesn't matter to you. The only thing that matters to you is winning and letting a killer like Dent go free."

Since that seemed to eat away at what little fuse Darcy had left, Nate took over. "You have any proof she took it? Security surveillance tapes? Eyewitnesses?"

"No." Edwin didn't glare. He just looked smug. "But who else would have done it? Adam did an inventory of that safe just minutes before she arrived, and when he checked the safe again later that afternoon, the cash was gone. Are you saying your own officers are thieves?"

"No." Nate could play the smug game, too. "I'm saying you two are troublemakers or liars. Maybe both. You honestly think Darcy would have done anything to endanger her son or my daughter?"

Darcy made a slight sound. Relief, maybe? Nate glanced at her and realized that's exactly what it was. Oh, man. Had she really thought he might believe she'd put her child in danger to clear a client?

But Nate took a mental step back.

Yesterday, he might have indeed believed it. Before he'd seen her reaction to Noah's kidnapping. Before he'd witnessed firsthand how terrified she was.

Before he'd kissed her.

Yeah, that was playing into this, as well.

The sweltering attraction. But Nate knew in this situation that the kiss wasn't clouding his judgment. Darcy hadn't taken that money, and she hadn't had anything to do with kidnapping the babies.

Grayson moved to the end of the table and sat down. He studied Edwin and Adam for a moment. "So, you're suggesting a lawyer with no criminal record would do something like this?" He didn't wait for them to respond. "Because she's not a suspect, and you two are."

"I did nothing wrong!" Adam shouted.

"Nor did I." Edwin's voice was almost calm. *Almost.*

"That remains to be seen," Nate let them know.

Edwin got to his feet. "Are you arresting us? Because this was just supposed to be an opportunity for us to tell you about her stealing that money and trying to clear her client. And I don't appreciate your intimidation tactics. If I'd known we would be grilled like this, I would have brought my attorney."

"Come on," Grayson fired back. "Did you really think you could walk in here and put this kind of spin on what happened? If Darcy had wanted to clear her client, she would have gone about it differently. Not using reverse psychology."

"And if she had criminal intent, she could have created and paid for a witness," Nate explained. "One that would have given Dent an airtight alibi. It would have been far cheaper. Far safer. And it wouldn't have put her baby's life on the line."

Nate leaned in so he could look them in the eyes. "But you two have a lot to gain if you put Dent behind bars. Or better yet, get him the death penalty."

"Dent made his own bed," Edwin insisted. "He's running scared because he's guilty. And he knows you can prove it. You've said so yourself that you believe he's guilty."

Nate had said that. He couldn't deny it. And maybe Dent was behind the kidnapping, but Darcy certainly wasn't. So, that meant either these two had been duped into thinking Darcy was guilty, or they were the ones trying to do the duping.

Edwin gave his suit an adjustment that it in no way needed. "We're done here. We've given you the information, and now we'll go to your captain at SAPD. We'll press him to file charges against..." He cut his eyes toward Darcy. And smiled an oily smile. "Well, whatever she is to you."

Nate didn't consider himself someone who had a bad temper, but Edwin's suggestion sent anger boiling through him.

"Who said we're done?" Nate fired back.

Surprise showed in Edwin's eyes. Adam seemed alarmed.

Grayson stood, gave Nate a nod. "I'll take things from here." He looked at the two men. "You have the right to remain silent—"

"You're arresting us?" Edwin howled.

"Detaining you for questioning and possible arrest for multiple felonies," Grayson clarified. "When you're done hearing your rights, I suggest you call a lawyer."

The two men started to protest, but Grayson glanced at Nate, and he knew what that glance meant. This was now an official interrogation. Not an interview. And that meant Darcy and he shouldn't be there.

"We can wait in Grayson's office," Nate said to her.

She looked ready to argue, and her gaze flew to Grayson as if he might allow her to stay. But Grayson only shook his head.

"Come on." Nate caught her arm and led her out of the room.

"Thank you," she whispered. "For sticking up for me in there."

He maneuvered her inside Grayson's office but didn't shut the door. Privacy and Darcy weren't a good idea, especially since her nerves were raw and right at the surface.

"It was a no-brainer. As I said, you love Noah too much to put him in danger."

Darcy looked at him and shook her head as if she didn't know how to respond to that. But she did respond. Man, did she. She stepped forward until she was pressed against him, and slipped her arms around him.

"I'm wired to handle stress," she whispered. "But not this kind."

Was she talking about Noah now, or this suddenly close contact between them? Nate wasn't sure, but that didn't stop him from pulling her into a hug.

Unfortunately, a hug he needed as much as she did.

He, too, was wired to handle stress, but it was different when his entire world was tipping on its axis. For so long he'd been living in a dark cloud of grief and pain over losing Ellie that he had nearly forgotten what it was like to feel something, well, good.

His body was burning for Darcy. There was no denying that. But that didn't make things easy. Or even acceptable. Wanting Darcy could put a wedge between him and his family.

Without breaking the armlock they had on each other, she eased back a little and looked up at him. A soft breath left her mouth. Like a flutter. And her face flushed with what he thought might be heated attraction.

Nate tested that theory by brushing his mouth over hers.

Yeah, attraction.

"We shouldn't act on this," Darcy whispered.

But she didn't back away. She kept her mouth hovering just beneath his. Her breath smelled like the cinnamon tea she'd had earlier, and he wanted to see if she tasted as good as she smelled.

But Nate didn't get the chance. The sound of the footsteps stopped him.

He braced himself for a face-to-face with one of his brothers, who would almost certainly notice all the heavy breaths and lust-filled eyes that Darcy and he had for each other. But it wasn't his brother.

It was Wesley Dent.

Nate stepped into the hall, directly in front of the man.

They knew each other, of course. Nate had interviewed and interrogated him at least a half-dozen times. Times that Dent apparently hadn't liked because his green eyes narrowed when he looked at Nate.

Unlike Edwin and Adam, there wasn't much polish here. Dent wore his usual jeans and untucked white button-down shirt that was fashionably rumpled. It was the same for his shoulder-length, highlighted, brown hair. As a rule, Nate didn't trust a man who got highlights and manicures. He especially didn't trust Dent.

Was he looking at the person behind the kidnapping?

Just the thought of it caused the anger to boil up inside him again.

"I heard about your daughter. And your son," Dent

said, glancing at Darcy before he brought his attention back to Nate. "You've arrested Edwin and Adam?"

"Not at the moment," Nate informed him. "They're here for questioning."

Dent's eyes narrowed again. "Why not just arrest them? They're behind this."

"Where's the proof?" Nate challenged.

"The motive is proof." Dent looked up, huffed, as if he couldn't believe Nate hadn't done the obvious— arrest his dead wife's ex and son. "Those two morons wanted you to set me up. To fix the investigation. If that isn't proof, I don't know what is."

"Maybe," Nate mumbled and he left it at that.

"How did you know about the kidnapping being tied to you?" Darcy asked. She stepped out into the hall with them.

Dent wearily shook his head. "It's all over the news. I tried to call your office, to make sure you and your son were okay, but your secretary said you were out indefinitely."

All over the news.

Though he hadn't turned on the TV or opened a newspaper, Nate didn't doubt that word had gotten out. Heck, this was probably a national story by now, especially with so many deaths and the kidnapping from a small-town preschool. But he did have to wonder how many of the details had been leaked. Details like the possible identity of the person who'd hired Ramirez to force Darcy and Nate into throwing the investigation.

"So, when will you be back at work?" Dent asked Darcy. "We need to discuss what's happened. *Alone,*" he added, sparing Nate a glance.

That was reasonable. After all, Darcy was his attorney, but Dent's remark stirred up other feelings inside Nate. Old wounds about Darcy and he being on opposite sides. And new wounds about his confused feelings for her.

"I'm not sure when I'll be back," Darcy let him know. She looked over her shoulder when the bell on the front door jangled.

Nate looked, too. After what had happened, he didn't feel completely safe even in the sheriff's office. He couldn't see who had arrived because Tina Fox, the dispatcher, stood to greet the person and blocked Nate's view. He did relax a little, though, because it was obvious Tina wasn't alarmed.

"Look, I know you've been through a lot," Dent complained to Darcy, "but my life is at stake. If the cops arrest me—"

"Mr. Dent, effective immediately I'm resigning as your lawyer," Darcy interrupted.

Both Nate and Dent stared at her, and Nate didn't know which of them was more surprised.

"I wouldn't be able to give my full attention to your defense," she continued. Her voice wavered a little but not her composure. "My secretary or assistant can give you other recommendations."

"I don't want another lawyer," Dent howled. "Good grief, the police are trying to pin my wife's murder on me. I need you to make sure that doesn't happen."

"I'm sorry." She shook her head. "But I simply can't represent you." She turned to go back into Grayson's office, but Dent stepped in front of her.

"You can't do this," Dent insisted. "I won't let you do it." He flung his hand toward Nate. "Is it because of him? Because he's turned you against me? Well, you're stupid to believe Nate Ryland. He's had it in for me since the moment Sandra drew her last breath."

Enough was enough. Nate stepped between Darcy and the man. "Dent, my advice is to make some calls. Find another attorney. Because you're probably going to want one with you when Sheriff Ryland questions you."

"Sheriff Ryland?" he said like profanity. "If any of you badge-wearing cowboys want to question me, then you get a warrant for my arrest because I'm done playing games." He aimed a glare at Darcy. "I'll settle things with you later."

Nate latched on to Dent's shirt and snapped the man toward him. "Is that a threat?"

Dent opened his mouth as if he might verify that, but he must have decided it would be a bad idea. He tore away from Nate's grip, cursed and turned, heading for the door.

Nate followed him, to make sure he did leave. Grayson would indeed want to question him, but that probably wasn't a good idea with Edwin, Adam and Darcy there. Besides, Dent needed a new attorney. Later, Nate would talk to Darcy about that, to make sure she was doing this for all the right reasons—whatever those reasons were.

For now, he watched.

Dent was moving at lightning speed. Until he reached the dispatcher's desk. And then he stopped and stared at the person on the other side of Tina.

That got Nate moving. Darcy, too. Nate wasn't sure who had captured Dent's attention, and he was more than a little surprised that it was Marlene. She had a bandage on her cheek, another on her arm, but she looked as if she'd physically weathered the kidnapping ordeal. Not mentally, though. The woman was practically cowering.

"Grayson said I needed to sign some papers," Marlene said, her head lowered, her bottom lip trembling.

"Papers?" Dent challenged, and his booming voice caused Marlene to look even more rattled. "Please don't tell me this woman had something to do with the kidnapping."

Nate put his hands on his hips and tried to figure out what the heck was going on.

"The gunmen took me hostage," Marlene explained. "I work at the Silver Creek Preschool and Day Care."

Dent stared at her. And then he laughed. "Oh, this is *good*."

That got Marlene's gaze off the floor. "I didn't do anything wrong," she insisted. And then she turned the pleading gaze on Nate and Darcy. "I swear."

"What do you mean?" Nate demanded. When Marlene didn't answer, Nate looked at Dent.

But the man just smiled and headed for the door. "Why don't you ask her? Or better yet, ask Edwin. I'm sure he'd like to tell you all about it."

Chapter Ten

Darcy kept watch out the SUV window while Nate drove back to the ranch.

Even though she didn't think anyone was following them, she wanted to make sure. With the eerie turn in the investigation, Darcy didn't want to take any chances with their safety. Or the babies'. She certainly didn't want a second wave of kidnappers trying to follow them to the ranch.

Nate was keeping watch, too, but he also had his cell phone clipped to the dash. Ready. And waiting for a call from Grayson that would hopefully explain why her former client had suggested Marlene was associated with Edwin. Grayson hadn't quite dismissed the semi-accusation, but he'd insisted that Nate and she head back to the ranch and leave him to handle the questions, not just for Edwin but for Marlene.

That was probably a good idea because the anger was already starting to roar through Darcy. Not just for Marlene's possible involvement but because she'd seen firsthand the venom inside Dent. She'd thought he was innocent, but she wasn't so sure of that now. Plus, there was the money taken from Sandra's safe. Dent could have stolen it and used it to fund the kidnapping.

Of course, the same could be said for Edwin or Adam.

"In all the interviews I did regarding Sandra Dent, Marlene's name never came up," Nate commented.

"Same here." But what had come up was the tyrannical way that Sandra had treated others—especially her husband, her ex and her son. It was that behavior, and her net worth, that had provided the possible motive for her murder.

Nate took the final turn to the ranch, and finally his cell rang. And Darcy saw that it was Grayson's name on the caller ID. Nate jabbed the button to answer and pressed the speaker function.

"Well?" Nate immediately asked.

Grayson huffed. "Edwin and Marlene know each other."

That kicked Darcy's pulse up a notch. "How?" Nate and she asked in unison.

"In the worst way possible for our investigation." Grayson sounded tired, frustrated and riled. "They had an affair."

"An affair?" Darcy challenged. "Those two don't exactly run in the same social circles."

"No," Grayson agreed. "But they apparently met at a bar in San Antonio. He bought her a drink, and things went from there."

Nate cursed, and it mirrored exactly how Darcy felt. "Any idea if Marlene had something to do with the kidnapping?" Nate pressed.

"She says no. So does Edwin. He puts the blame directly on Dent."

Of course, he would. Dent was putting the blame

on Edwin and Adam, and the finger-pointing was just going in circles.

"Edwin says the affair was short, just a few weeks, and that it ended months ago," Grayson continued. "Marlene echoed the same, but I got to tell you, I'm not sure I believe her. After all, she had an entire day to give me a heads-up about her relationship with Edwin, and she didn't even mention it. I have to ask myself why."

Darcy's pulse went up more than a notch. "Are you holding her?"

"No. I told her not to leave town, that I would have more questions for her once I did some checking. I'll get her phone records and go from there. Edwin's, too. If they put this kidnapping together, I'll find a way to prove it."

"Thanks," Nate told him.

"There's more," Grayson said before Nate could hang up. "The two deputy marshals are here to extradite Ramirez."

"Already?" Nate cursed. And Darcy didn't blame him. They'd hoped to have more time to get Ramirez to talk.

"Yeah. And the marshals want to leave immediately. I can't stop them from taking him," Grayson explained. "But I'll try."

Nate thanked his brother again, hit the end-call button and stopped the SUV in front of the ranch house. But he didn't get out. Neither did Darcy. They sat there trying to absorb what they'd just learned. A woman they had thought they could trust, a woman they had believed had helped them by writing those initials, could be the very person who had helped put their children in grave danger.

Darcy stared up at the iron-gray sky for a moment. Everything suddenly felt heavy. Dreary, even. Probably because a storm was moving in. Literally. But that storm was inside her, too.

They got out of the SUV, and Darcy glanced around at the lack of other vehicles in the driveway. Good. Fewer brothers to face. When they went inside, she could smell Bessie's lunch preparations, but none of the others were around. However, there were several notes on the table, which Nate stopped to read.

"Where is everyone?" she asked, automatically making her way to Nate's wing of the house. Maybe it was the news about Marlene, but she had to see her son and make sure everything was okay, and she headed in that direction.

Nate was right behind her. "According to the notes, Mason is in his office in the ranch hands' quarters. Kayla and Grayson's wife, Eve, are in San Antonio. Eve had a doctor's appointment."

Alarmed, Darcy stopped and whirled around to face him. "Is that safe? I mean, the person behind the kidnapping might go after members of your family."

He shook his head and ran his hand down her arm. "It's okay. Kade's with them. Grayson considered having Eve reschedule the appointment, but because of her age, her doctor here wanted her to see a specialist in the city. It's just a routine checkup."

"Routine," Darcy repeated under her breath. An impending birth that the family should be celebrating, but instead they were under this cloud of fear. Well, she was, anyway. Darcy didn't think she could forgive herself if something happened to another member of Nate's family.

"Come on." His gentle touch morphed into a grip and he led her in the direction of Kimmie's nursery.

There were no sounds. That was a cause for more alarm until Darcy realized both children were in the nursery. Sharing Kimmie's crib. And they were both asleep. Grace, the nanny, was seated in a rocking chair, a paperback in her hand, and she put her finger to her lips in a *shhh* gesture and joined them in the hall.

"They were both tuckered out," Grace whispered. "Fell asleep after their snacks so I decided to let them have a little nap."

Noah didn't normally take a morning nap, but Darcy figured he'd earned one because of the ordeal and the disruption in his routine.

"We'll be in my office," Nate whispered to the nanny. "Buzz me when they wake up."

Nate took Darcy toward the end of the wing until they reached his office. Like the rest of the rooms, it was large. There was a sitting area with a massive stone fireplace, several windows, but the remaining walls were filled with floor-to-ceiling bookshelves.

"I like to read," he commented when she stood in the doorway with her gaze shifting from one section of the shelves to the other.

Judging from the sheer number of books, that was an understatement, and it made her wonder when he found time to do that. Or exercise. But his toned body certainly indicated that he worked out, and the treadmill in the corner looked well used. It was the same for the desk, which was topped with all kinds of office equipment.

Including a red phone.

"Are you a secret agent or something?" she joked.

The corner of his mouth lifted. "It's a secure line. I need it sometimes if I'm here in Silver Creek and some sensitive SAPD business pops up."

She figured that was often. Nate was a lieutenant, an important man in SAPD. "It must be hard to live this far away from your headquarters."

"Sometimes. But it'd be harder if I didn't have my family around to help." Nate took two bottles of water from the fridge behind his desk and handed her one. His fingers brushed hers.

A totally innocent touch.

But like all of Nate's touches, it had a scalding effect on her.

And Nate noticed. "Sorry," he mumbled.

She tried to shrug it off and get her mind onto other subjects. It wasn't easy, but thankfully there were many things in the room—not just Nate—to distract her.

There were the monitors, for instance. A trio of flat screens had been built into the wall. They were all on, and she recognized the playroom and the nursery where the babies were sleeping. The third, however, was an exterior shot of a lush green pasture dotted with horses.

"A way for me to keep watch on the ranch," he explained.

Nate typed something on his computer keyboard, and the pasture scene switched to one of the outbuildings. She saw Mason talking with one of the ranch hands.

"We all pitch in to do what we can to run the ranch, but Mason has the bulk of the workload on his shoulders." There was regret in his voice. And fatigue.

Darcy strolled to the fireplace to study the photos on the mantel. As in the playroom, there was a picture of his murdered grandfather.

Nate's old baggage.

Funny that his old baggage was intertwined with some of her unfinished business. She took a sip of water, turned to him. "As the executor of Charles Brennan's estate, I can give you keys and access codes for all of his properties, including his safety-deposit boxes. If my assistant doesn't come up with anything, you might be able to find something that connects him to your late grandfather."

Nate blinked. "You'd do that?"

"Of course," Darcy said without hesitation.

But she was aware that just two days ago she would have done more than hesitate. She would have refused, citing her client's right to privacy, but her views weren't so black-and-white now. Being around Nate and having her life turned upside down had given her some shades of gray to consider. And since Charles Brennan had been a cold-blooded killer, she felt no obligation to hide his sins from the world.

Or from Nate and his family.

"Thank you," Nate said, his voice just above a whisper.

She shrugged and stared at the family pictures. "I know something about family love. And pain," she added. "About how complex relationships can be."

He studied her. "Are you talking about yourself now?"

Darcy smiled before she could stop herself. "Maybe. A little." But the smiled faded. "I'm responsible for my father's murder."

It was the first time she'd said that aloud, but mercy, it was always there. In her thoughts, dreams. Nightmares.

Always.

Nate put his water bottle on his desk, shoved his hands in his jeans pockets and walked closer. "You think you're responsible?" he challenged. "From what I remember, your father went after the eighteen-year-old thug who attacked you when you were sixteen."

She whirled around, her eyes already narrowing. "How do you know that?"

He slowly blew out his breath. "I always do background checks on the lawyers I come up against in court."

It felt like a huge violation of her privacy. And it was. But then she remembered she'd done the same thing to Nate and any other cop she might be grilling on the witness stand.

"Know your enemy," she mumbled. She lowered her head. "I hate that you learned that about me. I keep professing I'm a good person—"

"You are." And that was all he said for several seconds. "Why would you think you're responsible for his death?"

The pain from the memories was instant. Fresh and raw. It always would be. "Because I shouldn't have been out with Matt Sanders to begin with. My dad had forbidden me from dating him because he believed Matt was a rich bully. He was," Darcy admitted. "But I didn't learn that until it was too late." Her gaze flew back to his. "Please tell me you didn't see the pictures."

But his silence and suddenly sympathetic eyes let her know that he had. Pictures of the assault. Black eyes. A broken nose. Busted lip. Along with assorted cuts and bruises. All delivered to her face by Matt after Darcy had gotten cold feet about having sex with him.

"If someone had done that to Kimmie, I would have gone after him, too," Nate confessed.

"Maybe."

He took his hands from his pockets, touched her chin with his fingertips, lifting it so that it forced eye contact. "Your father made a mistake by carrying a gun to confront your attacker, but you did nothing wrong."

That was debatable. A debate she'd had often and lost. "My mother blamed me. Even on her deathbed." Dying from breast cancer hadn't stopped her from giving Darcy one last jab of guilt.

"Your mother was wrong, too." He sounded so sincere. So right. But Darcy couldn't feel that rightness inside her.

Her father had shot and killed Matt Sanders. And because they hadn't had the money for a good lawyer, the public defender had done a lousy job, and her father had been given a life sentence. Which hadn't turned out to be that long since less than a year later, he'd been killed while trying to break up a fight in prison.

"Your father is the reason you became a lawyer," Nate stated, as if he'd read her mind—again. His voice soothed her. A surprise. Nothing had ever been able to soothe her when it came to the subject of her father. "One day, maybe we'll both be able to remember the good without the bad mixed in."

Darcy wished that for both of them. Especially Nate. And that hit her almost as hard as learning that he knew all about her past. She'd known that her feelings for Nate were changing. She blamed the danger and the attraction for that change of heart. But she was more than surprised to realize that she cared about his healing.

About him.

And that went beyond the danger and the attraction.

Oh, mercy.

She was in huge trouble here.

The corner of Nate's mouth hitched. As if once more he knew what she was thinking. Maybe he did.

"I'm about to make a big mistake," he warned her. "Stop me?"

Right. She had less willpower than he did.

"Not a chance."

Nate frowned now. Cursed himself. Then cursed her.

Clearly he was not pleased that neither of them was going to do anything about this. He leaned in. Closer. Until she felt his warm breath brush against her lips. She also felt the pulse in his fingers that were still touching her chin.

And she felt his body.

Because he closed the distance between them by easing against her.

It flashed through her mind that while they shouldn't be playing with fire, it felt right. As if they should be doing this. And more. Then, he put his mouth on hers, and Darcy had no more thoughts. No more mind flashes.

The fiery heat took over.

It was as if they were starved for each other because Darcy wound her arms around him when he yanked her to him. They fought for position, both trying to get closer, but that was almost impossible.

Darcy's burning body offered her a quick solution for that.

Get naked and land in bed. Or in this case, the sofa, since it was only a few feet away.

But Nate didn't take her to the sofa. He turned her, anchoring her against his desk while he kissed the breath right out of her. His mouth was so clever, just the right pressure to make her beg for more. And then he gave her more by deepening the kiss.

The taste of him made those flames soar.

But it wasn't just the kiss. He touched her, too. First her face. Then her neck. Using just his fingertips, he traced the line to her heart. To her left breast. And to her nipple. It was puckered from arousal, and he used those agile fingers to work some heated magic there.

Darcy would have gasped with pleasure if her mouth hadn't otherwise been occupied by his.

She hoisted herself onto the desk so she was sitting. Behind her, things tumbled over, and she heard the sound of paper rattling. But that didn't matter. The only thing that mattered now was feeding this fire that Nate had started. So, she wrapped her legs around him and urged him closer.

Until his sex was against hers.

Yes, she thought to herself. This was what she needed, and judging from the deep growl that rumbled from Nate's throat, he needed it, too.

The kiss got even more frantic. It was the same for the touching. Each of them was searching for more, and Nate did something about that. He eased her down, so that her back was on his desk, and he followed on top of her. The contact was perfect. Well, except for their clothes, and Darcy reached to unbutton his shirt.

But Nate stopped her by snagging her wrist.

He looked her straight in the eyes. "This is just stirring up trouble," he mumbled. "I'm sorry for that."

For a moment, a really bad moment, Darcy thought he was about to call the whole thing off. But Nate shoved up her top and pulled down her bra. He put his mouth to her breasts and kissed her.

Okay, this was the opposite of stopping. She reached for his shirt again. However, Nate let her know that he was calling the shots because he got on the desk with her, pinning her in place with his body.

They were going to have sex, she decided. Right here, right now. And while she tried to think of the problems that would cause—and it would cause problems—she couldn't wrap her mind around anything logical.

Especially when Nate unzipped her jeans.

And slid his hand into her panties.

His first touch was like a jolt, and Darcy might have jolted right off the desk if he hadn't continued to pin her down. He kept up those maddening kisses to her breast and neck while he touched her in the most intimate way. It was making her crazy. Making it impossible to speak. Or move. Or do anything except lie there and take what his hand and mouth were dishing out.

Darcy felt herself racing toward a climax and tried to pull back so that Nate and she could finish this together. She wanted more. She wanted sex. But she was powerless to stop what Nate had already set in motion.

His fingers slid through the slick heat that his touch had created, and he didn't stop. Not with the touching. Not with the kissing. But what sent her over the edge was what he whispered in her ear.

"Let go for me, Darcy."

And she did. Darcy shattered, her body closing around his fingers as his mouth claimed hers. He kissed her through the shattering and deep into the aftermath.

Until reality hit her squarely between the eyes.

Mercy.

What the heck had she just done?

"Yeah," Nate mumbled. It was that "I'm right there with you" tone. "Trust me, though, it would have been, um, harder if we'd had sex."

Because Nate was indeed hard—she knew because of the way they were still pressed together. Darcy couldn't help herself. She laughed.

Nate's eyebrow rose, and he smiled. "I thought there'd be regret."

Oh, there was some of that. Nate was probably regretting it'd happened at all, and Darcy was regretting they hadn't just taken it to the next level.

"Hand sex crossed just as many lines as the real thing," she let him know. "Plus, it was only pleasurable for me."

He leaned in. Kissed her hard. "Don't think for one minute that you were the only one who enjoyed that."

And it seemed like an invitation for more. Darcy's body was still humming, but one look at Nate and she was ready for him all over again.

"It'll have to wait," he insisted.

For a moment Darcy thought the buzzing sound was all in her head, but then Nate let go of her. That's when she realized the sound was coming from his desk.

He pulled in several hard breaths as he made his way to the phone. Not the red one but the other landline. Nate snatched it up.

While she got off the desk and fixed her clothes, she

looked up at the monitors. The babies were still asleep, thank goodness. But her sense of relief faded when she saw the look on Nate's face.

"Where?" he demanded of the caller.

Nate cursed and punched some buttons beneath the monitor of the pasture and zoomed in on the high chain-link fence. Darcy saw nothing at first, but then the movement caught her eye.

There.

Someone was scaling the fence. Dressed in dark clothes with a baseball cap shadowing the face, the person dropped to the ground.

And that someone was armed.

"STAY PUT AND LOCK DOWN the house. I'm going out there to confront this SOB," Mason insisted.

"Be careful." Nate knew it was an unnecessary warning. Mason was always careful, and his brother would no doubt take a ranch hand or two with him. But the sight of a gunman meant plenty of things could go wrong.

Or maybe they already had.

Had Ramirez's boss hired someone else to come after them? Was this the start of another kidnapping attempt?

Nate hung up, and while he kept his attention on the monitors, he pressed in the code that would set the alarm for every door and window of the main house. He also took the gun from his desk drawer.

Beside him, Darcy was trembling now. She had her fingers pressed to her mouth. Her eyes were wide with concern and fixed on the screen with the intruder. An opposite reaction from what she'd had just minutes earlier.

Later, Nate would figure out why he'd had such a bad lapse in judgment by taking her that way on his desk. But for now, they had a possible kidnapper on the grounds.

"Please, not again," Darcy whispered.

Nate knew exactly how she felt. He didn't want the children, Darcy or anyone else to be in danger again. And in this case the danger didn't make sense. The person behind this had already failed to get Darcy and him to throw the investigation. Heck, Darcy was no longer even Dent's attorney.

But maybe this guy didn't know that.

"I need to go to the children," she insisted and headed for the door.

"No. Stay here. For now we just need to keep watch, to make sure Mason can handle this. There are no viewing monitors in the nursery, and it'll only upset the kids if you wake them from their naps."

Nate tapped the screen where the nursery and the babies were displayed on the monitor and hoped she would keep her focus there.

She didn't.

Darcy volleyed glances between the babies and the menacing figure making his way across the back pasture. Nate zoomed in on the intruder, trying to get a better look, but the baseball cap obstructed the man's face. Still, Nate had a sense of his size—about six-two and around one-eighty.

"How far is he from the house?" Darcy's voice was trembling, too.

"A good three miles. That part of the property is

near the county road." And that was probably why he was there. It wouldn't have been difficult to drive off the road and onto one of the old trails. Then hide a vehicle in the thick woods that surrounded the ranch. And maybe the intruder hadn't realized that any movement on the fence would trigger the security system.

"He's moving fast," Darcy observed.

Yes. He was practically jogging. While he kept a firm grip on his gun. A Glock, from the looks of it. There was something familiar about the way the man was holding it.

And that created an uneasy feeling inside Nate.

He flipped open his phone and called Grayson. "Tell me Ramirez is still behind bars."

Grayson didn't answer for a second or two, and that was an answer in itself. "Dade and Mel are on their way out there right now. It's possible Ramirez escaped."

Nate cursed. "He did. And he just scaled the west fence and is headed toward the ranch. How the hell did that happen?"

"Still trying to work that out, but neither of the marshals is responding."

Probably because they were dead. Nate didn't want to believe the marshals were in on this, that they'd let Ramirez escape, but later he'd have to consider it. If so, Ramirez's boss not only had deep pockets, he had connections.

"Dade is calling Mason now to tell him," Grayson explained.

Good. At least then Mason would know what he was up against. "How soon before Dade and Mel arrive?"

"Ten minutes."

That wouldn't be soon enough because once they

arrived, they would still have to make it out to the pasture. There was no way Mel and Dade would get there in time to give Mason immediate backup.

"I've tapped into the security feed," Grayson went on. "I can see everything that's happening, and I'll alert Mason if the gunman changes directions." With that, he hung up.

Nate could only curse again and watch the monitor. Yeah. It was Ramirez all right. But why come after them here? Why continue a plan that had already failed?

Those questions created an unsettling possibility.

"Ramirez will spend the rest of his life in jail if he's extradited," Darcy pointed out. "And his life might not be worth much since he killed a police officer. He must know he could die a violent death in prison." She paused. "This could be a suicide mission."

Oh, yeah. Death by cop. But Nate kept that agreement to himself.

He gave the security cameras another adjustment and located Mason. His brother was armed, of course, and was on horseback. One of the ranch hands was indeed with him, and they were both riding hard. It wouldn't take them long to close the distance between Ramirez and them.

When Nate went back to Ramirez, he saw that the man was now talking on a phone. Unless it was a prepaid cell, maybe they could trace the person he was calling. Nate opened his phone to request that trace, but he stopped cold.

"What's Ramirez doing?" Darcy asked. She moved closer to the screen.

Nate wasn't sure. Well, not sure of anything but the

obvious, and that was Ramirez had quit jogging. He rammed the cell into his pocket, turned and broke into a run—heading back toward the fence.

"He's leaving." There wasn't just fear in Darcy's voice. There was alarm.

Nate was right there with her. Even though it would put Mason in some danger, he wanted this situation to end now. He wanted Ramirez captured. Or dead. He didn't want him melting back into those woods so he could regroup and come after Darcy and the children again.

He turned to Darcy, knowing she wasn't going to like this, but also knowing there was no other choice.

"Go to the children," Nate ordered. "Lock the nursery door and don't come out until I give you the all clear."

She snapped toward him and grabbed his arm. "What are you doing?"

"I'm stopping Ramirez." Nate brushed a kiss on her cheek, shook off her grip and ran as fast as he could.

Chapter Eleven

Things were moving so fast that Darcy had trouble catching her breath.

She raced to the nursery as Nate had insisted and locked the door. She braced herself to explain everything to Grace, the nanny, but the woman was on the phone. Judging from her pale face and frantic tone, she was already aware of the danger. Thankfully, though, the children weren't.

Both Kimmie and Noah were still sound asleep.

"We're leaving," Grace said the moment she got off the phone. "When Dade and Mel get here, they're taking us to the sheriff's office. We're supposed to meet them at the front door." The woman hurried to the crib to scoop up Kimmie.

Darcy shook her head. "But what about Nate and Mason?" She didn't want to leave until she was certain they were safe.

"Grayson's orders," Grace explained. "He's worried that Ramirez could double back and get close enough to the house to shoot through the windows."

Darcy's heart nearly stopped.

She hadn't even considered the attack could escalate like that. Yes, she was still terrified for Nate and Mason, but she had to put the babies first.

Darcy grabbed a diaper bag, picked up Noah, who immediately started to fuss, and followed Grace out of the room, through the hall and foyer, and to the door. The timing was perfect because Dade and Mel pulled to a screeching stop directly in front of the steps.

"Hurry!" Dade insisted.

It was starting to drizzle, and Darcy tried to shield Noah with the diaper bag.

With his phone sandwiched between his shoulder and his ear, Dade continued to talk with someone. Grayson, she quickly realized. Dade rushed them into the backseat of the SUV, and Mel sped away. There were no infant seats so Darcy and Grace kept the babies in their laps.

Darcy wiped the rain from Noah's face, then Kimmie's, and looked out at the endless pasture, but she couldn't see Nate anywhere. That only caused her heart to pound harder. Not good. She felt on the verge of a panic attack, even though she knew it couldn't happen. Dade didn't have time to coddle her now, not while two of his brothers were in immediate danger.

"What if Nate and Mason need backup?" Darcy asked.

"They're cops," Dade reminded her. "Plus, the ranch hands are there." He sounded confident about that, but she noticed the hard grip he had on his gun, and his attention was glued on the pasture.

Soon, though, the pasture and the ranch were out of sight, and Mel sped down the country road toward town. Grace had her hands full trying to comfort a crying Kimmie. Noah was still crying, too. But Darcy

tried to hear the phone conversation Dade was having
with Grayson. She did. And heard something she didn't
want to hear.

"The marshals are dead?" Dade asked. "Both of
them?"

Oh, mercy.

She knew which marshals he meant—the ones who'd
been escorting Ramirez. And now Nate was out there
with a monster who'd killed before and wouldn't hesitate to kill again.

"Are you okay?" Grace whispered to her. Probably
because the nanny had noticed that Darcy was trembling from head to toe.

"Everything will be all right," Darcy answered, and
she repeated it, praying it was true.

Mel didn't waste any time getting them to the sheriff's office, and she pulled into the parking lot, angling
the SUV so they were at the back entrance. Both Dade
and Mel helped them into the building, and Dade locked
the door before he rushed ahead of them to Grayson's
office.

Grace stayed back a little, maybe so she could try
to calm Kimmie, but since Noah's cries were now just
whimpers, Darcy went with Dade in the hopes that
she'd be able to hear news about Nate and Mason.

But Grayson stepped into the hall first. One look at
his face, and Darcy knew something was wrong. "Is it
Nate?" she asked, holding her breath.

"He's okay." Grayson's attention went to Dade. "But
Ramirez got away."

That robbed her of her breath. This couldn't happen.
This nightmare had to end. "Nate's out there. Ramirez
could come after him."

Grayson shook his head. "Nate's already on his way back here."

Darcy was thankful for that, but she knew until he stepped inside the sheriff's building that he was essentially out there with a killer.

Dade started to curse, but he bit off the profanity when he glanced at Noah. "How did Ramirez escape?" Dade demanded, taking the question right out of her mouth.

Grayson shook his head again. "He made it back to the fence before Mason could get to him, and he disappeared. We'll keep looking," Grayson said first to Dade and then to her.

Darcy didn't doubt they would look, and look hard, but as long as Ramirez was a free man, then Nate, the children and she were all in danger.

"We're bringing in the rangers to assist in the search," Grayson explained. "The FBI, too."

"What do we do with them?" Dade hitched his thumb to Noah and her.

Grayson scrubbed his hand over his face and leaned closer to his brother so he could whisper. "Take them upstairs to the apartment. For now." He looked past Darcy and into the room behind her. "While we're waiting for news, I'll start this interview."

Darcy turned and saw Adam seated at the gray metal table. She turned to Grayson for an explanation as to why Adam was still there, but the young man got up and went to the door. However, he didn't focus on Grayson but rather Darcy.

"I didn't know," Adam said. "I swear."

"Didn't know what?" Darcy asked. And her mind began to whirl with all sorts of bad answers. She wasn't sure she could stop herself from going after Adam if he was about to confess to having some part in Ramirez's escape and the murder of those federal officers.

"About my father's affair with Marlene." Adam's forehead was bunched up. "He never said a word to me about it, and now I have to wonder—what else is he keeping secret?"

Darcy wasn't sure she had the focus or energy to deal with this, but as an attorney she knew it could be critical to the investigation.

"Do you think Marlene helped your father plan the kidnapping?" she asked, shifting Noah in her arms so she could face Adam head-on.

Adam didn't answer right away. He squeezed his eyes shut and groaned. "It's possible. It's also possible my father stole the money from the safe. He was there. I let him in myself, and I know he was in my mother's office."

"Did you see him take it?" Darcy pressed.

"No. But he had my mother's briefcase with him when he left the house." Adam opened his eyes and met her stare. "He could have used that seventy-five thousand to fund the kidnapping."

Grayson and Dade exchanged glances, and it was Grayson who stepped forward, right next to Darcy. "Why do you think that?" he asked Adam.

Again, Adam took several seconds to answer. "I heard him on the phone speaking to someone in Spanish. I don't speak the language myself, but I heard him say *pistolero*. I looked it up on the internet, and it means—"

"Gunman," Darcy and Grayson said in unison.

That admission changed everything. Father and son

were no longer in the camp of accusing Dent, and now Adam had just pinned both means and opportunity on his father. Edwin already had motive—revenge against his ex for divorcing him and marrying a much younger man. Plus, he had to be worried that Dent would cut off his allowance the moment he inherited Sandra's estate.

"I'll go upstairs with Grace and Kimmie," Mel volunteered. She took Noah from Darcy.

"I'll be up soon," Darcy let her know. But first she wanted to ask Adam a few more questions. "Why didn't you tell us this before now?"

"I didn't know about Marlene until today." He dodged her gaze. "And I didn't want to…believe my father could do something like this to my mother. Even though they were divorced, my parents were still in love, in their own way. It would have crushed my mother to know he was carrying on with a woman like Marlene."

Adam sounded sincere enough. There was even a slight quiver in his voice, especially when he said *my mother.* And maybe he did love her, even though after interviewing Sandra's so-called friends and family, Darcy was having a hard time believing that anyone actually loved the woman. But plenty of people loved her money. Of course, Adam would only benefit financially if his stepfather was convicted of the murder. Not his father.

But Darcy rethought that. Could Edwin benefit somehow?

It certainly wasn't an angle she'd researched, but she made a mental note to do just that. Maybe it was the kidnapping or Ramirez's escape, but she wasn't in a trusting mood.

"My father said Marlene is crazy in love with him," Adam went on. "Emphasis on the *crazy*. I think she'd do anything for him, with or without his consent. She might have believed this was a way to get him back in her life."

Darcy looked back at Grayson to see if he shared the same opinion, but the sheriff only lifted his shoulder. *Mercy.* That meant this investigation was about to head out on a new tangent. She didn't mind that in itself, but the more tangents, the longer it might take to figure out who was creating the danger and make an arrest.

"Put all of this in writing," Grayson told Adam. The sheriff pointed toward the paper and pen that were already on the table.

When Adam went back inside the interview room, Grayson shut the door. "Adam will have to wait. I've already asked for a check on Marlene's financials, but I doubt the woman had the money to hire gunmen."

True. After all, she worked at a day care and preschool. "Can you run Edwin's financials, too?" Darcy asked.

"Yeah." And Grayson didn't ask why, which meant he'd already considered that money might be playing into Adam's bombshell about his father's possible guilt. He tipped his head to the back stairs. "There's an apartment on the second floor where Mel and Grace took the children. Why don't you wait up there with them?"

Darcy wasn't about to argue with that, but before she could head in that direction, the back door flew open and someone walked in.

Nate.

She felt herself moving. Running toward him. Yes, it was stupid with his brother and heaven knows who else around. But she went to him. And was more than surprised when Nate closed the distance between them and pulled her into his arms.

"I'm okay," he whispered.

It was the same thing Grayson had told her, but this time she believed it. Still, the panic already had hold of her. Her breath broke, and Darcy disgraced herself by crying. Nate came to the rescue again and wiped the tears from her cheeks.

His hands were already damp. His hair, too. And the rain had soaked his shirt.

"How are the children?" Nate asked. He leaned down, cupped her face and looked her straight in the eyes.

It was the one subject that could get her to focus. "They're fine."

"Good." He pushed her hair from her face and brushed a kiss on her mouth. His lips were also wet from the rain. "Don't worry. We'll find Ramirez."

Again, she believed him and wished she could stay longer in his arms. But the sound of footsteps had them pulling apart. It was Grayson, and even though Darcy felt better, it was clear that Nate's brother didn't share her relief. No doubt because of the kiss he'd just witnessed.

"Where's Mason?" Grayson practically growled.

Nate kept his arm around her waist, causing Grayson's gaze to drop in that direction. "At the ranch, waiting for the rangers and the FBI," Nate told him. "After they arrive, he's driving Bessie to her sister's house."

Darcy hated that she was causing this tension between Nate and his brother, but she would hate even more having to distance herself from Nate. This attraction probably couldn't lead anywhere, but she wasn't ready to let go of it just yet.

Grayson continued to stare at the embrace for several moments. Then he mumbled something and headed back down the hall, saying what he had to say over his shoulder. "I have Adam Frasier in an interview room writing a statement. Darcy can fill you in on what's happening."

Well, at least Grayson hadn't said her name as if it were profanity.

"Adam says now that his father could be behind the kidnapping. Or Marlene," she explained. "Grayson is already digging to see if it's true. Or if Adam is just trying to cover up his own guilt."

Nate wearily shook his head. "Maybe when we catch Ramirez, we can get him to talk."

Darcy was about to remind him that at best Ramirez was a long shot, but then she heard the voices. One familiar voice in particular.

Wesley Dent.

She turned and spotted him making his way down the hall toward them. Tina, the dispatcher, was right behind him, telling him that he would have to wait in reception.

"It's okay, Tina," Nate assured the woman, and he stepped in front of Darcy. Probably because Dent looked riled enough to explode.

"You'd better not be here to threaten Darcy again," Nate warned.

"No threat. I'm here because I found something." Dent started to reach into his jacket pocket, and before he could get his hand inside, Nate had his gun drawn and pointed it right at the man.

Dent glanced at the gun. Then Nate. Dent looked as if he tried to smirk, but he failed. "I'm not the killer, Lieutenant Ryland." Now, he managed some smugness. "But I have something that could blow your investigation wide open."

That got her attention. Nate's, too. And Dent waited until Nate eased his gun back down before he reached into his pocket and extracted a small black leather-bound book. One look and Darcy immediately knew what it was.

Sandra Dent's missing diary.

"Read it," Dent said, thrusting it toward Nate. "And then you'll know who killed my wife."

Chapter Twelve

Nate didn't touch the diary, but he figured if this was the real deal, then any fiber or print evidence on it had already been compromised.

Still, they might get lucky.

With Grayson and Darcy right behind them, Nate led Dent into Grayson's office, took a sterile plastic evidence bag from the supply cabinet and placed it on the center of the desk. Nate motioned for Dent to place the diary there.

"Where did you find it?" Nate asked Dent. But he didn't look at the man. He grabbed a plastic glove, as well, and lifted the diary's cover.

"In the back of Sandra's closet. It'd been shoved into a coat pocket."

Nate was certain the cops had gone through Sandra's closet, but it was possible they'd missed it.

"Go to the last entry," Dent instructed.

Nate did, and Darcy and Grayson moved closer so they could look, as well. The handwritten words practically jumped off the page.

Adam and I argued tonight again. Money, always money. He's too much like his father. Let's see how sorry he is when his allowance is gone.

"Sandra was about to cut off Adam's allowance," Dent emphasized.

Nate mentally went back through his notes. Adam's allowance was a hundred thousand a year and was paid out through a trust fund, but it was a trust fund with strings. Adam could only get the hundred grand per year and that was it. He couldn't touch the principal amount itself for any reason.

A hundred thousand wasn't a huge sum by Sandra's standards, but maybe this was motive for Adam to kill her—especially since the allowance would have continued for the rest of his life. Well, it would continue unless Sandra managed to disown him and rewrite the conditions of the trust.

"Adam didn't say anything about this during his interview," Grayson mumbled, the disgust and frustration in his voice.

Nate understood that frustration. This case just kept getting more complicated, and they had to find the culprit soon so they could end the danger for the children.

"Adam's still here," Grayson added. "I need to talk to him again."

When Grayson walked out, Nate stayed and continued with the diary, but he quickly realized the page was the last thing Sandra had written. He checked the date at the top.

The night before she died.

Well, the timing was suspect. But then Nate noticed something else. The ragged edge, barely visible, indicating a subsequent page had been ripped out.

Nate looked up at Dent. "Know anything about this missing page?"

Dent seemed surprised by the question and had a look for himself. "No. I didn't see that until now. Maybe Adam tore it out?"

"You'd like them to think that, wouldn't you?" Adam snarled from the hall.

With Grayson right behind him, Adam marched into the room and looked at the diary. When he reached for it, Nate blocked his hand.

"It's evidence now," Nate informed him. "I'll have it couriered to the SAPD crime lab for immediate analysis." He pointed to the blank page beneath the one that had been torn out. "I think we might have impressions so we can figure out what your mother wrote."

Both Dent and Adam went deadly silent. For a few seconds, anyway.

"We don't even know if that is my mother's diary," Adam concluded.

"True," Nate acknowledged. "But we have her handwriting on file. It shouldn't take long for the lab to do a comparison."

The muscles in Adam's jaw turned to iron, and he snapped toward Dent. "You're setting me up." He whirled back to Nate. "Yes, my mother and I argued, but we worked out everything before someone murdered her."

"I didn't kill her," Dent calmly replied. He seemed to be enjoying Adam's fit of temper.

"Well, someone did. Either you or my father." Adam poked him in the chest with his index finger. "And if it was you, then I'm going to prove it."

That washed away Dent's calm facade, and Nate was concerned the two men might come to blows. He was too tired to break up a fight. "Are you done with Adam?" he asked Grayson.

His brother nodded.

"Both of you can leave," Nate told Dent and Adam.

"But what about the diary?" Adam demanded.

"We'll let you know what the lab says."

"And then they can arrest you," Dent concluded. He smiled and walked out.

Adam cursed him, but he didn't rush after his step-father. "Don't let him get away with murder," Adam demanded.

Nate huffed and motioned for him to leave. For a moment, he thought Adam might argue, but the man finally stormed out.

Grayson put on a pair of gloves and picked up the diary. "I'll have Tina fax the pages to the crime lab so they can do a quick comparison of the handwriting to make sure it's Sandra Dent's. Then, I'll have a courier pick it up."

Nate thanked him, and once Grayson was out of the room, he turned his attention to Darcy. She looked several steps beyond exhaustion. And worried. Because he thought they could both use it, he brushed a kiss on her mouth.

Yeah, he needed it, all right, and wasn't surprised that the kiss worked its magic and soothed him.

Man, he was toast.

"Why don't you go check on the kids?" he suggested. "I need to make some calls."

She didn't question that. Darcy only nodded, turned but then turned back. She kissed him. Like his, it was brief, barely a touch, but she pulled back with her forehead bunched up and a frown on that otherwise tempting mouth.

"We'll deal with this later," he promised, figuring she knew exactly what he meant. The only question was how they would deal with it.

Except that wasn't in question, either.

They'd deal with it in bed. With some good old-fashioned sex. And yeah, it would mess things up with his family. It might even become the final straw of stress that would break his proverbial back. But Nate was certain that sex would happen no matter how it messed up things.

She ran her hand down the length of his arm. "Just yell if you want me," Darcy whispered.

Despite the fatigue, he smiled. So did she—after she blushed.

Nate watched her walk away. He felt the loss, or something. And wondered when the heck Darcy had become such an important part of his life. Cursing himself and cursing her, he pushed that question aside and got to work. He called Sergeant Garrett O'Malley at SAPD headquarters, the cop working on the Dent case. And now the kidnapping, as well.

"Garrett," Nate greeted. "What do you have on Marlene Lambert's financials?"

"There's nothing much in her checking account, but something else popped up," he explained, and in the background was the sound of the sergeant typing on a computer keyboard. "Two months ago she sold some land she'd inherited from her grandparents. The buyer gave her a check for nearly fifty thousand, which she cashed, but that fifty grand hasn't shown up in her financial accounts."

Nate felt the knot twist in his stomach. This was a woman he'd known for a long time. A woman he'd trusted with the safety and care of his baby girl.

"Of course, Ms. Lambert might have a good explanation," Garrett went on, "but I'm not seeing it right now."

So, Nate knew what had to be done. Grayson would have to bring her back in for questioning and grill her until she told them everything. Fifty thousand probably wasn't enough to have pulled off the entire kidnapping plot, but it would have been enough to get it started.

"What about the financials on Edwin and Adam Frasier?" Nate asked. "I wanted someone to take a harder look at those."

"I did," Garrett assured him. "And if either of them spent an unexplained chunk of money from any of their accounts, I can't find it."

Those financials had been a long shot since neither man would have been stupid enough to have the money trail lead straight back to them. Especially when Adam or Edwin could have just stolen that money from the safe. But Nate had still hoped he could pin this on one of them. On anyone. He just needed this to end.

"I did see something that might be important," Garrett said a moment later. "Adam is the sole heir to his father's estate, and while Edwin doesn't have a lot of cash, he does own a house that he got from the divorce settlement. It's worth close to two million. If some-

thing happened to Edwin—jail, death, whatever—
Adam would be executor of his father's estate."

Interesting. Nate was betting Edwin would do something about that now that his son had implicated him
in the kidnapping. It was also interesting that if either
Dent or Edwin went down for Sandra's murder, then
Adam would benefit.

Yeah. That was motive, all right.

Of course, Dent had just as big a motive. And Nate
couldn't discount Edwin's jealousy of his ex-wife's new
boy toy. Or Marlene's possible misguided love.

In other words, he was still at square one. All four of
his suspects had motives, and worse, they could have
had the means and opportunity, as well.

Nate thanked the sergeant, hung up and was about
to check on Darcy and the children, but Grayson was
right outside the door. Waiting. And judging from his
brother's expression, something bad had happened.

"The children?" Nate automatically asked.

"Are fine," Grayson assured him. He stretched his
hand across his forehead and ground his thumb and
finger into his temples. "But I'm thinking we need to
get them to a safe house."

That nearly knocked the breath out of Nate. "What
happened?"

Grayson tipped his head in a follow-me gesture
and started toward the front of the building to the dispatcher's desk, where Tina was packaging the diary for
the courier.

"Did you find something in the diary?" Nate demanded.

"No. But Tina did fax copies, so we might know
something soon." Grayson went toward the computer

on Tina's desk. "While you were on the phone, I got a call from Kade. About twenty minutes ago, Ramirez was spotted on a security camera at a gas station off the highway. Less than five miles from town."

Oh, mercy. That was way too close for comfort. "Is Kade going out there to try to arrest him?"

Grayson shook his head. "Ramirez is already gone." He turned the computer monitor so Nate could see the feed from the security camera.

Yeah. It was Ramirez, all right, standing under the sliver of the overhanging roof of the gas station. And he wasn't alone. There was another broad-shouldered man with him. Both were wearing baseball caps and raincoats, but the bulkiness in their pockets indicated they were carrying weapons.

"We have this image and a description of the vehicle," Grayson pointed out, tapping the black four-door sedan stopped in front of the gas station.

But not just parked. It was directly in the line of sight of the security camera. Nate watched as Ramirez looked up at the camera.

Ramirez smiled.

The anger slammed through him, and Nate wished he could reach through the screen and teach this moron a hard lesson about endangering babies.

"What's he doing there, anyway?" Nate asked. Because it was clear Ramirez wasn't filling up the car or buying something.

"He's leaving a message," Grayson mumbled.

Yeah. That was obvious. "And that message is he's begging for me to go after him."

"Not quite."

Since Nate hadn't expected to hear Grayson say that, he snapped toward him. "What do you mean?"

"Just watch," Grayson instructed.

Nate did, and his heart started to ram against his chest. Within seconds, Ramirez pulled a folded piece of paper from his raincoat pocket, lifted it toward the camera and then tucked it into the glass door. He gave the camera one last smile, and the men got into the vehicle and sped away.

Not quietly.

The tires howled against the wet concrete and created enough noise to get the clerk's attention. The young man hurried to the door, opened it and caught the note before it dropped to the ground. He read it, his eyes widening with each passing second, and then he raced back into the station and grabbed the phone.

"The clerk called nine-one-one," Grayson supplied. "And in turn the dispatcher called here. He read me the note." Grayson took the notepad from the desk and handed it to Nate.

He knew this wouldn't be good, and Nate tried to brace himself for the worst.

But the message turned Nate's blood to ice.

Nate Ryland and Darcy Burkhart, you killed my brother and my men. This is no longer a job. It's personal, and I'm coming after both of you. Get ready to die.

"Uh, guys," Tina said, "I think we have a problem."

At first Nate thought she was talking about the note. Yeah, it was a problem, all right. A big one. But Tina was looking out the window.

"There." Tina tipped her head to the building just up the street.

The rain was spitting on the glass, but Nate could still see the shadowy figure using the emergency ladder on the side of the hardware store. The guy was climbing onto the roof.

And Nate reached for his gun.

"Wait," Grayson warned. "The windows here are tinted. He can't see us to shoot inside."

Grayson was right. Besides, the guy wasn't in a shooting stance. Once he reached the roof, he dropped onto his belly and pressed binoculars to his eyes.

"Recognize him?" Grayson asked.

Yeah. Nate did. It was the man who'd been with Ramirez on the surveillance footage. Nate automatically glanced around, looking for the man who'd just threatened to kill Darcy and him.

But Ramirez was nowhere in sight.

"You going out there?" Tina asked them.

"No," Grayson and Nate said in unison.

"Not right now," Nate finished.

Good. Grayson and he were on the same page, and Nate knew what he had to do. Darcy wasn't going to like it. Heck, *he* didn't like it. But it was necessary if he had any chance of keeping all of them out of the path of a killer.

Chapter Thirteen

Darcy read the note again. And again.

Each time it felt as if the words were razor-sharp knives slicing through her. A monster, a cold-blooded killer, was coming after Nate and her.

"I won't let him get to you," she heard Nate say.

Darcy believed that Nate would try. But Ramirez wasn't just after her. He was after Nate, as well.

She tore her attention from the note and looked at Nate, who was seated next to her. He'd made her sit on the sofa in the second-floor apartment at the sheriff's office before he'd handed her the note, and that was probably a good thing. After reading it, her legs were too wobbly to stand.

"We have a plan," Grayson explained. He was standing, his hands on his hips. Grace was behind him, seated on the floor and playing with the babies, trying to keep them occupied.

"Please tell me that plan includes making sure the children are safe." Darcy's voice cracked, and she hated feeling scared out of her mind for Noah and Kimmie. Nate, too.

"It does," Nate assured her. "We're going to set a

trap for Ramirez." He caught her shoulders and waited until they'd made eye contact. "And I'll be the bait."

Oh, mercy. That required her to take a deep breath. Thankfully, Grayson continued so she didn't have to ask about the details of this plan, which she already knew she didn't like. She wouldn't approve of anything where Nate made himself bait.

"First, we've made arrangements to move Grace, you and the children. We'll secretly take all of you to a safe house in a neighboring town, where both Mel and I will be with them. So will the town's sheriff and the deputy."

Okay. The security was a good start, but it wasn't enough. Maybe nothing would be with Nate's life at stake. And that required another deep breath.

"Secretly," Nate repeated. "Someone is watching the building."

"Who?" she immediately wanted to know. "Not Ramirez?" Darcy would have jumped off the sofa if Nate hadn't kept hold of her.

"No. It's a man who was on the surveillance video with him. Right now, he's on the roof of the hardware store just up the street. The dispatcher spotted him there about an hour ago. Once we knew he was there, Grayson and I sat down and came up with this plan."

Darcy shook her head. "Why don't you just arrest him? Make him tell you where Ramirez is."

"We considered it," Grayson explained. "But we figured the guy would die before giving up his boss. And we don't want a gunfight with the children here. So we decided to make it work for us."

"How?" she wanted to know.

"Soon, it'll be dark, and Nate will pretend to leave.

It's raining so we'll give him a big umbrella and bundles of something to carry. It'll look as if he has the children with him, but actually we'll sneak them and you out through the back and into my SUV. Kade will be here as additional protection just in case this guy comes off the roof. But we don't think he will."

Darcy tried to think that through. She wished her thoughts would settle down so she could figure out why this sounded so wrong. "You think he'll report to Ramirez that Nate's left and then he'll follow him?"

Nate nodded. "He'll follow me to the ranch. Ramirez will, too, and that's where we'll set the trap for them."

"The ranch?" she challenged. Now, she came off the sofa. "Your family is there."

Nate stood, slowly, and stuffed his hands into his pockets. "We've already moved them. Eve, Kayla and Kayla's son, Robbie, are already on their way to SAPD headquarters, where they'll stay until this situation with Ramirez is resolved."

Yes. And it wouldn't be resolved until Ramirez was dead. Darcy got that part, and she got other things, too. "There's a big flaw in your plan," she told them, even though they already knew it. "If Ramirez wants us both dead, then he won't be satisfied just trying to kill you. He'll want to come after me, as well."

Nate attempted a shrug but didn't quite pull it off. "He might."

"He *will*," Darcy corrected. "And if Ramirez gets lucky and finds me, he'll find the children, too."

Neither Grayson nor Nate could deny that. "We won't let Ramirez get near them."

Darcy took a deep breath and braced herself for the argument they were about to have. An argument she would win because there was no way she was going to give Ramirez a reason to go after Kimmie and Noah again.

"There's only one thing that makes sense—for both of us to lead Ramirez away from the children. Anything less than that puts them in danger."

Nate's jaw muscles stirred. "But coming with me puts you in danger."

"Yes." And she didn't hesitate. "We know what has to be done here. You don't have to like it. Heck, I don't like it. But I won't be tucked away at a safe house knowing that I could be putting our children in jeopardy."

He opened his mouth, probably to continue the argument, but Darcy nipped it in the bud. "You can't change my mind. I'm going with you."

Nate looked at Grayson, who only huffed and mumbled something. Nate looked as if he wanted to mumble some profanity, but he didn't. He sat down, his jaw muscles battling, and then he finally nodded.

Darcy tried not to look too relieved. It was easy to do, since she knew full well she was putting herself in the line of fire. Still, better her than the babies.

Nate simply nodded again. "If Ramirez knows we're at the ranch, he'll come after us so he can try to avenge his kid brother's death. But we'll be ready for him."

"How?" she asked.

Nate eased her down onto the sofa, but they both glanced back when the children giggled. Grace was reading them a story and making funny voices. The laughter certainly helped Darcy's nerves and reminded her of why this plan had to work.

"We think the man on the roof is the person who

helped Ramirez escape. We also believe he's the one who called Ramirez when he climbed over the fence. He probably told his boss to get out of there because he'd seen Dade and Mel driving out of the ranch. In other words, he's Ramirez's eyes and ears, and we want to feed this guy some info."

"Bad info," Grayson explained. "We want Ramirez to believe this storm has knocked out both the power and the security system for the ranch. We want him to come across that fence again. And when he does, we'll have Kade and a half-dozen federal agents waiting."

Darcy nodded but then thought of something. "What if Ramirez doesn't use the fence? What if he uses the road and comes directly to the house?"

"Mason and I will be waiting for him," Nate assured her. "And if he's managed to hire more goons to come with him, then we'll know because Kade will have someone watching the road." He paused again. "It's the fastest way to put an end to this."

She couldn't argue with that. Darcy couldn't argue with the plan, either. Nate was a good cop, and she trusted him with her life. But she couldn't discount that Ramirez was as driven to kill them as they were to stay alive and keep their children safe.

"How much time before you and the children leave for the safe house?" she asked Grayson.

He glanced out the window. "Not long."

So, she needed to say her goodbyes. Darcy got up, forcing her legs to move, and she got down on the floor next to the children. Both Noah and Kimmie were still involved with the story, but Noah climbed into her lap. Kimmie babbled some happy sounds and did the same.

Everything was suddenly better.

And worse.

They had so much at stake. Darcy hugged the babies close to her. Kimmie might have sensed something was wrong because she kissed Darcy on the cheek and put her head on Darcy's shoulder. The moment was pure magic, and Darcy realized she'd come to love this child as her own.

"I'll just freshen up and get ready for the drive to the safe house," Grace offered, and she disappeared into the bathroom, no doubt to give them some time alone.

Grayson mumbled something about having to make some calls and walked out, as well.

Nate sat down beside her, and Darcy expected Kimmie to switch to his lap, but she stayed put. It was Noah who made the shift when he spotted Nate's shoulder holster. But Nate distracted her son by unclipping his badge from his belt and handing it to Noah.

"Oooo," Noah babbled, obviously approving of the shiny object. He looked up at Nate and offered him a big grin.

The moment hit Darcy hard, partly because her son had never had a male figure in his life, and partly because everything seemed to fit. Kimmie in her arms. Noah in Nate's. Her heart and body, burning for this man.

A man she couldn't have.

Nate was just now healing from his wife's death, and he needed his family to help him and Kimmie through the rest of that process. She couldn't put that wedge between them.

She kissed the top of Kimmie's head and ran her fingers through those fiery curls. The little girl had her mother's looks, but that smile and those silver-gray eyes were genetic contributions from her daddy.

"Me," her son said, and he handed the badge to Kimmie. "Me," he repeated.

"I think he's trying to say her name." Nate smiled.

But the smile and the moment ended when Nate's cell phone buzzed. He took the phone from his pocket and glanced at the screen.

"It's the SAPD crime lab." Nate put the call on speaker. "Lieutenant Ryland," he answered.

"Sir, we got that handwriting comparison you requested on the faxed pages," the tech said. "It's a match to the sample of handwriting we have for the deceased, Sandra Dent."

So, the diary was real. Of course, that created more questions than answers. Had Dent really just found it, or had he known all along where it was?

"The handwriting is consistent through all the pages," the tech added.

And that meant Sandra had written the entry about quarreling with her son and planning to cut him out of her life. Maybe Adam knew that. Maybe not. But Dent might have just given them a motive for Adam to kill his mother.

"What about the pages that were torn out?" Nate asked.

"We can't get anything from the paper itself. There's not even any partial letter there, but there could be some DNA or trace fibers. The lab has it now and has started the testing. They're also looking at the indentations on the pages following the ones that'd been torn out."

"And?" Nate prompted.

"It doesn't look good, Lieutenant. It appears someone has actually rubbed or applied pressure to flatten out the indentations, but the lab will do what it can."

Nate wearily dragged his hand over his face, but then smiled when Noah attempted to do the same. "Call me if you find out anything else," Nate instructed the tech, and he ended the call.

The phone grabbed Kimmie's attention, and she dropped Nate's badge so she could go after it. Just like that, Nate had both kids in his lap, and he adjusted, giving them both room, as if it were second nature for him. However, even the half smile he gave the children didn't mask his frustration.

"It would have been nice to know what Sandra wrote on that last page," Darcy said. "She might have named her killer, or at least given us some hint of who that person might be. I mean, why else would the pages have been torn out?"

Nate didn't answer her, but something flashed through his eyes. He took out his phone again and put it on speaker.

"Grayson," he said when his brother answered. "Is our guest still on the roof of the hardware store?"

"Still there. He's getting soaked, but he hasn't moved."

Darcy hoped he'd stay put. And catch pneumonia.

"I just finished talking with the lab," Nate explained to his brother. "The handwriting matches Sandra's, but the indentations probably won't give us anything. What I want is for all four of our suspects to believe otherwise. I want them to think the lab uncovered what Sandra had written and that SAPD is making arrangements for an arrest."

Grayson made a sound to indicate he was contemplating the idea. Darcy thought about it, too. If it worked, they could have Sandra Dent's killer in custody within hours.

"You think this'll flush out her killer and cause him or her to go on the run?" Grayson asked Nate.

"Yeah, I do. But I don't think it'll cause the killer to come after Darcy, me or the children again. He or she must have figured out by now that they can't use us to fix the murder investigation."

Grayson made a sound of agreement. "I'll make some calls and have the roads and airports watched. And then we'll have to make the suspects believe that one of them is about to be outed. That'll be easy to do for Marlene since she's already here."

"Why?" Darcy and Nate asked in unison.

"Your guess is as good as mine, but she's insisting that she talk to Darcy and you, too."

Nate groaned and looked at her. "You up for this?"

Darcy nodded. She didn't want to waste any more time with Marlene, but the woman might actually be there to confess to orchestrating the kidnapping. If she was, then Darcy very much wanted to hear what she had to say.

Darcy gave both babies a kiss, and Nate did the same. Then she knocked on the bathroom door to signal Grace should come out. Once Grace was back on the floor with the kids, Nate and Darcy headed downstairs to confront Marlene.

They didn't have to go far.

Marlene was in the hall, just outside of Grayson's office, and the moment she spotted them, she walked toward them. Grayson stepped out of his office and joined them, too.

"I didn't help anyone kidnap your children," Marlene volunteered. "When I heard the kidnappers say they were taking us to the Lost Appaloosa, I wrote the initials so you'd find us."

"But the van where you wrote them was a decoy," Nate pointed out.

"I didn't know that, either. That's the van they put us in when they first took us, and then they moved us to another one. I wouldn't have done anything to help them take Noah and Kimmie, and you have to believe me."

"Maybe I will believe you," Nate told her, "if you'll explain what you did with the fifty thousand you got for selling the land you inherited."

Marlene flinched as if he'd slapped her. "That has nothing to do with the kidnapping."

Darcy folded her arms over her chest and stared at Marlene. "Then where's the money?"

Marlene looked around as if she wanted to be anywhere but there, and for a moment Darcy thought she might bolt. Would that mean Marlene was guilty?

"You're wasting our time," Nate accused.

Marlene shook her head, but it still took her several moments to say anything. "Someone's trying to kill me."

And she didn't add more. Just that little bombshell.

"Who's trying to kill you?" Darcy asked. "Ramirez?"

"No." But then Marlene paused. "Well, maybe it's him, but I don't think so. If he'd wanted me dead he could have killed me when I was his hostage."

"Were you?" Nate demanded, and then he clarified, "His hostage?"

"Yes. Those gunmen took me when they took the children, and it doesn't have anything to do with the money I got from selling the land."

Nate huffed. So did Grayson. "Look," Grayson warned, "either you explain about the money now, or I arrest you for obstruction of justice."

Marlene's eyes widened, and it seemed to hit her that she was in big trouble. "I gave the money to my sister in San Antonio." She paused again. "She was in debt to a man who was threatening to kill her. I had to pay him off."

Nate rolled his eyes. "Let me get this straight—someone's trying to kill both you and your sister, and not once did you consider telling Grayson about this?"

"I couldn't." Again, she shouted, but then she blinked back tears. "The loan shark would have killed my sister if she'd gone to the cops. And as for me, I don't think this man has anything to do with the threats on my life."

Darcy could practically feel the frustration coming off Grayson and Nate. She felt it, too, and only wanted this woman to spill it and get out of there. Soon, very soon, the children would be leaving for the safe house, and she wanted to spend a little more time with them.

"Explain why you think someone's trying to kill you," Grayson insisted, and it wasn't a gentle request.

Marlene hiked up her chin and clearly wasn't pleased that Grayson and Nate seemed to doubt her. If she was innocent, Darcy would apologize to the woman, but for now she wanted the same thing Nate and Grayson did—the truth.

"Someone's been following me," Marlene started. "And before the kidnapping, I was getting hang-ups."

Grayson, Nate and Darcy all looked toward the front of the building when the bell jangled, indicating someone had opened the front door. Nate stepped in front of Darcy. Grayson, too. And they both slid their hands over their guns.

Darcy held her breath, praying the man from the roof hadn't decided to come in and try to kill them. But the person who walked through the door was a familiar face, although not a welcome one.

It was Edwin.

He used his hand to swipe the rain from his face, and he stormed toward them. He didn't make it far. Tina, the dispatcher, stepped in front of him to block his path. Edwin did stop, but he aimed his index finger and a scowl at Marlene.

"Whatever she says, it's a lie," Edwin growled.

Marlene frantically shook her head. "It's true. Someone is trying to kill me. Or scare me at least. And I think it's *you*."

"Please." Edwin stretched out the syllables. "You were a cheap fling, nothing more, and I never gave you a minute's thought until that damn kidnapping."

Edwin's anger seemed genuine enough, and it seemed genuinely directed at Marlene. However, Darcy wasn't about to cross either of them off her list of suspects. Judging from Nate's expression, neither was he.

"Are you trying to kill her?" Nate asked him.

Edwin cursed. "She's not worth killing." He pointed at Marlene again. "I plan to do everything in my power to find proof that you set up the kidnapping so that Dent would be tossed in jail. Trust me, I want him in jail, but

I don't need or want your help for that. You're a stalking, obsessive wacko, and I want you out of my life."

Marlene opened her mouth, no doubt to return verbal fire, but Nate put up his hand in a *stop* motion. "In a few hours we'll know who killed Sandra."

Edwin and Marlene both seemed to freeze, and each stared at Nate. "What do you mean?" Marlene asked Nate.

"Dent found Sandra's diary—"

"It's a fake," Edwin interrupted.

Nate shook his head. "It's not. The lab just confirmed that the handwriting is hers."

His voice was so calm. He was all cop now, and Darcy watched as he took one menacing step closer to Marlene. But the woman wasn't the only one to earn some of his attention. Nate turned those suddenly cold gray eyes on Edwin, too.

"The next step is for the lab to lift the indentations Sandra made when she wrote the page that was torn out," Nate continued. "The page that sealed her fate and named her killer."

"Someone could have planted information to make me look guilty," Edwin snarled.

"Or me," Marlene piped up.

Nate lifted his shoulder again. "Then maybe you two should call your attorneys. Because I'm betting one or both of you will need a good lawyer before the night is over."

Edwin stood there, glaring, as if he would launch himself at Nate or Marlene, but then he cursed again, turned and walked back out into the rain.

"Excuse me," Grayson mumbled when his desk phone rang.

Marlene, however, didn't storm out with Edwin. In fact, she didn't budge an inch. "I believe Edwin is trying to scare me. Or worse." She groaned. "He's trying to make me look guilty because he's the one who put all of this together. He killed his ex-wife, and he wants Wesley Dent to go to jail because he hates him that much."

All of that could be true.

Or none of it.

"You got proof?" Nate asked.

Marlene groaned again, more softly this time, and she stared at Nate. "You really believe Sandra wrote her killer's name in her diary?"

"I do," Nate said, sounding totally confident.

"Good," Marlene whispered. Then she mumbled a goodbye and hurried down the hall.

Darcy didn't release the breath she'd been holding until Marlene was out the door.

"Lock it," Nate instructed Tina. "We've had enough surprise visitors today. Besides, I don't want anyone walking in when we're transferring the children into the van that will take them to the safe house."

Darcy shook her head. She'd thought it was too early for the children to leave, but she was wrong. It was still an hour or so before actual nightfall, but the rain and the iron-gray clouds made it seem like night.

The darkness was closing in.

And so was her fear.

Nate must have sensed what she was feeling because he gave her arm a gentle squeeze. He was still doing that when Grayson threw open his office door.

"Everything is ready for the children," Grayson told

them. There was both sympathy and concern in his voice. "It's time."

"Come on," Nate whispered to her. "We need to tell Kimmie and Noah goodbye."

Darcy swallowed hard. *Goodbye*. It hit her then that while their children would be safe, Nate wouldn't be. They would have to face the devil himself and somehow come out of it alive.

Or this was the last time they would ever see their children.

Chapter Fourteen

The plan was in place. Nate knew he'd done everything possible to make this work.

Well, *logically* he knew that.

But in the back of his mind, he hated that he couldn't guarantee all of them would come out of this unscathed.

He ended the call with Kade. One of many calls Nate had made over the past hour since Darcy and he had arrived at the ranch. More would no doubt have to be made.

"Well?" Darcy asked the moment he hung up.

She was in the doorway of his office, her hands bracketed on the door frame. All the lights in the house were off—that was part of their plan, to lure Ramirez with a fake power outage—but Nate didn't need to see her face to know she was worried and on edge. He could hear it in her voice. In that one word. In the air zinging around them. The storm brewing outside only added to the menacing feel.

"The children are fine," he assured her. "They're all tucked in for the night at the safe house."

Her breathing was way too fast, and he thought he could even hear her heartbeat. "Thank God," she whispered.

Nate echoed that. "So far none of our suspects has shown up at the airport or the border. None has withdrawn any money from their bank accounts. No suspicious activity of any kind even though Adam is out driving around. Dade is watching him, and we have surveillance on the others' houses."

Darcy shook her head. "But they could sneak out."

"They could," he admitted. "But if that happens, and the killer heads in this direction, we'll know. Kade and his men are scattering out all over the ranch to set up surveillance equipment."

"What about the man who was on the roof of the hardware store?" she asked.

"He left right after we did. On foot. He disappeared into the alley behind the stores."

That didn't help her breathing.

"We figure he's already joined up with his boss, Ramirez." He walked closer to her. "When all the equipment is set up and everything is in place, the ranch hands will pretend there's an emergency. A fence down from the storm. And they'll appear to leave the area. If Ramirez is watching the ranch, and we're almost positive he is, then he'll believe that's his opportunity to strike."

Her breath shivered, and Nate pulled her into his arms. It wasn't much of a hug, but it helped to relax her. Him, too. But it didn't help the attraction.

Not a good time for it.

But then, there'd never been a good time.

"Why don't you try to get some rest?" he said softly. Trying to stay calm. Trying not to let her hear the concern in his own voice.

A burst of air left her mouth. Not exactly a laugh.

"Rest? Right." And then she did something that shouldn't have surprised him. But it did.

Darcy put her arms around him and kissed him. Not a peck of reassurance. Not this. The kiss was long, hard and filled with way too much need. And urgency.

"Rest," he repeated. Not easily. That kiss had made him crazy in a bad way. He was starting to think that kissing and maybe adrenaline sex might be the way to get through the waiting.

Darcy pulled back and hesitated. The moments crawled by while he waited for her response.

"Rest with me," she insisted.

An *okay* nearly flew right out of his mouth before he remembered he had to set up the surveillance on his laptop. Not that he would actually be able to see anything in the dark and rain, but the motion detectors were on, and he would get the alert over the laptop if Ramirez did come across any part of the fence. His brothers and the ranch hands already had equipment to detect movement, but Nate wanted it as a backup for himself. And in case something went wrong with the exterior detection equipment.

"I'll be in my room," Darcy added, and she walked away.

Nate stared at the empty doorway for a second. And he cursed himself for what he knew would happen before the night was over. He should have one thing on his mind: Ramirez. But Ramirez wouldn't get anywhere near the place without Nate and the others knowing.

There was time to kill.

Or so he rationalized.

He could kill that time in his office, waiting and

watching. He could stay away from Darcy and give her the possibility of getting some rest.

But that didn't happen.

Nate turned on his laptop and tapped into the security feed. It didn't take long for the images to appear on the screen. And just as he'd figured, nothing was going on. He couldn't see a thing in the rainy darkness so he tucked the laptop under his arm, took a deep breath and launched into what would no doubt be a very pleasurable but stupid mistake.

He walked straight to Darcy's room.

The door was open, and he stepped inside so he could put his laptop on the table just a few feet away. He took off his shoulder holster, as well, and dropped it next to the laptop.

Bright white lightning flashed through the rain-streaked window. For a second Nate saw Darcy sitting on the edge of the bed. Her ivory-colored top, her blond hair, her pale skin all made her look a little otherworldly. A siren, maybe. Or a rain goddess.

But then the darkness took over the room again.

He stood there, letting his eyes adjust, waiting for another jolt of lightning. He didn't have to wait long. It came. Stabbing across the sky and giving him another look at her. He felt starved for the sight of her.

And he groaned at that somewhat sappy realization. "That bad, huh?" she asked.

He waited for the lightning again to see if she was smiling. She was. Well, sort of. "I'm thinking thoughts I don't usually think," he confessed. "Sappy ones."

He heard the mattress creak softly as she stood. Then heard her footsteps on the bare wood floor. "Good," she whispered.

Oh, man. Did she know how hot she sounded all breathy like that? Apparently, he was starved for the sound of her voice, too.

"Good?" he challenged when he remembered how to form words with his mouth. His body didn't want to contribute any energy to something that didn't involve getting Darcy naked. "You want me to think sap?"

She stepped closer so he could see the half smile, and her face. "You've done a number on my mind. My body. I figure it's only fair that you're sappily confused."

Nate sighed and slipped his arm around her waist. "Oh, I'm not confused, Darcy. I know exactly what I want—and that's *you*."

The slam of thunder gave his confession a little more punch than he'd intended, and Darcy laughed. It was smoky and rich, and Nate kissed her so he could feel that laughter on his lips.

"Good," she repeated. "Because I want *you*."

Yeah. He knew that.

And that was the problem. Neither was going to stop this getting-naked part. Ditto for some raunchy, memorable sex. The door was locked. They had some privacy for the first time in, well, forever. And even though there would be hell to pay, Nate eased her to him and deepened the kiss.

Later, he would pay hell.

Now, he just wanted to kiss her blind. For starters, anyway.

There was something about her, about that taste, that made him crazier than he already was, and he felt his body rev up to take her hard and fast.

Especially hard.

He considered something mindless, maybe even

sex against the wall. Sex where he didn't have to think of the consequences. But a rain goddess who tasted like sin deserved something better than that. And Nate wasn't surprised that he wanted to make love to her.

He leaned back, to make sure there wasn't any doubt in her eyes or expression. He could see her face, the rain shadows sliding down her body. She was beautiful. But he hadn't needed to see her face to remember that.

Nate scooped her up and headed for the bed. Even in this position, she fit, as if she belonged there in his arms. In his bed. Heck, maybe his life. He pushed that aside. It was too deep and too complicated to deal with now.

The lightning came again. And the thunder. As he eased her onto the bed, the mattress creaked softly and creaked some more when he followed on top of her. This fit, as well, and so did the way their mouths came together for the kiss.

It didn't take long, barely seconds, for the kisses to give way to touches. Darcy started it by sliding her hand down his chest. That did it all right. The simple, easy pressure of her hands on his body. And just like that, he was hard and aching to take her.

"You're like a fantasy," she whispered.

Despite his rock-hard body, Nate lifted his head to see what she meant by that.

"You are," she insisted. She didn't stop touching him or kissing his neck, and because she was apparently going for torture, she lifted her hips, brushed against the front of his jeans and caused his eyes to cross. "As in you're really hot. The kind of guy I always fantasized about…well, you know, in bed."

He couldn't imagine that he looked hot with crossed

eyes and the hard ache behind the zipper of his jeans, but at the moment he was just pleased that she wanted him as much as he wanted her. Especially since she was fulfilling a few of his own fantasies.

Her top had to go—more of his fantasy fulfillment—and Nate stripped it off. Her bra, too. And he kissed her breasts the way he wanted to kiss her, his tongue circling her nipple.

That brought her hips off the bed again, and she made a sweet sound of pleasure. A sound that slid right over him like the warm rain on the cool glass.

"You, too," Darcy insisted. And she went after his shirt.

While she fumbled with the buttons, Nate did some more sampling. He moved his mouth to her stomach and smiled when she made more of those pleasure sounds.

"I'm on fire," she let him know and gave his shirt a fierce tug.

Nate was pleased about that fire he'd helped build. Until her lips went to his chest. Oh, man. She wasn't a rain goddess. She was a witch, casting a spell with that mouth and setting him on fire.

When he could take no more of the scalding pleasure, he dropped to his side, pulling her on top of him so he could rid her of her jeans. Darcy didn't help much, mainly because she went after his zipper. He was hard and very aware of her touch.

Again, when he could take no more, he put her back on the mattress and shimmied her jeans and panties off.

The lightning cooperated.

Oh, yeah. She was beautiful all right, and Nate kissed her right in the center of all that heat.

She made another sound. This one had an urgency to it, but she didn't stop him. Darcy wound her fingers deep into his hair and took everything he was giving her.

Nate considered finishing her off like this, but he wanted more. He wanted to be inside her so he could watch and feel her shatter all around him.

"Your jeans," Darcy reminded him.

He was painfully aware that his remaining clothes were in the way of sex, and Nate helped her get off his boots and jeans.

But Darcy didn't play fair.

She was the one who removed his boxers, and she did it by sliding her hands down his lower back and his butt. And she didn't just use her hands. She used her knees and legs, and when she was done, when his boxers were dangling on her foot, she wrapped her legs around him.

Nate moved down as she moved up, and he slid into that tight, wet heat of her body. Stars. Yeah, he saw them. Hell, maybe fireworks, too. There was something exploding in his head, and the pleasure, well, it was something he was glad he didn't have to put into words.

He moved deep and hard inside her. But he didn't stop kissing her. Couldn't. After being so long without, he wanted it all. The taste of her in his mouth. Her scent on his skin. The feel of the hot, intimate contact of their sex.

"A fantasy," she repeated. Her eyes were wide, and she was staring at him.

Yes, it felt good enough to be her fantasy, and in the back of his mind he wondered if anything would ever feel this good again. But then the need took over, and his mind cleared of any thoughts except one.

Finishing this.

Turned out that was Darcy's goal, as well, because she met his thrusts, using her legs to pull him right back in. Over and over. Robbing him of his breath. Maybe his mind. Everything. Until all he could see and feel was Darcy.

She dug her fingers into his back when she climaxed, bucked beneath him, and her breath was mixed with hoarse sobs of pleasure.

Nate listened and watched her as long as he could. Cataloging every sound. Every move. Every expression. Until he could take no more. Until the ripples of her climax forced him into letting go.

The lightning came again. The thunder. And even over the thick rumble, Nate heard the single word he whispered.

"Darcy."

Chapter Fifteen

Darcy didn't want to move. Nor did she want to break the intimate contact with Nate.

But Nate apparently did.

He rolled off her and landed in a flop on his back. He didn't say anything, but Darcy could still hear the way he'd spoken her name in the last climactic moment.

Somehow, that had sounded more intimate than the sex itself.

In the back of her mind, she'd considered that Nate had been thinking about his late wife. That would have been, well, natural even though it was painful for her to consider. But it'd been Darcy's name on his lips. And he'd certainly made love to her as if she was the woman he wanted.

But did he?

Had this been a primal reaction to the danger?

She couldn't dismiss it, but she so wanted it to be real. She wanted Nate and not just his body—though Darcy wanted that, too.

And speaking of his body, she looked over at him. He was still naked, of course, and thanks to a jagged flash of lightning, she got a good look at him.

Oh, mercy.

Yes, she wanted to feel more of those toned muscles on his chest and stomach. More of his clever mouth and the kisses that could make her burn to ash. She wanted to be wrapped in his strong arms again. She wanted it all.

Darcy groaned and hoped the rumbling thunder concealed the sound that had escaped.

It didn't.

Nate tilted his head and looked at her. "Well?" he asked.

Sheesh. Where should she go with a question like that? Anything she said could make him regret what had just happened and might send him running for cover.

"Well," she repeated, giving herself some time to think, "the sex was amazing."

He stared at her. "Then why did you groan?"

That required another pause—and a deep breath. "Because this might have been easier for both of us if it hadn't been amazing."

Nate stayed quiet a moment and then made a sound of agreement. He brushed a kiss on her cheek, got up and started to dress.

Darcy wanted to smack herself for that stupid groan. It had reminded Nate of the trouble a possible relationship could stir up. That groan had broken the spell and caused him to move away from her.

Nate's phone buzzed, and he rifled through his clothes on the floor to find it. He glanced at the caller ID before he answered it.

"Kade," Nate answered.

Darcy prayed this was good news, but since Nate didn't put the call on speaker, she couldn't tell.

She got up, as well, and began to gather her clothes. Suddenly, Darcy felt awkward and uncomfortable about being stark naked in front of Nate. She dressed as quickly as she could. Not easy to do since her clothes were scattered everywhere.

"Did he have a suitcase or anything with him?" Nate asked his brother.

Again, she couldn't hear Kade's answer.

"A lot of people are watching the place," Nate responded. "If he shows up, we'll see him." And he hung up.

Darcy waited, her breath stalled in her lungs.

"It's Dent," Nate told her. "He left his house about a half hour ago, and he had a suitcase with him. He managed to lose the tail we had on him."

Darcy leaned against the wall and let it support her. She also put her hand over her breasts since she was still braless. Where was the darn thing?

"This doesn't mean Dent is a killer," Nate pointed out. He looked at her but then just as quickly turned away. "He could just be running scared."

True. But Darcy wasn't ready to trust Dent or any of the other suspects.

Nate finished dressing before her and went straight for his laptop, which he'd left on the table near the door. When he lifted the screen, it created a nightlight of sorts, and she was able to find her bra. It was dangling on the bedpost.

"No sign of Ramirez," he relayed to her, and he slipped his shoulder holster back on.

Ramirez. Just the thought of him chilled the remaining heat she felt after making love with Nate. How could she have forgotten, even for a few minutes, that a killer wanted them dead?

Sex with Nate wasn't just amazing.

It apparently caused temporary amnesia.

And stupidity.

Darcy finished dressing and saw that Nate was still staring at his laptop screen. "Is there a problem?" she said, praying there wasn't.

"No. I'm just reading an email from Grayson."

"Grayson?" She hurried across the room to see what the message said. "It's about the children?"

Of course, she immediately thought the worst, but what she saw on the screen wasn't the worst at all. There was a picture of both Kimmie and Noah. They were asleep side by side in a crib.

"Grayson snapped it with his cell phone and emailed it," Nate explained. "He thought it would make us feel better."

It did.

Darcy couldn't help herself. She touched the screen, running her fingers over those precious little faces. "I miss them so much."

"Them," Nate mumbled.

It hit her then that he might think she was trying to push her way into his life by using his daughter. Darcy frantically shook her head. "What I feel for Kimmie doesn't have anything to do with you."

He lifted his eyebrow and paused for what seemed an eternity, then nodded. "I know. You love kids." Nate added a shrug. "I love kids."

Darcy waited, but he offered nothing else. Especially nothing else about what he might be feeling for her. Or feelings about what had happened in that bed just minutes earlier. But because she was watching him so closely, she saw his expression change from that of a loving father to that of a very sad widower. He, too, touched the image on the screen, and Darcy suspected he was wishing that Ellie were alive.

"You miss your wife," Darcy said before she could stop herself.

"Yeah." No hesitation. Nate kept his gaze fixed on the screen for several seconds before he pulled back his hand and switched to the feed from the security system. He split the screen so that it showed six different camera angles at once.

She considered pushing a little and asking Nate to talk about his feelings. He'd no doubt rather eat razor blades than do that, so Darcy decided to give him the time and space to work out whatever was going on in his head. Heck, she needed that space, too.

But one look at the screen, and she realized her attention was going to be otherwise occupied. She saw movement in the top-left screen.

"Ramirez?" she managed to ask.

Unlike before, Nate didn't give her an immediate answer, but he did draw his gun from his shoulder holster. "I don't think so."

Whoever it was, the person wasn't on foot. Nor was he coming across the fence. This was a car, and the headlights were on, slicing through the thick rain. The vehicle was traveling on the ranch road.

Toward the house.

Oh, mercy. Darcy had thought she was ready for this. Well, as ready as anyone could be. But just the sight of that car made her heart spin out of control.

"I doubt Ramirez would drive right up to the front door," Nate added.

And that's exactly what the driver appeared to be doing. Darcy clung to that hope, that it wasn't Ramirez, but then she had to wonder, if it wasn't the killer, who was it? It was hardly the hour for guests, and all of Nate's brothers were occupied with either the children or setting the trap for Ramirez.

Nate's phone buzzed, and he answered it without taking his focus off the car. He clicked the speaker function.

"Nate," she heard Dade say. "Adam should be arriving at the ranch any minute now. I was tailing him, but I got…distracted. I spotted someone in the woods on the back side of the ranch, and I stopped. I think it might be our watcher from the roof. Can you deal with Adam on your own?"

"Sure," Nate answered. "What does Adam want?"

"Who knows. He checked into a hotel in Silver Creek, but about forty-five minutes ago, he came barreling out of the driveway like a man on fire. I guess he must have gone out to the parking lot through the emergency exit at the back of the hotel."

"Is he armed?" Nate wanted to know.

"Couldn't tell. I barely got a glimpse of him before he sped away from the hotel. I stayed back so he wouldn't spot me, but he didn't make it easy. He stopped on the side of the road twice, changed directions a couple of times, but then he finally headed out to the ranch."

"Any sign of Edwin, Dent or Marlene?" Nate asked.

"No. And I've been keeping my eye out for all of them in case they head out this way." In the background, Darcy could hear the storm winds howling. "You're positive you can handle Adam?"

"Don't worry about us. Just watch your back." Nate ended the call, picked up the laptop and started out of the room.

Darcy caught his arm. "You're not planning to let Adam in?"

"No. But I do want to talk to him. And I want to be closer to the door in case he decides to break in."

Darcy's grip melted off his arm. "Break in?" But she knew what Nate meant. Adam could have killed his mother, and the lie they'd planted about the diary could have sent him spinning out of control. With everything going on with Ramirez, she'd forgotten that someone had originally hired that monster to kidnap the children.

Was it Adam who'd done that?

And was he there to finish what he'd paid Ramirez to start?

Darcy followed Nate down the hall and toward the foyer, but he didn't go into the open area. Instead, he placed the laptop on the floor, and they crouched down where they could both still see it.

On the screen Darcy saw the car and then heard it come to a screeching halt. Adam certainly wasn't trying to conceal his arrival. Nate and she waited, watching, but Adam didn't get out. However, Nate's phone buzzed again, and when he flipped it open, it was Adam's name on the screen.

"What are you doing here?" Nate demanded when he answered the call. Darcy whispered for him to put it on speaker, and he did.

"I'm trying to stay alive, and you have to let me in. I

need to be in protective custody." Adam sounded scared
out of his mind. Of course, Darcy knew it could all be
an act.

"And you thought the way to stay alive was to come
here?" Nate tossed right back.

Adam mumbled something she didn't catch. "Dent
is trying to kill me. He murdered my mother, and now
he's trying to kill me so he can inherit her entire estate
and my trust fund. I want him arrested *now*."

"There's still no proof to arrest him. Or you, for that
matter," Nate added. "But we might soon have proof
with the diary."

"Yes," Adam mumbled. "The diary." He said it in
the same tone as he would profanity. "Dent doctored
that diary, and I'm betting he did that to make either
me or my father look guilty of murder. When your lab
people check those so-called indentations, they'll be
fake, added by the real killer. And that real killer is
Dent."

Darcy certainly couldn't discard that theory. But
Dent had been the one to find the diary, and if her
former client thought for one minute that it could have
implicated him in his wife's murder, then he wouldn't
have brought it to Grayson and Nate.

So, Dent was either innocent or stupid.

"If you really believe someone is trying to kill you,"
Nate said to Adam, "then go the sheriff's office or
SAPD headquarters. Dent won't come after you there."

"No. But his hired gun would, and I'd rather have
you protecting me than the deputy at the sheriff's
office." Adam cursed. "I know Dent hired that psycho,
Ramirez. He took the money from my mother's safe to

pay him. And now he's hired Ramirez to come after me. And Darcy and you, too."

Nate glanced at her, and Darcy saw some doubt, but Nate wasn't totally dismissing what Adam had accused Dent of doing.

"What makes you think Ramirez is after you?" Nate demanded.

"I *know* he's after me. He came to my hotel room." Adam's voice cracked on the last word. "I'm sorry. He gave me no choice."

Darcy felt the icy chill go through her. "What do you mean?"

Adam took his time answering. "I mean Ramirez came here in the trunk of my car, and he got out just a few minutes ago—before we got to the security camera at the end of the road.

"I'm sorry," Adam repeated. "But Ramirez is on the grounds."

Chapter Sixteen

Nate prayed that Adam was lying. Or playing some kind of sick joke.

Yes, Nate was fully aware that Ramirez was after Darcy and him, but if Adam had hand-delivered a killer to their doorstep, then there would be a bad price to pay.

"I don't see Ramirez," Darcy said, her voice filled with nerves, her breath racing. She dropped to the floor, grabbed the laptop screen and moved closer, frantically studying it.

Nate looked, as well, and saw the same six screens he had earlier. All showed different parts of the ranch, including the front of the house, where Adam was parked. He didn't see Ramirez, either, but the thought had no sooner crossed his mind when white static filled the screen.

Hell.

"Ramirez," Darcy mumbled. "He did this?"

"Maybe." Nate sandwiched his cell between his shoulder and ear and sat next to Darcy. He took the laptop and typed in the security codes again to adjust the cameras.

Nothing.

"Ramirez jammed your security system, didn't he?"

Adam asked. The man didn't sound smug. He sounded as concerned as Nate felt. "He said he would. Said he had the equipment to do it. Now he can come after you, and you can't even see where he is."

"How do I know you didn't do this?" Nate fired back. "After all, you're the one who claims to have brought Ramirez here to the ranch." Nate mentally cursed when he tried the codes again. And they failed, again.

"It's not a claim. It's the truth," Adam insisted. "I had to bring him here or he would have killed me on the spot. He broke into my hotel room, put a gun to my head and forced me to drive him here. I couldn't just let him shoot me."

"He'll kill you, anyway," Nate pointed out.

He gave up on reactivating the exterior cameras and checked to make sure the intruder alarms for the doors and windows were still armed.

Thank God. They were.

"I'm not sitting out here in the open any longer," Adam said. "Ramirez could decide to come after me before he finishes you two off." At least that's what Nate thought the man said, but he couldn't be sure because Adam gunned the engine.

Darcy's gaze flew to his, and she started to get up from the floor, but Nate caught her shoulder to keep her where she was. Right now, the floor was the best place for her, especially since it meant she was away from the windows. The security system would trigger the alarms if anyone tried to break in, but Ramirez could still shoot through the glass.

"Adam's getting away," she reminded him.

"For now. And that's not a bad thing. I don't want to

have to deal with him right now. Only Ramirez." Besides, if Ramirez attempted to kill Adam, Nate would have to do something to stop it. He only wanted to concentrate on keeping Darcy and his brothers alive.

"We need another weapon," he said. He handed her his cell phone. "Stay put and call Mason to let him know what's going on. Tell him that Ramirez is probably headed straight for the house."

She gave a shaky nod, but her eyes widened when he handed her his gun. "It's just a precaution," he added. And maybe it would stay that way—a precaution—but Nate doubted it. Ramirez was a crazy man on a mission of murder.

He ran back down the hall while Darcy made the call to Mason. Nate tried to listen to the conversation, but thanks to the relentless storm, Darcy's voice soon faded from hearing range when he hurried into his office.

Where there were windows.

The windows were the reason he'd wanted Darcy to stay put.

Nate tried to make sure Ramirez wasn't lurking outside one of them, but the rain streaks on the glass and the darkness made it impossible. So, he stayed low and went to his desk. To the bottom drawer. It had a combination safety lock, and once again the darkness wasn't in his favor, but he finally entered the correct code and jerked open the drawer.

Two guns.

He slid one in his holster, held on to the other one and crammed some extra magazines of ammo into his pockets. It was more than enough to fight off one man, but Nate had no way of knowing if Ramirez had brought backup.

The moment Nate stepped back into the hall, his attention went to Darcy. She wasn't talking on the phone, but she was staring at the laptop screen.

"Did you get Mason?" he whispered. Also a precaution. Even though it was a long shot, he didn't want Ramirez to hear them and know where to shoot.

She nodded, still not taking her wide eyes from the screen. "Look," she insisted.

Nate cursed. He didn't have to guess that something was wrong. Darcy's expression said it all. And Nate soon knew what had caused her reaction.

Five of the security screens were still filled with static, but the sixth was working. Working, in a bad way.

Ramirez's face was on the screen.

He was clearly soaked, but he was giving them that slick grin that made Nate want to come through the computer and rid the man of his last breath.

"Can he see us?" Darcy asked.

"No." The security cameras didn't have a two-way feed. But Nate could certainly see Ramirez.

"Where is he? Can you tell?" she wanted to know.

Nate really hated to say this aloud. "I can't tell from the screen." Mainly, because Ramirez was blocking the entire camera. "It's camera five, and it's on this wing of the house."

"Oh, mercy," she mumbled.

And Nate had to agree. Ramirez had gone directly to the spot where they were, and Nate didn't think that was a coincidence. He studied the screen, looking for any sign that the man had an infrared device with him, but Nate could only see that face. That grin. And the evil in his eyes.

As a cop, Nate had faced cold-blooded killers before, but Ramirez was the worst of the worst.

"What's he saying?" Darcy asked when Ramirez's lips began to move.

There was no audio, but it didn't take Nate long to figure out that Ramirez was repeating the same three words.

Ready to die?

Judging from the gasp Darcy made, she had figured it out, as well.

"Mason said he'd let everyone know that Ramirez is on the grounds," Darcy relayed. "They're moving closer to the house so they can try to spot him."

Good. That meant in ten minutes or so, Darcy and he would have plenty of backup. Of course, Ramirez might have plenty, as well, and he needed to warn his brother that they might be walking into an ambush. Mason would already be prepared for that, but Nate wanted to make it crystal clear.

He took his phone back from Darcy. Just as Ramirez moved. Ramirez stepped to the side, and Nate then saw the other person behind Ramirez.

A man several yards away from the camera.

And this man wasn't a stranger. Far from it.

"What the heck is he doing here?" Darcy asked.

Nate cursed. He wanted to know the same damn thing.

WESLEY DENT'S FACE STARED back at Darcy.

But not for long. The screen went fuzzy again. A Ramirez mind game, no doubt. The man was trying to keep Nate and her off-kilter.

It was working.

Instead of focusing on the impending attack, Darcy was wondering what her former client was doing outside the ranch house with Ramirez. Was Dent there to try to kill them, too? And if so, why?

She tightened her grip on the gun and hoped she would have answers soon. So much for believing in Dent's innocence. He looked pretty darn guilty to her.

Crouched next to her, Nate flipped open his phone.

"You're calling Mason?" Darcy asked.

But Nate didn't have time to answer. Darcy heard the cracking sound and prayed it was a violent slash of lightning. But no. This was violence of a different kind.

A bullet slammed through a window.

Nate automatically shoved her lower to the floor, even though they weren't directly in front of the window. *Any* window. But it was certainly nearby because she could hear the broken glass clatter to the floor.

"The guest room," Nate supplied.

Her pulse kicked up a notch, and the blood rushed to her head. The guest room was where they'd made love less than a half hour earlier.

Nate made the call to Mason and warned him what was happening. The moment he ended the call, he moved her, positioning her behind him so that he was facing the side of house where that shot had been fired.

"Please tell me Mason is nearby," Darcy whispered.

"He's on his way."

On his way didn't seem nearly close enough, and yet she didn't want Mason or anyone else walking into gunfire.

The jolt of lightning lit up the hall, but the crashing

noise from the following thunder was minor compared to the next shot that slammed into the house.

More broken glass fell to the floor.

"That was also in the guest room," Nate explained. He took out an extra clip of ammo and handed it to her. "Just in case," he added.

That gave her another slam of adrenaline.

So did the next bullet.

No broken glass. Just a loud, deadly-sounding thud.

"It went through the wall," Nate whispered. She could hear the adrenaline in his voice, too, but his hand seemed steady.

Unlike hers.

Darcy was afraid she was shaking too hard to aim straight. The one good thing in all of this was that the children were safe. As bad as it was having Ramirez shoot at them, it would have been a million times worse if Kimmie and Noah had been anywhere nearby.

"Watch the foyer," Nate instructed, and he angled his body so that his aim was fastened to the guest-room door.

Darcy turned, as well, and watched, though it was hard to see anything in the pitch-black foyer. However, she was certain if Ramirez managed to come through the front door, then she would hear him. And the alarms would go off.

Another shot slammed through the wall.

Beside her, Nate's phone buzzed, and he answered it without taking his aim off the doorway. Since Darcy was so close, she could actually hear the person on the other end of the line.

Adam, again.

"You have to let me inside," Adam demanded. "I tried to leave, but someone fired a shot at me."

Darcy hadn't heard such a shot, but it could have happened far enough away that the storm could have drowned it out.

"Not a chance," Nate informed him. "We're under attack and going to the door to let you in would be suicide for all of us."

"Then what the hell am I supposed to do out here?" Adam yelled.

"My advice? Keep your voice down so Ramirez doesn't hear you. Then, find a place to take cover." Nate didn't wait for Adam to respond. He snapped his phone shut and crammed it back into his pocket.

Darcy wanted to ask if Nate thought Adam was in on this. Or Dent. But the next shot stopped her cold. Again, no broken glass. This was a heavy thudding sound, but in the murky darkness, she saw the drywall dust fly through the air.

Oh, no.

The shot hadn't gone through just the exterior of the wing, it had actually made it through the interior wall.

Just a few yards away from them.

She heard Nate's suddenly rough breath, and he glanced around as if trying to decide where to move. Any direction could be dangerous.

And the next bullet proved that.

The blast was louder, much louder than the others, and she saw the large hole it made in the hall wall.

Closer this time.

"Ramirez is using heavier artillery," Nate whispered. "Get all the way down on the floor."

But he didn't wait for her to do that. He put his hand

on her back and pushed her, hard, until her face was right against the hardwood.

Just as another bullet tore through the wall.

Sweet heaven. This one was even closer.

Maybe Ramirez was using infrared to find them, but if so, why hadn't he just aimed at them right from the beginning?

"Shhh," she heard Nate say, and he brushed the back of his hand over her cheek.

It took her a moment to realize he was doing that because her breathing was way too fast and shallow. She was on the verge of hyperventilating, and that couldn't happen. She couldn't fall apart because Nate needed her for backup in case Mason didn't get there in time.

Darcy concentrated on leveling her breath. And her heartbeat. She fixed her mind on Noah's smiling face. Kimmie's and Nate's, too, and just like that, her body started to settle down. She fought to hang on to her newly regained composure even when the next bullet slammed through the wall.

This one was just inches away.

"We have to move," Nate whispered, and he caught her arm.

Darcy wasn't even off the floor yet when there was another sound. Not a bullet this time.

Something much worse.

The security alarm blared, the noise seemingly shaking the walls. And she gasped. Because she knew what that sound meant.

Ramirez was inside the house.

Chapter Seventeen

Nate knew the nightmare had just gotten worse.

The clanging of the security alarms was deafening, but that wasn't his biggest concern. With that noise, he couldn't hear Ramirez or anyone else. And he needed to hear because in addition to Ramirez, he had both Adam and Dent on the grounds. For that matter, Marlene and Edwin could be at the ranch, as well.

Anything was possible.

Plus, he had to watch out for his brothers and everyone else trying to stop Ramirez.

Nate tried to keep watch all around them, but he had no idea where the intruder had entered. It could be any window or door in the house.

"I have to turn off the alarms," Nate shouted, though Darcy only shook her head and touched her fingers to her ear.

Nate grabbed her, lifted her from the floor and turned her to the side so she could keep watch at the back of the foyer. He would take the front door and the hall, the most likely point of entry since the shots had come from that direction.

Trying to make sure they weren't about to be ambushed, Nate led her into the foyer. Darcy kept her gun ready and aimed. Nate did the same. And they made their way across the open space.

Too open.

The sidelight windows around the door were especially worrisome because a gunman could fire right through those.

He held his breath, prayed and moved as fast as he could to the keypad panel on the wall between the foyer and the family room. His mind was racing. His heart, pounding. And it took several precious seconds to recall the code. The moment he punched in the numbers, the alarms went silent.

Nate lifted his head. Listened. The rain was battering against the door and windows, but he heard the wind, too. Not from the storm. This wind was whistling through the broken windows. He tried to pick through all those sounds so he could hear what he was listening for.

Footsteps.

They barely had time to register in his mind when a bullet slammed into the wall next to them. Darcy gasped and dived toward the family room. Nate was right behind her, and he fired in the direction of the shooter.

"You missed!" someone yelled out.

Ramirez.

It was true. The killer was inside.

As quietly as he could, Nate positioned Darcy behind the sofa. It wouldn't be much protection against bullets, but it was better than nothing. He cursed himself for this stupid bait plan and wondered how the devil he could get Darcy out of this alive. And how soon.

Where were Mason and the others?

Maybe someone had managed to nab Dent, Adam or anyone else outside waiting to help Ramirez.

Ramirez fired another shot at them. "You killed my brother," he shouted. "Did you really think I wouldn't make you pay for that?"

Nate didn't answer him. He didn't want Ramirez to use Nate's voice to pinpoint their position. However, Nate let his aim follow Ramirez's voice.

He sent another bullet toward the man.

Nate couldn't see him, but he was pretty sure he missed. Ramirez's laughter confirmed it. He'd moved. Maybe to the rear of the foyer?

If so, he was getting closer.

"Before I kill you," Ramirez shouted, "I think it's only fair I should tell you who hired me to kidnap your little brats."

Darcy's breath rattled, and she tried to come up from behind the sofa, but Nate pushed her right back down. He put his finger to his mouth in a stay-quiet warning. He hoped she realized that this was a trick that could get them killed, but he knew the firestorm Ramirez's offer had created inside her. She was afraid, yes, but like Nate, she wanted justice.

"Maybe you'd like me to take care of my boss before I punish you?" Ramirez asked.

The only thing Nate wanted was a name because when this was over, he would deal with that SOB, too. For now, though, he waited and listened for Ramirez to come into view. All Nate needed was one clean shot.

"Well?" Ramirez prompted.

There. In the deep shadows of the foyer, Nate saw what he'd been watching for. The silhouette of a man. He took aim. But before he could squeeze the trigger, there was god-awful sound of wood splintering, and the man ducked out of sight.

The door.

Someone had kicked it down.

Nate didn't fire because it could be one of his brothers, and because of that, he had to break his silence. "Ramirez is in the house!" Nate warned.

"What the hell?" Ramirez snarled.

And a shot tore through the foyer.

EVERYTHING SEEMED TO FREEZE, and Darcy felt the sickening dread slice through her.

The bullet wasn't the same as the others. There had been no sound of the metal ripping through drywall or glass.

No.

This was a deadly thud. Followed by a gasp. And Darcy knew. The bullet had been shot into *someone*.

She shoved her hand over her mouth so she couldn't cry out. This couldn't be happening. Ramirez couldn't have shot Mason or Kade. She couldn't be responsible for Nate losing anyone else in his life.

Darcy tried to get up, again, but once again Nate kept her pinned behind the sofa. "Stay put," he warned.

Nate, however, didn't heed his own warning. Neither did the person in the foyer because she heard footsteps. Someone was running, probably trying to escape.

With his gun aimed and his attention pinned to the foyer, Nate started walking. Slow, inch-by-inch steps. Darcy wanted to tell him to stop, but she couldn't. If one of his brothers was hurt or worse, then Nate would need to go to him. He would have to help. Or at least try.

It might be too late for help of any kind.

And then there was the flip side. Someone had already been shot, but Ramirez was still alive. Still armed. He would shoot Nate or anyone else if he got the chance, and that's when Darcy knew she couldn't obey Nate.

She had to help him.

Darcy eased up from behind the sofa and took aim in the same direction as Nate.

Nate mumbled some profanity, and that's when Darcy spotted the body on the foyer floor. She couldn't see the man's face because he was sprawled out on his stomach, but he was dressed all in black.

No. God, no.

Was it Mason?

Nate obviously thought it was his brother because she heard the shift in his breathing. Heard him whisper a prayer.

Darcy followed Nate to the edge of the foyer, but she waited, watching in case someone came through the now-open front door. Ramirez had perhaps gone out that way, but it didn't mean he wouldn't be back.

Nate inched closer, his gaze firing all around, and when he reached the body, he leaned down and touched his fingers to the man's neck. No cursing this time, but he groaned, a painful sound that tore right through her heart.

And he flipped the body over.

Nate froze for just a second, and Darcy started to go to him, to try to comfort him. But there wasn't time. He stood, and in the same motion, Nate whirled back around to face her.

Darcy shook her head, not understanding why he'd

done that. She didn't get a chance to ask because someone karate chopped her arm, causing her weapon to go flying through the air. But she felt another gun, cold and hard, when it was shoved against her back.

"Move and your boyfriend dies," the person behind her growled in a hoarse whisper.

Her breathing went crazy, started racing. As did her heart. And she looked past Nate's suddenly startled face and stared at the body on the foyer floor.

Not Mason.

It was Ramirez.

Darcy's stomach went to her knees. Because if Ramirez was there, lifeless and unmoving, then who had a gun jammed in her back?

"Sorry about this," the person whispered. It was a man, but she couldn't tell who. "You have to be my hostage for a little while."

Darcy had no intentions of being anyone's hostage.

She moved purely on instinct. She jerked away from her captor and dived to the side. But so did he, and he hooked his arm around her and held her in place. Still, she didn't give up. She didn't stop struggling.

Until the blast from a gun roared through her head.

Everything inside her went numb, and it took her a moment to realize she hadn't been shot. That it was the deafening noise from the bullet that had caused the pain to shoot through her. In fact, the gun hadn't even been aimed at her. The shot had been fired over her head.

"Darcy?" Nate called out.

She tried to answer him but couldn't get her throat unclamped. Darcy cursed her reaction and forced herself to move. She didn't intend to die without a fight so she rammed her elbow into her captor's stomach. It wasn't much, but it was enough for her to break the hold he had on her and scramble away.

She got just a glimpse of her attacker's face.

But a glimpse was all she needed to recognize him. It was Adam.

He fired another shot, again over her head, and it slammed into the wall just a fraction of a second before he hooked his arm around her throat and put her in a choke hold.

Oh, mercy. She couldn't breathe. That caused panic to crawl through her. And worse, Nate was coming closer. Putting himself out in the open so that Adam could kill him, instead.

"Stop fighting me," Adam warned her. "Or Nate dies. Your choice."

That was no choice at all. She stopped fighting and prayed it would save Nate.

"Good girl," Adam whispered in a mock-sweet tone. But he did loosen the grip on her throat. Darcy frantically pulled in some much-needed air and hoped it was enough to stop her from passing out.

"Adam, give this up," Nate ordered. "You can't get out of here alive."

"No?" Adam answered. He kept his arm around her neck but aimed his gun at Nate. "So far, so good. Ramirez is dead."

"Yeah." With his own gun aimed at Adam, Nate inched closer, but he stayed in the foyer, out of Adam's direct line of fire. "You killed him before he could tell us that you were the one who hired him to set up the kidnapping."

Adam didn't deny it, and Darcy realized it was true.

Adam was the one who'd put the children in danger. Her fear was replaced by a jolt of anger.

How dare this moron do that!

"All this for money," Nate continued. He moved again. Just a fraction. And Darcy realized he was trying to get into a position so he could take Adam out.

Good. She wanted Adam to pay for what he'd done.

"Hey, it's always about money," Adam joked. He started inching toward the foyer. "If you'd just arrested Dent and tossed his sorry butt in jail, then my mother's estate would have been mine, and we wouldn't be here right now."

"But Dent isn't guilty," Nate concluded.

"No. But Dent is dead," Adam confessed. "I killed him about ten minutes ago."

Dead? Darcy tried hard to hang on to her composure. She was already losing that battle before Adam fired a shot into the foyer. She heard herself scream for Nate to get down, and somehow he managed to duck out of the way.

Adam cursed. "Move again, Lieutenant, and I'll shoot Darcy in the shoulder. It won't kill her, but it won't be fun, either." He shoved her forward, keeping his choke hold and his gun in place.

"Don't you have enough blood on your hands?" Nate asked. "First your mother with a lethal dose of insulin. Then, you kill Dent. Now, Ramirez. All of this to cover up what you've done. My theory? You knew what your mother had written in her diary so you tore out the page that would have incriminated you. But something happened, something that prevented you from destroying it."

"Yeah," Adam readily agreed, "and that was my

mother's fault. She saw me rip out the page, and she grabbed the diary and ran. She hid it before I found her and then wouldn't tell me where she'd put it. That's when I killed her."

Darcy could almost see it playing out. Sandra, terrified of her own son as he shoved a needle into her arm. She understood that terror because she was feeling it now.

"Unless you do something to ruin my plan," Adam went on, "the diary is what will keep you both alive."

"What do you mean?" Darcy asked.

But Adam didn't answer her. He nailed his attention to Nate. "I want you to give me the diary so I can destroy it."

"Impossible," Nate fired back.

"No. It's doable for a man in your position. I'll take Darcy someplace safe while you go to the crime lab. When you bring me the diary, then I'll let Darcy go. Well, after I've cashed in my mother's estate and escaped, of course."

The adrenaline and the anger were making it hard for her to think, but Darcy could still see the faulty logic. Adam wouldn't let them go. If he got his hands on the diary and Sandra's money, he would kill them so he could cover up his crimes.

Or rather, he'd try to kill them.

"There's no need to take Darcy," Nate bargained. "I can call and have the diary brought to us."

She latched on to that, hoping Adam would agree. If they could somehow prevent him from leaving the ranch with her, then she would have a better chance of escape.

But Adam shook his head.

"Not a chance. As long as I have Darcy, you'll do whatever it takes to cooperate." Adam tightened his grip on her and muscled her into the foyer and toward the front door. "Lieutenant, tell your brothers and anybody else out there to back off." He shoved Darcy forward again, toward the door.

Nate's gaze slashed from Adam's gun to her own eyes, and she saw the raw, painful emotions there. Nate was blaming himself for this. She wanted to tell him that it wasn't his fault. But there was no time to tell him anything. Because Adam dragged her out onto the porch, down the steps and toward his car, which was parked behind Nate's SUV. Adam had obviously pretended to drive away from the ranch.

The storm came right at her, assaulting her. The rain stung her eyes, but that didn't stop her from seeing the shadowy figure on the side of the house.

Mason.

He had his gun drawn, like Nate, who was now in the doorway, but neither could fire. The way Adam was holding her would make it next to impossible for either of them to get a clean shot.

"Lieutenant, tell your brother to back off," Adam warned, forcing Darcy into the yard.

But Mason stepped out. "She makes a lousy hostage," Mason snarled. "She's a good six inches shorter than you, and that means somebody out here has a good chance at a head shot. *Your* head."

She felt Adam's arm tense, and he crouched farther down behind her. Maybe Kade or one of the others was behind them, but that still didn't mean there'd be a clean shot. After all, the bullet could go through Adam and into her.

"I'd make a better human shield," Mason offered. He shrugged as if he didn't have a care in the world. "I'll take her place."

Part of her was touched that Mason would even make the offer, but she didn't want to place Nate's brother in even more danger. Apparently neither did Nate because he inched down the steps.

"What a dilemma, Lieutenant," Adam mocked. He clucked his tongue. "Your brother or your lover. So, which one will it be?"

Oh, mercy. Darcy hadn't thought this could get any worse, but she'd been wrong. It was sick to force Nate into making a choice like this.

"It's okay," Darcy insisted. "I'll go with him." Well, she would, but she would also try to escape. She wasn't about to give up.

"No, you won't go with him," Nate said. "If Adam won't take me, then Mason will go."

Adam made a sound of amusement. "You're choosing her over your own blood?"

Nate gave him a look that could have frozen Hades. "Mason's a cop. Darcy's a civilian."

Mason just shrugged again and then nodded.

Adam didn't respond right away, and she couldn't see his expression. However, she could feel his muscles tense again. "No deal," Adam finally said. "She'll be a lot easier to control than either of you. Besides, Darcy knows if she doesn't cooperate, I'll just go after her son again."

It took a few seconds for those words to sink in, and they didn't sink in well. How dare this SOB threaten Noah again.

Her hands tightened to fists.

And that was for starters.

The slam of anger created a new jolt of adrenaline, and it wasn't just her hands that tightened. The rest of her body did, too. Suddenly, she was primed and ready for a fight and needed someplace to aim all this dangerous energy boiling inside her.

She saw the anger—no, make that *rage*—go through Nate's eyes, and she knew he was within seconds of launching himself at Adam. That couldn't happen because Adam would shoot him. But maybe there was something she could do to improve Nate's odds.

Darcy frantically looked around her. There was nothing nearby that she could grab. No shrubs, rocks or weapons. But the car was directly behind them, and Darcy watched. And waited.

Until Adam reached to open the door.

She used every bit of her anger and adrenaline when she drew back her elbow and rammed it into Adam's ribs. He sputtered out a cough and eased up on his grip just enough to give her some room to maneuver. Darcy lifted her foot, put her weight behind it and punched her heel into his shin.

"Get down!" Nate yelled to her.

Darcy had already started to do just that, but Adam latched on to her hair. The pain shot through her, but she kicked him again. And again. Fighting to get loose from him.

She succeeded.

Darcy fell facedown onto the slick driveway, the rough, wet concrete grating across her knees and forearms. She immediately tried to scramble for cover behind the car.

But it was too late for that.

From the corner of her eye, she saw Adam lift his gun. Take aim.

And he fired.

Chapter Eighteen

Nate felt the searing pain slice through him.

Just like that, his legs gave way, and he had no choice but to drop to the ground.

Hell.

Adam had shot him.

That, and the pain, registered in his mind, and he maneuvered his gun so he could try to protect Darcy. He had to stop Adam from taking her.

Or worse.

The sound of another gunshot let him know that worse could have already happened.

"Darcy?" Nate managed to call out.

She didn't answer, and he couldn't see her, but there was the sound of chaos all around him.

Another shot.

Mason shouted something that was drowned out by the thunder, and suddenly there was movement. Footsteps. Some kind of scuffle. A sea of people—FBI agents and the ranch hands. All of them converged on Adam and took him to the ground.

"Darcy?" Nate yelled.

He had to make sure she was safe. He had to see for himself. If Adam had managed to shoot her... But he couldn't go there. Couldn't even think it. Because he was responsible for this.

No.

It was more than that.

Nate couldn't lose her. It was as simple as that. He couldn't lose her because he loved her.

He would have laughed if it hadn't been for the god-awful pain searing his left shoulder. It was a really bad time to realize just how he felt about Darcy.

"Nate?" he heard someone say.

He lifted his head and amid that swarm of people, he saw her. Darcy. She had mud on her face and clothes, and he couldn't tell if she'd been shot. But she was moving.

Or rather, running.

She hurried to him and pulled him into her arms. He saw the blood then and had a moment of rage where he wanted to tear Adam limb from limb.

But then he noticed that the blood was his.

Thank God. Darcy was all right.

"You're hurt," she said, her voice shaking almost violently.

Yeah, he was, but that didn't matter now. "Are you okay?"

"No." She made a sobbing sound, and her tears slid through the mud on her cheeks. "I'm not okay because you've been shot."

Oh. That. The relief didn't help with his pain, but it helped with everything else.

Darcy was okay.

Adam hadn't managed to shoot her, after all.

"Can you stand?" she asked. "I don't want to wait for an ambulance. I'll drive you to the hospital."

Nate hated the worry in her eyes. Hated those tears. But he couldn't refuse her offer. Even he wasn't too stubborn to refuse a trip to the hospital—though he did want to first make sure that Adam had been neutralized. Nate glanced around, but he couldn't tell. Because he couldn't actually see the man who'd just tried to kill him.

However, he did see Mason.

His brother broke from the group and made a bee-line for him. "Hurt much?" Mason asked. But he didn't wait for an answer. With Darcy on one side of him and Mason on the other, they got Nate to his feet and headed toward his SUV.

"What about Adam?" Nate wanted to know.

"Kade is on him." Mason glanced back at the huddle of activity. "Literally. He's not going anywhere except to jail."

Good. One less thing to worry about right now. Later, he would deal with his hatred for this SOB who'd nearly cost Nate everything.

Darcy pressed her hand to his shoulder, right where it was burning like fire, but he guessed she was doing that to stop the blood flow and not to make him wince in pain.

"Are you okay?" Darcy whispered as they hauled Nate onto the backseat of the SUV. Darcy followed right in beside him and crouched on the floor. Mason peeled out of the driveway, the tires of the SUV kicking up gravel and rain.

"I'm okay," Nate tried.

"Are you really?" she questioned.

Since she sounded very close to losing it, Nate decided to give her some reassurance. He slid his hand around the back of her neck, pulled her to him and kissed her. He wasn't surprised when it gave him some reassurance, too.

"Can't be hurt that bad if you can do that to her," Mason growled.

"I'm not hurt that bad," Nate verified. And he was almost certain that was true. It was hard to tell through the blistering pain.

"You were shot," Darcy pointed out. The frantic tone was back in her voice. "Adam could have killed you."

"He could have killed you, too," Nate reminded her.

But it was a reminder that cut him right across the heart. He would see Adam in his nightmares. Darcy would, too. And Nate would never forgive Adam for that and for placing Noah and Kimmie in grave danger.

"Adam got some blood on his hands tonight," Mason said, his attention glued to the wet road. The wipers slashed across the windshield. "I'm the one who found Dent just a few seconds before he died from a gunshot wound to the chest. He told me Adam had called him to come to the ranch and said that he had proof it was Edwin who'd killed Sandra."

Dent had been stupid to fall for that, but then Adam had probably convinced him that he'd be safe at the ranch with a cop, an FBI agent and a deputy sheriff.

"What about Ramirez's partner?" Nate asked. "Someone needs to make sure he doesn't try to help Adam."

"He can't help anybody," Mason assured him. "Right before Adam grabbed Darcy, Kade found Ramirez's partner—dead."

Adam, no doubt. With Ramirez and Sandra Dent, that meant Adam had killed at least three, maybe four people. A lot of murder and mayhem all for the sake of money. But the high body count along with the kidnapping charges meant there was no way Adam could escape the death penalty.

"How much longer before we get to the hospital?" Darcy asked.

"Not long," Mason assured her. "One of the ranch hands is calling ahead so the E.R. will be expecting us."

She kept her hand pressed over his wound and kept mumbling something. A prayer, he realized.

"The pain's not that bad," he lied.

But more of her tears came, anyway, and they were followed by a heart-wrenching sob. "I should have held on to Adam's arm. I should have kicked him harder." Darcy shook her head. "I should have done something to stop him from firing that gun."

"Hey, don't do this." Nate touched her chin and lifted it. "I'm the one who planned for us to be bait."

"The plan worked," Darcy reminded him, though she had to draw in a deep breath before saying it. "What didn't work was that I allowed Adam to take me at gunpoint. That's when things went wrong."

He could have told her that things went wrong when Adam killed his mother, but Nate didn't think Darcy would hear the logic. No, she was hurting and worried, and he was the cause of that.

Nate hoped he could also be the cure.

He pulled her back to him for another kiss. And another. And he kept it up until oxygen became a big concern for both of them. But he figured he might need her a little breathless for what he was about to say.

"I don't want to lose you," he let her know.

She shook her head, smeared the tears from her

cheeks. "Adam isn't a threat anymore. Nor Ramirez. We'll be safe."

Yeah. But that wasn't where Nate was going with this. "I don't want to lose you," he repeated.

Darcy blinked. Shook her head again.

"Part of me will always love Ellie," he explained. "But I can't live in the past, and she was my past...."

"We're here," Mason announced, and he braked to a screeching halt directly in front of the E.R. door.

Nate choked back the pain that was blurring his vision and gathered his breath. He wanted to finish this now.

"Darcy, will you marry me?"

She opened her mouth, but nothing came out. *Nothing.* And then the moment was gone.

Everything started to move way too fast. Two medics threw open the SUV's door and hauled him onto a gurney. Nate got one last glimpse of Darcy's startled, bleached face before the medics whisked him away.

DARCY WAS AFRAID if she sat down, she'd collapse. So, she kept pacing and waiting. Something she'd been doing for nearly an hour. It felt more like an eternity.

"SAPD is booking Adam right now," Mason relayed to her from the chair in the corner of the waiting room. He had his feet stretched out in front of him as if he were lounging, and he'd been on and off the phone— mainly on—since they'd arrived at the E.R.

Mason certainly didn't seem crazy scared, like she did. But then, neither did Dade, who had his shoulder propped against the wall. He, too, was on the phone, with his fiancée, and from the sound of it, both Kayla and Grayson's wife, Eve, were on their way to the hospital to see Nate. Kade was the only Ryland who showed signs of stress. He was seated, elbows on knees, his face buried in his hands.

"What about Marlene and Edwin?" Darcy asked. Because it occurred to her if Adam had killed Dent, his mother and Ramirez, he might have killed others.

"They're safe and sound," Mason answered. "Neither appears to have had anything to do with this. According to Mel, Edwin's pretty torn up."

Of course. His son would be facing the death penalty.

"Adam was chatty when he arrived at the sheriff's office," Mason went on. "He admitted to trying to make his father look guilty. He wanted the blame placed on anyone but him. Edwin might not be so torn up when he learns that sonny boy was willing to let him take the fall for murder." Mason's phone buzzed again.

Darcy continued to pace until she heard Mason mention Grayson's name, and that stopped her. She certainly hadn't forgotten about the children, but with Nate's injury, she'd put him at the top of her worry list.

Until now.

She hoped Grayson wasn't phoning because there was a problem. She moved closer to him so she could try to hear, but the call ended quickly.

"Grayson and the kids are on their way here," Mason relayed. "Everybody's okay."

The blood rushed to her head. A mix of relief and happiness overcame her when she realized she would soon get to see Noah and Kimmie. But Darcy knew there wouldn't be total relief until she saw Nate. Until she talked to him.

Until she asked him about that *question.*

Heaven knows how long that would be. Besides, he might not even know what he'd said. Nate had been in so much pain, and mixed with the blood loss and the shock, he might have been talking out of his head.

Everything suddenly felt still and silent. None of the Rylands were on their phones. Like her, they were fully in the wait mode. Except for Mason. He was studying her with those intense, steely eyes.

"Well?" he asked.

Darcy froze. Because even though that one word hardly qualified as a question, she was positive what Mason meant. After all, Mason had been in that SUV, and he'd almost certainly heard Nate's question.

Kade lifted his head. Looked at Mason. Then at her. "Well what?"

Oh, no. She hadn't wanted to do this tonight and especially not before she'd had a chance to speak with Nate.

But apparently Mason did. "Right before the medics took him into the E.R., Nate asked Darcy to marry him."

The room was suddenly so quiet that Darcy could hear her own heartbeat. It was racing.

All three Rylands stared at her. And stared. But it was Dade who walked toward her. He stopped just a few inches away, and she braced herself for a good tongue-lashing about how she'd played on Nate's vulnerability.

"What was your answer?" Dade asked.

She managed to shrug, somehow, though her muscles seemed frozen in place. "There wasn't time for an answer."

Dade waited, still staring, and it became clear that he expected her to reveal what that answer would be.

"I want to tell Nate first," she explained. And she braced herself for Dade to demand to know.

But he reached out, put his arm around her and eased her to him. He brushed a kiss on her forehead. "I hope you'll say yes."

Darcy couldn't have been any more stunned. "You do?"

The corner of his mouth lifted, probably because all that shock had made it into her voice. "You're good for Nate."

Kade stood, crammed his hands in his pockets and walked closer, as well. "You are good for him," he verified. "It's nice to see Nate happy for a change."

Again, she got another dose of being stunned. "I'm in love with him," she blurted out. *Oh, mercy.* She hadn't expected to say that. Not to them, anyway.

"Does he know that?" Dade asked.

Darcy shook her head, causing Kade and Dade to grumble under their breaths. "You need to tell him," Dade insisted.

She would. Once she could speak. And once she got past the whole "maybe Nate was talking out of his head" thing. Maybe he wouldn't remember proposing to her.

"I hope like the devil that you two get married the same time as Kayla and Dade," Mason mumbled. "No way do I want to wear a monkey suit twice."

Kade huffed. "Ignore Mr. Congeniality over there. You name the date for him to be in a monkey suit, and he'll be in one. There are four of us and one of him."

Mason matched that huff. "Yeah, and it'll take all

four of you weenies to try." He sounded serious enough, but Darcy suspected he was joking.

She was about to ask for clarification, but the door behind them swung open.

And there was Nate.

His shirt was open, exposing the bandage on his shoulder, and his left arm was in a pristine-white sling. He looked exhausted. And really confused when his gaze landed on all of them.

Darcy hurried to him, slipped her arms around his waist and tried to give him a gentle hug. "You're okay?" she asked. And she cursed the tears that came automatically.

"I am," Nate verified. "The bullet went straight through. No real damage. The doctor says I'll be fine in about a week or so."

Now, here was the flood of relief that she'd waited for. Nate was all right.

He brushed a kiss on her cheek and ducked down to make eye contact. "Is something, uh, wrong?"

"No," Darcy jumped to answer. Unfortunately, Dade and Kade jumped to answer with their own noes.

Mason just made a snorting sound. "I told them about your marriage proposal. And Darcy told us that she's in love with you." He looked at Nate. "Yeah, we were surprised, too. We didn't consider you, well, all that lovable."

That brought on some snickers from Kade and Dade, but Nate just kept looking at her. "Did you tell them the answer to my proposal?"

Suddenly all eyes were on her again. "No. I said I needed to talk to you first."

Nate's face dropped, and around her she heard the

murmurings of the Ryland brothers as they started to leave, giving them some time alone to absorb what she was about to say. Of course, judging from the sudden mood in the room, they thought she was about to say no.

So, Darcy tried one of Nate's ploys.

She kissed him. She didn't keep it exactly gentle, either. It was best if he knew just how deep, and how hot, her feelings were for him. She didn't break the mouth-to-mouth contact until Mason cleared his throat, a reminder that Nate and she weren't alone, after all.

Darcy eased back and looked Nate in the eyes. "I'm in love with you."

Nate smiled that little smile that made her want to kiss him again. And haul him off to bed.

But bed could wait.

"Yes," she added. "I want to marry you."

Nate's smile suddenly wasn't so little. "Good. Because I'm in love with you, and I definitely want to marry you." He hooked his uninjured arm around her and hauled her closer to him for a perfect kiss.

One that caused Dade and Kade to whoop.

Nate and she broke away laughing. And then kissed again.

Darcy hadn't thought this moment could get any better, but then she heard the familiar voices. Grayson was making his way toward them, and he was carrying both babies. Amazingly, both were wide-awake and were squirming to get down. Grayson eased them both onto the floor, and the two toddled into the waiting area.

"Here," Kade said, peeling off his jacket and slipping it on Darcy.

That's when Darcy realized she had blood on her top. Nate's blood. And she didn't want the children to see that. "Thank you," she whispered to Kade.

"Anything for my new sister-in-law." He brushed a kiss on her cheek and moved away so she could kneel down and give both babies a big hug.

Kimmie started babbling as though trying to tell Darcy all about their adventure at the safe house, and Darcy scooped up both of them so that Nate wouldn't have to bend down for all-around kisses.

"Boo-boo," Noah announced when he spotted the bandage on Nate's shoulder, and when he kissed it, Kimmie repeated the syllables and kissed it, as well.

"Your mom and I are getting married," Nate told Noah. "How do you feel about that?"

Noah looked pensive for a moment, then grinned and babbled some happy sounds.

Her son was obviously okay with this. "And what do you think?" Darcy asked Kimmie.

Kimmie looked at her uncle Mason. "Your call, curly locks," he told her.

Even though there was no way Kimmie knew what that meant, she giggled and clapped her hands.

Darcy had never thought she could feel this much happiness, but then she saw Grayson, the only person in the room who hadn't given some kind of thumbs-up. She wouldn't take back her yes. She loved Nate too much to walk away because his brother disapproved, but she wanted it just the same.

"I'm in love with Nate," Darcy told Grayson, just in case he'd missed that part.

Grayson nodded. "Then I guess that leaves me with

just one thing to say." He leaned in and brushed a kiss on her cheek. "Welcome to the family."

A breath of relief swooshed out of her, causing Kimmie to laugh and try to make the same sound. Darcy looked at Nate and saw the love he had for all of them.

Nate kissed her despite the fact he had to maneuver through both kids to do that. "Ready to go home?" he whispered against her mouth.

Darcy didn't even have to consider this answer. "Yes."

And with Nate's arm around her, they took their first step toward their new life together.

* * * * *

This was his baby. His little girl.

He felt the punch, and it nearly robbed him of his breath.The doctor was right. He should have sat down for this.

The love was there. Instant and strong. Deep in his heart and his gut, he knew the test had been right.

Even though he'd had no immediate plans for fatherhood, that all changed in an instant. He knew he loved her, would do whatever it took to be a good father to her. But he also knew she'd been abandoned. That left Kade with one big question.

Where was her mother?

This was his baby. His little girl

He felt the panic and a nearly unbearable longing of his friend. The doctor was right. He should have sat down for this...

The love was there, instant and strong. Deep to his heart and he just knew the rest from there on.

Even though he had no immediate plans for fatherhood, that affection for the infant was there. He loved her, would do whatever it took to be a good father to her, but he also knew she deserved a mother. That thought struck with one big question:

Where was her mother?

KADE

BY
DELORES FOSSEN

First published in Great Britain 2013
by Mills & Boon, an imprint of Harlequin (UK) Limited,
Eton House, 18-24 Paradise Road, Richmond, Surrey TW9 1SR

© Delores Fossen 2012

ISBN: 978 0 263 90344 7
ebook ISBN: 978 1 472 00693 6

46-0213

Harlequin (UK) policy is to use papers that are natural, renewable and recyclable products and made from wood grown in sustainable forests. The logging and manufacturing processes conform to the legal environmental regulations of the country of origin.

Printed and bound in Spain
by Blackprint CPI, Barcelona

Imagine a family tree that includes Texas cowboys, Choctaw and Cherokee Indians, a Louisiana pirate and a Scottish rebel who battled side by side with William Wallace. With ancestors like that, it's easy to understand why *USA TODAY* bestselling author and former air force captain **Delores Fossen** feels as if she were genetically predisposed to writing romances. Along the way to fulfilling her DNA destiny, Delores married an air force top gun who just happens to be of Viking descent. With all those romantic bases covered, she doesn't have to look too far for inspiration.

Chapter One

Special Agent Kade Ryland raced up the steps of the
Silver Creek hospital. Whatever was going on, it was
bad. No doubt about it. The voice message from his
brother had proven that.

Get to the hospital now, Grayson had ordered.

Since his brother Grayson was the sheriff of Silver
Creek, it couldn't be good news. Nor was the fact that
Grayson wasn't answering his phone—probably be-
cause he was in the hospital, a dead zone for reception.

Kade prayed that someone wasn't hurt or dead, but
the odds were that's exactly what had happened. He had
four living brothers, three sisters-in-law, two nephews
and a niece. Since all his brothers were in law enforcement and one of his sisters-in-law was pregnant, there
were lots of opportunities for things to go wrong.

The automatic doors swished open, and he hurried
through, only to set off the metal detector's alarm. Kade
mumbled some profanity for the delay. He'd just come
from work and was still wearing his sidearm in a shoulder holster concealed beneath his jacket. He also had
his backup weapon strapped to his boot. He didn't want
to take the time to remove either of them.

The uniformed guard practically jumped from the
chair where he was reading a battered copy of the

Silver Creek Ledger. His name was Rowdy Dawkins, a man that Kade had known his whole life. But then Kade could say that about half the town.

"The sheriff's waiting for you in the emergency room," Rowdy said, waving Kade through the metal detector. His expression was somber. His tone dripped with concern.

Oh, man.

Kade didn't even take the time to ask Rowdy for details, though the man no doubt knew what was going on. He didn't just hurry—Kade ran to the E.R. that was at the other end of the building. The hospital wasn't big by anyone's standards, but it seemed to take him an hour to reach the E.R. waiting room.

No sign of his brother or any other family member.

Kade's heart was pounding now, and his mind was coming up with all sorts of bad scenarios. He'd been an FBI agent for seven years, not nearly as long as his brothers had been in law enforcement, but that was more than long enough to fuel the worst sort of details about what could be wrong.

"Your brother's in there with Dr. Mickelson," a nurse volunteered as she pointed the way. She, too, gave him a sympathetic look, which meant he was probably the only person in the whole frickin' town who didn't know what the heck was going on.

Kade mumbled a thank-you to her and hurried into the doctor's office, the first door in the hall just off the waiting room. He tried to brace himself for what he might see, but he hadn't expected to find everything looking so…normal.

Well, almost.

Grayson was indeed there, standing, and looking fit as a fiddle as his granddaddy Chet would have said. He looked as he usually did in his jeans and crisp white shirt with his badge clipped to his rodeo belt.

Dr. Mickelson, the chief of staff, was there, as well, practically elbow to elbow with Grayson. Nothing looked out of the ordinary for him, either. The two had obviously been expecting him.

"I was in the middle of an arrest when you phoned," Kade started. "That's why your call went straight to voice mail, but I tried to get in touch with you after I got your message. I tried your office, too, and the dispatch clerk said her orders were for me to speak directly to you. What's wrong? Who's hurt?"

"No one's hurt," Grayson said, but then he wearily shook his head. "At least no one that we know about." He stepped closer and looked directly into Kade's eyes. Ice-gray eyes that were a genetic copy of Kade's own.

Oh, yeah. This was bad.

And downright confusing.

"What do you mean by that?" Kade asked.

Grayson and the doctor exchanged glances. "You'd better sit down. We have something to tell you." The doctor tipped his head to the chair next to his desk, which was cluttered with folders, computer equipment and papers.

The one thing Kade didn't want was to sit. "Does someone in the family have cancer or something?"

Or God forbid, had there been a suicide? It wasn't something the average person would consider high on their list of worries, but since his own mother had committed suicide when he was barely eleven, it was never far from Kade's mind.

"No one has cancer," the doctor answered. He flexed his graying eyebrows, but he didn't add more.

Like the security guard, Kade knew Dr. Mickelson.

The doctor had been the one to deliver him thirty-one years ago, but Kade couldn't read the doctor as well as he could read Grayson. So, he turned to his brother.

"Tell me what happened," Kade pushed.

Grayson mumbled something under his breath. "I would if I knew where to start."

"The beginning's usually a good place." Kade's stomach was churning now, the acid blistering his throat, and he just wanted to know the truth.

"All right." Grayson took a deep breath and stepped to the side.

Kade saw it then. The clear bassinet on rollers, the kind they used in the hospital nursery.

He walked closer and looked inside. There was a baby, and it was likely a girl since there was a pink blanket snuggled around her. There was also a little pink stretchy cap on her head. She was asleep, but her mouth was puckered as if sucking a bottle.

"What does the baby have to do with this?" Kade asked.

"Everything. Two days ago someone abandoned her in the E.R. waiting room," the doctor explained. "The person left her in an infant carrier next to one of the chairs. We don't know who did that because we don't have security cameras."

Kade was finally able to release the breath he'd been holding. So, this was job-related. They'd called him in because he was an FBI agent.

But he immediately rethought that.

"An abandoned baby isn't a federal case," Kade clarified, though Grayson already knew that. Kade reached down and brushed his index finger over a tiny dark curl that peeked out from beneath the cap. "You think she was kidnapped or something?"

When neither the doctor nor Grayson answered, Kade looked back at them. Anger began to boil through him. "Did someone hurt her?"

"No," the doctor quickly answered. "There wasn't a scratch on her. She's perfectly healthy as far as I can tell."

The anger went as quickly as it'd come. Kade had handled the worst of cases, but the one thing he couldn't stomach was anyone harming a child.

"I called Grayson as soon as she was found," the doctor went on. "There were no Amber Alerts, no reports of missing newborns. There wasn't a note in her carrier, only a bottle that had no prints, no fibers or anything else to distinguish it."

Kade lifted his hands palm up. "That's a lot of *noes*. What do you know about her?" Because he was sure this was leading somewhere.

Dr. Mickelson glanced at the baby. "We know she's about three or four days old, which means she was abandoned either the day she was born or shortly after. She's slightly underweight, barely five pounds, but there was no hospital bracelet. We had no other way to identify her so we ran a DNA test two days ago when she arrived and just got back the results." His explanation stopped cold, and his attention came back to Kade.

So did Grayson's. "Kade, she's yours."

Kade leaned in because he was certain he'd misheard what his brother said. "Excuse me?"

"The baby is your daughter," Grayson clarified.

Because that was the last thing Kade expected to come from his brother's mouth, it took several seconds to sink in. Okay, more than several, and when it finally registered in his brain, it didn't sink in well.

All the air vanished from the room.

"That's impossible," Kade practically shouted.

The baby began to squirm from the noise. Kade's reaction was just as abrupt. What the devil was going on here? He wasn't a father. Heck, he hadn't been in a real relationship in nearly two years.

Grayson groaned and tipped his eyes to the ceiling. "Not impossible according to the DNA."

Kade did some groaning, as well, and would have spit out a denial or two, but the baby started to cry. Grayson looked at Kade as if he expected him to do something, but Kade was too stunned to move. Grayson huffed, reached down, gently scooped her up and began to rock her.

"The DNA test has to be wrong," Kade concluded.

But he stared at that tiny crying face. She did have dark hair, like the Rylands. The shape of her face was familiar, too, similar to his own niece, but all babies looked pretty much the same to him.

"I had the lab run two genetic samples to make sure," the doctor interjected. "And then Grayson put the results through a bunch of databases. Your DNA was already in there."

Yeah. Kade knew his DNA was in the system. Most federal employees were. But that didn't mean the match had been correct.

"Who's the baby's mother?" Kade demanded.

Because whoever she was, all of this wasn't adding up. A baby who just happened to match an FBI agent's DNA.

His DNA.

A bottle with no fingerprints. And the baby had been abandoned at the hospital in his hometown, where his family owned a very successful ranch.

All of that couldn't be a coincidence.

"We don't know the identity of the child's mother," the doctor answered. "We didn't get a database match on the maternal DNA."

And that did even more to convince Kade that this was some kind of setup. But then he rethought that. Most people didn't have their DNA recorded in a law enforcement system unless they'd done something to get it there.

Like break the law.

"Since you haven't mentioned a girlfriend," Grayson continued, "you're probably looking at the result of a one-night stand. Don't bother to tell me you haven't had a few of those."

He had. Kade couldn't deny there had been one or two, but he'd always taken precautions. *Always.* The same as he had in his longer relationships.

"Think back eight to nine months ago," Grayson prompted. "I already checked the calendar you keep on the computer at the ranch, and I know you were on assignments both months."

Kade forced himself to think and do the math. He could dispel this entire notion of the baby being his if he could figure out where he'd been during that critical time. It took some doing, but he picked through the smeared recollections of assignments, reports and briefings.

The nine-month point didn't fit because he'd done surveillance in a van. Alone. But eight and a half months ago he'd been in San Antonio, days into an undercover assignment that involved the Fulbright Fertility Clinic, a facility that was into all sorts of nasty things, including genetic experiments on embryos, questionable surrogates and illegal adoptions.

Kade froze.

"What?" Grayson demanded. "You remembered something?"

Oh, yeah. He remembered *something*.

Kade squeezed his eyes shut a moment. "I teamed up with a female deep-cover agent. A Jane we call them. She already had established ties with someone who worked in the clinic so we partnered up. We posed as a married couple with fertility issues so we could infiltrate the clinic. We were literally locked in the place for four days."

Kade had been on more than a dozen assignments since the Fulbright case, the details of them all bleeding together, but there was one Texas-size detail about that assignment that stood out.

Bree.

The tough-as-nails petite brunette with the olive-green eyes. During those four days they'd worked together, she'd been closemouthed about her personal life. Heck, he knew hardly anything about her, and what he did know could have been part of the facade of a deep-cover agent.

"We didn't have sex," Kade mumbled. Though he had thought about it a time or two. Posing as a married couple, they'd been forced to sleep in the same bed and put on a show of how much they *loved* each other.

"There must be someone else, then," Grayson insisted.

"Alice Marks," Kade admitted. "But the timing is wrong. Besides, I saw Alice just a couple of months ago, and she definitely wasn't pregnant…"

Everything inside Kade went still when something else came to him. It couldn't be *that*.

Could it?

"The Jane agent and I posed as a couple with fertility problems, and the doctors at the Fulbright clinic had me provide some semen," Kade explained.

"Could the doctors have used it to impregnate the mother?" Grayson asked.

"I'm not sure. Maybe," Kade conceded. "The investigation didn't go as planned. Something went wrong. Someone at the clinic drugged us, and we had to fight our way out of there. But maybe during that time we were drugged, they used the semen to make her pregnant."

The doctor shook his head. "If the birth mother was an agent, then why wasn't her DNA in the system?"

It was Grayson who answered. "If she was in deep-cover ops, a Jane, they don't enter those agents' DNA into the normal law enforcement databases. The Bureau doesn't want anyone to know they work for the FBI."

His brother was right. The odds were slim to none that Special Agent Bree Winston's DNA would be in any database other than the classified one at FBI Headquarters in Quantico, Virginia.

Kade forced his eyes open, and his gaze immediately landed on the baby that Grayson was holding. The newborn was awake now, and she had turned her head in his direction. She was looking at him.

Kade swallowed hard.

He felt the punch, and it nearly robbed him of his breath. The doctor was right. He should have sat down for this.

The love was there. Instant and strong. Deep in his heart and his gut, he knew the test had been right.

This was his baby.

His little girl.

Even though he'd had no immediate plans for fatherhood, that all changed in an instant. He knew he loved

her, would do whatever it took to be a good father to
her. But he also knew she'd been abandoned. That left
Kade with one big question.

Where was her mother?

Where was Bree?

And by God, if something had gone on at the clinic,
why hadn't she told him? Why had she kept something
like this a secret?

Kade pulled in his breath, hoping it would clear his
head. It didn't, but he couldn't take the time to adjust
to the bombshell that had just slammed right into him.

He leaned down and brushed a kiss on his baby girl's
cheek. She blinked, and she stared at him as if trying
to figure out who the heck he was.

"Take care of her for me," Kade said to his brother.
"I'll be back as soon as I can."

Grayson nodded and stared at him, too. "You know
where the mother is?"

He shook his head. Kade had no idea, since he hadn't
heard anything from her since that assignment eight
and a half months ago at the Fulbright clinic. Right
now, he was sure of only one thing. If the baby was
here and Bree wasn't, that meant she was either dead
or in big trouble.

Kade had to find Bree *fast*.

Chapter Two

Bree heard the pitiful sound, a hoarse moan, and it took her a moment to realize that the sound had come from her own throat.

She opened her eyes and looked around for anything familiar. Anything that felt right.

Nothing did.

She was in some kind of room. A hotel maybe. A cheap one judging from the looks of things. The ceiling had moldy water stains, and those stains moved in and out of focus. Ditto for the dingy, paint-blistered walls. The place smelled like urine and other things she didn't want to identify.

What she did want to identify was where she was and why she was there. Bree was certain there was a good reason for it, but she couldn't remember what that reason was. It was hard to remember anything with a tornado going on inside her head.

She forced herself into a sitting position on the narrow bed. Beneath her the lumpy mattress creaked and shifted. She automatically reached for her gun and cell phone that should have been on the nightstand.

But they weren't there.

Something was wrong.

Everything inside her screamed for her to get out

right away. She had to get to a phone. She had to call…
somebody. But she couldn't remember who. Still, if
she could just get to a phone, Bree was certain she'd
remember.

She put her feet on the threadbare carpet and glanced
down at her clothes. She had on a loose dress that was
navy blue with tiny white flowers. She was wearing a
pair of black flat leather shoes.

The clothing seemed as foreign to her as the hotel
room and the absence of her gun and phone. She wasn't
a dress person, and she didn't have to remember all the
details of her life to realize that. No. She was a jeans
and shirt kind of woman unless she was on the job, and
then she wore whatever the assignment dictated.

Was she on some kind of assignment here?

She didn't have the answer to that, either. But the
odds were, yes, this was the job. Too bad she couldn't
remember exactly what this job was all about.

Bree took a deep breath and managed to stand. Not
easily. She had to slap her hand on the wall just to stay
upright, and she started for the door.

Just as the doorknob moved.

Oh, God. Someone was trying to get in the room,
and with her questionable circumstances, she doubted
this would be a friendly encounter. Not good. She could
barely stand so she certainly wasn't in any shape to
fight off anyone with her bare hands. Still, she might
not have a choice.

"Think," she mumbled to herself. What undercover
role was she playing here? What was she supposed to
say or do to the person trying to get in? She might need
those answers to stay alive.

"Bree?" someone called out. It was followed by a
heavy knock on the rickety door.

She didn't answer. Couldn't. The dizziness hit her hard again, and she had no choice but to sink back down onto the bed. *Great.* At this rate, she'd be dead in a minute. Maybe less.

"Bree?" the person called out again. It was a man, and his voice sounded a little familiar. "It's me, Kade Ryland. Open up."

Kade Ryland? The dizzy spell made it almost impossible to think, but his name, like his voice, was familiar. Too bad she couldn't piece that hint of familiarity with some facts. Especially one fact...

Could she trust him?

"Don't trust anyone," she heard herself mumble, and that was the most familiar thing she'd experienced since she'd first awakened in this god-awful room.

She braced herself for the man to knock again or call out her name. But there was a sharp bashing sound, and the door flew open as he kicked it in.

Bree tried to scramble away from him while she fumbled to take off her shoe and use it as a weapon. She didn't succeed at either.

The man who'd called himself Kade Ryland came bursting into the room, along with a blast of hot, humid air from the outside.

The first thing she saw was his gun, a Glock. Since there was no way she could dodge a bullet in the tiny space or run into the adjoining bathroom, Bree just sat there and waited for him to come closer. That way, she could try to grab his gun if it became necessary.

However, he didn't shoot.

And he didn't come closer.

He just stood there and took in the room with a sweeping glance. A cop's glance that she recognized because it's what she would have done. And then he turned that intense cop's look on her.

Bree fought the dizziness so she could study his face, his expression. He was in his early thirties. Dark brown hair peeking out from a Stetson that was the same color, gray eyes, about six-two and a hundred and eighty pounds. He didn't exactly look FBI with his slightly too-long hair, day-old stubble, well-worn jeans, black T-shirt and leather jacket, but she had some vague memory that he was an agent like her.

Was that memory right?

Or was he the big bad threat that her body seemed to think he was?

"Bree?" he repeated. His gaze locked with hers, and as he eased closer, his cowboy boots thudded on the floor. "What happened to you?"

She failed at her first attempt to speak and had to clear her throat. "I, uh, was hoping you could tell me." Mercy, she sounded drunk. "I'm having trouble remembering how I got here. Or why." She glanced around the seedy room again. "Where is *here* exactly?"

He cursed. It was ripe and filled with concern. She was right there on the same page with him—but that didn't mean she trusted him.

"You're in a motel in one of the worst parts of San Antonio," he told her. "It isn't safe for you to be here."

She hadn't thought for a minute that it was. Everything about it, including this man, put her on full alert.

But how had she gotten to this place?

"I was at my apartment," she mumbled. Was that right? She thought about it a second. Yes. That part was right. "But I don't know how I got from there to here."

Kade shut the door, though it was no longer connected to the top hinge, and he slipped his gun back into the leather shoulder holster beneath his jacket.

"Come on," he said, catching onto her arm. He gave a heavy sigh. "I need to get you to a doctor."

"No!" Bree couldn't say it fast enough. She didn't want to add another person—another stranger—to this mix. She shook off his grip. "I just need a phone. I have to call someone right away."

"Yeah. You need to call your boss, Special Agent Randy Cooper. Or Coop as you call him. But I can do that for you while you're seeing the doctor."

Coop. That name was familiar, too, and it seemed right that he was her boss. It also seemed right that she'd get answers from him. Especially since this cowboy agent didn't seem to be jumping to provide her with the vital information that she needed. She had to know if she could trust him or if she should try to escape.

Bree stared up at him. "Am I on assignment?"

Kade stared at her, too. Stared as if she'd lost her mind. He leaned down, closer, so they were eye to eye. "What the heck happened to you?"

She opened her mouth and realized she didn't have an answer. "I don't know. How did I get here?" She tried to get up again. "I need to call Coop. He'll know. He'll tell me why I'm here."

"Coop doesn't have a clue what happened to you."

That got her attention and not in a good way. "What do you mean?"

Kade moved even closer. "Bree, you've been missing nearly a year."

Oh, mercy. That info somehow got through the dizziness, but it didn't make sense. Nothing about this did. What the heck was wrong with her?

Bree shook her head. "Impossible."

He shoved up the sleeve of his black leather jacket and showed her a watch. He tapped his index finger on the date. June 13.

"June 13?" she repeated. Obviously, he thought that would mean something to her. It didn't. That was because Bree had no idea what the date should be. Nor did she know the date of that last clear memory—when she'd been at her apartment.

"I didn't know you were missing at first, not until a little over a month ago," he continued. His voice trailed off to barely a whisper, but then he cleared his throat.

"What's the last thing you remember before this place?" Kade asked. But he didn't just ask. He demanded it. He seemed to be angry about something, and judging from his stare turned glare, she was at least the partial source of that anger.

But what had she done to rile him?

She cursed that question because she didn't have an answer for it or any of the others.

Bree pushed her hair from her face. That's when she noticed her hands were trembling. Her mouth was bone dry, too. "Someone drugged me, didn't they?"

"Probably. Your pupils are dilated, and there's not a drop of color in your face," he let her know. "What's the last thing you remember?" he repeated.

She forced herself to think. "I remember you. We were on assignment together at the Fulbright Clinic. Someone figured out I was an agent, and they drugged us. We had to shoot our way out of there."

Bree glanced down at the thin scar on her left arm where a bullet had grazed her. It wasn't red and raw as it should be. It was well-healed. But that couldn't be right.

"And?" Kade prompted.

Bree shook her head. There was no *and*. "How long ago was that?"

"Nine and a half months." His jaw muscles turned to iron. She might have been dizzy, but she didn't miss the nine month reference. *Nine months.* As in just the right amount of time to have had a baby.

Her gaze flew back to him. This time Bree took a much longer and harder look at the cowboy. His face was more than just familiar. Those features. That body. Kade Ryland was drop-dead hot, and yes, she could imagine herself sleeping with him.

But had she?

She wasn't a person who engaged in casual sex or sex with a fellow agent.

"We didn't have sex, did we?" she asked.

Something shot through his ice-gray eyes. Some emotion she didn't understand. "No," he concluded. "But there was an opportunity for you to get pregnant. We were in a fertility clinic, after all."

Oh, mercy. Had the doctors in the clinic done something to her? No, Bree decided. She would have known. She would have remembered that.

Wouldn't she?

"After the shoot-out, other agents moved in to arrest the two security guards who tried to kill us," Kade continued. "But we didn't manage to apprehend everyone involved. Key evidence was missing, but the FBI decided to send in other agents to do the investigation since my identity had been compromised."

Yes. That sounded right. It wasn't an actual memory, though. None of this was, and that nearly sent Bree into a panic.

"And then you called your boss," Kade continued,

his voice calm despite the thick uneasiness in the room. "You said you were taking some vacation time."

Still no memory. Bree just sat there, listening, and praying he would say something to clear the cobwebs in her head and that it would all come back to her.

"Two weeks later when you were supposed to check back in with Coop, you didn't. You disappeared." Kade caught her chin, forced it up. "Bree, I need you to think. Where have you been all these months?"

Again, she tried to think, to remember. She really tried. But nothing came. She saw flashes of herself in Kade's arms. He was naked. And with his hard muscled body pressed against hers. He'd kissed her as if they were engaged in some kind of battle—fierce, hot, relentless.

Despite the dizziness, she felt her body go warm.

Bad timing, Bree, she reminded herself.

"You, uh, have some kind of tattoo on your back? It's like a coin or something?" She phrased it as a question just in case she was getting her memories mixed up, but she doubted she could ever mix up a man like Kade with anyone else.

"A concho," he supplied. "With back to back double *R*'s, for my family's ranch. You remember that?"

A ranch. Yes, he looked like a cowboy all right. She'd bet he wasn't wearing those jeans, Stetson and boots to make a fashion statement. No, he was a cowboy to the core, and that FBI badge and standard issue Glock didn't diminish that one bit.

"We kissed," she recalled. Now, *here* was a crystal clear memory. His mouth on hers. A fake kiss with real fire. And a cowboy with an unforgettable taste. "To create the cover of a happily married couple."

"But we didn't have sex," he clarified.

No. They hadn't, and she was reasonably sure she would have remembered sleeping with Kade. She glanced at him again and took out the *reasonably* part.

She would have remembered *that*.

"How did you find me?" Bree asked. There were so many questions and that seemed a good place to start.

"I set up a missing person's hotline and plastered your picture all over the state. I didn't say anything about you working for the FBI," he added, just as she was on the verge of protesting.

The last part of his explanation caused her to breathe just a little easier. As a deep-cover agent, the last thing she wanted was her picture out there. Still, his plan had worked because here he was. He'd found her.

But why had he been looking?

Was he working for her boss, Coop?

"An hour ago, I got a tip from an anonymous caller using a prepaid cell," Kade continued. "The person disguised their voice but said I'd find you here at the Treetop Motel, room 114. The person also said you were sick and might need a doctor."

An anonymous caller using a prepaid cell. That set off alarms in her head. "Someone drugged me and dumped me here. That same someone might have been your caller."

"That's my guess." He paused, huffed and rubbed his hand over his forehead as if he had a raging headache. "Look, there's no easy way to say this, so I'm just going to put it out there so you can start dealing with it. I think someone in the fertility clinic inseminated you with the semen they got from me…."

Kade hesitated, maybe to let that sink in. But how the heck could that sink in?

Bree gasped and looked down at her stomach. "I'm

not pregnant. If I were, I'd be about ready to deliver."
She stretched the dress across her stomach to show him
there was no baby bulge.

"You've already delivered, Bree. A baby girl. She's
about seven weeks old."

She heard that sound. A hoarse moan that tore its
way from her own throat. "You're lying." He *had* to
be lying.

Kade didn't take back what he'd said. He just stood
there, waiting.

Bree tried to figure out how she could disprove the
lie, and she glanced down at her stomach again.

"Go ahead," Kade prompted. "Look at your belly.
I don't know if you'll have stretch marks or not, but
there'll likely be some kind of changes."

Bree frantically shook her head, but her adamant denial didn't stop her from standing. Still wobbling, she
turned away from Kade and shoved up the loose dress.
She was wearing white bikini panties that she didn't
recognize, but the unfamiliar underwear was only the
tip of the proverbial iceberg.

Just slightly above the top of her panties was a scar.

Unlike the one on her arm, this one still had a pink
tinge to it. It had healed, but the incision had happened
more recently than the gunshot injury.

Probably about seven weeks ago.

Bree let go of the dress so it would drop back down.
"What did you do to me?" She turned back to him. She
would have pounded her fists against his chest if he
hadn't caught her hands. "What did you do?"

"Nothing. It wasn't me. It was someone in the Fulbright Clinic." Now it was Kade's turn to groan, and
that was her first clue that he was as stunned by this
as she was.

They stood there, gazes locked. Her heart was beating so hard that she thought it might come out of her chest.

"Who did the C-section?" she demanded.

Kade shook his head, cursed. "I don't know. Until now, I didn't even know you'd had one, though the doctor in Silver Creek guessed. He said Leah's head was perfectly shaped, probably because she'd been delivered via C-section."

What little breath Bree had vanished. *"Leah?"*

"That's what I've been calling her. It was my grandmother's name."

"Leah," she mumbled. Oh, mercy. None of this was making sense. "What makes you think she's our child?"

"DNA tests," he said without hesitation. "I got your DNA from the classified database in Quantico and compared it to Leah's. It's a match."

There was so much coming at her that Bree could no longer breathe. Was this all true? Or maybe Kade and this baby story were figments of her drug-induced imagination. One thing was for certain. She needed to contact her boss. Coop was the only one she could trust right now.

And Coop had better tell her this was all some kind of misunderstanding.

"I need to use your cell phone," she insisted.

"You can use it in the truck." He took her by the arm. "Something bad obviously happened to you, and we need to find out what. That starts with a visit to the doctor so you have a tox screen."

Bree didn't dispute the fact that she might indeed need medical attention, but she had no reason to blindly trust Kade Ryland.

"I want to make that call now," she demanded.

Kade stared at her, huffed again and reached in his coat pocket. But reaching for his phone was as far as he got. There was a noise just outside the door, and despite the drug haze, it was a sound that Bree immediately recognized.

Footsteps.

Kade drew his gun, and in the same motion, he shoved her behind him.

But it was too late.

Bree heard a swishing sound. One that she also recognized. Someone had a gun rigged with a silencer.

And a bullet came tearing through the thin wooden door.

Chapter Three

Kade threw his weight against Bree to push her out of the line of fire. She landed hard against the wall, and Kade had no choice but to land hard against her.

Another bullet came through the door, splintering out a huge chunk of the already-rickety wood. No one called out for them to surrender. No one bashed in the room to hold them at gunpoint.

And that meant the gunman had one goal: to kill Bree and him.

Later, he would kick himself for coming here without backup, but he'd been in such a hurry to rescue Bree that Kade had put standard procedures aside so he could get to her before she left the motel. Or before she was killed or kidnapped again. Finding her had been critical. But now the challenge was to get her out of there alive.

It was a risk, anything was at this point, but Kade moved from the wall so he could kick the dresser against the door. He gave it another shove to anchor it in place.

"That won't stop him for long," Bree mumbled.

No. It wouldn't. But if the gunman had wanted to get inside, he could have easily knocked down the door before he started shooting. Firing through the door had likely been his way of trying to strike first without risk-

ing a direct showdown. If so, he knew Kade was armed.
Maybe he even knew that Kade was an agent.

But who was he?

And why attack them?

Kade wanted those answers, and maybe he could get
them from this Bozo if he could keep the guy alive. Of
course, rescuing Bree was his first priority.

Kade had to do something to keep some space between the danger and Bree, so he fired directly into
the door. Unlike the gunman's shots, the one he fired
was a loud thick blast that echoed through the room.
He didn't wait to see if he'd hit the target. He had to get
Bree out of there.

Unfortunately, their options sucked.

Kade shoved her into the bathroom, such as it was.
Barely five feet across with only a toilet and what was
once a shower stall.

The tile was cracked and filthy, but the room had
one redeeming feature: a window that faced the back
side of the motel. He knew it was there because he'd
done a snapshot surveillance of the place before he ever
knocked on Bree's door. The gunman would have to
run around the entire length of the building to get to
that window. Well, unless he had a partner with him.
Kade hoped that wasn't the case. One gunman was more
than enough.

Another shot came into the bedroom.

Kade returned fire, this time a double tap that would
hopefully send a message—he would kill to get Bree
out of there. He darn sure hadn't come this far to lose
her before he got the answers to his questions.

Bree was still more than a little unsteady on her feet
so Kade shoved her deeper in the bathroom, kicked the
door shut and locked it. The lock was as rickety as the

rest of the place, and it wouldn't give them much protection if the gunman came blasting in, but it might buy them a few critical seconds, just enough time to get out.

He hurried to the window. It popped right open, and he looked out in the thin alley that separated the motel from an equally seedy-looking bar. Both ends of the alley were open, and there were no signs of a backup gunman, but it would still be a long dangerous run to his truck.

"I'll go first to make sure it's safe," he told Bree. "You follow me. Got that?"

She gave him a look, and for a moment he thought Bree might refuse. For a good reason, too. She didn't trust him.

And why should she?

Bree was no doubt trying to absorb everything he'd just dumped on her, and Kade knew from personal experience that coming to terms with unexpected parenthood wasn't something that could happen in five minutes—especially after the trauma Bree had been through. And the trauma wasn't over.

"You have no choice," Kade told her. He moved his truck keys from his jeans pocket to his jacket so they'd be easier to reach. "If we stay here, we both die."

She shook her head as if trying to clear it, or argue with him, but still didn't move. Not until another bullet bashed through the room.

And more.

Someone was moving the dresser that Kade had used to block the door. That *someone* was now in the motel room just a few yards away with only a paper-thin wall and equally thin bathroom door between them.

Bree's eyes widened. She obviously understood what was happening now. She caught his arm and shoved him against the window. Kade grabbed the sill, hoisting himself up and slithered through the narrow opening. He landed on his feet with his gun ready, and he looked up.

No Bree.

For one heart-stopping moment Kade thought she might have decided to take her chances with the gunman, but then he saw her hand on the sill. She was struggling to keep a grip. And Kade cursed himself again. The drugs had made her too weak to lever herself up.

While he tried to keep watch on both sides of the alley, Kade latched onto her wrist and pulled hard. She finally tumbled forward and landed with a jolt right in his arms. He didn't have time to make sure she was okay or even carry her since he had to keep his shooting hand free. Kade put her on her feet, grabbed her by the shoulder and started running in the direction of his truck.

They were already on borrowed time. By Kade's calculations, it'd been twenty seconds or longer since the gunman had fired. That meant he could have already made it into the bathroom and have seen that they weren't there. He could try to kill them by shooting through the window, or else he could be heading around the building straight toward them.

"I should have a gun," Bree mumbled.

Yeah, she should. That would be a big help right about now because Kade knew for a fact she could shoot. However, since he couldn't take the time to pull his backup weapon from his ankle holster, he ran as fast as he could with a groggy, dazed woman in tow.

Finally, he spotted his dark blue truck.

But Kade also heard something.

He glanced behind them and saw someone he didn't

want to see. A guy wearing camo pants and jacket came around the far end of the building. He was also armed, and he pointed a handgun directly at Kade and Bree.

There wasn't time to get to his truck. No time to do much of anything except get out of the line of fire. So Kade shoved Bree to the ground, right against the exterior wall of the hotel, and he followed on top of her. Not a second too soon. The guy pulled the trigger.

The shot slammed into the wall.

Kade turned, took aim and returned fire.

Their attacker dived to the side but not far enough. Kade could still see him, and he wanted the SOB temporarily out of the picture so he could get Bree safely out of there. Of course, he might have to settle for killing the guy. That would mean no answers, but it was better than the alternative.

Kade sent another shot his way.

And another.

He cursed when the guy moved, causing the bullets to strafe into the ground. But the third was a charm because the gunman finally scrambled back behind the building.

Bree was trembling and as white as paper when Kade came off the ground and yanked her to her feet. She had been under fire before, but probably not while defenseless. Kade kept watch behind them, but he got them running toward the truck again. He also did some praying that a second gunman wasn't near his vehicle.

Kade fired another shot in the direction of the gunman. Maybe it would keep him pinned down long enough for them to escape.

Maybe.

He let go of Bree so he could take out his keys, and he pressed the button to unlock the doors. Thankfully,

Bree ran without his help, and they made a beeline for the truck.

Kade saw the gunman again, but he didn't stop to fire. Instead, he threw open the truck door. Bree did the same on the passenger's side, and they both dived in.

"Watch out!" Bree shouted. "He's coming after us."

"I see him," Kade let her know.

He lowered the window, just enough to allow himself room to fire another shot. Just enough to keep the gunman at bay for a few more seconds.

Kade started the engine and slammed his foot on the accelerator. He didn't exactly make a silent exit out of the parking lot. The tires howled against the asphalt, but Kade figured anyone within a quarter mile had already heard the gunfight and either reported it or run away.

In this neighborhood, he was betting it was the latter.

"Keep watch," he told Bree.

While he took out his phone, he glanced around to make sure they weren't being followed. Then, he glanced at Bree.

Man, she was still way too pale, and she was sucking in air so fast she might hyperventilate. In the four days he had spent with her undercover, he'd never seen her like this, and Kade hoped she could hold herself together for just a little while longer until he could get her out of there and to a doctor.

Since he didn't want to spend a lot of time making all the calls he needed, Kade made the one that he knew would get the ball rolling. He pressed in the number for his brother, Lt. Nate Ryland, at San Antonio police headquarters. Nate answered on the first ring because he was no doubt waiting for news about Bree.

"I found her at the Treetop Motel," Kade said. That alone would be a bombshell since over the past month they'd had nine false reports of Bree's location. "But there was a gunman. Caucasian. Brown hair. About six-two. One-seventy. No distinguishing marks."

Nate cursed and mumbled something about Kade being a stubborn ass for not waiting for backup. "I'll get a team out there right away," Nate assured him, and it was the exact assurance Kade needed. "What about you? Where are you taking her?"

"The hospital. Not here in San Antonio. I'm driving her to Silver Creek." Kade didn't say that too loud, though Bree no doubt heard it, anyway. "Call me if you find anything at the hotel. I'll let you know when I have answers."

"I don't want to go to a hospital," Bree said the moment he ended the call. She was trembling, but she had her attention fastened to the side mirror, no doubt checking to see if they were being followed. "I just want to find out what happened to me."

So did Kade. But first he had to make sure the gunman wasn't on their tail. Then the hospital whether she wanted to go there or not.

While Bree was being checked out by a doctor, he could start the calls and the paperwork. It wouldn't be pretty. He would have to explain to his boss and his brothers why he hadn't waited for backup after receiving that anonymous tip about Bree's location. It probably wasn't going to fly if he told them that he had a gut feeling that she was in danger.

And he'd been right.

Still, gut instincts didn't look good on paper, and he would get his butt chewed out because of it. Kade figured it would be worth it. After all, he'd gotten Bree out of harm's way.

Well, for now.

"He's not following us," Bree concluded. She swallowed hard and looked at him.

Kade looked at her too out of the corner of his eye. She had certainly been through an ordeal. Her dark brown hair had been choppily cut and was mussed well beyond the point of making a fashion statement. And then there was the dress. It hung on her like a sack. There were dark circles under her drug-dazed eyes. Her lips were chapped raw. Still, she managed to look darn attractive.

And yeah, he was stupid enough to notice.

It was also easy to notice that Bree had passed on those cat-green eyes to their daughter.

She opened her mouth, and for a moment Kade thought she might ask about Leah. But she didn't. She snatched his phone from his hand.

"I'm calling my supervisor," Bree insisted.

Kade didn't stop her, though he knew Randy Cooper didn't have the answers that Bree wanted. That's because Kade had spent a lot of time with the agent over the past month and a half.

She must have remembered the number because she pressed it in without hesitation and put the call on speaker. "Coop," she said when the man answered.

"Bree," he said just as quickly. "Are you all right?"

"No." With that single word, her breath broke, and tears sprang to her eyes. She tried to blink them back, but more just came.

"The last lead paid off," Kade informed Coop. "She was at the Treetop Motel here in San Antonio, but so was a gunman. The informant could have set us up to be killed."

Coop cursed. "Either of you hurt?"

"I'm fine," Kade assured him. "Not so sure about Bree—"

"Where have I been all these months?" she interrupted.

"I don't know," Coop answered. He gave a weary sigh. "But trust me, we'll find out."

Yeah. They would. Step one was done. Kade had located Bree, and now that he had her, he could start unraveling this crazy puzzle that had resulted in the birth of their daughter.

"I need to see you ASAP," Coop told her. "How soon can you get her here, Kade?"

"Not soon," Kade let him know. "Someone drugged her, and even though it looks as if it's wearing off, she needs to see a doctor."

"I can arrange that," Coop insisted.

Of course Coop could, but if Kade took Bree to FBI headquarters, she'd be sucked into the system. Exams, interviews, paperwork. That had to wait because the FBI wouldn't put Leah first.

Kade would.

He had to find out if the gunman meant Leah was now in danger, too. Kade had a hard time just stomaching that thought, but it wouldn't do him any good to bury his head in the sand.

"Is it true, Coop?" Bree asked. "Did I really have a baby?"

Coop took some time answering. "Yes," was all he said.

Bree groaned, squeezed her eyes shut and the phone dropped into her lap. She buried her face in her hands. She wasn't hyperventilating yet, but she was about to fall apart.

"Coop, we'll call you back. In the meantime, my

brother Lt. Nate Ryland is on his way to the hotel crime scene and is trying to track down this gunman. We need to find this guy," Kade emphasized, though Coop already knew that.

Because the gunman could be the key to unraveling this. Well, unless he was just a hired gun. But even then, that was a start since they could find out who'd paid him to kill them.

Coop began to argue with Kade's refusal of his order to bring Bree in, but Kade took the phone from her lap and ended the call. He also made another turn so he could check to make sure they weren't being followed. Things looked good in that department but not with Bree. She kept her hands over her face. Clamped her teeth over her bottom lip. And then she made that sound. Half groan, half sob.

Hell. That did it.

Kade hooked his arm around her and dragged her across the seat toward him. Much to his surprise, she didn't fight him. She dropped her head on his shoulder.

For a moment, anyway.

Just a moment.

Her head whipped up, and she met his gaze. She blinked. Shook her head and got a strange look in her eyes.

"I have to keep watch," she insisted. Bree moved back across the seat and glanced at the mirror. Her breathing got faster again. "There's a black sedan behind us."

"Yeah." Kade was fully aware of that. "But I don't think it's following us. It just exited onto this road." To prove his point, he made another turn, and the car didn't follow.

That didn't settle Bree's breathing much. She started

to chew on her bottom lip. "You told Coop that your brother was helping us. He's a cop?"

Kade nodded. "San Antonio PD. All four of my brothers are in law enforcement. We've been working to find you ever since someone abandoned Leah at the hospital."

"Leah," Bree repeated, and she slid her hand over her stomach. "We didn't have sex," she tossed out there.

"No. But someone in the fertility clinic obviously inseminated you."

"Hector McClendon," Bree said, and it wasn't exactly a question.

Kade suspected the man, as well. Hector McClendon had been head of the Fulbright Fertility Clinic and was the main target of their undercover investigation that had started all of this.

"McClendon said he wasn't aware of the illegal activity going on at his own clinic," Kade reminded her.

"Right," she mumbled, sarcasm dripping from her voice. "Stored embryos were being sold without the owners' permission or knowledge. Illegal immigrants were being used as surrogates and kept in deplorable conditions. Babies were being auctioned to the highest bidder. We were pretty sure McClendon knew what was going on." Bree looked at Kade. "Please tell me he's behind bars."

Kade hated to be the bearer of more bad news. "No. None of the evidence we got from the clinic implicated McClendon in any of the serious crimes."

And it hadn't been for Kade or the FBI's lack of trying.

"But McClendon ordered those two security guards to kill us," Bree pointed out.

"No proof of that, either. The guards are in custody,

but they're insisting they acted alone, because they thought we were a threat to the other patients. They claim they had no idea we were agents."

"Right," she repeated.

Kade had to agree with that, too. But the guards weren't spilling anything, probably because they knew it would be impossible to prove their intent to murder without corroboration from someone else. So far, that hadn't happened, and Kade suspected the guards would ultimately accept a plea deal for much lesser charges.

"The only two people arrested so far have been Mc-Clendon's son, Anthony, who was a doctor at the clinic and a nurse named Jamie Greer," he explained. "They're both out on bond, awaiting trial."

Bree repeated the names. "Just because there's no evidence, it doesn't mean McClendon's innocent of kidnapping and doing God knows what to me."

Kade tried to keep his voice calm. "True, but if he did it, he's not confessing. Still, he has the money and the resources to have held you all this time."

She shook her head. "But why?"

Now it was Kade's turn to shake his head. "I don't know. There were no ransom demands for you. Leah wasn't hurt. In fact, she was dropped off at the hospital probably less than a day after she was born."

She shuddered, maybe at the thought of her kidnapping. Maybe at the way Leah had been abandoned.

"And if McClendon had wanted me dead," Bree finished, "then why not kill me after the C-section? Heck, why not just kill me after taking me from my apartment?"

This is where Kade's theory came to an end. "I was hoping you'd have those answers."

Bree groaned. "I don't! I don't remember any of that."

He reached over and touched her arm. Rubbed lightly. Hoping it would soothe her. "But you can with help. That's why I'm taking you to the hospital."

She opened her mouth, probably to repeat that she didn't want to go, but she stopped. And gasped. "What if the gunman goes after the baby?"

"He won't." Kade hoped. "She's at my family's ranch with my brother. He's a deputy sheriff and can protect her."

Bree frantically shook her head and pushed his hand away so she could latch onto his arm. "Hurry. You have to get to her now."

There's no way Kade could stay calm after that. "Why?"

"Hurry," Bree repeated. Tears spilled down her cheeks. "Because I remember. Oh, God. I remember."

Chapter Four

The memories flooded back into Bree's mind. They came so fast, so hard, that she had trouble latching onto all of them. But the one memory that was first and foremost was the danger to the baby.

Her baby.

Even though that didn't seem real, Bree had no more doubts about the child. She had indeed given birth, and at the moment that was the clearest memory she had.

"You have to get to the baby," Bree insisted.

"I'm headed there now," Kade assured her. His voice sounded more frantic than hers. "What's wrong?" he demanded. "What do you remember?"

"Pretty much everything." And Bree tested that by starting with the first thing she could recall. "The night after the botched assignment at Fulbright Fertility Clinic, I was kidnapped by a person wearing a mask."

"How did that happen?" Kade wanted to know. "And what does it have to do with Leah?"

"It has everything to do with Leah." Because it was the start of her becoming pregnant. "I came out of my apartment that night, and the person was waiting for me just outside the door. He popped me on the neck with a stun gun. I went down like a rock before I could even fight back. Then, the guy used chloroform." Yes, definitely. She recalled the sickly sweet smell of the drug.

"Chloroform," he repeated, but there was impatience in his voice now. Concern, too. "Did you get a good look at the person before you lost consciousness?"

"No." In fact, not a look at all, good or otherwise. The guy never took off his mask. "When I finally came to, I was at a house in the middle of nowhere, and the guy wasn't alone. A masked woman was with him." Bree had to pause and regroup. "You were right—they inseminated me with your baby."

He had a death grip on the steering wheel and was flying through traffic. "Why did they do that, and why do we have to hurry to get to Leah?"

Oh, this was crystal clear. Well, part of it, anyway. "More than once they said that the baby was to get me and you to *cooperate*."

"Cooperate?" he questioned. "With what?"

"I don't know. And it's not that I don't remember. They didn't say how they would use the child. But I'm figuring they'll go after her, especially now that they no longer have me."

Kade cursed, snatched up his phone and made a call. Hopefully to one of those brothers he'd mentioned that were in law enforcement.

"Lock down the ranch," Kade instructed to whomever was on the other end of the line. "There could be trouble. I'll be there in about twenty minutes."

He jabbed the end call button so hard that she was surprised the phone didn't break. "Who held you captive, and if they planned to use Leah to get to you and me, then why abandon her at the hospital?"

That part wasn't so crystal clear, but Bree had a theory about it. "Something must have gone wrong. Not at the beginning, but later."

Much later.

The memories came again. Like bullets, slamming into her. "I woke up after the delivery and heard my kidnappers talking," she continued. "The man told the woman he didn't get the money they'd been promised. He was furious. He was going to kill me right then and there." A shiver went through her. "Maybe the baby, too."

Kade's jaw muscles turned to iron. "What stopped them?"

Bree had to take a moment because she was reliving that horrible fear as if it were happening all over again. "The woman talked the man out of it. She said she'd take care of the baby." Bree had to choke back the emotions she'd felt then. And now. "I thought that meant…"

She couldn't finish, but she'd thought she would never see her baby alive.

"This woman must have been the one who dropped Leah off at the hospital," Kade said through clenched teeth. He turned off the interstate at the Silver Creek exit. "Leah wasn't harmed."

Relief flooded through Bree. But it didn't last long. "If the man who kidnapped me knows that she's alive…" She couldn't finish that, either.

"No one will get onto the ranch without my brothers being alerted," he promised. He didn't say anything else for several moments. "How did you escape?"

"The woman helped me again. She had on a prosthetic mask, one of those latex things that makes it impossible to see any of her real features. And she used a voice scrambler so I never heard her speak normally.

But a few hours after she disappeared with the baby, she came back and got me."

Now, here's where her memory failed. No more bullets. Only bits and pieces of images and conversations that Bree wasn't sure she could trust. Were they real or part of the nightmare she'd had all these months?

"She drugged me then and I don't know how many times after. A lot," Bree settled on saying. "The woman moved me, too. Usually to and from hotels, but a time or two, she took me to a house. I think she was trying to save me."

"Sure. And she might have made that call to let me know you were at the motel," he suggested. "The person who contacted me used a voice scrambler, too."

If so, then Bree owed that woman her life many times over. Not just for saving her, but for delivering Leah to Kade.

Except the woman had also been one of Bree's kidnappers.

If she hadn't helped keep Bree captive, then maybe none of this would have happened. And since Kade and she had come darn close to dying today, Bree wasn't ready to give the woman a free pass just yet.

"This has to go back to the Fulbright clinic," Kade said. "Hector McClendon could have masterminded all of it. His son, Anthony, and that clinic nurse, Jamie Greer, could have helped with the kidnapping. And with the delivery since Anthony is a doctor."

She couldn't argue with that. Plus, she'd seen what they really were at the clinic—criminals—and believed them capable of murder. After all, someone had tried hard to cover up everything that had gone on there.

"You said Anthony and Jamie were out on bond awaiting trial?" Bree asked.

"Yeah. And their lawyers have been stonewalling the investigation and the trials."

Great. So, not only were they suspects, both had the means and opportunity to have done this to her. In fact, they could be working as a team.

"Maybe they were looking for another way to get some leverage over us," Kade went on, "since we're the only two people who could or would testify against them. That could be why the kidnappers said they would use the baby for leverage."

True, and McClendon could have done the same, as well. Of course, if she remembered correctly, there wasn't any hard evidence against him except for some minor charges that wouldn't warrant much jail time, if any at all.

Not so far, anyway.

Nor could Kade and she testify that they'd seen him do anything illegal because they hadn't. McClendon had stayed away from the dirt, and even though Bree had tried, she hadn't been able to make a direct connection between him and the crimes.

Still, McClendon could have feared that some evidence would surface that would support their testimony. After all, Kade and she had failed to find the missing disks to the clinic's surveillance systems. Those systems were dated and still did hardcopy backups. If they'd found those, then McClendon might be in jail right now, and he couldn't have kidnapped her.

If he had been the one to honcho the kidnapping.

The agent in her reminded her to look at all the angles. To examine the evidence and situation with an unbiased eye. But it was hard to do that when someone had made Kade and her involuntary parents, and might now be placing their daughter in danger.

"You heard your male kidnapper speak," Kade continued. He took a turn off the main highway and turned onto Ryland Ranch Road. "Was it Anthony or McClendon?"

Bree had to shake her head. "Maybe. The man also used a voice scrambler whenever he was around me." Which wasn't very often. He always kept his distance from her and only came into the room after she'd been given a heavy dose of drugs. "But if I could hear interviews with Jamie and Anthony, I might be able to pick up on speech patterns."

Kade didn't respond except to pull in a long hard breath. And Bree soon realized why. He stopped directly in front of the sprawling three-story house that was surrounded by acres and acres of pasture and outbuildings.

It looked serene. Inviting. Like pictures of ranches that she'd seen in glossy Western magazines. There definitely wasn't any sign of kidnappers, gunmen or danger, but Bree still felt panic crawl through her.

The baby was inside.

Oh, mercy. She wasn't ready for this. Maybe she'd never be ready. But she especially wasn't ready with her mind in this foggy haze.

"I need a minute," she managed to say. A minute to get her breath and heartbeat tamped down. Her composure was unraveling fast. "For the record, I'd never planned on having children."

When Kade didn't say anything, Bree looked at him. She didn't exactly see empathy there. Well, not at first. But then he gave a heavy sigh and slipped his arm around her. As he'd done before, he pulled her across the seat until she was cradled against him. It felt better than it should.

Far better.

Bree knew she should be backing away. She should be trying to stay objective and focused on what had happened. Besides, she'd learned the hard way that taking this kind of comfort from a man, any man, could be a bad mistake. Especially since she could feel this steamy attraction for Kade simmering inside her. It'd been there from the first moment she'd laid eyes on him.

And it was still there now.

Getting worse, too. The comforting shoulder was getting all mixed up with the confusion, the attraction and the fact that he'd just saved her life.

Bree took another deep breath and gathered her composure. "Let's do this," she said, pushing herself away from him.

Kade lifted his eyebrow but didn't question her. Not verbally, anyway. He got out of the truck and started toward the porch. Bree followed him, and with each step she tried to steady her nerves.

She finally gave up.

Nothing could help in that department.

But then, Kade reached out and took her hand.

It was such a simple gesture. And much to her surprise and concern, she felt herself calm down. It lasted just a few seconds until Kade threw open the front door, and Bree spotted the armed dark-haired man.

Kade's brother, no doubt.

But this Ryland had a hard dangerous look that had her wanting to take a step back. She didn't. However, she did pull her hand from Kade's.

"This is my brother Mason," Kade explained. He took off his Stetson, put it on a wall hook where there were two similar ones, and he glanced around the massive foyer.

Bree glanced around, too, looking for any threats,

any gunmen. Anything other than the brother that might set off alarms in her head.

Like the house's exterior, this place screamed *home*. It looked well lived in and loved with its warm weathered wood floors and paintings of horses and cattle. There were more pictures and framed family shots in the massive living room off to her left.

"Where are the others?" Kade asked when he'd finished looking around.

"Dade's in his office watching the security cameras. After you called, I had a couple of the ranch hands take Kayla, Darcy, Eve and the kids to Grayson in town. They'll stay at the sheriff's office for a while."

Since Bree didn't recognize those names, she looked at Kade.

"Dade's another brother," he clarified. "He's a deputy sheriff like Mason here. Kayla, Darcy and Eve are all my sisters-in-law." He turned his attention to Mason but didn't say anything.

Something passed between them. A look. And Mason tipped his head to the room off the left side of the foyer. Kade caught Bree's arm and led her in that direction.

For one horrifying moment she wondered if she'd been a fool to trust Kade. After all, someone had kidnapped her and done heaven knows what to her. But that horrifying moment passed and settled like a rock-hard knot in her stomach when they walked into the living room and Bree saw the petite woman with reddish graying hair.

The woman was holding a bundle in a pink blanket.

"This is Grace Borden, one of the nannies here at the ranch," Kade said. "Grace, this is Bree Winston."

Grace offered Bree a tentative smile and then walked

toward her. As she got closer, Bree saw the tiny hand as it fluttered out from the blanket. The knot in Bree's stomach got worse. It got even tighter when Grace stopped in front of her, and Bree could see the baby nestled inside all that pink.

"This is Leah Marie Ryland," Kade volunteered. He led Bree to the sofa and had her sit down, probably because she didn't look too steady on her feet. And she wasn't. "The names of both my grandmothers."

A lot of family tradition for such a tiny little thing. "You said she's healthy?"

Kade nodded. "She just had her checkup, and she's nearly eight pounds now."

Bree had no idea if that was good or bad. And the terrifying feeling returned in spades when Grace came closer and held out the baby for Bree to take. The nanny must have picked up on Bree's uneasiness because she shot Kade a questioning glance. The moment he gave another nod, Grace eased the baby into Bree's arms.

It probably wasn't a normal reaction, but Bree gasped.

She'd never held any living thing this tiny, and Leah felt too fragile for Bree to trust her hands. Her breath stalled in her throat. In fact, everything seemed to stop.

"I'll be in the kitchen if you need me," Grace whispered.

"I need you to call Dr. Mickelson," Kade told her. "If he can, have him come out to the ranch right away to give Bree a checkup. Explain that she'll need lab work done."

That made sense. Maybe they could learn what she'd been drugged with. Considering the female kidnapper had seemingly tried to keep Bree alive, maybe the drug wasn't addictive or harmful. Ditto for the drugs they'd given her when she was pregnant.

Grace verified that she would indeed call the doctor and walked out of the room. The silence came immediately. Awkward and long. Bree couldn't say anything. She could only stare at the baby's face.

"She's got my hair and coloring," Kade said. "Your green eyes, though."

Yes, those curls were indeed dark brown, and there were lots of them. Bree couldn't see the baby's eyes because she was sound asleep. But she could see the shape of her face. That was Kade's, too.

Until Bree had seen the baby, she'd been about to question the DNA test that Kade said he'd run. She had figured to ask him to repeat it, just to be sure. But a repeat wasn't necessary. Kade was right: Leah was a genetic mix of Ryland and Winston blood.

And that required a deep breath.

Because she knew this baby was indeed hers.

Oh, mercy. Not good. She had lousy DNA, and that's why she'd never intended on passing it on to a helpless little baby.

"Here," Bree managed to say, and she quickly handed Leah to Kade. Despite her wobbly legs, she got up so she could put some distance between Kade and her.

Kade cuddled the baby closer to him, brushed a kiss on her cheek. The gesture was so loving. But the glare he aimed at her wasn't. Far from it. She'd obviously riled him again, and he had no trouble showing it.

"I don't have a normal life," Bree blurted out. "I'm always deep undercover. Always living a lie."

That didn't ease his scowl.

"Besides, I'm no good with kids." Even though looking at that tiny face made her wish that she was. There

was something about that face that made her want to
do what Kade had done—brush a kiss on her cheek.

Kade's scowl ended only because Leah made a
sound. Not a cry exactly, more like a whimper. And he
began to rock her gently as if it were the most natural
thing in the world.

"I was raised in foster care," she added. Heaven
knows why she'd volunteered that. Maybe to stop him
from scowling at her again. Yes, it was true, and it was
also true that her childhood had been so nightmarish
that she'd vowed never to have children of her own.

And technically she hadn't broken that vow.

But someone had overridden her decision, and Kade
was holding the proof in his arms.

Kade kissed the baby again, stood and placed her
in a white carrier seat that was on the coffee table just
inches away. Leah stirred a little, but she didn't wake
up. He put his hands on his hips and stared at Bree.

"It's all right." His jaw was tight again, and his gray
eyes had turned frosty. "I don't expect anything from
you."

It felt as if he'd slugged her, and it took Bree several
moments to recover and gather her breath. "What the
heck does that mean?"

Kade shrugged. Not easily. The muscles were obviously locked tight there, too. "It's clear you're not comfortable with this."

"And you were?" Bree fired back.

"I am now. She's my daughter, and I'll raise her."
He started to turn away, but Bree caught his arm and
whirled him back around to face her.

"Now, just a minute. I didn't say I wouldn't raise her.
I just need time. You've had seven weeks to adjust to
being a dad," she reminded him. "I've had an hour, and

for a good part of that time we've been ducking bullets and nearly getting killed."

The mini tirade drained her, but Bree stayed on her feet so she could face him. They weren't exactly eye to eye since she was a good seven inches shorter than he was, but she held his gaze.

And she saw the exact moment he backed down.

Kade mumbled some profanity and scrubbed his hand over his face. "I'm sorry. It's just that I love Leah, and I figured you'd feel the same."

"I do!" The words came flying out of her, and so did the heart-stopping realization that followed.

Bree looked at that tiny face again. Her daughter. The baby she'd carried for all those months while being held captive. She felt the tears burn her eyes, and Bree cursed them and tried to blink them back.

"I tried not to think of her as a real baby," Bree said, her voice barely a whisper. "Because I wasn't sure we would make it out of that place alive."

Oh, mercy. The confession brought on more blasted tears. Bree hated them because she wasn't a whiner, and she darn sure didn't want Kade to think she was trying to milk some sympathy from him.

Kade cursed again and called himself a bad name before he moved toward her. Bree wanted to tell him it wasn't a good time to offer her a shoulder to cry on. She was too weak and vulnerable. But Kade pulled her into his arms before she could protest.

And then she was glad he had.

Bree dropped her head on Kade's shoulder and let his strong arms support her. She felt that strength, and the equally strong attraction.

Good grief.

Didn't she have enough on her plate without adding

lust to the mix? Of course, maybe it was a little more than lust since Kade and she had this whole parenthood bond going on.

She pulled back, looked up at him. "This holding is nice, but it's not a good idea."

His left eyebrow cocked. "Considering what you've been through, you've earned the right to lean on somebody."

But not you.

She kept that to herself, but it was best if she kept Kade out of this emotionally charged equation. There was still so much to figure out. So many questions…

First though, she wanted to get acquainted with her daughter.

Bree eased out of Kade's grip and walked to the carrier seat that was lined with pale pink fabric and frilly lace. She touched her finger to Leah's cheek, and Bree was more than a little surprised when the baby's eyes opened.

Yes, they were green like hers.

Leah stared at her. Studying Bree, as if trying to figure out who she was.

"I'm your mother, little one," Bree whispered. "Your mom," she corrected. Less formal. Even though both felt foreign to Bree's vocabulary. "And you're the one who kicked me all those months. With all those hard kicks, I thought you'd be a lot bigger."

The corner of Leah's mouth lifted. A smile! It warmed Bree from head to toe. Yes. Now she knew what Kade meant when he said he loved this baby. How could he not? It was something so strong, so deep that if Bree had been standing, she wouldn't have managed to stay on her feet for long.

"This is potent stuff," she mumbled.

"Oh, yeah," Kade agreed. "Wait until she coos."

Bree wasn't sure she could wait. She stood, reached into the basket and brought her baby back into her arms. Bree drew in her scent. Something that stirred feelings she thought she'd never have.

Magic. Pure magic.

It hit Bree then. This was the only person she had ever truly loved. Someone she would die to protect.

Of course, that brought back on the blasted tears, but rather than curse them, Bree sank down on the sofa and gave her daughter a good looking over. She pulled back the blanket.

"Ten fingers, ten toes," Bree mumbled.

"And a strong set of lungs," Kade supplied. He sank down next to her. "You'll hear just how loud she can be when she wants her bottle at 2:00 a.m."

Bree turned to him. "Will I be here at 2:00 a.m.?"

Kade nodded, but it wasn't exactly a wholehearted one. Yes, he'd given her that hug and some much-needed empathy, but he was holding back. And Bree didn't blame him. She was holding back, too. The problem was she didn't want to be separated from Leah.

Correction: she couldn't be.

Yes, she'd just laid eyes on her for the first time, but Bree felt like something she'd thought she would never feel.

She felt like a mother.

An incompetent one but a mother nonetheless.

"You can stay while we sort things out," Kade finally said.

Again, it wasn't a resounding yes, but Bree would take it. At this point, she would take anything she could get that would allow her to stay with this precious child.

"Things," she repeated. A lot fell under that umbrella. The danger. And the custody, of course. Living arrangements, too. She probably no longer had an apartment since she'd been gone all this time and hadn't paid rent.

Heck, did she even have a job?

"Take one thing at a time," Kade said, his Texas drawl dancing off each word.

She returned the nod. "So, what's first?"

But Kade didn't get a chance to answer. That's because Bree and he turned toward the footsteps. A moment later, Mason appeared in the doorway.

One look at his face, and Bree knew something was wrong. *No.* Not again. She automatically pulled Leah closer to her.

"We got trouble," Mason announced, and he drew his gun.

Chapter Five

Trouble. Kade was positive they'd already had enough of their share of that today.

"What's wrong?" Kade asked his brother.

Mason tipped his head toward the front of the house. "About a minute ago, a strange car turned onto the ranch road, and Dade ran the plates. The vehicle is registered to none other than Hector McClendon."

Beside him, Bree gasped. Kade knew how she felt because McClendon shouldn't be here at the ranch. After all, he was their lead suspect in too many crimes to list—including Bree's own kidnapping that had led to Leah's birth.

That stirred some strong conflicting feelings in Kade.

He loved Leah so much that he couldn't imagine life without her, but someone would pay for what had happened. His baby didn't deserve the rough start she'd gotten in life.

Kade got to his feet, the questions already forming in his head. He hadn't wanted this meeting with McClendon, but maybe they could learn something from it. Right now, he'd take any answers he could get—as long as he got them while keeping Leah safe.

Bree, too, he mentally added.

Yes, she was a trained federal agent, but she was in no shape right now to face down a snake like McClendon.

"Wait here," he told Bree. "I'll deal with this."

But she stood, anyway, and eased Leah back into the carrier. "You're not letting him near the baby."

"Not a chance. I'm not letting him in the house, period. But I do want to talk to him and see why he came. He's never been out here to see me before now, and I don't like the timing."

It was past being suspicious since it'd been less than an hour and a half since Kade had rescued Bree from that motel. Was McClendon here to finish off the job that the hired gunman had failed to do?

Kade drew his gun and headed toward the front door.

Of course, Bree didn't stay put as he'd ordered. She was right behind him.

"Have Dade keep monitoring the security feed," Kade instructed Mason. This could be a ruse that someone could use to get gunmen onto the ranch, but Mason probably already knew that. "And take Leah to Grace. I want them to stay at the back of the house until McClendon is off the grounds."

Mason hesitated, glancing first at Leah in her carrier seat and then out the front window at the approaching silver Jaguar. His brother was probably trying to decide if he should stay and play backup, but Mason thankfully picked up the carrier and hurried out of the room.

Good. That was one less thing to worry about. One less *big* thing.

Kade gave Bree one last try so he could take another worrisome issue off his list. "McClendon could be dangerous, and you're still feeling the effects of that drug."

Her chin came up, and even though he didn't know

her that well, Kade recognized the attitude. Bree wouldn't back down. Something he understood since he would have reacted the same in her position. However, because she wasn't duty ready, he eased her behind him when he headed for the door.

Kade paused at the security system so he could open the door without setting off the alarms. By the time he'd done that, McClendon was already out of his car and walking up the porch steps. His driver—aka his armed goon bodyguard, no doubt—stayed by the open car door.

Even though it'd been months since Kade had seen the man, he hadn't changed much. The same salt-and-pepper hair styled to perfection. A pricey foreign suit. Pricey shoes, too. The man was all flash. Or rather all facade. McClendon appeared to be a highly successful businessman, but at the moment he was basically unemployed and living off the millions he'd inherited from parents. Old money.

The man was also old slime.

And Kade was going to have to hang on to every bit of his composure to keep from ripping McClendon's face off. If this arrogant SOB was behind Bree's kidnapping and the insemination, then he would pay for it.

Kade positioned himself in the center of the door, blocking the way so that McClendon couldn't enter. He also blocked Bree so she couldn't get any closer. She was already way too close for Kade's comfort.

"Why are you here?" Kade demanded.

McClendon ignored the question and looked past Kade. His attention went directly to Bree, who was on her tiptoes and peering over Kade's shoulder.

"I got a call about her." McClendon jabbed his index finger in Bree's direction. "I thought I was rid of you.

Guess not. But if you're back to make more accusations about me, then you'd better think twice."

Despite Kade's attempts to block her, Bree worked her way around him, stepping to his side, and she faced McClendon head-on. "Who called you?"

McClendon's face stayed tight with anger, but he shook his head. "It was an anonymous tipster. The person used some kind of machine to alter his voice so I couldn't tell who it was. I couldn't even tell if it was a *he*. Could have been anybody for all I know."

Like the call Kade had gotten about Bree. "This person told you Bree was here? Because I only found her myself a little while ago."

"No, the person didn't say she was here, only that she was with you. I figured out the ranch part all by myself since this, after all, is your family home," Mc-Clendon smugly added.

"It's a long drive out here just to talk to Bree," Kade remarked.

The man made a sound of agreement. "Let's just say the anonymous caller piqued my interest. Plus, I wanted to make sure Agent Winston here wasn't trying to pin more bogus charges on me."

Kade wished he had a charge, any charge, he could pin on the man. Maybe he could arrest him for trespassing, but that wouldn't get him behind bars.

"So, why do you look like death warmed over?" Mc-Clendon asked Bree.

"Because I've had a bad day. A bad year," she corrected in a snarl. "Someone kidnapped me. Maybe you? Or maybe someone working for you? Maybe even the Neanderthal standing by your car." Bree aimed her own finger at him, though unlike McClendon's, hers was shaky. "And that someone had me inseminated. What do you know about that, huh?"

McClendon flexed his eyebrows. Maybe from surprise, but Kade seriously doubted it. In fact, McClendon might have personal knowledge of every detail of this investigation.

"I know nothing about it," the man insisted. "And it's accusations like that I'm here to warn you against. I have plans to open a new clinic in the next few months. One that will help infertile couples. *Real couples.* Not FBI agents hell-bent on trying to ruin me and my reputation."

"Your own shady dealings ruined you," Kade fired back. "You used illegal immigrants as gestational carriers and surrogates. Hell, you didn't even pay them. Just room, board and minimal medical care." And for each of those women, McClendon and the clinic had collected plenty of money.

"Prove it," McClendon challenged.

"Give me time and I will. And while you're here, you could just go ahead and make a confession." Though Kade knew that wasn't going to happen.

McClendon looked ready to jump in with a smug answer, but instead, he pulled in a long breath. "I knew nothing about the illegal activity that went on." No more flexed eyebrows or surprise, feigned or otherwise. Fire went through McClendon's dust-gray eyes. "That was my son's doing and that idiot nurse, Jamie Greer. They'll be tried, and both will pay for their wrongdoings."

"Yes, they will," Kade assured him. "But that doesn't mean there won't be more charges. Ones that involve you spending a lot time in jail."

Now, the venom returned. "I'm not responsible for

those two losers' actions, and I refuse to have any of
Anthony and Jamie's mud slung on me. Got that?"

McClendon didn't wait for Kade or Bree to respond
to that. He turned and started off the porch.

"If you did this to Bree…to *us,*" Kade corrected, calling out to the man. "I'll bring you down the hard way."

McClendon stopped and spared them a glance from
over his shoulder. "Careful, Agent Ryland. You just
might bite off more than you can chew. Trying to bring
me down will be hazardous to your health. And anyone
else who happens to get in my way."

Bree started after him, probably to rip him to shreds
as Kade had wanted to do, but Kade caught her arm. She
wasn't in any shape to take on a man like McClendon,
and besides, assaulting an unarmed civilian wouldn't
be good for the investigation.

And there would be an investigation.

That's how Kade could wipe that smug look off this
rat's face. He didn't believe for one second that Mc-
Clendon had stayed clean from all the illegal junk that
went on at the clinic.

"An anonymous tipster," Bree mumbled. Her mind,
too, was obviously on the investigation. Good. Because
they needed answers and they needed them fast. That
was the only way to make sure Leah remained safe.

Bree, too.

Even though Kade doubted she'd agree to let him
protect her. Still, he had to do something to make things
as safe as he could. McClendon had just thrown down
the gauntlet, and it could be the start of another round
of danger.

Kade's phone buzzed, and on the screen he could see
it was from his brother, Dade. "Make sure McClendon

leaves the grounds," Kade said to him as he watched the Jaguar speed away.

"I will," Dade assured. "But someone else is coming up the driveway. It's Dr. Mickelson, and he should be there any minute. Who's sick?"

Kade looked at Bree, who was still glaring at McClendon's retreating Jag, and he hoped that she didn't fall into that sick category. Heaven knows what her kidnappers had done to her these past ten and a half months. Hopefully nothing permanent, but he doubted they'd had her health and best interest at heart. There were a lot of nasty addictive drugs they could have used to force her to cooperate.

"The doc's here for Bree," Kade told his brother, and he ended the call just as he saw the doctor's vehicle approaching. Not a sleek luxury car. Dr. Mickelson was driving a blue pickup truck.

"This checkup is just for starters," Kade reminded Bree, just in case she planned to fight it. "Once we're sure Leah is safe, I want you at the hospital for a thorough exam."

She opened her mouth, probably to argue like he'd anticipated, but her fight was somewhat diminished by the dizzy glaze that came over her eyes. No doubt a residual effect of the drugs, or maybe crashing from the adrenaline that kept her going through the gunfight.

Kade caught her to keep her from falling. When she wobbled again, Kade cursed, holstered his gun and scooped her up in his arms.

Of course, she tried to wiggle out of his grip. "I'm not weak," Bree mumbled.

"You are now," Kade mumbled back. "Thanks for coming," he said to the doctor.

"This is Leah's birth mother?" the doctor asked.

Unlike their previous visitor, the doctor had concern all over his expression and in his body language. With his medical bag gripped in his hand, he hurried up the steps toward them.

"Yep, the birth mother," Kade verified.

The sterile title worked for him, but he didn't know if it would work for Bree. Especially not for long. He'd seen the way she had looked at Leah right before McClendon had interrupted them, and that was not the look of a *birth mother,* but rather a mother who loved her baby and had no plans to give her up.

"This way," Kade instructed the doctor, and he carried Bree up the stairs toward his living quarters.

There was probably a guest room clean and ready. There were three guest suites in the house, but Kade didn't want to take the time to call Bessie, the woman who managed the house. And she also managed the Rylands. Bessie was as close to a mother as he had these days. Heck, for most of his life, since his mother had passed away when he was barely eleven.

"I can walk," Bree insisted.

Kade ignored her again, used his boot to nudge open his door, and he walked through the sitting-office area to his bedroom. He deposited her on his king-size bed.

Funny, he'd thought about getting Bree into his bed from the moment he first met her on the undercover assignment, but he hadn't figured it would happen this way. Or ever. After Bree and he had escaped that clinic, he hadn't thought he would see her again. Now her life was permanently interlinked with his.

"She'll need blood drawn for a tox screen," Kade reminded Dr. Mickelson.

"Will do. Any possibility there's something going

on other than drugs?" the doctor asked. "Maybe an infection or something?"

Kade could only shake his head. "I'm not sure. She's been held captive for months. I have no idea what all they did to her. And neither does she."

"I'll run a couple of tests," Dr. Michelson assured him, and he motioned for Kade to wait outside.

That made sense, of course, because Dr. Mickelson would want to check Bree's C-section incision. Maybe other parts of her, too. Kade didn't want to be there for that, especially since Bree had already had her privacy violated in every way possible.

Kade eased the bedroom door shut, leaned against the wall. And waited. It didn't take long for the bad thoughts to fly right at him.

What the devil was he going to do?

McClendon's visit was a hard reminder that he hadn't left the danger at the motel in San Antonio. It could and maybe would follow them here to the ranch, the one place he considered safe.

He couldn't bear the thought of his baby girl being in harm's way, though she had been from the moment of her conception. What a heck of a way to start her life. But there was a silver lining in all of this. Leah was too young to know anything about her beginnings. She knew nothing of the danger.

Nothing of a mother who wasn't totally acting like a mother.

Yeah. That was unfair, and it caused Kade to wince a little. Bree needed to get her footing, and when she did...

Kade's thoughts went in a really bad direction.

When Bree got that inevitable footing, what if she wanted full custody of Leah? Until now, Kade hadn't thought beyond the next step of his investigation—and that step was to find Bree. Well, he'd found her all right. Now what?

It sent a jab of fear through him to even consider it, but could he lose custody of his baby?

He shook his head. That couldn't happen. He wouldn't let it happen. Besides, Bree was a Jane and by her own admission not motherhood material. She worked impossible hours on assignments that sometimes lasted months. Then there was that whole confession about her being raised in foster care and never having planned to be a mother.

But Kade hadn't thought he was ready to be a father until he had seen Leah's face. Just the sight of her had caused something to switch in his head, and in that moment Leah became the most important person in his life.

He would die to protect his little girl. But his best chance of protecting Leah was to stay alive. And keep Bree alive, as well. There were probably some much-needed answers trapped in Bree's drug-hazed memories, and this exam by the doctor was the first step in retrieving those memories.

Kade's phone buzzed, and he saw on the screen that the call was from Mason. Mercy, he hoped nothing else had gone wrong. He'd had his *gone wrong* quota filled for the day.

"I've got news," Mason answered. As usual, there was no hint of emotion in his brother's voice. Mason definitely wasn't the sort of man to overreact, even when all hell was breaking loose. "I just got off the phone with Nate."

Kade breathed a little easier. Well, at first. Nate was handling the situation at the Treetop Motel in San Antonio where the gunman had tried to kill Bree and him. "Please tell me nothing's wrong," Kade commented.

"Not that I know of. But then all I got was a thirty-second update. Nate wanted me to tell you that he has his CSI folks out at the motel. They're going through the room where Bree was. His detectives also plan to comb the area to look for anyone who might have seen Bree come in."

That was a good start. "Any chance of surveillance cameras?"

"Slim to none. That neighborhood isn't big on that sort of thing."

Probably because it was a haven for drug dealers, prostitutes and a whole host of illegal activity. Still, they might get lucky. CSI could maybe find something that would help him identify Bree's kidnappers. That was step two. Then, once he had the culprits behind bars, he could think about this potential custody problem.

And Bree.

There was something stirring between them. Or maybe that was just lust or the uneasiness over what could turn out to be a potentially nasty custody dispute. Kade hoped that was all because lust and uneasiness were a lot easier to deal with than other things that could arise.

"I want to talk to Anthony McClendon and Jamie Greer again," Kade insisted. Both were suspects, just like Anthony's father, and he hadn't officially questioned them in months. "Can you set up the interviews and get them to the Silver Creek sheriff's office?"

That way, his brothers could assist, and he wouldn't have to be too far away from Leah or Bree. Though judging from her earlier behavior, Bree might want to get far away from here. He couldn't blame her after

McClendon's threats. The man hadn't named Leah specifically, but it had certainly sounded as if he were threatening the baby.

"Sure, I can get Anthony and Jamie out here. McClendon, too. But you have a couple of other fires to put out first. Special Agent Randy Cooper just called and demanded to see Bree. I take it he's her FBI handler or whatever it is you feds call your boss?"

"Yeah." Kade couldn't blame the man for wanting to see Bree, but the timing sucked.

"He seems kind of possessive if you ask me," Mason went on. "You sure he's just her handler?"

No. Kade wasn't sure of that. In fact, he didn't know if Leah had a boyfriend stashed somewhere. The only thing he knew about her was what he'd managed to read in her files. Which wasn't much. There wasn't a lot of paperwork and reports on undercover FBI Janes, and sometimes the files were nothing but cover fronts.

"Tell Coop he'll have to wait until tomorrow to see Bree," Kade said. "After the doctor finishes the exam, she'll need some rest."

That was the next step in his *for starters*. Maybe there wouldn't be anything that rest and time couldn't fix. Kade really needed her to recall more details of her captivity.

Mason made a sound of agreement. "Don't worry. I'll stall Coop." He paused. "Hold on a second. I just got a text from Nate. Might be important."

Kade could only hope this wasn't more bad news.

"There's another problem, little brother," Mason said. *"A big one."*

Chapter Six

Bree woke up to the sound of voices. Voices that she didn't immediately recognize.

She reached for her gun and phone. Not there. And an uneasy sense of déjà vu slammed through her. She sprang from the bed, her feet ready to start running when they landed on the thickly carpeted floor. Bree stopped cold.

Where the heck was she? And why hadn't there been a gun on the nightstand?

She glanced around the massive sun-washed bedroom, decorated in varying shades of blue and gray. At the king-size bed. The antique pine furniture. And it took her a moment to remember that she was at the Ryland ranch in Silver Creek.

More specifically, she'd been in Kade's bed.

She looked around again, first in the bathroom through the open door, then the massive dressing room. No sign of Kade.

So, she'd been in that bed alone.

And was apparently safe and sound since she had slept hard and long. After the ordeal she'd been through, she was thankful for that. Well, maybe. She was thankful *if* she hadn't missed anything important.

Which was possible.

After all, Leah was in her life now, and Kade and she were in the middle of a full-scale investigation. Yes, the potential for missing something important was sky-high, and she had to find Kade.

After she got dressed, that is.

Bree glanced down at the pink cotton pjs. They weren't familiar, either, but she did remember the doctor helping her change into them before he insisted that she sleep off the effects of the drugs her kidnapper had given her. She hadn't had a choice about that sleep, either. The fatigue and drugs had mixed with the adrenaline crash, and Bree hadn't been able to keep her eyes open at the end of the exam the doctor had given her.

Another glance, this time at the clock on the nightstand.

Oh, sheez.

It was nine, and she doubted that was p.m. because light was peeking through the curtains. It was nine in the morning, and that meant she'd been asleep at the ranch for heaven knows how many hours. Not good. She was certain she had plenty of things to do. But first, she needed to locate some clothes, the source of those voices and then see if she could scrounge up a phone and a strong cup of black coffee to clear the rest of the cobwebs from her head.

She hurried to the bathroom to wash up, but since she couldn't find a change of clothes, Bree gave up on the notion of getting dressed, and instead, she headed to the sitting room wearing the girlie pink pjs. She prayed nothing was wrong and that's why Kade had let her sleep so long. Too bad the thoughts of ugly scenarios kept going through her mind.

Bree threw open the door that separated the rooms in the suite and saw Kade. That was one voice. He was holding Leah and talking to someone. The other voice belonged to an attractive brunette that had her arm slung around Kade's waist.

The pang of jealousy hit Bree before she could see it coming.

"Oh," the woman said, her voice a classy purr.

Actually, everything about her was classy including her slim rose-colored top and skirt. Her hair was so shiny, so perfect, that Bree raked her hand through her own messy locks before she could stop herself. What was wrong with her? With everything else going on, the last thing she should care about was her appearance.

The woman smiled and walked toward her. "You must be Bree." Her smile stayed in place even when she eyed the pajamas. "I'm glad they fit."

"They're yours?" Bree asked.

The woman nodded.

Of course, they were. This woman was girlie, and she was also everything that Bree wasn't. Bree could see the love for her in Kade's eyes.

Another pang of jealousy.

Bree smoothed her hair down again before she could stop herself.

"I'm Darcy Ryland." The woman extended her hand for Bree to shake.

"Darcy is Nate's wife," Kade supplied. "He's the cop at SAPD who's helping us with the investigation."

Kade had a funny expression on his face as if he knew that Bree had been jealous.

Bree tossed him a scowl.

He gave her another funny look.

"I'm also the Silver Creek assistant D.A. and the mother of two toddlers who are waiting for me to bring them their favorite books and toys." Darcy checked her watch. "And that means I should have already been out of here. Good to meet you, Bree. We'll chat more when things settle down."

"Good to meet you, too," Bree mumbled.

Darcy tipped her head to the plush sofa. "I left you some other clothes—ones that aren't pink. Toiletries, too. And if you need anything else, just help yourself to my closet. Nate's and my quarters are in the west wing of the house. Just be careful not to trip over the toys if you go over there."

Bree added a thanks and felt guilty about the unflattering girlie thoughts and jealousy pangs. So, Kade's sister-in-law was, well, nice despite her picture-perfect looks.

Darcy walked back to Kade and picked up her purse from the table. In the same motion, she kissed him on the cheek and then kissed Leah. Using her purse, she waved goodbye to Bree and glided out of the room on gray heels that looked like torture devices to Bree.

Bree didn't waste any time going to Leah. No blanket this morning. The baby was wearing a one-piece green outfit that was nearly the same color as her eyes. She was also wide-awake and had those eyes aimed at Kade. Leah seemed to be studying his every move.

"I slept too long," Bree commented, and she touched her fingers to Leah's cheek. The baby automatically turned in her direction. "You should have woken me up sooner."

Bree wondered if there was a time when that wouldn't seem like such a huge deal. She hoped not. Because now everything seemed like a miracle, and just looking at her baby washed away all her dark thoughts and mood.

"You needed sleep," Kade insisted.

When he didn't continue, Bree looked up at him.

And she waited. Clearly, he had something on his mind, and thankfully he didn't make her wait long to deliver the news.

"The doctor got back your lab results."

That hung in the air like deadweight. Bree couldn't speak, couldn't ask the question that put her breath in a vise—had the drugs permanently harmed Leah or her?

"You had a large amount of Valium in your system. It caused the grogginess and the temporary memory loss." He paused. "It was temporary, right?"

She nodded and felt relief. Well, partly. "Any chance they gave me Valium when I was pregnant?"

"It's hard to tell, but Leah is perfectly healthy," Kade assured her. "I suspect because they wanted to use the baby for leverage that they didn't do anything that would risk harming her."

Good. That was something, at least. And with that concern out of the way, Bree could turn her full attention back to Leah.

"The doctor said any gaps in your memory should return," Kade explained. "So, it's possible you'll remember other details about your kidnappers."

She had a dozen or more questions to ask Kade about the test results and an update on the case, but Bree couldn't get her attention off Leah. She had to be the most beautiful baby ever born.

Or else Bree's brain had turned to mush.

"How is she this morning?" Bree asked.

"Fine. She just had her bottle." He motioned toward the empty one on the table.

She felt a pang of a different kind. Bree wished she'd been awake to feed her, and she cursed the long sleep session that had caused her to miss all these incredible moments.

"How long before she'll want another bottle?" Bree asked.

"Around one or two." He paused again. "There's a problem," Kade said.

Bree's gaze flew to his because she thought he was going to say that something was wrong with Leah, after all. She held her breath, praying it wasn't that.

"Late yesterday, Nate's detectives at SAPD found the gunman who shot at us," Kade finished. "He's dead."

Bree groaned. So, the problem wasn't with Leah, but it was still a big one.

"Please tell me he managed to make a confession before he died?" Bree asked.

"Afraid not. His name was Clyde Cummings. We ID'd him from his prints since he had a long rap sheet. In and out of trouble with the law most of his life." Another pause. "Word on the street is he was a hired gun."

That didn't surprise Bree. Whoever had masterminded her kidnapping had no doubt hired this goon. A goon who would have succeeded in killing her if Kade hadn't arrived in time to save her.

"Cummings didn't die in a shoot-out with the cops," Kade continued. "When Nate's men found him, he was already dead." Kade paused again. "He died from a single gunshot wound to the back of the head."

Oh, mercy. An execution-style hit on a hit man. That meant someone didn't want Cummings talking to the cops, or maybe this had been punishment for allowing Kade and her to get away. It didn't matter which. The bottom line was this case was far from being over.

Bree looked at Leah and hated that Kade and she had to have a conversation like this in front of her. A baby deserved better, even if Leah was too young to know what they were saying. Still, she might be able to sense the tension in the room. Bree could certainly feel it, and it had her stomach turning and twisting.

"Since we don't know who hired Cummings," Kade went on, "my sisters-in-law and the kids are leaving town for a while. Darcy came back to pack some things."

That gave Bree something else to be frustrated about. The monster after her had now managed to disrupt the entire Ryland family. Now, all of them were in possible danger, and that included Kade's nephews and niece.

Kade ducked down a little so that they were eye to eye. "I think it's a good idea if Leah goes with Darcy and the others."

"No," flew out of her mouth before Bree could stop it. But she immediately hated her response and hated even more that she might have to take it back.

"I'm just getting to know her," Bree mumbled, and she kissed Leah's cheek as she'd seen Kade do. Each kiss, each moment was a gift that she didn't deserve but would take, anyway.

Bree pulled in a long breath and tried to push away the ache. But no, it was still there. It hurt her to the core to think of her daughter being whisked away when she'd only had a few real moments with her. It hurt even more though to know that Leah was in danger and would continue to be until Kade and she put an end to it.

"Whoever killed Cummings could hire someone else," Bree said, more to herself than Kade. She had to make her heart understand what her brain and instincts already knew. Her training and experience forced her to see scenarios and outcomes that ripped away at her.

"Just where exactly is this safe place that the others and Leah could go?" she asked.

"My other sister-in-law, Kayla, has a house in San

Antonio. It's an estate with a high wrought-iron fence
and security system surrounding the entire grounds and
house. SAPD will provide additional protection. Plus,
Dade and Nate would be with them."

It sounded like a fortress. Ideal for keeping her baby
safe. But Bree knew that bad guys might still try to get
through all those security measures.

"You could go, too," Kade quietly added.

"No." And this time, Bree wouldn't take back her
response. Just the opposite. It was the only answer that
made sense. "Wherever I go, the danger will follow. I'm
the one this person wants dead, and I don't want Leah
anywhere around if and when he hires another hit man
to come after me."

Kade didn't argue. Because he knew it was the truth.
The more distance between her baby and her, the better.

Still, that didn't ease the ache that was quickly turning into a raw, throbbing pain.

"This is much harder than I thought it would be,"
Bree whispered.

Kade only nodded, and she could see the agony in
his icy gray eyes. So much emotion that it prompted
Bree to touch her fingertips to his arm. She wasn't big
on providing comfort, and her job had required her not
to sympathize with anything or anybody, but she and
Kade shared this heartbreak.

"When would Leah have to go to Kayla's house?"
she asked.

Kade lifted his shoulder and sank down on the
sofa. "Soon. This morning," he clarified. "But maybe
it wouldn't be for long."

Maybe.

And maybe it would be far longer than Bree's heart
could handle.

An uncomfortable silence settled between them, and Bree eased down on the sofa right next to him. She waited. Hoping. And it wasn't long before Kade sighed and placed the baby in her arms.

It was far better than anything else he could have done.

It soothed her. And frightened her. It filled her with a hundred emotions that she didn't understand. But even that seemed trivial.

She was holding her baby.

And it was breaking her into pieces.

Until this moment she hadn't realized she could love someone this much. Or hurt this much because she might lose her, even for only a day or two.

"What are we going to do?" Bree said under her breath.

When Kade didn't answer, she looked at him and saw his jaw muscles set in iron.

Handsome iron, she amended.

Because his good looks weren't diminished by a surly expression or the possible impending danger. Again, she blamed it on their shared situation. And on the close contact between them. After all, they were arm to arm. Hip to hip. Breath to breath. Except she doubted Kade was thinking about the close contact in a good way.

That expression let her know that he hadn't told her everything, and the part that he had left out would be something that would only add to the pain she was already feeling.

"Okay, what's wrong?" Bree demanded.

He didn't answer right away. He'd mulled over his answer. "I'm not giving up Leah."

For a moment she thought he meant that he'd changed

his mind about the baby going to the San Antonio estate, but then she got it.

Oh, yeah.

She got it all right.

Kade had physical custody of Leah since she was just a few days old. Plus, he had something that Bree didn't—a home, a supportive family and money from the looks of it. There was also the fact that he had strong ties in the community. That meant ties with people who could help him keep custody of their child.

Still, that was just one side of it.

"I'm her mother," Bree said when she couldn't think of another argument. It certainly wasn't a good one, and it didn't mean she had what it took to raise a child. But the other side was that she loved this child with all her heart.

Kade nodded. "And I'm her father."

Frustrated, she stared at him. "Does this mean we're at some kind of stalemate?"

"No." And that's all he said for several moments. "It means we have some things to work out. Things that will be in Leah's best interest."

Bree could see where this was going, and she didn't like the direction one bit. "You think you can be a better parent than me."

He didn't deny it.

She couldn't deny it, either. He certainly looked at ease with Leah. So did the other members of his family that she'd met. Leah was a Ryland.

But she was Bree's baby, too.

Bree huffed. "I'm not just giving her up, either." Even though it didn't make logical sense, it made sense to her. As a mother. Yes, it was a new role, new feelings.

New everything. But it was a role she would embrace with as much devotion and love as she had her badge.

Kade didn't huff, but he mumbled something under his breath. "Be reasonable about this. You're a Jane for heaven's sake."

Bree jumped right on that. "And I could become a regular agent. Like you."

In the past that would have caused her to wince. Or laugh because she had thought a regular job would be a boring death sentence. But she wasn't wincing or laughing now. In fact, she was on the verge of crying at the thought of losing this child that she hardly knew.

With those iron jaw muscles still in place, Kade leaned forward and picked up the little silver object from the table. Bree recognized the design. It was the same as the tattoo on his shoulder. He began to roll it like a coin across his fingers. Maybe as a stress reliever. Maybe so he wouldn't have to look at her. Whatever, it was working.

Well, for Kade.

Bree didn't think anything could relieve her stress, but she shoved that aside and tried to reach a solution. Even a temporary one. She sure needed something to get her through this morning.

"We only have a few hours to spend with Leah before she leaves," Bree conceded. "We can table this discussion until after...well, after," she settled for saying.

Because she refused to admit this could end badly. The stakes were too high for that.

"Later, then," Kade agreed, and he looked back at her. His expression let her know that *later, then,* wasn't going to happen immediately.

"There aren't a lot of rules for situations like this. And we don't know each other very well." He kept rolling the concho. "In fact, I don't know much about you at all."

It wasn't a gruff or barked observation. It was conversation, that's all, and he had genuine concern in his voice. Bree knew this could turn ugly, but since he was trying to make nice, she tried, too.

"Bree is my real name. Bree Ann Winston. I'm twenty-nine." She paused. Frowned. "Wait. What's the date?"

He glanced at his watch. "June 14."

That required a deep breath. "Okay, I'm thirty." She'd missed a pivotal birthday by two months.

Ironically, it had been a birthday that she'd been dreading since many Janes didn't last long after their mid-thirties. They were either dead or moved to a regular agent position. However, after the ordeal she'd just been through, turning thirty didn't seem so bad, after all.

"Both of my parents are dead," she continued, addressing another touchy subject. "They were killed in a meth lab explosion when I was nine. Let's just say they weren't stellar parents and leave it at that. I spent the rest of my so-called childhood in foster care."

Hellish foster care that she didn't discuss. Ever. With anyone.

Bree took another deep breath. She hadn't intended to confess all of that dirty laundry, but she figured this wasn't a good time to keep secrets. Besides, if it came down to a custody fight with Kade, he'd find out, anyway. Kade would learn that prior to becoming an FBI agent, she'd been a mess. A juvenile record for underage drinking. Truancy. And running away from foster care. Especially that. Bree had lost count of how many times she'd run. In fact, she always ran when things got tough.

Or rather she had.

She wouldn't run now.

"So, there's the dirt on me," she concluded. "Nothing like your life, I'm sure."

He made a sound that could have meant anything and followed it with a deep breath to indicate it was his turn to spill his guts. "I'm Kade Jason Ryland. Age thirty-one. And I've lived here at this ranch my entire life. Wouldn't want to live anywhere else."

She could see him here as a little boy. Learning to ride those magnificent horses that she'd seen in the painting in the foyer. Running through this sprawling house surrounded by older brothers and other family who loved him the way Bree loved Leah. It was so far from what she'd experienced as a kid that it seemed like a fantasy.

Kade's next deep breath came with a change of expression. His forehead bunched up, and he dodged her gaze. "When I was ten, my grandfather was murdered. He was the sheriff then, and well, I was close to him. All of us were. He was gunned down by an unknown assailant, and the case has never been solved."

"I'm sorry." And that was genuine. An injustice like that ate away at you. Obviously, that's what it'd done to Kade. She could see the hurt still there in his eyes.

He shrugged, and she saw the shield come down. He was guarding himself now. Bree knew, because she was a master of doing it.

"A few days after my grandfather was murdered, my father gave me and my five brothers a custom-made silver concho." He held it up for her to see.

"That was nice of him." Though there was something about his tone that said differently.

"It was a guilt gift." Kade didn't continue until he'd

taken Leah from her and put the baby in the carrier seat on the table in front of them. "After that, my father walked out on us. My mother killed herself because she was severely depressed, and my older brother, Grayson, had to forgo college, life and everything else so he could raise all of us and keep the ranch going."

Kade met her gaze. "So, there's the dirt on me."

Okay. Bree hadn't expected anything other than a fairy tale family story to do with the idyllic family ranch, but that was more a nightmare. The sympathy came, and it didn't feel as foreign to her as she thought it would.

"I'm sorry," she repeated.

He waved her off. "Yeah. I'm sorry about your life, too."

It was the first time she ever remembered anyone saying that and really meaning it. And much to her surprise, it felt good. Too good. And it set off more warnings in her head. Her motto of *don't trust anyone* was slowly being chipped away.

By Kade.

She looked up at him, to thank him, not just for the reciprocal sympathy but also for taking care of their baby when she hadn't been around to do it.

Kade looked at her, too. And her *thank you* died on her lips when he put his arms around her and pulled her to him.

"We have to be together on this," he whispered.

It wasn't exactly the kiss that she'd braced herself for. Just the opposite. He was holding her as if trying to comfort her.

His arms were warm and strong. So welcoming. Of course, she'd been in his arms before at the fertility clinic. She'd been naked then. Kade had, too. And his body had definitely given her dreams and food for thought.

Not now, of course.

And Bree wanted to believe that.

Too bad those memories warmed her far more than they should have. It'd been a job, she reminded herself. And that job was over now. Kade's naked body was just a memory, and it had to stay that way.

Bree wanted to believe that, too.

He pulled back, met her gaze. His breath was warm, as well, and he moved closer. Closer. Until his mouth brushed against hers. Bree tried to brace herself again, but what she didn't do was move away.

"I'd kiss you," he drawled, "but we both know that'd be a bad idea."

She was about to agree with him, but Kade leaned in and touched his mouth to hers again. Still not a kiss, but it heated her as thoroughly as if it had been one.

"A bad idea," she repeated. Mercy. She sounded like a wimp. And she still wasn't moving. Bree could see what was happening. Like a big train wreck. Except this was a wreck that her body was aching to experience.

What would a real kiss feel like with Kade?

The fake ones had been amazingly potent, and she figured a real one would pretty much melt her into a puddle.

"Bad," he mumbled without taking his eyes off her.

Bree could see a kiss coming. Could feel it. And she heard herself say *uh-oh* a split second before Kade snapped away from her.

Okay.

No kiss, after all. She didn't know who looked more disappointed or more confused—Kade or her.

He cursed. Some really bad words. And Bree thought

that was it. The end of the possible lethal kiss. But then he came back at her. He grabbed her and put his mouth on hers. And it wasn't for just a peck this time.

This was a Kade Ryland kiss.

Yes, this was so different from the fake ones, and they weren't even naked to enjoy the full benefits. Still, there were benefits. His mouth moved over hers as if he'd been born to kiss her like this.

The heat washed through her, head to toe. It cleared the haze and fogginess from her mind while it created some haze of a different kind. Her body was suddenly on fire.

From one blasted kiss!

How could he do that to her body? How could he dissolve all her defenses and make her want him like this?

Bree wasn't sure she wanted to know the answer. But she was certain that she wanted the kiss to continue. And it couldn't. For one thing, Leah was in the room. For another, neither Kade nor she was in a good place for this to be happening.

Still, she wasn't the one to stop. Kade did. Later, much later, after her body cooled down, she might actually thank him for it.

He pulled back, dragged his tongue over his bottom lip and made a sound of approval. Or something. Whatever the sound, it went through her as fiery hot as the kiss.

Bree didn't ask for clarification on what that sound meant. She didn't need it. That kiss had held up to the fantasies she'd had after those naked fake kisses at the clinic.

"I'm sorry," Kade said.

She didn't have time to repeat that lie to him because someone cleared their throat and both Bree and Kade turned toward the open doorway. It was Mason, and he obviously hadn't missed the close contact between them. He didn't look too pleased about it, either, but then he hadn't looked pleased about much since her arrival.

"You got a visitor," Mason said, his attention landing on her. "SA Randy Cooper."

Coop. The very person that she should have called by now. Sheez. How could she have forgotten that? But then Bree remembered.

Sleep, baby and kisses.

Yes. That had really eaten into her time, but she had to get her mind back on track. She had to think like an agent because that was the best way to keep her baby safe.

"I had him wait on the front porch," Mason explained. "Just in case you didn't want to see him."

Oh, she wanted to see him all right. She turned to Kade. "I need to change my clothes. Best if I don't talk to my boss while wearing these pink pjs."

He nodded and picked up Leah in the infant carrier. "Mason can watch Leah. Meet me downstairs in the living room after you've changed."

"There's more," Mason said, and that stopped both Kade and her midstep. "Somebody else called the sheriff's office and left a message for you. And it's a call I think you'll need to return before you speak to Agent Cooper."

Bree shook her head, not understanding that remark. "Who wants to talk to us?" she asked cautiously.

"To *you*," Mason corrected, staring right at her. "It's Anthony McClendon."

One of their suspects. She glanced at Kade, wondering if he knew why Anthony would be calling her, but he only lifted his shoulder.

"What does he want?" Kade demanded.

"Apparently a lot. He's either lying through his teeth or else you should rethink seeing Agent Cooper. That's why I left him on the porch and locked the front door. I reset the security alarm, too."

Bree lifted her shoulders. "Why would you take those kinds of measures for a federal officer?" she added. "And why would you listen to a piece of scum like Anthony McClendon?"

It was Mason's turn to shrug. "Because he says he has proof that Cooper is dirty."

"Proof?" Kade challenged.

Mason nodded. "Oh, yeah. And he says he's also got evidence that Cooper is the one who wants Bree dead."

Chapter Seven

"Proof," Kade mumbled while he waited for Bree to change her clothes.

He was eager to hear exactly what that would be or if such a thing even existed. Kade had already tried to return Anthony's call, but it had gone straight to voice mail.

"So-called proof coming from a confirmed suspect awaiting trial," Mason interjected. He dropped down on the sofa and gave Leah's foot a little wiggle. His brother didn't smile, but it was as close to a loving expression as Mason ever managed. "Anthony could be just blowing smoke."

Under normal circumstances that reminder would have been enough to calm some of Kade's concerns. But it wasn't enough now.

His daughter was in the house.

The very house that Coop was waiting to get inside. Yeah, Mason would protect Leah, and Kade could do the same to Bree, but he hated the possibility of danger being so close. Bree already had enough danger dumped on her, and judging from her still-sleepy eyes and unfocused expression, she wasn't anywhere near ready to face down someone who might not be on their side.

Especially when it was someone she thought was on their side.

"I'm ready," Bree announced, hurrying out of the bathroom. No more cotton candy pajamas. She wore loose black pants and a pale purple top. Darcy's colors. But they didn't look so bad on Bree, either.

Kade also saw the change in her body language. No more lack of focus. Hers was the expression of an agent who wanted some answers. Or maybe she just wanted to throttle Anthony for making that accusation against her boss.

"I know, I know," she mumbled when she followed his gaze. She went to Leah and kissed her forehead. "The clothes aren't my usual style."

"You look good," he settled for saying.

Bree glanced down at the outfit and grumbled a distracted thanks. Her mind was obviously locked on seeing their visitor.

Kade aimed for the same mind lock. He pushed her clothes, Leah, the kiss and this attraction for her aside so he could deal with something potentially dangerous.

"You trust Coop?" he came right out and asked.

"Of course." She answered without hesitation, but she stopped on her way to the door. Now, she paused and shook her head. *"Of course,"* she repeated it and slowly turned back around to face him. "What did Anthony have to say about Coop wanting me dead?"

"I wasn't able to reach him, but I left a message and told him to call my cell."

"Well, I'm sure whatever comes from Anthony's mouth will be a lie," she added and headed out of the room. "Coop's not the enemy. I can't say the same for Anthony, especially since he's facing criminal charges."

Kade hoped she was right about Coop, but just in

case, he kept his hand over his gun. He also moved ahead of Bree, hoping that he could keep himself between Coop and her until he could determine if there was a shred of truth to Anthony's allegations.

The maneuver earned him a huff from Bree.

He gave her a huff right back.

Kade disarmed the security system and looked out the side window. It was Coop all right. Kade had had many conversations with the lanky blond-haired man while he'd been searching for Bree. Conversations where Kade had been sure that Coop's actions were the right ones.

He hoped he continued to feel that way when he opened the door.

"Bree," Coop said on a rise of breath as if he truly hadn't expected to see her. The man stepped forward, and Kade had to make a split-second decision about letting him in.

But Bree made the decision for him. She stepped around Kade and pulled Coop into her arms for a hug. The man hugged back and kept repeating her name. It was a regular warm and fuzzy reunion.

"I never thought I'd see you again," Coop whispered, though it was plenty loud enough for Kade to hear.

"It was touch-and-go yesterday," Kade offered.

"Yes." Coop eased away from Bree and had the decency to look a little uncomfortable with his public display of affection for his subordinate.

Coop then turned his attention to Kade. "I heard about the shooting in San Antonio. About the dead gunman, too. You should have called me the second you got that anonymous tip."

That would have been protocol, yes, but Kade hadn't exactly been operating on a logical level. "No time for calls," Kade answered. "As it was, I barely had time to get her out of there alive."

Coop still seemed annoyed that he hadn't been looped in. "Thanks for getting her out."

"I didn't do it for you." Kade should have probably kept that to himself, but there was something about this reunion that riled him. Hopefully, it was Anthony's accusation and not the possessive way Coop was holding on to Bree.

Coop took something from his pocket and handed it to her. Her badge. Bree closed her fingers around it, then slipped it into her pocket. "Thanks."

"I got it from your apartment after you went missing," Coop explained. "I figured you'd want it back right away. You always said you felt naked without it."

Coop smiled.

Kade didn't.

And he hated that at a critical time like this the naked comment had an effect on him. A bad one. The kiss had been a huge mistake, and worse, he wanted to make that mistake again. He hoped he didn't feel that way because of the shot of jealousy he'd just experienced.

"I talked to the doctor who examined you," Coop volunteered, dropping the smile. "He wouldn't tell me much, other than you were okay. He did say there'd be no lasting complications from the delivery or your ordeal."

"Other than the threat to her life," Kade spoke up. He looked at Bree to give her a chance to ask Coop about what was on both their minds.

She flexed her eyebrows and sucked in a quick breath. "Anthony McClendon called the ranch. He made some, uh, accusations against you."

Coop's eyes widened, and he tossed his concerned

gaze first to Kade and then back to Bree. "What kind of accusations?"

"Anthony said you were *dirty,*" Bree explained, then paused. "And that you're the one who's trying to kill me." She waved it off before he could say anything. "He's lying, of course."

"But he said he had proof," Kade added.

"Then he's lying about that, too," Coop said as gospel.

Coop caught Bree's arm and turned her to face him. "Anthony's guilty of a lot of things that went on at the Fulbright clinic. It was pure luck on his part that we didn't get those missing surveillance backups that would have no doubt proven that he's guilty of even more serious charges. If he's trying to put a spin on this, it's because he knows I'm going to put his sorry butt in jail."

Kade agreed that Anthony was likely guilty of something more than harboring illegal immigrants, theft and embezzlement, but he still wanted to hear what the man had to say. Especially what he had to say about Coop.

"What's the status of the Fulbright investigation?" Bree asked.

"It's still active," Coop said. "Kade and you gave us a good start with your undercover work, and I'm still digging. Trying to connect the dots. I do know that Anthony was skimming money from the clinic, and that's why father and son are now at odds."

Kade had learned the same thing, but realized that he hadn't brought Bree up to speed on the case. Of course, there hadn't been much time for that between dodging bullets and sleeping off the Valium.

"And what about the shooting yesterday?" Bree

pressed. "Any word on who might have hired a hit man to come after me?"

"Nothing yet. It's SAPD's jurisdiction. For now. But I've requested that the FBI take over, since the shots were fired at two agents."

Yeah, but moving it to the FBI would take Nate out of the investigative loop. Kade preferred his brother in on this. Nate had an objective eye, and Kade needed that right now. Clearly, his objectivity had taken a hike. First the kiss. Now the jealousy.

He wasn't on a good track here.

Bree blew out a long, weary breath. "Is there any evidence about why someone would have kidnapped me in the first place?"

Coop shook his head and gave her arm a gentle squeeze. "I'm sorry. I'm trying hard, but I haven't been able to prove anything. Of course, my theory is that McClendon did all of this so he'd have some leverage over the investigation."

"But he hasn't contacted Bree, me or you to try to tamper with evidence or anything." Kade tried not to make it sound like a question. He also tried not to be so suspicious of a fellow agent.

Oh, man. He couldn't let a suspect like Anthony play these kinds of mind games.

"McClendon hasn't contacted me *yet*," Coop verified. "I figured it would happen as Anthony's and Jamie's trial dates got closer. But since Bree managed to escape and since the baby is here and safe, the person responsible has lost their leverage."

Kade wanted to believe that, because if it were true, then that meant the danger to Bree and Leah had lessened. Well, maybe. That didn't mean the person wouldn't try to kidnap them again. But at least both were safe now.

And it had to stay that way.

Even if he had to check out Anthony's crazy allegation. Kade would do that and anything else that it took. He made a mental note to recheck all the security measures at the ranch. And to try to convince Bree to take him up on his offer to send her to a safe house.

"So, what are your immediate plans?" Coop asked Bree. But he didn't wait for her to answer that. "How soon are you returning to work?"

She glanced at Kade, and he was certain that he looked as surprised as she did. The timing was all off, but Kade didn't jump to answer for her.

"I'm not sure," she finally said. Not an answer, but it appeared that was all she was going to give him. She fluttered her hand toward the stairs. "I want to spend some time with my daughter. Get to know her."

Coop's forehead bunched up. "I thought you'd want to figure out who kidnapped you right away."

"I will." But then she paused. "I just need some time."

Coop's gaze shifted to Kade, and the man instantly frowned. "Not too much time, I hope. Bree, you haven't worked in nearly a year."

"That wasn't exactly her fault," Kade pointed out.

Coop's frown deepened, and he moved even closer to Bree. "Officially, you were listed as missing in the line of duty, but we both know your Jane identity was compromised when things went wrong at the Fulbright clinic. Your face was on those surveillance videos, and your cover was blown."

Kade couldn't deny any of that. But what he still didn't know was how their cover had been blown. It was definitely something he wanted to learn, but for now, he had other things that were much higher priority.

"What are you saying?" Bree asked Coop. "That I can no longer be a Jane? Well, that's okay. It would have been hard to pull off deep-cover assignments now that I have Leah."

Coop looked as if she'd slugged him. "I didn't think you'd ever give that up without a fight." He shook his head and stared at her as if she'd lost her mind. Or as if Kade had brainwashed her. "But that's not the only problem we have here. Bree, there are people in the Justice Department who feel you brought this kidnapping on yourself. That you didn't take the proper security precautions."

Kade tamped down the rush of anger and stepped by Bree's side. "They're blaming the victim?"

Coop huffed. "No. I'm not saying that—"

But he didn't get to finish because Mason appeared at the top of the stairs. He had Leah's carrier in his left hand, and he had the baby positioned behind him in a protective stance.

"We have another problem," Mason called down to Kade. "The ranch hand that I've got watching the security cameras just called, and we have some more visitors. He's running the plates, but it looks like Anthony McClendon and Jamie Greer."

"Good," Coop spat out, and he drew his gun. "Because I can confront the SOB about the lies he's spreading about me."

Kade look at Bree, and her expression verified how he felt. This wasn't *good*. Far from it. Two of their suspects were way too close for comfort, and they had a riled agent with his gun drawn.

"Keep your gun down," Kade ordered Coop. "And

you need to stay with Leah," he added to his brother. "Call a couple of the ranch hands to the front in case I need backup."

"I'm your backup," Coop snarled, and with his gun ready, he stormed out onto the porch.

Kade caught Bree's arm to stop her from following. "I know you won't wait upstairs with Mason." He reached down and pulled the Colt .38 from his ankle holster. Kade had no idea if she had a steady aim yet, but even if she didn't, he preferred Bree to be armed.

"Thanks," she mumbled, but her attention was on the stairs where Mason had just left with Leah. "He's a good cop?" she asked.

"Yeah. And we're not letting anyone get past us."

She nodded, licked her lips and looked a little shakier than Kade wanted. However, he couldn't take the time to soothe her because he didn't want bullets to start flying this close to Leah. Even though Coop was a well-trained agent, he seemed to be working on a short fuse when it came to Anthony.

Kade stepped onto the porch, with Bree behind him, just as the white Lexus stopped next to Coop's car. It was Anthony and Jamie all right. Kade had interviewed them enough to recognize them from a distance.

Anthony got out first. He definitely didn't look like a killer or even a formidable opponent. The man was lanky to the point of being skinny, and his black hair was pretty thin for a man in his early thirties. But Kade knew that Anthony had some strength. During their undercover assignment, Kade had watched Anthony get into a shoving match with an irate illegal immigrant father who was looking for his daughter. Anthony had some martial arts skills to make up for all that lankiness.

The man wore no scrubs today, as he'd worn in all his interviews with Kade. He was dressed in khakis and a white shirt. He looked like a nerd. If he was carrying a concealed weapon, Kade didn't see any signs of it. That didn't mean Kade would let down his guard. Neither would Coop. Or Bree.

"No reason for those guns," Anthony called out. "I'm just here to talk."

"You mean you're here to lie," Coop shouted back.

Oh, yeah. This could turn ugly fast, and Kade was thankful when he spotted the three armed ranch hands round the east corner of the house. The men stopped Anthony in his tracks, probably because they were armed with rifles that no amount of martial arts could match.

But those rifles didn't stop Jamie from getting out of the car.

Jamie spared the ranch hands a cool, indifferent glance before she slid on a pair of dark sunglasses and strolled toward them as if this were a planned social visit. No nerd status for her. Jamie was tall and lean, and she had her long auburn hair gathered into a sleek ponytail. Kade had always thought Jamie looked more like a socialite than a nurse.

"How did you know I was here?" Coop demanded.

"I didn't." Anthony looked past him and put his attention on Bree. "I came here to see you. It's all over the news about the shooting, and since Agent Ryland wasn't at his office in San Antonio, I thought he might bring you here. Obviously, I guessed right."

Kade hoped it was a guess, and that Anthony didn't have any insider knowledge. Of course, Anthony could have learned Bree's location from his father, but Kade didn't think the two were on speaking terms.

"Why'd you want to see Bree?" Kade demanded while Anthony and Coop started another glaring contest with each other.

"Because SAPD has been hassling us again," Jamie calmly provided. "And Anthony and I thought we'd better nip this in the bud."

"What are you planning to nip?" Kade asked, and he didn't bother trying to sound friendly. He wanted all three of these people off his porch and off his family's property.

"You, if necessary." Jamie turned toward Kade, though with those dark shades, he couldn't tell exactly where she was looking. "You had your shot at investigating us, and you found nothing on me other than a few charges that you can't make stick."

"Not yet. But at least you'll do some time in jail. That'll be enough for now." Kade knew it sounded like a threat, and he was glad of it. "Bree's been through hell and back, and someone will pay for that."

Anthony pointed toward Coop. "What about him? He should be the one paying."

"I warned you about those lies." There was a dark, dangerous edge to Coop's voice.

Still, Anthony came closer, but he pleaded his case to Bree, not Coop or Kade. "Did Agent Cooper tell you that he provided *security* to the Fulbright clinic and that he was paid a hefty amount for his services?"

"Security?" Kade repeated over Coop's profanity-punctuated shouts that this was all a crock.

Anthony nodded, and Jamie strolled closer until she was near the bottom step and standing next to Anthony. "It's true. Anthony's father told me that Agent Cooper kept the local cops from digging too deeply into what was going on."

Coop turned that profanity tirade to Jamie, but it didn't stop the woman from continuing.

"Hector said Cooper was stunned when he realized Bree, one of his own agents, had been sneaked into the undercover assignment at the clinic that could ultimately land him in jail." Jamie paused, a trace of a smile on her dark red lips. "And Anthony here has proof."

Anthony had a bit of a smile going on, as well. Kade could understand why—*if* there was proof. And it was that possibility of proof that kept Kade from latching onto them and giving them the boot.

"Anthony and you have nothing on me," Coop fired back. "Neither does Hector McClendon."

But Jamie only shrugged. "You're investigating the wrong people, Agent Ryland. You need to be looking closer to home. You need to investigate Agent Cooper."

Bree huffed and stepped around Kade, between Coop and him. But she didn't say anything. She just studied Jamie from head to toe, and Kade had to wait just like the others to hear Bree's take on all of this.

"Are you the woman who held me captive all those months?" Bree asked.

With all the other accusations flying around about Coop, Kade certainly hadn't expected such a direct question from Bree. But he waited for Jamie's answer and watched her expression. He wished he could strip those glasses off her so he could see her eyes because he was certain that question had hit some kind of nerve.

Jamie shifted her posture and folded her arms over her chest. "I did nothing wrong," she insisted.

Kade looked at Bree to see if she believed Jamie, but Bree only shook her head. It made sense. After all, Bree had said her kidnappers had kept on prosthetic masks, but he'd hoped that she would recognize something about Jamie or Anthony.

Of course, maybe there was nothing to recognize because they hadn't been the ones to hold her captive.

"Did. You. Hold. Me. Captive?" Bree repeated. Her anger came through loud and clear.

Jamie shifted again. "No." She paused. "Are you accusing me so you can protect your boss? My advice? Don't. Because accusing me won't do anything for your safety. Or your baby's safety." Jamie leaned in and lowered her voice as if telling a secret. "Investigate him, and you'll learn the truth, even if it's not what you want to hear."

That got Coop started again. "I want to see this so-called proof of my guilt," Coop demanded.

Anthony lifted his hands, palms up. "You think I'm stupid enough to bring it with me? *Right*. Then you just kill me and take it."

"I'm an FBI agent," Coop fired back, "and I'm not in the habit of killing people just because they're telling lies about me."

"I'm not lying, and you know it." Anthony turned to Kade and Bree. "I have an eyewitness who'll testify that Agent Cooper here had a meeting with my father at the clinic, less than an hour before your cover was blown."

Oh, that was not what Kade wanted to hear, and by God, it had better not be true. If so, Coop would pay and pay hard.

"That witness will also tell you that Cooper took money from my father," Anthony smugly added.

It took a moment for Kade to get his teeth unclenched. Bree had a similar reaction. She was hurling daggers at Anthony with a cold glare, but she wasn't exactly giving Coop a resounding vote of confidence, either.

"Sounds like I need to talk to this witness," Bree commented.

"No, you don't." Coop walked toward Jamie and Anthony with his finger pointing at the man who'd just accused him of assorted felonies. "I'm not going to let you get away with this."

Because Kade didn't want Coop to do something they'd both regret, he grabbed his fellow agent. He held on until he was sure Coop would stay put.

"We're not dealing with this here at the ranch," Kade informed Anthony, Jamie and Coop. He shifted his attention to Anthony. "Bring the witness to the Silver Creek sheriff's office. And while you're at it, both of you come prepared to answer some more questions because this investigation is just getting started."

Jamie groaned softly and mumbled something. "I've had enough questions to last me a lifetime."

Kade tossed her a glare. "Then you'll get a few more. Be there when Anthony brings in this secret witness."

Much to Kade's surprise, Anthony nodded, and his smile wasn't so little now. The man was smirking when he headed back to his car. "Come on, Jamie. We're finished here, for the moment."

But Jamie paused a moment and glanced over her shoulder at Anthony before she spoke. "I don't trust Anthony," she said in a whisper. "And neither should you. The man is dangerous."

Bree and Kade exchanged a glance, and she was no doubt thinking the same thing—what the heck was this all about? One minute ago Jamie had been ice-cold and unruffled. Now she looked on the verge of panicking.

"If Anthony is dangerous, then why did you come here with him?" Bree asked.

Jamie didn't answer right away. She glanced over her shoulder again as if to make sure Anthony wasn't close enough to hear. "Because sometimes the only choice you have is to cooperate." And with that, she turned and followed Anthony to the car.

"They're liars," Coop repeated before Anthony even started the engine. "It's a mistake to give them an audience for whatever it is they're trying to pull."

Kade shrugged. "I have to start somewhere to get to the bottom of what happened to Bree."

"What happened to Bree is *my* concern," Coop snapped.

That was *not* the right thing to say, especially after those heated accusations that Anthony had just made. Kade had to fight once more to hang on to his temper, but Bree beat him to the punch.

"Kade and I became parents," she reminded him. And there was a bite to her voice. "What happened is most definitely his concern."

That didn't cool down the anger in Coop's face. He opened his mouth, no doubt ready to argue, but there was no argument he could give that would make Kade back off from this investigation. His baby girl's safety was at stake.

Coop gave her a look that could have frozen hell. "Be careful who you cast your lot with, Bree. It could come back to bite you."

Bree faced him head-on. "I'm always careful."

That obviously didn't please him because he cursed. "I'm giving you forty-eight hours." Coop's voice had that dangerous edge to it again. "If you're not at headquarters by then, you'll never see your badge again."

Chapter Eight

Bree watched Leah sleep and hoped the baby would wake up before Kade's brother Grayson arrived to take her to the house in San Antonio. These last minutes with her daughter were precious time, and she needed every second to count.

"Grayson will be here in about a half hour," Kade informed her when he got off the phone.

Bree had listened in on the flurry of calls that Kade had made after their guests' departures, but her main focus had been on Leah.

And her badge.

It was hard to push that aside completely, even though that's exactly what Bree wanted to do.

She'd been an agent for five years now, after she'd slogged her way through college night classes at the University of Texas and cruddy jobs so she could get her degree. And Coop had helped with that. In fact, he'd helped with a lot of things to put her on track and keep her there. He hadn't just been her boss but also her mentor and friend.

"All three of the nannies will be at the estate in San Antonio," Kade explained. "So, Leah will have lots of attention from them and her three aunts."

Still, it hurt that she wouldn't be there to share it.

"I've never thought of family as being a good thing," she mumbled. "But I'm glad Leah has yours."

"So am I." He walked back to the sofa where she was seated. "It's not too late, you know. You can go to San Antonio with them."

Mercy, that was tempting, just so she wouldn't have to leave Leah, but Bree had to shake her head. "Too big of a risk, especially since all of our suspects know I'm with you."

Bree's gaze whipped to his. "Please tell me that Grayson will take precautions when driving Leah to San Antonio. McClendon and the others can't follow him."

"They won't follow," Kade promised. "Grayson's a good lawman. And besides, his pregnant wife is at the house. He wouldn't put her or any of the rest of the family at risk."

Further risk, Bree mentally corrected. Because the risk was already there.

He sank down on the sofa next to her and touched Leah's cheek. The baby stirred a little but went straight back to sleep. Bree repeated what Kade had done and got the same results.

"Don't worry," Kade said. "You'll have time with her after this is over."

Yes, and that was another unsettled issue to go with the others. Leah. A custody arrangement. And the man next to her.

Her mind was already spinning with some possibilities. "Maybe I can move to Silver Creek. And get a regular job with the FBI." Those were things she'd considered *before* Coop's visit. "If I still have a badge, that is."

"You will," Kade promised. "Coop was just, well,

I think he was pissed that you didn't jump to go back with him. He's pretty territorial when it comes to you."

That sent her gaze back to his. "There's nothing personal between Coop and me."

"Didn't think there was on your part, but Coop's reaction could be because of guilt. He failed to protect you, and now he's trying to make sure nothing else goes wrong."

She stared at him. "Or?"

Kade shrugged. "Or Anthony's accusations could be true. We have to at least consider that Coop might be in on this. I'm having someone check his financials to see if there's a money trail that leads to the Fulbright clinic or any of our suspects."

Before today, Bree would have jumped to defend her boss. But that was before someone tried to kill her. "What about this witness that Anthony claims he has?"

Another head shake. "Anthony won't give names, but both Jamie and he are supposed to show up at the sheriff's office tomorrow. Grayson told them they'd better have proof and the witness."

That caused her stomach to churn, because she didn't want to believe that Coop could have endangered her this way. But it also gave her some relief. If Anthony maybe had proof that could lead to an arrest, then Bree wouldn't have to be away from Leah very long.

Of course, that might not end the danger.

Coop could be just a small piece in all of this. An insignificant piece. But Bree still didn't like that he could have kept a secret that would have an impact on the investigation. Not just for the Fulbright clinic but for the aftermath and what had happened to her.

"When are Anthony's and Jamie's trial dates?" she asked Kade.

"Two more weeks. I'll testify. They'll want you to do the same."

Yes, because their testimony was what would convict them of the worst of the charges since there wasn't a lot of hard evidence.

"Nothing else on those missing surveillance backups?" she pressed.

"No. We have agents looking for them, though. Agents who don't work for Coop," he added before she could voice her concern. "Even if we don't find them before the trial dates, our testimony should be enough to convict Jamie and Anthony of at least some of the charges. The security guards, too."

Because those guards had tried to kill Kade and her on that undercover assignment. Plus, she could testify about the two illegal immigrant surrogates she'd ferreted out while there. The women had said both Jamie and Anthony were responsible for them being at the clinic. Of course, the women had also since disappeared and hopefully were alive somewhere, but Bree's testimony should be sufficient.

Unless…

"McClendon's lawyers could use my ordeal to question how reliable my memories are." That didn't help with the acid in her stomach. "And we don't have proof that McClendon, Anthony or Jamie was the one who had me kidnapped."

Kade nodded and eased his arm around her. He also eased her to him. "Two weeks is a long time, Bree. Anthony's witness could pan out."

And if so, that meant Coop would be arrested or implicated in something bad. It was a long shot and one she hoped she didn't have to face.

"What if an arrest doesn't end the threat against us?" she asked.

"Then, we keep looking."

Kade pulled in a deep breath and brushed a kiss on her forehead. He didn't look at her, and it didn't seem as if he'd noticed what he had done. That made it even more scary. Had they become so comfortable with each other that a benign peck was standard?

Apparently so.

The danger was responsible for that. And Leah. Kade and she were joined at the hip now, and that wasn't likely to end anytime soon. Their situation was bringing them closer together and keeping them there. For now. But Bree knew that bubbles often burst.

"I know you're uncomfortable with all of this," Kade said. He glanced at his arm slung around her and then at the spot where he'd kissed her.

So, he had been aware of what he'd done.

"I'm comfortable," she corrected. "And that's what makes me most uncomfortable."

He laughed. It was smoky and thick. All male. And she realized it was the first time she'd heard him do that. It made her smile in spite of the mess they were in. And then the easy way she'd smiled only added to the discomfort.

Sheez.

She was in trouble here in more ways than one.

"If you take the danger out of the situation," he continued, "then what's happening between us might not be a bad thing. I mean, I'm attracted to you, and I'm pretty sure you're attracted to me. That's better than having us at each other's throats."

That created an image that she tried to push aside.

Fast. Of Kade kissing her throat. Her, kissing his. Heck, she was just fantasizing about kissing him, period.

"The attraction isn't going to make this easier," she reminded him.

He paused, made a sound of agreement. Then, made another sound that could have meant anything. "Not easier, but I can't seem to stop it. I dreamed about you."

She risked looking at him, even though that put them face-to-face with their mouths too close together. Another kiss wouldn't send them into a wild scramble to have sex on the sofa. Because Leah was there. But if the baby hadn't been, then all bets were off.

And Grayson would arrive soon to take Leah.

What then?

More dreams, no doubt.

She didn't question Kade about his dream. Didn't need to hear the details. She'd had enough hot dreams about him when they'd played under the covers at the clinic. She doubted his dreams about her could be as hot as the ones she'd had about him.

The corner of his mouth lifted, and a dimple flashed in his cheek. That smile no doubt caused many women to melt into a puddle.

And it was doing the same to her.

But the puddle cooled down when she heard the sound. It was slight. Like a little squeak. However, it was enough to send Kade and her looking down at Leah. The baby squirmed, made another of those sounds.

And her eyes finally opened.

"About time you woke up," Kade told her, and he kissed the baby on her cheek.

Bree did the same. A puddle of a different kind. How could she possibly love someone this much?

"I'll miss her," Bree whispered. And that was a huge

understatement. It would kill a piece of her to see Grayson take her baby out that door.

"Yeah," Kade agreed. It sounded as if he had a lump in his throat. He opened his mouth to say more, but another sound stopped him.

Footsteps.

And that meant Grayson had likely arrived to take Leah away. Bree instantly had to blink back tears.

However, it was Mason who appeared in the doorway, and while he wasn't exactly out of breath, he had obviously hurried. He was also carrying a laptop. "We have another problem," he told them.

Bree groaned. "Not another visitor?"

"Of sorts," Mason verified. "You guys are real popular today. Someone just scaled over the fence. And that someone is armed."

KADE CURSED AND DREW HIS GUN. He didn't want a confrontation with a gunman. Especially not with Leah still in the house. Not with Bree there, either.

Mason put the laptop on the table in front of them. The screen was split into six frames, each of them showing the feed from the various security cameras positioned around the grounds. Mason pointed to the top right where Kade could see an armed man behind a tree. He was armed all right.

A rifle with a scope.

Bree pulled Leah even closer to her. "How far away is he from the house?"

"Half mile," Mason answered.

But the moment Mason spoke, the guy darted out and raced for cover behind another tree. He was moving closer to the house. Closer to Leah.

"I've alerted the ranch hands," Mason continued. He drew his gun. "And I'm about to head out there myself."

Kade wanted to go with him. He wanted to be the one to confront this SOB and one way or another get some answers from him.

But that would mean leaving Bree and Leah alone. He couldn't do that. Too big of a risk.

"I'll watch the surveillance and call you if there's a problem," Kade assured his brother.

Mason nodded, switched his phone to the vibrate mode so that it wouldn't be heard, and he hurried out of the room.

Bree moved closer to the laptop screen, her attention fastened on the man who was wearing dark camouflage pants and shirt. He had a black cap that obscured the upper part of his face.

"How tall do you think he is?" Bree asked.

"Six feet, maybe." He glanced at her. "Why? Do you recognize him?"

She kept studying him. "Maybe. I think it could be the man who kidnapped me. There's something about the way he's holding that rifle that looks familiar."

Then Kade wanted the man alive. Of course, his brother already knew that. Because this goon could give them answers. Kade wasn't sure if he could keep his temper in check if this was the man who'd put Bree through hell and back.

"Your captor held a rifle on you?" Kade wanted to know.

Bree nodded, and that only added to the anger he'd felt. Each little piece of information only worsened the description of hell that she'd been put through.

The gunman moved again, going behind another tree. The shift in position only highlighted more of his face. Kade couldn't see the guy's eyes, but they had a clearer image of his mouth and chin.

"Recognize him?" Kade pressed.

Bree shook her head. "I never saw his face," she reminded him. "Nor the woman's."

Still, it was obvious that she thought this could be the guy, and that was enough for Kade.

Kade looked at Leah to make sure she was okay, and thankfully she'd fallen back asleep. His baby girl didn't have a clue what was going on, but he didn't want her sensing any of Bree's fear. Except maybe it wasn't fear because Bree was staring at the man as if she wanted to rip him limb from limb.

Good.

Fear was natural, but it was determination and some luck that would get them through this.

"There aren't any more trees between that part of the pasture and the house," Kade let her know. "So, if he wants to get closer to fire that rifle, he'll have to do it out in the open."

Where Mason and the ranch hands could spot him. And hopefully stop him. But just in case the guy managed to get off a shot, Kade needed to take some more precautions.

He grabbed the laptop and took it toward the other side of the room. Toward the front of the house and far away from the windows on the rear where the gunman would no doubt be approaching. Kade helped Bree onto the floor behind the sofa. The bathtub would have been safer if it weren't for the two windows in there.

Kade kept his gun ready, and he watched. On one screen he could see Mason and three ranch hands. All armed, all headed toward the gunman. The gunman stayed put behind the tree, but he took a small device from his jacket pocket and aimed it toward the house.

"The gunman has infrared," Kade mumbled along with some profanity.

Kade fired off a text message to let Mason know that the gunman now had a way to get a visual of who was in the house. He wouldn't be able to see actual images, but he could tell from the heat blobs on his screen where they were.

"He came here to kill us." Bree's voice was barely a whisper, and Kade heard the fear now.

She turned so that her body was between Leah and the gunman. She was protecting their child, and Kade moved in front of them to do the same.

Kade braced himself for the gunman to come closer, especially now that he no doubt knew where they were.

But the man didn't do that.

He dropped the infrared device and fired. Not at the house. He fired in the direction of Mason and the ranch hands. They all dived to the ground as the bullets pelted around them.

"They're pinned down." The fear in Bree's voice went up a notch.

Kade felt his own fear rise, too, and he frantically searched the screen to see if any other ranch hands were close enough to respond and provide Mason and the others with some backup.

They weren't.

Probably because Mason had ordered everyone to stay away from possible gunfire. And they were doing just that. At least a dozen of them were guarding the house, but it wouldn't do Mason and the others any good.

"I have to go out there," Kade told Bree. He hated

to tell her this, but he had no choice. "I can approach him from this direction." He tapped the screen to the gunman's right. "While he's keeping my brother pinned down, I can sneak up on him."

Bree shook her head, but then she groaned and squeezed her eyes shut a second. She knew this had to happen.

"Be careful," she said.

"That's the plan." Kade gave Leah and her one last look. Hopefully, a reassuring one, and he grabbed the Colt .38 from the table so he could put it by Bree's side. Things would have to have gone to hell in a handbasket if she had to use it, but Kade didn't want to leave her defenseless.

He raced out of the room, barreling down the steps and out the front door. He stopped just long enough to holster his handgun and grab a rifle from the weapons' safe just off the foyer.

"Text Mason for me," Kade instructed the ranch hand guarding the front of the house. "Tell him I'm approaching the shooter from the west side."

The shots kept coming. Not rapid fire any longer, probably because the guy wanted to conserve ammunition, but the bullets were spaced out just at the right pace to keep Mason and the others on the ground.

Kade ran to the side of the house and peered around, but the angle was wrong for him to see the gunman. He headed toward the first outbuilding—the stables— and he raced along the side until he reached the back.

Now, he had the right angle.

The shooter was still a good distance away, but the guy wasn't looking in Kade's direction. Or, thankfully, the direction of the house.

Kade took aim. Not for a kill shot. But for the man's right arm.

And he fired.

The shot blasted through the air. Kade saw the man's body snap back when the bullet slammed into his shoulder.

But the shooter didn't drop the rifle.

Despite the bullet wound, the guy pivoted, lightning fast, aimed at Kade. And he fired.

Kade ducked behind the stables in the nick of time. The shot slammed into the exterior wall in the exact spot where his head had just been.

Whoever this guy was, he wasn't an amateur.

Kade stayed low, glanced around the stables, but before he could get a good look, another shot came at him.

Then another.

Kade tried to see this as a good thing. This way, Mason might be able to return fire, but it was hard to see the good side of things with the bullets coming at him.

He got even lower to the ground and looked out again. The man had taken aim but not at Kade.

At the house.

His heart went to his knees. Yes, Bree and Leah were somewhat protected, but this guy could maybe get off a lucky shot.

Kade couldn't risk that.

He came out from the stables, his rifle already aimed at the intended target. No arm shot this time. He went for the kill.

And Kade pulled the trigger.

Even from this distance, he heard the sickening thud of the bullet tearing into the shooter's body. The man's rifle dropped to the ground.

Seconds later, so did the man.

Kade started running toward him.

Maybe, just maybe, he could get to him in time, before he took his last breath. And then Kade could learn the identity of the person who'd sent this monster after Bree and his baby.

Chapter Nine

Bree almost wished the latest adrenaline crash would numb her to the fear and desperation that she was feeling. Not for herself.

But for Leah.

Their situation wasn't getting better, and judging from Kade's stark expression, he felt the same way. He sat across from her, his elbows on his knees and his face in his hands.

"I'm sorry," he repeated to her.

"You had no choice but to kill him." Bree knew that was true because she'd watched the nightmarish ordeal play out in front of her on the laptop screen.

First, she'd been terrified that Kade, his brother or one of the others would be killed. Then, her terror had skyrocketed when the shooter took aim at the house. For a couple of horrifying moments, Bree had thought he might shoot. That a bullet could tear through the walls and reach Leah.

But Kade had made sure that didn't happen. The gunman hadn't even had time to pull the trigger again before Kade shot him.

And killed him.

She'd watched that, too, while she'd held her baby close and prayed that nothing else bad would happen.

Leah was okay, thank God. But the shooter hadn't been able to say anything before Kade got to him. No dying confession to clear his conscience, and that meant they were right back at square one.

Well, almost.

Kade's brother Grayson had arrived just minutes after the fatal shooting and immediately taken over the necessary mop-up of an inevitable investigation. Grayson was pacing their suite while talking on the phone, and from what Bree could glean from the conversation, he was within minutes of turning over the investigation to one of his deputies so he could leave for San Antonio.

With Leah, of course.

That was good, Bree kept reminding herself. However, in this case *good* felt like something beyond bad.

"We're doing the right thing sending Leah with Grayson," she whispered. She tried not to make it sound like a question, but it did, anyway. She prayed she wasn't sending her baby from the frying pan into the fire.

Kade eased down his hands, looked at her. Then looked at Leah, who was in Bree's lap. "Yeah." He no doubt knew everything Bree was feeling because he was feeling it, too. He paused. "I also need to make arrangements for you."

Bree shook her head. "Once Leah is away from the danger, what I'd really like is a showdown with whoever's responsible for this."

That sent another jolt of anger through her. She wanted to find this person fast and be the one to put them in jail or do what Kade had just done. End it with a bullet.

"You're up for that?" Kade questioned.

Probably not. Her hands were still shaky, and she felt years removed from her FBI training. Right now, she felt like a mother with a child who'd just been placed in harm's way. And that was a far stronger motivation than she'd ever had to bring down a criminal.

Bree touched her daughter's cheek, and even though Leah's eyes were closed, she gave Bree one of those baby smiles. The feeling of warmth replaced the anger. But not the determination for Bree to keep her safe.

However, Leah wasn't the only person for her to be concerned about.

"Are you okay?" she asked Kade. "And before you give me a blanket *I'm fine* answer, I'd like the truth."

Kade stayed quiet a moment. "Ever killed a man in the line of duty?"

"Once." A cut-and-dried case of defending herself, just as Kade had done.

"It doesn't get easier," Kade mumbled.

Bree rubbed his arm and hoped that would help. But how could it? He'd done what he had to do, but he'd also have to come to terms with taking a life.

Yet something else they had in common.

As if they needed more.

Sometimes, like now, Bree felt that Kade and she were speeding headfirst, no helmets, into a brick wall. One of them, or both, would get hurt, but there didn't seem to be anything that would stop it. She didn't know whether to fight it or just save her energy and surrender.

Grayson ended his call, and when he didn't make another one, both Kade and Bree looked at him.

"The dead shooter's name is Tim Kirk," Grayson explained. "He worked as a security guard at the Fulbright clinic during your undercover investigation."

Maybe that's why he'd seemed familiar to Bree. "Kirk's connected to one of our suspects?" And she

didn't include Coop in that list, despite what Anthony
had told them during his visit to the ranch.

"He is. And he's also connected to the man who tried
to kill you at the motel. Mason checked Kirk's cell,
and yesterday morning he called the prepaid phone of
the triggerman who turned up dead." Grayson paused.
"However, the last person he called was Anthony."

Anthony, who'd accused Coop of wrongdoing. Of
course, that accusation hadn't gotten Anthony's name
off their suspect list. Now he was at the top of it.

"SAPD is sending someone over to Tim Kirk's apartment to check it out now. There might be more evidence linking him to Anthony. Or one of the others,"
Grayson added.

Maybe Coop, judging from Grayson's tone. Well,
good. Bree wanted them to look, but she was sure they
wouldn't find anything.

"While they're at Kirk's place, I hope they'll search
for those surveillance backups that went missing from
the Fulbright clinic," Kade reminded him.

"They will." Grayson shrugged. "But unless Kirk
was planning to use them to pin the blame on someone else, those backups might have been destroyed."

Yes, Bree had considered that. She had also considered if that had happened, they might never have
enough evidence to convict any of their suspects to
long jail sentences. Heck, it was possible that even with
a conviction Anthony and Jamie would get as little as
probation.

Kade and she needed more evidence.

Grayson looked at Bree. "Any luck remembering
where you were held during your pregnancy? Because
there might still be some evidence there we can use."

Bree pushed her hair from her face and forced herself to think. "It was a house in the country." Which she'd already told them. "High brick fence with guard dogs. Dobermans." She shook her head. "I can remember the rooms clearly now, but I can't tell you what was past that fence."

If that disappointed Grayson, he didn't show it. "When one of the kidnappers helped you escape, do you have any idea how long it took you to get from the fenced house to the motel?"

Those images weren't so clear. In fact, they were nonexistent.

"I don't have a clue about the time frame, but I do know we didn't go directly from the house to the Tree-top motel. We went to another hotel first. In Austin, I think. And she gave me a heavy dose of drugs before we left." Bree stopped a moment. "But she was in a hurry. The man wasn't there, and she said we had to get out before he came back because he was going to kill me."

Since Kade's leg was touching her, she felt him tense. "Why did he want to kill you?" Kade asked. "Leah was gone by then. Why did he or his boss feel you were no longer of any use to them?"

Again, Bree forced herself to think. "Maybe I saw something. Or maybe something changed in his situation. His boss might have found a different kind of leverage to tamper with the investigation."

But what?

Bree drew a blank on all counts.

"It sounds as if you were around the female kidnapper a lot," Grayson commented. "Any chance it was Jamie Greer?"

"A good chance," Bree admitted. "The height and body build are a match." Still, she had to shake her head. "But she certainly didn't dress like Jamie, and the prosthetic mask was very good. I couldn't see any of her features behind it." She shrugged. "Of course, the drugs probably helped with that. Hard to see a person's features when they're swimming in and out of focus."

"Keep trying to remember," Grayson insisted after a nod. He checked the time and blew out a weary breath. "McClendon, Anthony and Jamie are all on their way to my office. Or they sure as heck better be. If not, I warned them they'd all be arrested."

Good. Maybe they would defy that order, and that would get them tossed in jail. A temporary stay was better than nothing.

"I need you to help Mason question them," Grayson added, his attention on Kade. "Are you up to it?"

"Absolutely." Kade got to his feet. "Anthony accused Bree's boss of being a dirty agent, said he had a witness. Maybe he'll bring that witness with him."

Bree adjusted the baby to the crook of her arm and stood, too. "I'd like to get in on this."

The brothers exchanged glances and were no doubt thinking she wasn't mentally or physically ready for this. She wasn't, but that wouldn't stop her. "When I hear what they have to say, it might help me remember where I was held captive."

Grayson finally nodded. "Tape the interviews and follow the rules. If one of them is guilty, I don't want them slipping through the cracks on a technicality."

Bree was on the same page with that. Someone would pay for what had happened. Hopefully, it wouldn't be Kade, her or Leah.

"It's time," Grayson said, and with those two little words, Bree knew exactly what he meant.

Kade did, as well, because he leaned over and kissed

Leah's cheek. "This won't be for long," he promised the baby in a whisper.

Bree kissed her, as well, but she didn't trust her voice to speak. Oh, mercy. This was much harder than she'd imagined it would be; something she hadn't thought possible.

"Three of the ranch hands are making the drive with us," Grayson let them know. He picked up the diaper bag, looped it over his shoulder and then walked closer.

Waiting for Bree to hand Leah over.

Bree gave her baby one last kiss. Kade did the same. And she eased Leah into Grayson's waiting arms.

"I'll take good care of her," Grayson promised. And just like that, he hurried out of the room.

Bree's heart went with him.

Tears stung her eyes, and she blinked them back when Kade slipped his arm around her.

"Everything will be okay," he said, his voice clogged with emotion. He cleared his throat. "And the sooner we question our suspects, the sooner we can maybe end this."

So that Leah could come home.

Well, come to the ranch, anyway. It was her home, of course, but Bree knew that might change when Kade and she worked out some sort of custody arrangement.

"Let's go to the sheriff's office," he insisted, and with his arm still around her, he led her to the door where Grayson had just exited.

Kade stopped.

He looked down at her and opened his mouth. Closed it. Then shook his head. "Later," he mumbled.

Bree nearly pressed him for an answer, but she wasn't sure she wanted to open any cans of worms with Kade right now. One thing at a time, and the first thing was to get through these interrogations.

By the time they made it outside to Kade's truck, Grayson had already driven away. *To safety,* Bree reminded herself again. And if Kade and she could do their jobs and make an arrest, their time apart from Leah would be minimized. That was all the motivation she needed to end this quickly.

"What if Anthony produces a witness who says that Coop is dirty?" Kade asked her. He started his truck and headed for town.

"Then, I'll assume Anthony paid off the person to lie." Bree figured this wasn't the answer Kade wanted to hear. She stared at him. "Why are you so willing to believe Coop worked for McClendon?"

He stayed quiet a moment, mumbled something she didn't quite catch. "For the worst of reasons." Another pause. "I think I might be jealous of him."

"What?" Bree couldn't get that out there fast enough.

"This is hard for me to admit, but Coop seems possessive of you."

"In a boss to employee sort of way," she clarified. "There has never been anything personal between Coop and me."

"You're sure he knows that?"

Again, she jumped to answer, but then stopped. And Bree remembered something that'd happened over a year ago. "Coop kissed me."

"He did what?" Kade volleyed glances between the road and her.

"He'd had too much to drink. And he apologized."

Kade made a *yeah-right* sound.

"Hey, you kissed me, and you apologized," Bree reminded him.

"The apology was a lie. I'm attracted to you and so is Coop." He cursed. "But that attraction probably means he wouldn't betray you."

Bree felt relieved. For a moment. However, the uneasy feeling came. "I pushed him away that night," she recalled. "I told him I didn't feel that way about him."

She waited for Kade to say something about a scorned man seeking revenge, but he only shrugged. "If you hadn't been kidnapped, he probably would have tried again. I would have," Kade added in a mumble.

Bree stared at him. Yes, he would have. "If you hadn't, I would have," she confessed. "And if you think that pleases me, think again."

Despite the seriousness of the conversation, the corner of his mouth lifted, and she got a hint of that killer smile once more. "I just don't want you to think that the attraction I feel for you has anything to do with Leah."

She'd been on the verge of smiling herself, but that stopped it. Bree shook her head.

"I'm not trying to work out custody issues with you in bed," he clarified.

Oh.

At first there was a jolt of anger, that maybe Kade would think that's what she was trying to do. But she kept staring at him and didn't see any sign of it.

The only sign she saw was the confirmation that what she felt for him had zilch to do with Leah. Or with the danger. It had to do with the fact that he was, well, hot.

She groaned and leaned her head against the window. "Sex should be the last thing on my mind right now."

"Yeah," Kade agreed.

That didn't make it true.

Both of them knew that.

"I'm thinking when you're a hundred percent, we just get it over," he continued. "I mean, we worked ourselves up on the assignment. Now the close contact is steaming things up again. If we could just find the time to jump into bed, that might cool us down."

Her smile came, anyway. "Is that some kind of invitation to your bed?" Oh, yes. Headfirst into that brick wall.

He took her hand, lifted it and brought it to his mouth to kiss. "I already have you in my bed, but you're not in any shape for sex."

Her mind agreed.

Her body didn't.

And Bree was about to blurt that out when Kade's phone buzzed. He answered it but said little so she couldn't tell if the caller was Grayson. Soon, she'd want to contact Kade's brother and make sure the trip to San Antonio had gone smoothly.

Bree prayed it had.

"Let me know if you find anything," Kade said to the caller, and he hung up. "That was Nate, my brother at SAPD. It's not about Leah," he quickly added.

Good thing, too. Her mind wasn't going in a good direction on this.

"Nate sent one of his detectives to Tim Kirk's apartment, but it's been ransacked. His wall safe had been opened, and it was empty."

Definitely not good. Any potential evidence had probably been destroyed or contaminated. Still, Bree had a gut feeling that Kirk was the person who'd kidnapped her. Proving it, though, would be a bear.

But then, as Kade was pulling into the parking lot of the sheriff's office, she saw someone who could maybe clear all of this up.

Anthony.

He was heading inside the front door of the building. For the interview no doubt, but he clearly wasn't happy about being there. And he was alone.

No witness.

However, that wasn't the only thing Bree wanted to question Anthony about. It was that phone call that Kirk had made to him.

Kade and she got out of the truck, and both checked their surroundings. Old habits. Plus, the events of the morning still had her on edge. Bree wished that she'd at least brought a firearm with her just in case someone had already hired another hit man, but she'd given Kade back the little Colt that he carried in his ankle holster.

They stepped inside the back entrance, but the sound of the voice stopped them. A voice that Bree recognized.

Hector McClendon.

And whomever he was talking to, it wasn't a friendly conversation. McClendon was speaking in whispers, but the anger in his tone came through loud and clear.

Kade pointed to the last room on the right and put his finger to his mouth in a stay-quiet gesture. Bree did, and she listened.

"I don't know what game you're trying to play," McClendon snarled. "But I'm warning you to keep your mouth shut. If you don't, Bree Winston isn't the only person who'll be on the business end of a rifle."

Chapter Ten

Kade couldn't wait to see the face of the person that Hector McClendon had just threatened. He stepped into the doorway.

And saw Jamie Greer.

Both McClendon and Jamie snapped toward Kade and Bree. Jamie's eyes were wide, and she appeared to be shaken. Not McClendon, though. He just cursed. It was ripe, raw and aimed at Kade and Bree.

Especially Bree.

The venomous look the man gave her made Kade want to punch his lights out. *Great.* No objectivity left, and while punching McClendon might make him feel a little better, it wouldn't do anything to help their investigation.

"Eavesdropping," McClendon barked. "Figures."

Kade shrugged. "If you want your death threats to be more private, maybe you shouldn't do them in a sheriff's office."

"It wasn't a death threat. It was a warning."

"Sounded like a death threat to me," Bree spoke up.

Kade waited, gauging Jamie's reaction, but the woman didn't have much of one other than the obvious fear.

"Deputy Garza is waiting to interview me," Jamie

said, and she stepped around the three of them and headed up the hall.

Deputy Melissa Garza, known as Mel, would no doubt fill in Kade later if Jamie volunteered more about the threat.

"And your brother is waiting to interview me," Mc-Clendon informed them.

Bree blocked the man's path when he started out of the room. "Just to let you know, your intimidation tactics won't work. I'm testifying against Anthony and Jamie, and I'll testify against you too the second charges are filed. And they will be filed."

"Really?" McClendon stayed calm and cool. "You'd testify against me? You think a jury will listen to a woman who has gaps the size of Texas in her memory?"

Bree looked ready to demand how he knew about her memory issues, but she stepped back. The man was on a fishing expedition, probably, and Kade didn't want Bree to provide him with anything that he could in turn feed to his team of attorneys.

Well, McClendon couldn't have known about the memory gaps unless Coop had told him. But Kade had enough on his plate without looking for another angle on this. And the biggest thing on his plate came walking up the hall toward him.

Hector McClendon's son, Anthony.

He spared his father a glance. The two didn't speak. The senior McClendon walked off and disappeared into one of the interview rooms where his attorneys and Mason were no doubt waiting for him.

"I told you that Coop would try to silence you," Anthony said to Bree the moment they were alone.

Kade didn't respond, but he did step into the interview room across the hall, and he motioned for Anthony and Bree to join him. Once they were inside, Kade made a show of hitting the record button on the camera that was mounted in the corner.

Anthony's eyes narrowed, first at the camera, then at Bree.

"I stand by what I said," Anthony insisted. He sank down into one of the chairs.

Bree leaned against the wall. "But yet you didn't bring the witness who could corroborate your allegation."

His eyes narrowed even more. "The witness wasn't available at such short notice. Tomorrow."

Kade wouldn't hold his breath. He took the chair across the table from Anthony, whirled it around and sat with the chair back facing Anthony.

"Today, we'll talk about Tim Kirk," Kade started. "Oh, and for the record, you do know you have the right to remain silent and the right to have an attorney present—"

"You're reading me my rights? Well, I already know them." He paused only to draw breath. "You planning to take me back in into custody, Agent Ryland? Because I have to tell you that I'll press to have your badge removed for an illegal detainment."

"Won't be illegal if I have cause," Kade tossed back.

"Tim Kirk," Bree prompted. She moved closer, propped her hip on the edge of the table and put on her best law enforcement face. "He tried to kill us earlier."

Anthony couldn't have looked more disinterested. "So?"

"So, guess who was the last person Kirk called before the attempted murder of two federal agents, a deputy sheriff, multiple civilians and a seven-week-old baby?"

Now Anthony was interested, and those once-narrowed eyes widened. "He didn't call me."

Kade nodded. "Yeah. He did. And unlike your mystery witness, I have real proof of it. I have Kirk's cell phone."

"Well, I don't have mine. It went missing yesterday." Anthony stopped and groaned. "I thought I'd lost it, but it's obvious someone stole it so they could set me up."

Kade huffed. Of course the man would come up with something. "Who would do that to you?" Kade pressed. And he would bet his next paycheck that Coop's name was going to roll off Anthony's tongue.

But it's a bet he would have lost.

"My father," Anthony answered.

Bree flexed her eyebrows. "And why would he do that?"

"To make me look guilty, of course. Don't you see? He's desperate, especially since his overpriced lawyers haven't been able to stop the investigation. Now that you're back in the picture, he's got to be thinking he's just days away from being arrested on something more serious than misdemeanors."

Bree and Kade exchanged glances, and she was probably thinking about the encounter they'd just overheard between McClendon and Jamie. Anthony was right about one thing—his father was indeed desperate.

"You have any proof that your father stole your phone?" Kade asked.

Anthony shook his head. "But he had the opportunity because he came to see me last night. He could have taken it when I stepped out of the room to take a call on my house phone."

Bree stared at the man, probably trying to determine if everything coming out of his mouth was a pack of lies.

Or the truth that made his father look very guilty.

"Why did he visit you?" Bree questioned.

"Probably to steal my phone," Anthony practically yelled, but he settled down almost immediately. "He said he was worried about you, that the person who kidnapped you probably wasn't done. That he or she would want you dead because you might remember something that would get the person arrested."

"Persons," Bree corrected. "Two people held me captive, and I think one of them was Tim Kirk. He's linked to you with that phone call."

"Keep digging. He's linked to my father, too, because dear ol' dad is the one who hired Kirk to work at the clinic. Security," he added with a smirk. "The man was as dirty as they came, and my father hired him."

That may be, but it still didn't mean McClendon had paid Kirk to kidnap Bree or to try to kill her.

"Go ahead, access my cell phone records," Anthony insisted. "Maybe you'll be able to see that the phone wasn't at my house. I tell you, my father stole it."

Kade wasn't sure he could get that kind of info from the records, but he'd try. After all, he was pretty sure McClendon was a criminal for the things that had gone on at the clinic, and it wasn't much of a stretch for the man to try to put the blame on someone else.

Including his own son.

Anthony stood. "I think I should consult my lawyer now. Because it's clear I'm not making any headway with you two. Believe what you will. But watch your backs when you're around my father or any of his cronies. That includes Agent Cooper."

Kade considered stopping Anthony. Maybe putting

him in lockup for a few hours until his lawyer could arrive. But that wouldn't accomplish much other than to give Kade some satisfaction that someone was paying for what'd happened to Bree. The problem was, he wasn't sure Anthony was the right someone.

So he let the man walk.

Kade stood, turned off the camera just as Bree huffed.

"How soon can you get someone on Anthony's cell records?" she asked.

"I can do that with a phone call." Kade paused. "And while I'm doing that, I can see what's happening with the search into Coop's financials."

That hit a nerve. Bree dodged his gaze, huffed again. "I'm guessing the agents have found nothing or they would have called."

"Yeah, that's my guess, too." Another pause. "That doesn't mean they won't find something eventually."

"I know." She nodded. "I know. But unless they do, McClendon and Anthony are looking better and better for this. Is there a chance we can get Anthony's bond revoked, or bring some charges, any charges, against McClendon?"

"It's possible." And Kade would try. "There were some financial irregularities at the clinic that we could use to arrest McClendon. But either of them could still try to get to you even if they're behind bars."

He ran his hand down the length of her arm. Felt her shudder. She was no doubt reliving the worst of the moments of the attacks that had led up to this.

"Let's go back to the ranch. Mason and the other deputies can handle these interviews, and I'll see about setting up a video call with Grayson."

Her eyes lit up. "So we can see Leah."

Yeah. Seeing images of their baby would have to do for now. And maybe it wouldn't be long before they had the real thing.

Kade led her into the hall, but they'd made it just a few steps before Jamie stepped into the hall, as well.

"I have to speak to you," she mouthed. And she looked all around as if she expected them to be ambushed.

That put Kade on full alert, and he eased Bree behind him. He put his hand on the gun in his holster.

"What do you want?" Kade asked, and he didn't use his polite voice. He was sick and tired of all the suspects and just wanted to get Bree out of there.

Jamie looked over her shoulder again and reached into her purse. That had Kade tightening the grip on his gun, but Jamie didn't draw a firearm. She pulled out a small folded piece of paper and handed it to Bree.

"Read it," Jamie instructed. "Not here. And don't let anyone else know that I gave it to you. If anyone else is involved, I'll call the whole thing off."

Kade had no idea what Jamie was talking about. Apparently neither did Bree because she started to unfold the note.

"Not here," Jamie repeated, her voice still barely above a whisper. "It's not safe for anyone else to know."

And with that cryptic warning hanging in the air, Jamie turned and walked back into the interview room.

BREE LOOKED AT JAMIE'S note again, even though she already knew what it said. The message was simple:

I'll call you to arrange a meeting for tomorrow. By then, I'll have the answers you need.

"Answers," Bree mumbled.

Well, Kade and she were certainly short of those, but she wasn't sure that Jamie would be the one to provide them.

Neither was Kade.

"It could be a trap," Kade said, glancing at the note while he drove them back to the ranch.

Yes, it could be. Plus, there was another question. "Why didn't Jamie just give us these *answers* while we were at the sheriff's office?"

Kade lifted his shoulder. "Maybe because McClendon was there. Or maybe she doesn't have them *yet*."

Well, McClendon had threatened her just minutes earlier, so Jamie could be afraid of him. Still, something didn't add up. Bree wanted to suggest that they go back to the office and demand information, but that might cause Jamie to take back her offer.

Right now, that offer was pretty much all they had.

"So, what? We just wait for Jamie's call?" she asked.

He nodded though he didn't seem very eager to walk into a trap. Of course, doing nothing was just as dangerous. Bree was willing to do whatever it took to speed up the investigation and get Leah back.

Kade parked his truck directly in front of the ranch house porch, and even though there were several ranch hands there for their protection, Kade didn't dawdle. He held on to Bree and practically raced inside. Once he had the door shut, he armed the security system.

Bree stood there a moment to catch her breath and try to absorb everything that'd happened. Kade must have needed the same thing because he leaned against the door and drew in a long breath. But the breath-taking moment was over quickly.

"Our cook is at the estate in San Antonio, but I'll fix you some lunch," he said.

However, Kade had barely made it a step when his phone rang.

Kade mumbled something and pushed the button to answer the call on speaker.

"You're having me investigated," Coop immediately said. "You had someone dig into my financials."

"I did," Kade readily admitted. "It's standard procedure. Anthony McClendon made an accusation about you providing security to the clinic, and I had to check it out. Just as I've done with all leads."

"It's a witch hunt, and you know it." Coop's voice was so strained with anger that Bree barely recognized it.

She thought of the conversation earlier when Kade had admitted that he might be jealous of Coop. Bree was still trying to wrap her mind around that, but she didn't think for one second that jealousy was what had motivated Kade to investigate Coop.

"This had to be done, Coop," Bree spoke up. "We had to rule you out as a suspect. Standard procedure. You would have done the same thing if you were in my place."

Silence.

Her heart skipped a beat. "The investigation will rule you out, right?" And Bree hated that it was a question.

More silence, followed by more profanity. "It'll only muddy the waters more than they already are."

When Coop didn't add more, Bree glanced at Kade. And then she tried to brace herself for whatever they were about to hear from a man she'd been positive she could trust.

"I take security jobs on the side," Coop finally said.

"It helps with the child support and my old college loans."

Oh, mercy. "Did you work for McClendon at the Fulbright clinic?" Bree demanded.

"Not in the way you think," Coop snapped. But he paused again. "A friend of a friend put me in contact with McClendon about eighteen months ago. McClendon said he thought he had some employees skimming profits, and he wanted me to set up a secret security system in addition to the basic one they already had. So I did."

Each word was like a slap to the face, and Bree reached for the wall to steady her suddenly weak legs.

"Give me details," Kade ordered.

"McClendon paid me ten grand to set up equipment in his son's and Jamie Greer's offices. I monitored the surveillance for a couple of months, and then he said my services were no longer needed. That happened weeks *before* the two of you were sent in there undercover."

That wasn't exactly comforting, but it was something.

If it was true.

Bree just didn't know anymore.

"Why didn't you tell anyone this before now?" Bree asked, and she held her breath.

"Because I knew it would look bad. And I also knew it didn't have anything to do with the case. Like I said, this just muddies the waters. The whole time I was monitoring those phone taps and hidden cameras, I didn't see anything illegal going on."

Kade groaned softly and shook his head. "Are you telling me that during all of this, you didn't hear anything about the FBI's investigation of that clinic?"

"Not a word," Coop insisted.

That was possible because the investigation had been kept close to the vest, but Coop still should have come forward when he finally had heard about it.

And that brought Bree to another question that she didn't want to ask. But she had to.

"When did you learn about Kade's and my under-cover operation?"

Another stretch of silence. "Three days into it," Coop answered.

Her legs got even shakier. "The day our cover was blown and someone tried to kill us."

"I had nothing to do with that!" Coop snapped. "And I want all of this talk and accusations to go away. I've told my boss all about it, and it's the end of it. *Period.*"

Maybe the official end as far as the FBI was con-cerned, but it gave Bree some major doubts. Still, she couldn't believe that Coop would have known about her kidnapping and not tried to do something to stop it.

"Are you satisfied, Ryland?" The anger in Coop's voice went up a notch.

"No," Kade readily answered. "Not even close. If I find out you did something to endanger Bree and our daughter—"

"I didn't," Coop interrupted. "And everyone at the Bureau believes me. They know I'm a good agent." He paused again. "Bree, I need to see you. We need to talk alone. Say the word, and I'll drive out to see you right now."

Yes, they did need to talk, but it couldn't happen *right now.* "I'll call you when I can," she let him know.

Bree gave Kade a nod, and he pressed the end call button. They both stood there, silent, while Bree tried to absorb what she'd just learned. But that wasn't possible.

"Coop's the reason I have a badge," she managed to say.

Kade just nodded and pulled her into his arms. Until he did that, Bree hadn't known just how much she needed to be held.

This hurt, bad.

"Just wait until all the evidence is in, and we'll see where this goes," Kade said, and he pressed a kiss on her forehead. "It might not even lead back to Coop."

She eased back, looked up at him. "Even if Coop isn't dirty, he still should have said something about having worked for McClendon."

Kade could only make a sound of agreement.

And Bree felt as if her world had fallen apart.

The soft sobbing sound left her mouth before she could stop it, and it caused Kade to pull her back into his arms.

"Shhh," he whispered, his breath brushing over her face. "It'll be okay."

Bree wasn't sure she believed that and looked up to tell him, but everything seemed to stop. Not the pain. That was still there. So was the ache at being separated from Leah. But the whirlwind of thoughts about Coop and the investigation came to a grinding halt. She was instantly aware of Kade. Of his arms. Of the way he made her feel.

Without thinking, she came up on her toes and kissed Kade.

He made a sound, too. A low rumble that came from deep within his throat, and he snapped her to him until her body was pressed against his.

And he kissed her right back.

But he did more than that. Oh, yeah. More. Kade

took control of things. His mouth moved over hers, and he parted the seam of her lips with his tongue.

The taste of him roared through every inch of her. She'd known the attraction was there. Had felt it. But this was more. It was a burning fire that the kiss fanned until it seemed more like a need.

His fingers dived into her hair, anchoring her head so that he controlled the movement. He didn't stop there. He turned her and put her back against the wall. And he put himself against her.

The sensations hit her hard. Not just the heat and the need, but the feel of his body on hers. It didn't help when he took that kiss to her neck.

Bree fought to get in a different position so that she could feel more of him, and she got it finally. The alignment brought his sex against her, and the intimate contact along with his lips and tongue on her neck were making her insane. She was within seconds of dragging him to the floor so they could do this the right way.

Or the wrong way.

She caught his chin and lifted it, forcing eye contact. "Are we ready for this?" she asked.

It no doubt sounded like a joke, but there was nothing humorous in Kade's eyes. That icy gray had turned fiery hot, and it was clear that he wanted her as much as she wanted him.

"Ready?" he repeated as if it were painful just to ask the question. He dropped back an inch.

"Sex will complicate things," she settled for saying.

He thought about that a few seconds. "Yeah." And he put another inch of space between them.

Bree hated the loss of his touch and the heat, but she was also aware that both could return in a snap. What she felt for Kade wasn't just going to disappear.

"When we have sex," he said, "it probably shouldn't happen on the foyer floor."

For some reason that made her smile. "The place is optional," she let him know. "But the timing isn't."

Almost reluctantly, he nodded. "Soon, then." And he came back at her with a kiss that could melt metal.

He pulled away, leaving her breathless and making her rethink her decision to delay this, just as Kade's phone buzzed again. She groaned because she thought it might be Coop, but this time it was Jamie.

As he'd done with Coop's call, Kade took the call on speaker. "We read your note," Kade greeted. "You have answers? Well, I'd like to hear them *now*."

"Not yet," Jamie answered, her voice strained with fear.

Or something.

Bree wasn't about to take anything this woman said at face value.

"Meet me tomorrow morning, both of you," Jamie explained. "Nine a.m. at the pond that's in the park on the edge of town. If you bring anyone else with you, the meeting is off. You'll never learn the truth."

Bree got a very uneasy feeling about this.

Apparently, so did Kade. "What truth?" he demanded.

Jamie groaned softly. "The truth about what *really* happened to Bree after she was kidnapped."

Chapter Eleven

Kade wasn't at all sure this meeting should happen, and Jamie's one condition had made him even more concerned.

They were supposed to come alone, or the meeting was off.

Kade understood Jamie's fear—feigned or otherwise—but he had a greater need to keep Bree safe. That's why he was taking precautions without violating Jamie's *come alone* command.

He ended the call with Mason and glanced over at Bree on the passenger's seat beside him. Her attention was fastened to the rearview mirror, no doubt making sure no one was following them. She also had her hand on the gun in the shoulder holster that he'd lent her.

After all, they could be driving into a trap, and he hadn't wanted her unarmed. Since he couldn't tuck her away safely, the next best thing was to use her agent's training to get them out of this.

"Mason's in place at the park," Kade relayed to her. "He's across from the pond and hidden in some trees. Jamie arrived a few minutes ago."

"Good." She paused. "Was Mason able to secure the area before Jamie got there?"

"More or less." It was the *less* part that was giving

Kade some second and third thoughts about this, and it wasn't too late to turn his truck around and head back to the ranch.

But then, they wouldn't be any closer to ending this investigation.

"Mason is armed with a rifle in case something goes wrong, and he has one of the ranch hands with him," Kade explained. "But there are a lot of places to hide in that park. Jamie could already have someone in place."

And by someone, he meant another hit man.

"You could wait at the sheriff's office," he suggested. After looking at her, he didn't want her in danger. So much for relying on her training. "I'll call Jamie and renegotiate another meeting place. A safer one."

"She'll just say no, and one restless night away from Leah has been enough. I want this to end."

Yeah. He couldn't disagree with that. Being away from Leah had sucked, but this meeting and Bree had also contributed to his lack of sleep.

Kade blamed himself for the Bree part.

The kissing session had left his body burning for her, and even though she'd slept in the guest room just up the hall from him, that brainless part of him below the waist hadn't let him forget that Bree was nearby. Brainless had also reminded him repeatedly that if he pushed, he could have Bree in his bed.

But it was wrong to push.

Even if he wanted to badly.

No, this was one of those situations where he had to leave the decision making to his brain.

Kade kept driving, through town and past the sheriff's office. Deputy Melissa Garza was inside and monitoring the lone security camera at the park. It wasn't at the best angle, but if she saw someone approaching the pond area, she had instructions to call Mason.

Not a foolproof plan, but maybe they'd get lucky.

He took the turn into the park and was thankful to see it practically deserted. Probably because it was a weekday, and it was still a little too early for an outing. Kade drove to the pond that was on the back side of the twenty-acre area, and he parked as close to it as he could. He had no trouble spotting Jamie.

The woman was seated at a picnic table and was wearing a dark green pants outfit that blended in with the summer grass and the leafy trees. She had on her usual sunshades and a baseball cap—probably her attempt at a disguise. Hard to disguise that bright auburn hair. She stood the moment Kade and Bree stepped from his truck.

"You came," she said on a rise of breath. Her skeptical tone let Kade know that she hadn't expected him to follow through.

Or else she was acting.

"You didn't give us much choice," Bree informed her. Like Kade, she kept watch on their surroundings. And on Jamie. Bree kept studying the woman to make sure she didn't draw a weapon on them.

"Let's make this quick," Kade told her right off the bat. "Give us the *answers* so we can get the hell out of here."

Jamie nodded, swallowed hard. "I want to make a deal. Immunity from prosecution in exchange for information."

Interesting. But somewhat predictable. Jamie was facing some jail time. "What information?"

But Jamie shook her head. "I need your word that you'll help me work a deal with the D.A."

Kade didn't jump to answer but finally said, "Sure." It was a lie. Maybe. If Jamie did help them end this, then he would see what he could do.

Jamie didn't jump to answer, either, and she sank back down on the table's bench. "About ten months ago I got a call from Tim Kirk, and he said there was a security problem that had to do with something going on at the clinic. He gave me an address to a house in the Hill Country, and when I got there, he was holding Bree captive. She'd been heavily drugged."

Bree pulled in a quick breath, and Kade figured she'd be taking a lot of those in the next few minutes.

"Why didn't you call the police or the FBI?" Bree asked.

Jamie glanced around again. "Because Kirk was blackmailing me. I signed off on one of the questionable surrogate deals."

"You mean an illegal deal," Kade corrected.

"Yes," Jamie said, her mouth tight now. "I didn't want to go to jail, and I thought he was only going to hold Bree long enough to try to influence the investigation."

"Influence?" Bree repeated. She cursed. "You let him inseminate me."

"I also helped you!" But the burst of energy seemed to drain her, and Jamie groaned. She turned that shaded gaze in Kade's direction. "I don't know who was paying Kirk, but the plan was to force you to destroy all the evidence that could incriminate anyone. Including me."

Ah, he got it now. "That's why you went along with it." So that there would be no evidence against her. But there was a problem. "The FBI doesn't have all the possible evidence so there's no way Bree or I could have destroyed it all. There are missing surveillance backups."

Jamie shook her head. "I have the backups."

Kade didn't know who looked more shocked—Bree or him. Now, this was something he hadn't expected to hear in the meeting.

"Where are they?" he demanded.

"Hidden safely away. They're my insurance that Kirk's boss won't come after me. He knows there's enough incriminating evidence on them to put him in jail for years. McClendon knows I have them, too."

Well, that explained the threat McClendon had made at the sheriff's office.

"McClendon knows you're trying to cut a deal with us?" Bree asked her.

"I don't think so." But Jamie didn't sound at all convinced of that. "McClendon threatens me a lot, but I've told him that if something happens to me, then those backups will find their way to the FBI."

Kade gave that some thought. If what Jamie was saying was true, this gave McClendon motive for trying to use Bree. Of course, maybe those backups showed someone else engaged in criminal activity.

Like Coop.

Anthony.

Or even Jamie herself.

"You can give us a copy of the backups," Kade suggested. "And that way you'd still have the originals to keep yourself safe."

"The backups can't be copied," Jamie explained. "It's the way McClendon set up the system. The backups have an embedded code to wipe them clean if anyone tries to burn a copy."

Well, hell. Now Kade had to figure out a way to get the originals from Jamie. If the woman really had them, that is.

He wasn't sure she was telling the truth. About this. Or about anything else.

"I wasn't there when Kirk or whomever did the insemination on Bree," Jamie went on. "I wasn't there for the C-section, either. But later Kirk told me that the obstetrician had been killed." Jamie shivered. "He even showed me a picture of a mutilated body and said the same thing would happen to me if I didn't keep my mouth shut."

Kade huffed. "You're an accessory to murder."

Jamie frantically shook her head. "No. I swear, I didn't know until afterward, and that's when I knew I had to do something. Kirk was saying they didn't need Bree anymore, that the baby was leverage enough to get you to cooperate."

Yes, and it might have worked. Kade would have done anything to protect Leah.

"So, how did you talk Kirk into keeping me instead of Leah?" Bree asked.

"I didn't. Couldn't," Jamie corrected. "He ordered me to take the baby to a house in San Antonio where a nanny was waiting and when I returned he was going to kill you. Instead, I drove the baby to the Silver Creek hospital and left her there."

Because Bree didn't look too steady on her feet, Kade moved closer to her. Not too close, though, because he wanted them both to have room to draw their guns if something went wrong. There was still a chance of that happening. Whoever had hired Kirk wouldn't want Jamie to spill this.

"Kirk couldn't have been pleased about you not delivering the baby to San Antonio." Kade made a circling motion for Jamie to continue.

Jamie touched her hand to her lips. Her fingers and

mouth were trembling. "He wasn't. I told him someone
had run me off the road and kidnapped her. He was
furious and said he had to see his boss immediately. I
knew I had to get Bree out of there, too."

"But you didn't, not right away," Bree reminded her.
"Why?"

"Because Kirk kept watching me. He didn't trust me
after what happened with the baby. Then one night I
slipped him a drug, and that's when I went on the run
with you. When I was sure I wasn't being followed, I
left you at that motel and then made the anonymous
call so Kade could come and get you. Before Kirk did."

Well, it had worked. So far. Bree and Leah were both
alive, and the man partly responsible for what had happened—Kirk—was now dead.

Kade moved closer to Jamie, hoping it would make
her nervous enough to tell them whatever else she was
keeping from them. "Who was Kirk's boss?"

"I don't know." She answered without hesitation.
"Kirk used to call him, but I never heard him say the
person's name. I always assumed it was McClendon."

Good assumption.

But it could be a bad one.

Kade glanced at Bree and realized she was no doubt
thinking the same thing.

Bree cleared her throat. "Did Kirk do anything else
to me?"

Jamie looked in her direction for a moment. "No.
Nothing like rape or torture. He just kept you drugged
as much as he could. More so after the C-section."

Kade was relieved that other horrible things hadn't
been done to Bree, but Jamie was wrong about the torture. Being held captive while pregnant was the stuff

of nightmares, and he figured those nightmares would be with Bree for the rest of her life.

And someone would pay for that.

Kade took out the small notepad he kept in his pocket and dropped it on the table by Jamie. "Write down the address of the house where Bree was held."

Jamie shook her head. "They burned the place to the ground. Kirk told me that when he called to threaten me to stay silent."

Hell. But still a burned-out house was better than nothing. "I want the address, anyway," Kade insisted. He'd get a CSI team out there ASAP. Maybe they could find something that would give them clues about the identity of Kirk's boss.

Of course, the biggest clue might be sitting in front of them.

When Jamie finished writing the address, he took the note paper but kept staring at her. "I want those surveillance backups."

"I can't. I told you they're my insurance so that Kirk's boss won't kill me." Jamie yanked off her glasses, and he could see that her eyes were red. Maybe from crying. Kade had to consider that she was truly afraid, but he couldn't put that above Leah's and Bree's safety.

"You can give them to us." Bree also moved closer to the woman. "And you will. In exchange we'll provide you with protection."

Jamie jumped to her feet. "You can't protect me. No one can. My advice is for both of you to leave town for a while. Get lost somewhere and enjoy the time with your baby. Because as long as you continue this investigation, the danger will be there for all of us."

She turned as if to walk away, but Kade stepped in

front of her. "The backups," he reminded her. "I won't let you leave until you tell us where they are."

The threat was real and had no sooner left his mouth when he caught the movement out of the corner of his eye. Something in the trees. And it wasn't the spot where Mason had said he would be. This was farther down by the end of the pond.

Bree must have noticed it, too, because her head turned in that direction. "Get down!" she yelled.

But Kade was already moving. He latched onto Bree and Jamie and dragged them down with him. It wasn't a second too soon.

A bullet sliced across the top of the wooden table above them.

Chapter Twelve

Bree didn't take the time to berate herself for coming to this meeting in such an open place, but she might do that later. However, the bullet meant Kade and she were in a fight for their lives.

Again.

Since Kade was already holding Jamie and her, Bree drew her weapon and scrambled forward, using the table for cover. It wasn't much, but it was the nearest thing. The trees and their vehicles were yards away.

Mason, too.

Though maybe Mason was already trying to figure out how to stop what was happening.

Another bullet bashed into the table. Then another, until they were coming nonstop. Jamie screamed with each one and covered her head with her hands.

Kade turned, took aim in the direction of the shooter and fired.

Bree was ready to do the same, but Jamie's screams got louder, and the woman tried to bolt from the table. She probably thought she could make it to her car that was parked nearby. But Bree knew that once Jamie was out in the open, she'd become an easy target.

"The shots are going over us," Kade mumbled.

Somehow, Bree managed to hear him over the noise

of the shots, Jamie's screams and the sound of her
own heartbeat pounding in her ears. She listened and
watched.

Kade was right.

The first two shots had gone into the table, but these
were much higher.

Bree kept a grip on Jamie's arm, and she looked
where the bullets were landing. In the trees near Kade's
truck and Jamie's car.

"He's not shooting at us," Bree said. If Jamie heard
her, it didn't stop the woman from struggling.

There was another shot. Different from the others.
From the sound of it, it had come from a rifle.

Mason.

Thank heaven. Because the shooter stopped firing.

Bree shifted so she could try to see what was going
on, but in the shift, Jamie threw off Bree's grip. She
reached for the woman again, but Jamie bolted out from
beneath the table.

"Get down!" Bree yelled to her.

Jamie didn't listen to that, either. She got to her feet
and started running to her car.

She didn't make it far.

Another shot tore through the air, and Bree watched
in horror as it smacked into Jamie. The woman screamed
and fell to the ground.

Bree didn't think. She started toward Jamie, but she
felt Kade put a hard grip on her shoulder.

"No. You can't," he insisted.

And Bree knew he was right. If she went out there,
she'd be shot, too. In fact, that was probably what the
shooter wanted her to do.

Bree waited and watched while Jamie squirmed on
the ground and clutched her left arm. There was blood,

but thankfully it didn't appear to be too much. And the wound seemed to be limited to her arm. Still, she needed medical attention.

"I need your phone," Bree told Kade.

With his attention fastened on the area around the shooter, he retrieved it from his pocket and handed it to her. She called the emergency dispatcher to request backup and an ambulance.

"Stay down," Bree called out to Jamie the second she finished the call. Maybe, just maybe, Jamie would listen this time.

"No more shots," Bree heard Kade say.

He was right. There hadn't been another shot since the one that injured Jamie. And that meant either Mason had managed to neutralize the shooter or...

The thought had no sooner crossed her mind when Kade's phone buzzed. "It's Mason," Bree said.

"Answer it," Kade instructed since he was still keeping watch.

Bree pressed the answer button.

"He's getting away," Mason said. "I'm in pursuit through the east side of the park."

Oh, God.

This wasn't over.

"I heard," Kade let her know, and he moved out from beneath the table. "Stay with Jamie. I'm going after this SOB."

KADE KEPT LOW, STARTING away from Bree and Jamie, and he headed for the area around the pond where Mason had said he was in pursuit.

It was a risk.

And he had to do this in such a way that he could

still keep watch to make sure the shooter didn't double back and come after them again.

Specifically Jamie, since she seemed to be the target this time around.

He hoped her injuries weren't life-threatening, and while he was hoping, he added that the ambulance would be there soon. Backup, too.

Kade didn't want to leave Bree and her without as much protection as possible, but if Mason and he could catch this gunman then that could put them one step closer to making an arrest.

Behind him, Jamie was still yelling, and he could also hear sirens in the distance. Thank God. Kade threw a quick glance over his shoulder. Bree had stayed put under cover of the table, and she had her gun aimed and ready.

Good.

Kade followed along the edge of the pond. It wouldn't save him, but if the gunman started firing again, at least he could dive into the water. He hoped it wouldn't come down to that. Bree had already had enough shots fired near her today. Jamie, too.

He saw movement in the trees but didn't fire. Good thing, because it was Mason. His brother motioned to his right and then disappeared into the trees.

Kade hurried.

Mason was a good cop, but he didn't want him facing down a professional hit man on his own.

If that's what the shooter was.

Something wasn't right about all of this, but Kade couldn't put his finger on exactly what was wrong.

Kade heard the ambulance come to a stop behind him so that meant Jamie would soon have the medical care she needed. Added to that, the gunman hadn't fired in minutes so he was probably trying to get out of the area. Not stopping to take aim.

Neither did Kade.

He broke into a full run to the spot where he'd seen Mason. No sign of him yet, but he zigzagged his way through the trees and underbrush. Kade knew what was on the other side of the trees.

The back parking lot.

He listened for the sound of a car engine, but Kade couldn't hear anything over his own heavy breath and the sirens from both the ambulance and a deputy's car. Kade shoved aside some low hanging branches and ran out into a clearing that led to a hill.

Mason was there.

He had his left hand bracing his right wrist, and his gun was aimed at the parking lot.

His brother fired.

That made Kade run even faster. He barreled up the hill and caught just a glimpse of the black car before it disappeared around a bend in the road.

Mason cursed.

Kade did the same.

"Did you get a look at him?" Kade asked.

Mason cursed again and shook his head. "He was wearing a ski mask." He pulled out his phone and hit a button. A moment later, Kade heard the emergency dispatcher answer. "The assailant is driving a late model black Chevy on Elmore Road. He's armed and dangerous."

Kade knew the dispatcher would send out all available deputies to track down this guy, but he also knew it would only be a matter of minutes before the shooter reached the interstate. Once there, he'd be much harder to find.

"I'll do everything I can to catch up with him," Mason promised, and he started running toward the road where he'd no doubt left his truck.

Kade would have liked to go in pursuit, as well, but with the shooter already out of sight, he had to check on Bree and Jamie. He could still see through the trees, but he wouldn't breathe easier until he'd talked to Bree.

He made his way back through the wooded area and came out at the pond. There was a lot of activity already going on. An ambulance and two cruisers, one of which was speeding away—hopefully out to search for the shooter.

But Kade picked through all the chaos to find Bree.

She was there, next to the medics who were lifting Jamie onto a stretcher. Bree spotted him, and she hurried toward Kade, meeting him halfway. She went straight into his arms.

Right where Kade needed her to be.

"Are you okay?" she asked in a whisper.

He nodded. "You?"

"Okay."

But he checked her just in case. No signs of injury, thank goodness.

Kade automatically brushed a kiss on her forehead, looped his arm around her and went to the medic, Tommy Watters, who was strapping Jamie onto the stretcher.

Jamie's face was paper-white, and she was shaking from head to toe. "Did you catch him?" she asked Kade.

"No. But Mason is after him. We might get lucky."

Jamie groaned, and tears spilled down her cheeks. "You can't rely on luck. You have to catch him because he nearly killed me."

Kade assured her they would do everything to find

the shooter, and he turned to Tommy. "How is she?" Kade asked.

"Not bad. Looks like a flesh wound to me." The young medic followed Kade's gaze to those straps that Tommy was adjusting. "All this is just safety procedures. I'll take her straight to the hospital and have the E.R. doc check her."

"We need to be there in case the doctor releases her," Kade whispered to Bree.

She nodded, and they hurried to his truck. Later, there'd be a ton of paperwork to do—there always was when it came to a shooting—but it could wait. Jamie had said a lot of things, made a lot of accusations, and Kade didn't want her slipping away before she told them the whereabouts of those missing surveillance backups.

They got into his truck and followed right behind the ambulance as the siren wailed.

"You're sure you're okay?" Kade asked when Bree didn't say anything. She kept checking the area all around them. "Because I think that gunman is long gone."

"I agree." She squeezed her eyes shut a moment. "But I also think something about this wasn't right. The gunman wasn't really shooting at us. He kept the shots high despite the fact Jamie was under that table with us."

Yeah. Kade's thoughts were going in the same direction. "What are you thinking?"

"I hope I'm wrong, but maybe Jamie set all of this up to make herself look innocent."

Again, his thoughts were right there with Bree. "If so, it was working. Still is. After all, she got shot. That's a way to take blame off yourself."

Bree nodded. "But I watched her when you were running after the shooter, and she was stunned. And angry. I know people have a lot of reactions to being wounded, but something about this felt like a setup."

Kade made a sound of agreement. "Maybe we can press her for more info while she's at the hospital."

If her injuries were as minor as the medic seemed to think. If they weren't, then Bree and he would have to rethink their theory about this being a setup.

Kade stopped his truck in the hospital parking lot and got out, but he'd hardly made it a step when he saw the man walking toward them.

Anthony.

Kade stepped in front of Bree and slapped his hand on his gun.

Anthony held up his hands in mock surrender, but didn't stop until he was only a few feet away. He hitched his thumb to the ambulance that had stopped directly in front of the E.R. doors.

"I was at the sheriff's office when the call came in about the shooting," Anthony said. "Who's hurt?"

Kade considered being petty and not answering, but Anthony would learn it sooner or later. "It's Jamie. She was shot."

Anthony made a sound of stark surprise and dropped back a step. He looked at the medics as they lifted Jamie out of the ambulance and whisked her into E.R.

"Is she alive?" Anthony asked.

"Yes," Kade and Bree answered in unison.

It was Bree who continued. "In fact, according to the medic she'll pull through just fine." She stared at Anthony. "Bet you're all torn up about that."

His stark surprise turned to narrowed eyes. "I don't wish Jamie any harm, but she was a fool to think she could trust my father. Or Agent Cooper."

Bree huffed and folded her arms over her chest. "And you think one of them is responsible for this?"

"Who else?"

"You," Kade quickly provided. And he silently added Jamie's name to that list of possibilities.

"You're wasting your time trying to pin any of this on me." Anthony tapped his chest. "I've told you who's behind all of this, and yet both are still out on the streets. How many more shootings will it take for you to haul my father and his lackey FBI friend in for questioning?"

Right now, speaking to Jamie was his priority.

"Come on." Kade slipped his arm around Bree and started for the E.R. entrance.

"Jamie accused me of all of this, didn't she?" Anthony called out. "I'll bet she said she had some kind of proof of my wrongdoing. But let me guess, she didn't have that proof with her."

Kade and Bree stopped, and Kade eased back around to face him. Not because he wanted to see Anthony, but he wanted to make sure the man wasn't about to pull a gun on them.

"She doesn't have proof of anything," Anthony went on, "unless it's crimes she committed."

"I thought Jamie and you were friends of sorts," Kade reminded him.

"No. She's a viper. My advice? Watch your back around her, and don't believe a word she says."

Kade didn't intend to believe any of them, and this conversation was over. Even though Anthony continued to bark out warnings, Kade and Bree went to the E.R. and entered through the automatic doors.

The first person Kade saw was Tommy Watters, and he made a beeline toward them. "The shooting victim is in the examining room."

Good. Maybe it wouldn't take long, and then Kade could get Bree out of there. Even though she'd been stellar under fire, the spent adrenaline was obviously getting to her. It was getting to him, too. Besides, he needed to call Grayson and check on Leah.

Kade didn't stay in the waiting area since he wanted to keep an eye on Jamie and talk to the doctor about her injury. He led Bree past the reception desk and into the hall where there were examining rooms on each side. The first was empty. The second had a sick-looking kid with some very worried parents by his bedside.

Bree walked ahead of him, checking the rooms on the other side of the hall. She made it to the last one and whirled around.

"Where's Jamie?" she asked.

That was not a question Kade wanted to hear, and he started his own frantic search of the room. He cursed.

Because Jamie was nowhere in sight.

Chapter Thirteen

Bree had no idea what to think about this latest mess.
Had Jamie left on her own, or had she been coerced
into leaving the hospital?

Unfortunately, Kade and she didn't know the answer.

But after a thorough search of the area and the entire hospital, they hadn't been able to find the woman.
Heck, they hadn't even been able to find anyone who'd
even seen her. Jamie had simply vanished.

And without her, they couldn't get those backups.

Bree had pinned her hopes on the backups. Kade's
latest phone call was to his brother Mason, who still
was at the hospital reviewing the surveillance feed of
the two newly installed cameras. One in the hospital
parking lot. The other, fixed at the E.R. entrance where
just weeks earlier someone had left Leah. It was because of Leah's abandonment that the city had put the
cameras in place.

Kade was seated at Mason's desk at the sheriff's office, the phone sandwiched between his ear and shoulder, while he fired off messages to the rangers that he'd
asked to assist in the search for Jamie. That's because
all the deputies were tied up either providing protection
for Leah and the others or investigating the shooting.

Bree had personally verified the protecting Leah part

because, despite the need to find Jamie, she had an even greater need to make sure her baby was okay. Grayson, his wife and both sisters-in-law had assured Bree that all was well, but she wouldn't be convinced of that until she held Leah in her own arms.

Kade hung up the phone and shook his head.

Bree's hopes went south for a quick end to this.

"Nothing," Kade verified. "The camera angles are wrong to film someone leaving out the side exits."

Which Jamie had no doubt done since one of those side exits was very close to the examining room where the EMT had left her to wait for the doctor.

"What about the backups?" Bree asked. "Has SAPD had time to search her house for them?"

"They're there now, but they haven't found anything so far."

She groaned even though the search had been a long shot. Her house was probably the last place Jamie would have left them. But where could they be?

"The rangers and deputies will keep looking for Jamie and the shooter," Kade continued. "And we'll look for a money trail. If she's going into hiding, she'll need cash."

Bree rubbed the back of her neck and the pain that was starting to make its way to her head. "She'll need money if she left voluntarily."

Kade nodded, stood and went to her. He took over the neck massage. At first, it felt too intimate for his brother's office—for any place—but after a few strokes of those clever fingers, Bree heard herself sigh.

"Thanks," she mumbled.

"Why don't we get out of here so you can get some rest? Maybe we can do another video call to Grayson and check on Leah."

Until he added that last part, Bree had been about to say no, that they needed to stay and assist with the search and investigation. But she was tired, and more than that, she wanted to see her daughter's face.

Bree walked into the hall, but the sound of footsteps had her turning in the direction of the dispatcher's desk.

Coop was there.

And judging from his expression, he was not a happy man.

Great. Something else to add to her already nightmare of a day.

"The dispatcher's trying to stop me from seeing you," Coop called out. He nudged the woman aside, flashing his badge, and he headed right for Bree.

"I heard about the shooting," Coop said. "Are you both all right?"

"Fine," Kade said and stayed right by her side. "The deputies have things under control so Bree and I were about to leave."

"I have to talk to Bree first." Coop's tone was definitely all FBI. Oh, yes. This would not be fun.

"About what?" she asked. Bree didn't even try to take the impatience out of her tone. She really wanted out of there now and didn't want to go another round of pressure from Coop.

Coop, however, didn't budge. "You haven't called, and I thought I made it clear that you had a decision to make."

Oh, that.

Bree hadn't forgotten that Coop had ordered her into work, but there hadn't been time. "Put me on unpaid leave," she suggested.

But Coop only shook his head. "I've been keeping the powers that be off your back, but I can't do it any

longer, Bree. They want you in for some evaluations—
both physical and mental. You have to come with me
now."

"Now?" Kade and she asked in unison.

Coop lifted his shoulder. "I warned you this could
happen."

"Did you tell those powers that be that Bree is as-
sisting with an investigation?" Kade fired back. "And
that she's in danger?"

"Part of the reason she's in danger is because she's
here with you." Coop's mouth tightened. "If she'd come
into headquarters when I asked, she wouldn't have had
shots fired at her."

When Kade tried to maneuver himself in front of
her, maybe to take a verbal swing at Coop, Bree positioned herself so that she was face-to-face with Coop.
There was no need for Kade's career to suffer from this.

"My daughter is in danger," Bree stated as clearly
as she could to Coop. "I don't have time to go to headquarters for evals."

"Then you leave me no choice." Coop held out his
hand. "Surrender your badge. Because if you don't come
with me, you're no longer an FBI agent."

Bree's breath stalled in her lungs. Those were words
she'd certainly never expected to hear. Not from Coop,
not from anyone. The badge and her job had been her
life for so long now that they were *her*.

"You can't do this to her," Kade insisted.

Coop shook his head. "She's given me no choice.
But Bree can fix it all just by coming with me now."

If she went to headquarters, she'd get caught in the
whirlwind of paperwork and evals. There wouldn't
be time to search for Jamie or those backups. There
wouldn't be time for a video call to see Leah.

Bree suddenly felt drained and overwhelmed, but she knew exactly what she had to do. She took her badge from her pocket.

And handed it to Coop.

Coop's tight jaw went slack, and he just stared at her. Kade didn't say anything, either, but he gave her a questioning look.

"I'm sure," she said to Kade. "Let's go."

"You can't just go!" Coop practically shouted. He latched onto her arm, his grip hard and punishing. "You can't throw your life away like this."

Kade moved to do something about that grip, but Bree didn't want a fight to start, so she glared first at the grip and then at Coop.

"You asked for my badge and you got it. You're no longer my boss, and you'd better get your hand off me."

Coop let go of her, shook his head and stepped back. He added some raw profanity, too, and turned that profanity on Kade. "You've brainwashed her. Or else she's still too high on drugs to know what she's saying."

Bree had to fight not to slap him. "I'm not high. I'm tired—of you and this conversation." She headed for the back door and hoped Kade would follow rather than slug Coop.

With his voice low and dangerous, Kade said something to Coop, and she finally heard Kade's footsteps behind her. Thank goodness. She'd had enough violence for today. For the rest of her life.

"I'm sorry," Kade said, catching up with her. He hooked his arm around her waist. "I'll call my boss at headquarters and have him intervene. You'll get your badge back."

"Thanks, but I'm not sure I want it back." And Bree was surprised to realize that was true.

"You're a good agent," Kade pointed out.

"I *was*." She didn't say more until they had gone outside and were in Kade's truck. "But I can't go back to being a Jane. You said it yourself—motherhood and being a deep-cover operative aren't compatible."

"I said that because I didn't want to lose custody of Leah." He groaned, started his truck and headed toward the ranch.

"It's true," Bree insisted. "Besides, I'd like to take some time off and work out things in my head. And with you."

His eyebrow slid up.

"Not that way," she answered. But then she shrugged. Yes, maybe that way. "I have some savings," Bree went on. "I'm thinking about finding an apartment or a small house to rent in Silver Creek. That way I can be close to Leah." And Kade. But she kept that last part to herself.

Kade stayed quiet several moments. "You could stay at the ranch."

It was a generous offer but one she couldn't take. "Probably not a good idea while we're trying to work things out."

Several more quiet moments. "You could marry me."

Bree turned her head toward him so quickly that her neck popped. "What?"

"It makes sense. You could live at the ranch, and you wouldn't have to work. We could raise Leah together."

Bree just stared at him. "A marriage of convenience?" She shook her head. "Or more like a kept woman." Because in all of that, Kade darn sure hadn't mentioned anything about a real marriage.

"Just think about it," he snarled.

She didn't have to think about it. There was only one reason she would ever marry, and it was for love.

Period. And Kade obviously didn't love her because there'd been no mention of it.

Bree didn't love him, either.

But she was falling hard for him in spite of his making stupid, generous offers like the one he'd just made.

She mentally cursed herself. Falling for Kade would only make this more complicated. She didn't need a broken heart on top of everything else.

With the snarl still tightening his mouth, Kade took the turn toward the ranch. Where they'd likely be *alone* inside the house. Bree hadn't given that much thought, but she thought about it now—after his offer. She didn't want a fake marriage from Kade, but she did want *him*. And that meant being alone under the same roof with him wouldn't be easy.

His phone buzzed, and he put the call on speaker as he pulled to a stop in front of the house.

"This is Sgt. Garrett O'Malley at SAPD. Your brother asked me to call you."

"You found Jamie Greer?" Kade immediately asked.

"No. But we searched a storage facility that Ms. Greer had rented, and we got lucky. We found the surveillance backups that were missing from the Fulbright Clinic investigation."

Chapter Fourteen

Kade sat on the foot of his bed and waited for Bree to finish her shower. She'd been in there awhile, and he figured she wouldn't end it anytime soon.

Probably because she was trying to work out what had happened.

Kade could still see the look on Bree's face when Coop had demanded her badge and when she'd handed it to him. Coop had given her no choice, but that didn't mean Bree wasn't hurting. And Kade was hurting for her. The badge was a big part of who they were, and it had no doubt cost her big-time to surrender it.

Kade could also still see Bree's face when he'd suggested they get married. The timing had sucked, of course. And he hadn't meant to blurt it out like that. But it was something that had been on his mind since she'd first arrived at the ranch. While a marriage of convenience didn't sound ideal, it was a way for both of them to raise Leah and not have to deal with split custody.

Still, he'd made it seem more like a business merger rather than a proposal.

The question was—would Bree take him up on it?

He groaned, moved his laptop to the nightstand and dropped back on the bed. Kade was too afraid to close his eyes even for a minute because as tired as he was, he might fall asleep. To say the day had been long was a massive understatement.

It wasn't just the proposal. There'd been the meeting with Jamie. The shooting and her disappearance from the hospital. The confrontations with both Anthony and Coop. Followed by SAPD recovering those backups. They were in the process of reviewing them, and the sergeant had told Kade that once they finished the initial review, the backups would be delivered to the ranch by courier in a couple of hours.

It would take more than a couple of hours to go through them.

Maybe all night.

That's why Bree and he had gone ahead with the video call to Grayson and Leah before her shower. Their daughter had slept through the entire call, but it'd been good to see her precious little face.

When the bathroom door opened, Kade snapped back up and tried to look alert. Suddenly, it wasn't that hard to do when he caught sight of Bree. Fresh from her shower, her hair was damp. Her face, too. And the heat and steam had put color back in her cheeks.

No pink pjs but she was wearing a pink bathrobe that hit well above her knees.

"Darcy must have a thing for pink clothes," Bree said apologetically.

Obviously. And even though it wasn't Bree's usual color, it looked good on her. Too good. Especially the parts of her that the robe didn't cover. Those parts were the ones that latched onto his attention.

"Darcy said it was okay to check her closet." Bree fluttered her hand toward the doorway. "So, I thought I'd look for a pair of jeans."

She took a step but then stopped. Stared at him. "Is

something wrong? Is there a problem with the back-ups?"

"No problem." He stood, and to give his hands something to do, he crammed them into his jeans pockets. "They should be here in a couple of hours."

Hours, as in plenty of time to do something about whatever it was that was happening between them.

Bree nodded.

Kade figured the best thing to do would be to keep his distance from Bree. The air between them was changing. Heating up from warm to hot. He blamed it in part on the clingy bathrobe, but the truth was, Bree could be wearing anything and he would have had the same reaction.

Heck, he'd reacted to her while they were undercover.

She stood there, staring at him. Waiting, maybe. Kade didn't make her wait long. He started toward her just as Bree started toward him.

He pulled her into his arms.

The kiss was instant, hungry, as if they were starved for each other. That wasn't too far from the truth. Kade had wanted her for a long time now.

He eased back just a fraction to make sure she wasn't planning to stop this. She wasn't. Bree hooked her arms around him and pulled Kade right back to her.

The fire slammed through him. The need, too. And he knew he had lost any chance of looking at this with reason and consequences. Sex wasn't about reason. It was about the burning need to take this woman that had turned him inside out.

"Kade," she whispered with her mouth against his. It wasn't a soft romantic purr, either. There was an urgency to it.

Something Kade understood because he felt the same urgency.

They fell backward onto the bed, and the kiss continued. So did the fight to get closer. Body to body.

Kade took those kisses to her neck. And lower. He snapped open the robe and kissed her breasts. Bree arched her back, moving closer, and she made a sound of pure feminine pleasure.

A sound that kicked up the urgency a notch.

"Now," Bree insisted.

She meant it, too. She went after his shirt, pulling the buttons from their holes and shoving it off his shoulders. It was easier for Kade. All he had to do was pull off that robe, and underneath was a naked woman.

Well, almost.

Bree wore just a pair of white panties, and Kade would have quickly rid her of those if she hadn't played dirty. She ran her hand down his bare chest. To his stomach.

And below.

That crazy frantic touch let him know exactly what she wanted.

Kade turned her, rolling on top of her so he could work his way out of his jeans. Bree didn't help with that, either. She kept kissing him. Kept touching. Until he was certain he'd go crazy. But somehow, he managed to get off his boots and Wrangler jeans.

"Hold that thought," he mumbled when she dropped some kisses on his chest.

He leaned across to the nightstand and took out a condom. Good thing he remembered. With the fire burning his mind and body, and with Bree pulling him closer and closer, he was surprised he could remember anything, including his name.

Bree pulled him back to her the moment he had the condom on, and Kade landed with his body on hers. Perfect. Or not. Bree maneuvered herself on top, and in the same motion she took him inside her.

No more frantic touches or kisses.

Both stilled a moment, and their gazes met.

Kade saw the surprise in her eyes and figured she saw it in his. He'd expected this to be good. But not this good. This felt like a lot more than sex.

She started to move, rocking against him and creating the contact they needed to make that fire inside him flame high. The need built. Little by little. With each of the strokes inside her. However, even through his sex-hazed mind, Kade took a moment to savor the view.

Oh, man.

Bree was beautiful.

He'd known that, of course, but this was like a fantasy come true.

She pushed herself against him. Harder and faster. Until Kade felt her shatter. His own body was on the edge, begging for release, but still he watched her. He watched as Bree went right over the edge.

"Kade," she said. This time, it was a purr.

And he gathered her in his arms, pushed into her one last time and let himself go.

BREE COULDN'T CATCH HER breath, and she wasn't sure she cared about such things as breathing.

Every part of her was on fire but yet slack and sated.

At peace.

Strange. She'd thought that sex with Kade would cause immense pleasure followed by the feeling that they'd just screwed things up worse than they already were.

Well, the pleasure had been immense all right.

Maybe it would take a while for the screwed-up feeling to set in.

But for now, she would just pretend that all was right with the world while they lay there naked and in each other's arms.

Kade made a lazy, satisfied sound. A rumble deep within his throat, and as if it were something they did all the time, he pulled her against him and kissed her. The moment was magic. Perfect. And even though Bree tried to keep the doubts and demons at bay, she couldn't stop the thoughts from coming. Well, one thought, anyway.

What now?

She couldn't accept his marriage proposal. Yes, she cared for Kade. Was hotly attracted to him and vice versa. But that wasn't the basis for a real marriage. For that matter, neither was the fact that they had a child together.

Kade made another of those sounds, gave her another kiss. "I'll be right back." And he headed into the bathroom.

The walk there was interesting, and she got a good look at his backside. Oh, yeah. The man was hot, and that body appealed to her in a down-and-dirty kind of way. Too bad the rest of him appealed to her, as well.

Because this could lead to a crushed heart for her.

With that miserable idea now in her head, Bree got up, located her bathrobe and slipped it on. She was trying to locate her panties when the bathroom door opened, and Kade came back in the room.

Naked.

She got a good frontal view this time and went all

hot again. Mercy. She'd just had him. How could she want him this much again so soon?

His eyebrow lifted in not an approving way at the bathrobe.

"The backups will arrive soon," she reminded him. It was the truth, but it was that fear of a crushed heart that had her putting on the terry cloth armor.

He frowned, walked to her and pulled her back onto the bed. Kade also slipped his hand into the robe and cupped her breast. "We have at least another hour," he drawled. "My suggestion? We stay naked."

Bree laughed before she could stop herself.

And just like that, the moment was perfect again. No doubts. No worries of hearts. Kade sealed the moment with another of those searing, mind-draining kisses that reminded her that yes, they were indeed naked. Or almost. He shoved open the robe and kissed his way down from her mouth to her stomach.

At first Bree thought the sound was the buzzing in her head, but when Kade cursed, she realized it was his phone.

He rolled off the bed, grabbed his jeans from the floor and jerked out his phone. He glanced at the screen and shook his head.

"The caller blocked the number," Kade mumbled, and he put the call on speaker. "Special Agent Ryland."

"Agent Ryland," the person answered.

And with just those two words, Bree's blood turned to ice. Because it wasn't a normal voice. The caller was speaking through a voice scrambler.

"Who is this?" Kade demanded.

"Someone you're going to meet in an hour at the Fulbright Clinic in San Antonio."

The voice sounded like a cartoon character, making

it impossible to recognize the speaker. But that didn't mean she couldn't figure out who it was. After all, there weren't many people who would make a demand like that.

"The Fulbright is closed," Kade reminded the caller. "It's an abandoned building now."

"Yes." The caller paused. "And that's exactly why it's a good place for us to meet. Show up in one hour alone. Just you and Bree. And when you come, bring those missing surveillance backups with you."

Kade glanced back at her and groaned softly. This was no doubt one of their suspects. But which one? McClendon, Anthony, Jamie?

Or heaven forbid, Coop?

"We don't have the backups," Kade said.

"Yes, but you can get them from SAPD. And trust me, it'll be in your best interest to get them and bring them to me at the clinic."

The caller didn't raise his voice, didn't change his inflection, but the threat slammed through her.

"Leah," she mouthed.

Kade shook his head, pulled her down to him and whispered in her ear, "Grayson would have called if something had gone wrong with Leah."

True. If something hadn't gone wrong with Grayson, too. Maybe the missing shooter or one of the suspects had gotten into the estate and was holding them all captive.

"Call him," Kade whispered, and he pointed to the house phone on the nightstand next to Kade's laptop. And he mouthed the number.

"It won't do any good to try to trace this call," the voice on the phone said. "Prepaid cell. And I'll toss it once we're done here."

Bree kept one ear tuned to what was being said, but she grabbed the house phone and went to the other side of the room. Grayson answered on the first ring.

"Is Leah okay?" she whispered.

"Of course. Why? What's wrong?"

The breath swooshed out of Bree, and the relief nearly brought her to her knees. "Are you all okay? Is anyone there threatening you?"

"Not a chance. I have this place locked up tight with Nate and Dade standing guard. Why?"

Bree couldn't get into details, mainly because she had to figure out what exactly the details were. "We might have a problem. Kade will call you when he can." And she hung up so they could finish this puzzling call.

"Leah's okay," she relayed in a whisper to Kade.

The relief was quick and obvious.

"Give me one reason," he said to the caller, "why Bree and I would meet you and give you evidence?"

"One reason?" the person repeated. "Oh, I have a big one reason. Well, actually a small one, but I think it'll be a very big reason to Bree and you. Check your email."

Bree's heart was still pounding like crazy, and she wanted to dismiss all of this as some kind of ploy, but that didn't stop Kade and her from moving toward his laptop. It was already on so he clicked into his email and found a new one with an attachment.

"Click onto the link in the attachment," the caller ordered.

Kade did, and the link took them to an online video. One with very poor quality. It appeared to be a dark room, so dark that Bree couldn't make out anything in it.

"Let me move closer to the camera," the caller said.

There was the sound of footsteps. Still no light. But

as the footsteps got louder, she could just make out the image of someone. An adult. The person was cloaked in black. Maybe a cape with a hood. And the person was seated in a chair.

He or she was holding something.

Bree drew in her breath. Waited. And zoomed in on whatever was in the person's arms.

Oh, God.

It was a baby.

"Leah!" she practically screamed when she saw the baby's face.

"It's not her," Kade said, but he didn't sound convinced. "It's some kind of trick."

Yes. Bree forced herself to remember that Grayson had just told her that Leah was all right. Kade's brother wouldn't have lied, and he hadn't sounded under duress when he'd answered her.

"No trick," the caller assured them, the cartoon voice sounding smug. "But the baby isn't Leah."

Bree shook her head. It was a real baby all right. Dressed in a pink dress and wrapped in a pink blanket, she was asleep, but Bree could see the face.

A face identical to Leah's.

"Confused?" the caller mocked. "Well, I've been keeping a little secret. And the secret is the reason you'll both come alone to the clinic and bring me those tapes."

"Who's baby is that?" Kade demanded.

The caller laughed. "Yours. Yours and Bree's," he corrected.

"What?" Bree managed to say. She had no choice but to drop down onto the bed.

Kade didn't look too steady, either. "What do you mean?"

"I mean seven weeks ago, Bree gave birth to identical twin girls."

"Oh, God," Bree mumbled, and because she didn't know what else to do, she kept repeating it.

She stared at the face, at the shadows, and could only shake her head. What was going on?

"Here's the bottom line," the caller continued, the horrible voice pouring through the room. "If you don't want your second daughter to be sold on the black market, then you'll be here alone at the clinic in one hour. I'll trade the baby for the backups."

Chapter Fifteen

"Wait!" Kade shouted into the phone.

But it was too late. The caller had already hung up. And his computer screen went blank. Someone had pulled the plug on the video feed.

Behind him, Bree was gasping and shaking her head.

"It is possible?" Kade asked. "Could you really have had twins?"

She looked at him, her eyes filled to the brim with tears. "I suppose so. They sedated me for the C-section."

Kade cursed. Yes, it was possible this could be some kind of elaborate hoax, but it was too big of a risk to take to ignore it.

He wiped away her tears. "Get dressed. We're going after the baby."

Bree nodded, and even though she was shaky, she hurried to the bathroom where she'd left her clothes. Kade dressed, too, and he called his brother Grayson.

"We have a problem," Kade said when Grayson answered. "I don't have time to sugarcoat this or explain it other than to say I need those surveillance backups from SAPD. Someone called and wants the backups in exchange for a baby. A twin girl that Bree might have delivered when she had Leah."

"What?" Grayson snapped.

Kade ignored his brother's shock and the questions Grayson likely wanted answered now. "Just have an SAPD officer, one you can trust, meet us at the intersection of Dalton and Reyes in San Antonio."

"The Fulbright Clinic is near there. Kade, you're not thinking—"

"Bree and I have to go in alone. That's the condition."

Grayson cursed. "But it could be dangerous. It could be a trap."

Both of those were true. "What would you do if it were your child?" Kade fired back.

Grayson cursed again. "At least let me arrange to have some backup in the area."

"Only if they stay far away and out of sight. I'm figuring this guy has already set up some kind of perimeter surveillance. They'll know if we have someone with us."

"Who did this?" Grayson pressed.

"When I know, I'll you let know. For now, just get me those backups."

Kade ended the call, knowing his brother would make it happen. After all, his other brother Nate, was an SAPD lieutenant, and he could do whatever it took to have those backups ready and waiting for them.

He hurried, dressing as fast as he could, and by the time he'd finished, Bree ran out of the bathroom. Dressed and looking ready to panic.

"We can do this," he promised her and hoped it wasn't a lie.

Kade put on his shoulder holster and ankle strap, filled both with guns and extra ammunition, and he took his backup weapon from the nightstand and handed it to Bree. She also grabbed some extra magazines of bullets and stuffed them into her pockets. They couldn't go in there with guns blazing, not with a baby's safety at stake, but Kade had no plans to go in unarmed, either.

They both ran down the stairs, but Kade used the security monitor by the door to make sure no one had sneaked onto the ranch. When he was sure it was safe, they hurried outside to his truck, and he drove away fast.

"What about the backups?" she asked.

"Grayson will get them."

She nodded and made what sounded to be a breath of relief. But Kade knew neither of them would be in the relief mode until they figured out what the heck was going on.

"Think back," he told her. He flew down the ranch road and onto the route that would take them to the interstate. "When you were pregnant, did you have any indications there was more than one baby?"

"Maybe." Her forehead bunched up. "There was a lot of movement from the baby, a lot of kicking and moving around and I felt huge. But I figured plenty of pregnant women felt that way."

"They do." He'd gone through his sister-in-law's pregnancy and now Grayson's wife, and both had complained about their size. "What about an ultrasound?"

"They did one, but they didn't let me see the monitor."

Hell, probably because they hadn't wanted her to know that it was twins.

But why keep that from her?

One baby or two, Bree wasn't going to fight them back for fear of harming the child. Her captors had her exactly where they wanted her.

"The second baby is their ace in the hole," Bree mumbled. And she groaned. "I remember Kirk using that term, but I thought he was talking about me. Or Leah. I had no idea he was talking about another baby."

Kade mentally groaned, too. "What did Kirk say exactly?"

She lifted her hand in a gesture to indicate she was thinking about it. "He said it wouldn't do any good for me to escape, that he had an ace in the hole." Her gaze rifled to him. "But why would Kirk's boss wait all these weeks to tell us about the other baby?"

Unfortunately, Kade had a theory about that. "Maybe the boss thought you were dead and if so, you couldn't testify against him. When you resurfaced, that meant you became a threat."

She turned in the seat toward him. "But Jamie's the real threat because she's the one who had those back-ups."

He shook his head. "She wasn't a threat as long as she kept the backups hidden. After all, those backups implicated her in a crime, too. She didn't want the cops or us to have them. She wanted to hang on to them as her own ace in the hole."

Bree pulled in her breath, nodded. "Then SAPD found the backups and now all of this has come to a showdown."

A showdown where his baby could be in danger.

"Twins," he said under his breath. He had to accept that it was possible. And that meant he had to do everything humanly possible to save his child.

"I'm sorry," Bree whispered, her voice shaking hard. "I should have put all the little things together to know there was a second baby."

"You couldn't have known. This was all part of some sick plan, and keeping you in the dark was essential." He took the ramp to the interstate. "But Jamie should have known. Even if she wasn't there for your C-section, she must have heard Kirk talking to someone about it."

"Yes," Bree agreed. "So, why didn't she say anything at the park?"

Kade could think of a reason. A bad one. Maybe Jamie was the person behind all of this. Those backups could have been her protection from Kirk's boss.

Or Jamie could be the boss.

"This might be Jamie's way of getting the backups back," Kade pointed out.

Bree stayed quiet a moment and then nodded. "That would explain why we're just now getting the news of the other baby." Another pause. "There must be something incriminating that we don't know about on those backups."

Kade agreed. And the bad flip side to that was SAPD hadn't had time to review them. Neither had Kade and Bree.

"It's too big of a risk to take in fake backups," Bree said. "And we can't give him or her just one or two. This person knows how many backups there are."

She took the words right out of his mouth. No, the person would almost certainly verify they were real before he or she handed over the baby.

And then what?

Kade didn't like the scenarios that came to mind. But there was a possible good outcome.

Well, semigood.

"The person disguised his or her voice," Kade explained, playing this through in his mind. "So, it's possible we can do a safe exchange. The backups for the baby."

"And we just walk out of there," Bree added in a mumble.

Yeah. That was the best-case scenario. Kade didn't want to do any bargaining with this SOB while the baby was still in the picture. Later, once they were all out of there, he'd move Bree, the twin and Leah to another safe location.

Then, he'd go after the person who'd orchestrated this.

Of course, that was just the beginning. If the second baby was real, then he had another child. To love and raise. To protect. Another custody issue to work out with Bree.

Since all of that was only clouding his mind, he pushed it aside and focused just on now. And *now* started with getting the backups.

Kade drove into San Antonio and kept an eye on both Bree and the clock. The caller had given them only an hour to deliver the backups, and half that time was already gone. He hated to think of what would happen if they were late.

He slowed down when he reached the intersection of Dalton and Reyes, and Kade's heart nearly stopped when he didn't see anyone waiting for them. But then, his brother Nate stepped from the side of a gas station. Kade mumbled a prayer of thanks and pulled in, stopping right next to Nate.

"The backups," Nate said. He handed the evidence envelope to Kade when he lowered the window.

"Thanks." Kade dropped the envelope on the seat between Bree and him. "Did this put your badge on the line?"

Nate shrugged. Meaning, it had.

"I'm sorry," Kade told him. And he was. He knew how much the badge meant to Nate, but he also knew how much family meant to him. "Grayson told you about the baby?"

"Yeah." Nate looked over his shoulder in the direction of the Fulbright clinic only a block away. "I put some SWAT guys on the roof." He hitched his thumb to the three-story building not far from where they stood. "And I have six others waiting to respond. We haven't seen anyone outside the clinic, but we've only been here about ten minutes."

Kade mumbled another thanks, took out his phone and set it so that he could reach Nate with just the touch of one button. "What about using infrared to get a glimpse of who's inside?"

Nate shook his head. "We tried. No luck. The place used to be a radiology clinic, and infrared won't penetrate the walls."

Bree made a frustrated sound, and even though the timing sucked, Kade remembered that he hadn't introduced Bree to this particular brother. But it would have to wait.

"Be careful," Nate said, and he stepped back from the truck.

Kade nodded and drove away, making his way toward the clinic. Less than a year ago, Bree and he had to battle their way out of here and had run along this very street.

Maybe they wouldn't have to do that again.

The thought of trying to escape with a baby under those circumstances sickened him.

Bree pulled in a hard breath when Kade came to a stop in the clinic's parking lot. It was empty. Not another vehicle in sight. No lights, either. Even the ones in the parking lot were out—maybe because the caller had disabled them.

There was also a problem with the windows. Each one facing the parking lot had burglar bars. Thick metal rods jutting down the entire length of the glass. It would be impossible to use those to escape.

The moment Kade turned off the engine, his phone buzzed. The caller's info had been blocked, just like before.

"Agent Ryland," the scrambled voice greeted him when Kade answered. "So glad you made it. Do you have the backups?"

"I do," Kade hesitantly answered.

"Excellent. Both of you enter the clinic through the front door. I've already unlocked it. You're to put all your weapons and the backups on the floor—"

"I'll give you the backups when you give us the baby," Kade interrupted.

There was silence for several heart-stopping moments. "All right," the caller finally said. "Then, let's get this show on the road."

The person ended the call, and Kade looked at Bree to make sure she was up to doing this. She was. Yes, she'd cried earlier, but there weren't tears now. Just the determined face of a well-trained federal agent who would do anything to get her baby out of harm's way.

"If something goes wrong," Kade whispered, "I want you to take the baby and get out of there. I'll run interference."

She shook her head, and the agent facade waivered a bit, but she couldn't argue. The baby had to come first.

"We're all coming out of there alive," Bree whispered back. And she leaned over and kissed him.

Kade wanted to hold on to that kiss, on to her and that promise, but there wasn't time. "Stay behind me," he added, "and hide your gun in the back waist of your pants."

After she'd done that, he stepped from his truck. He waited until Bree was indeed behind him before they walked to the double front doors. He wished they were glass so he could see inside but no such luck. They were thick wood. Kade said another prayer and tested the knob.

The door opened.

Like the exterior of the building and the parking lot, the entrance was pitch-black, and he could barely make out what appeared to be a desk and some chairs. This was the reception area, and if anyone was there, he couldn't see, hear or sense them.

"Here's my gun," Kade called out, and he took his weapon and one of the extra magazines and put them on the floor.

"Now, the other weapons." The voice boomed over an intercom. The same scrambled voice as the caller.

"Weapon," Kade corrected. And he motioned for Bree to surrender her gun, as well.

Kade could feel her hesitation, but she finally did it. That only left them with the small gun in his ankle holster, and he hoped like the devil that the SOB on the intercom didn't know about it.

Behind them, there was a sharp click. Not someone cocking a gun. But maybe just as dangerous.

Someone had locked the door. That someone had no doubt used a remote control because Nate wouldn't have let anyone get close to the exterior side of the door.

"Kick the weapons down the hall," the voice ordered.

Kade did it, the sound of metal scraping across the tiled floor.

"Here," Kade whispered to Bree, and he handed her

his cell so if necessary she could make that emergency call to Nate. It would also free up his hands in case he had to go for the ankle holster.

"Where's the baby?" Kade asked, holding up the envelope with the backups.

"I'll have to verify the backups first. Walk forward, down the hall. Keep your hands in the air so I can see them at all times."

The *dark* hall. Where they could be ambushed and the backups taken from them.

"How about you meet us halfway?" Kade asked.

"How about you follow orders?" the person snapped.

"Because your orders could get us killed. Either meet us halfway, or show us the baby now."

More silence. And with each passing second, Kade's heartbeat revved up. Bree's breathing, too. Since her arm was against his back, he could feel how tense she was.

"Okay," the person finally said. "Start walking. I'll do the same."

It was a huge risk, but staying put was a risk, too.

Kade took the first step, then waited and listened. He heard some movement at the end of that dark hall, and he took another step. Then another. Bree was right behind him and hopefully would stay there.

If this goon sent in someone from behind, through those front doors, Nate's men would stop them. The same if a gunman tried to shoot through one of the windows.

So, the danger was ahead.

"There are two rooms ahead off the hall," Bree whispered. "One on the left. The other on the right."

Kade hadn't remembered that about the clinic layout, but he was thankful that Bree had. He would need to make sure no one came out of those rooms to ambush them.

Another step.

The person at the end of the hall did the same.

Now that Kade's eyes were adjusting a little to the darkness, he could see the shadowy figure better. Well, the outline of the person, anyway. He couldn't make out any feature and couldn't tell if it was a man or woman. The person seemed to be wearing some kind of dark cloak.

"When you get to the spot where the reception area meets the hall," the voice instructed, "take the backups from the envelope and hold them up so I can see them."

Kade made several more steps to get to that spot, and with his attention fastened on the figure ahead of him, he took out the backups and lifted them in the air.

Overhead on the hall ceiling, a camera whirred around, the lens angling toward Kade's hand. Either this guy had backup inside the building or else he was using a remote control device.

Kade was betting he had backup.

Behind him, he heard a buzzing sound. His phone. And Kade mentally cursed. "Answer it," he whispered to Bree, hoping that the person at the end of the hall hadn't heard.

She didn't say anything, but she pressed a button and put the phone to her ear. A moment later, she froze.

"What's wrong?" Kade asked, still trying to keep his voice low.

"You're sure?" she asked.

Kade was about to repeat his *what's wrong* question, but Bree latched onto his arm.

"It's a trap," she said. And Bree started to pull him to the floor.

But it was already too late.

The shot slammed through the air.

Chapter Sixteen

Bree pulled Kade to the right, out of the line of fire of the person in the hall.

Just as the bullet slammed into the locked door.

Kade and she slammed onto the floor. Hard. It knocked the breath right out of her, but Bree fought to regain it so she could get them out of harm's way.

If that was even possible now.

Thankfully, Kade could breathe and react because he grabbed her by the shoulder and dragged her onto the other side of the desk. He also drew the small Colt .38 from his ankle holster. It wasn't much firepower considering their situation.

And their situation was *bad*.

"Stop shooting!" Kade yelled. He shoved the back-ups inside his shirt. "You could hit the baby."

The person laughed, that cartoony voice echoing through the dark clinic. Bree knew the reason for the sickening laughter.

"There's no second baby?" Kade whispered to her on a rise of breath.

"Not here. That was Mason on the phone. About ten minutes ago a woman dropped off a baby at the Silver Creek hospital. A baby who looks exactly like Leah. She's all right. She hadn't been harmed."

The sound that Kade made deep in his throat was a mixture of relief and dread. Relief because their baby was all right, away from the monster who'd fired that shot at them. But the danger for Kade and she was just starting.

"Thank you for cooperating with my plan," the figure called out. "And see? I'm not such a bad person, after all. The woman I hired to take the baby to the hospital did exactly as I asked. So, all is well."

Kade cursed. "If all is truly well as you say, then you'll let us go."

"Can't do that."

Another bullet blasted into the door.

Kade's brother Nate would likely have heard the shots. He no doubt knew about the baby being dropped off at the hospital. But there was no way Nate could come in with guns blazing. Still, if Kade and she could make it to the window, they might be able to figure out a way through those burglar bars. Then Nate might be able to provide enough cover for them to get out of there.

Later, when this was over, she'd try to come to terms with the fact that the second baby was real. That she'd delivered twins. But right now, she had to focus on keeping Kade and her alive.

"You can have the backups," Bree told the shooter. She latched onto Kade and inched toward the window. "And we don't know who you are. There's no reason for you to kill us."

"Oh, there's a reason." And that's all the person said for several moments. "You both know too much. Especially you, Bree. You're too big of a risk because I have no idea what you might have overheard when Kirk was holding you. You might know who I am, and I can't risk you testifying against me."

Bree tried to figure out who was speaking. All of their suspects probably thought Kade and she knew *too much*. Especially since all their suspects were tied in some way or another to this clinic.

"I didn't overhear anything that would identify Kirk's boss," she explained, hoping the sound of her voice would cover Kade's and her movement toward the window.

"Can't take that chance," the shooter fired back.

He also fired another shot into the door.

"Oh, and if I were you, I wouldn't try to get out through the window—they're locked up tight and they have thick metal security bars. So, you might as well stop where you are. Well, unless you want his brother to die."

Oh, mercy.

Kade and she froze. The shooter must have a camera in place so that they were watching their every move.

"What the hell does my brother have to do with this?" Kade shouted.

"A lot actually. Before your cop brother arrived to put some of his men on the roof near here, I already had a gunman in place. In the catbird seat, you might say."

Kade cursed. "He could be lying," he whispered to Bree.

But it didn't sound like a lie. This person had had plenty of time to set all of this up.

"My hired gun has a rifle trained on your brother right now," the person added.

That didn't sound like a lie, either, and even if it was, it was too big a risk to take. Nate had come to help them, and she didn't want him dying.

Bree knew what she had to do. Now it was just a matter of convincing Kade to let her do it.

"I'm the threat to your identity," she shouted, levering herself up a little so that she could peer over the desk. "Not Kade. Let him go. So he can raise our daughters," Bree added so that it would remind Kade of what was at stake here.

If both of them died in this clinic, their twins would become orphans.

"You're not doing this," Kade immediately said, and he pulled her back down behind the desk.

The shooter laughed. "I'm not looking for a sacrificial lamb. I'm afraid both of you have to die."

Her stomach twisted, but Bree wasn't about to give up. There had to be some kind of argument she could use to get at least Kade out of this alive.

There was a sound. Some kind of movement at the end of the hall. And Bree tried to brace herself for the person to come closer.

Where Kade could shoot to kill.

"These are copies of the backups," she tried. "Not the originals. Those are in a safe place."

"Liar," the shooter answered.

Was it her imagination or did the person sound farther away than before?

"The backups can't be copied," the voice continued. "And I should know because it's a security check that I put in place. Didn't want anyone copying them to use them for blackmail."

"They're not coming closer," Kade whispered.

She'd been right about the moving away part. But why would the person do that?

Unless he or she was trying to escape?

But that didn't make sense, either. Kade and she had the backups.

"I'm afraid I have to say goodbye now." And footsteps followed that puzzling comment.

Was the person just leaving them there?

No, her gut told her that wouldn't happen and that something was terribly wrong.

Kade must have realized it, too, because he got to his feet and hurried to the door. He rammed his shoulder against it, but it didn't budge.

And then he cursed.

Bree stood, trying to figure out what had caused his reaction, and she spotted the tiny blinking red light on the wall. Except it wasn't just a light.

The blinks were numbers.

Ticking down.

Seven, six, five…

"It's a bomb!" Kade shouted.

He grabbed Bree and they started to run.

KADE HAD TO MAKE A split-second decision because a few seconds were all they had left.

The door behind them was locked. No way out there. It was the same with the windows. He could risk pulling Bree behind the desk, but he could see the fistful of explosives attached to the timing device. The reception area and the desk were going to take the brunt of the impact.

So, with his left hand vised around Bree's arm, he raced down that dark hall.

Yeah, it was a risk. The shooter could be waiting for them to do just that, but at the moment the bomb was a bigger risk, especially since the shooter had also made a run for it.

"Hurry!" Kade shouted to Bree, though she no doubt understood the urgency.

They raced down the hall, past the first two rooms that were nearest to the lobby, and he pulled her into the next door. He dived toward a desk, pulling her underneath it with him. Kade also put his body over hers.

The blast tore through the building.

The sound was deafening, and the blast sent debris slamming into the desk and a chunk of the wall slammed into Kade's back. He'd have a heck of a bruise, but Bree was tucked safely beneath him.

He got his gun ready, in case he had to shoot their way out of there, but the sound made him realize they had bigger things to worry about than the shooter.

The ceiling groaned, threatening to give way.

"Run!" Bree shouted.

She fought to get up, just as Kade fought to get the debris off him. They finally made it to their feet and raced out of the room. What was left of it, anyway. It was the same for the hall. Walls had collapsed, and there was junk and rubble everywhere.

Bree hurdled over some of the mess and continued down the hall. Cursing, Kade caught up with her, and shoved her behind him. Of course, that might not be any safer, what with the ceiling about to come down, but there were other rooms ahead. An exit, too. And he didn't want that shooter jumping out from the shadows.

After all, Kade still had the backups.

Maybe the guy thought the blast would destroy them, along with Bree and him. Especially Bree, since the bozo clearly thought she was the biggest threat. Still, this could be all part of some warped plan to get them out and into the open so he could gun them down.

Behind them, another chunk of the ceiling fell. It

slammed into the tile floor and sent a new spray of debris their way. They kept on running until they reached the back exit. Kade hit the handle to open it.

Hell.

It was locked.

He cursed, grabbed Bree again and ducked into the room to their left. He couldn't be sure, but he thought this would lead them to the quarters where the infertile couples stayed. As Bree and he had done. There were more exits back in that area. Maybe, just maybe, not all of them would be locked.

His phone buzzed, and since Bree was still holding it, she pressed the button to put the call on speaker.

"Are you okay?" the person asked.

Not the shooter. It was Nate.

"Barely," Kade answered. "Did you see anyone leave the building?"

"No."

Kade cursed again and kept watch around them. "Bree and I are trying to make our way to an east side exit."

"Good. My men and I are converging on the building now."

Kade wanted to ask about the baby, how she was doing after being dropped off at the hospital, but it would have to wait. Right now, he had to get Bree out of there. Bree closed the phone and they started running as fast as they could.

Her breath was gusting. His, too. They meandered their way through the maze of rooms and furniture until they came to another hall. There were more windows in this part of the building. Good thing because it allowed him to see.

There was a door ahead.

"Stay behind me," Kade reminded her once again. He lifted his gun and made a beeline to the door.

They were still a good ten feet away when the second blast ripped through the hall.

Chapter Seventeen

Bree didn't have time to get down. The blast came right at them, and she felt herself flying backward. Everything seemed in slow motion but fast, too.

Her back collided with the wall.

Kade hit the concrete block wall beside her, and despite the bone-jarring impact, he managed to hang on to his gun. He also yanked her to her feet. Kade didn't have to warn her that they had to get out of there.

She knew.

Because there had already been two explosions, and that meant there could be another.

So far Kade and she had either gotten lucky or this was all some kind of elaborate trap.

"This way," Kade said, and he led her away from the part of the hall where the door had once been. It was now just a heap of rubble—a mix of concrete, wood and metal—and it was dangerous to try to get through it.

They hurried in the other direction, back through the rooms where Kade and she had stayed nearly a year ago when they were undercover.

Each step spiked her heartbeat and tightened the knot in her stomach. Because each step could lead them straight into another explosion. For that matter, the entire place could be rigged to go up.

Kade and she made their way into another hall, one with windows. And it was the thin white moonlight stabbing its way through the glass that allowed Bree to see the movement just ahead of them.

Kade pulled her into the room.

Just as a shot zinged through the air.

There was another jolt to her body when Kade and she landed on the floor. Another shot, too. But it slammed into the doorjamb and thankfully not them.

Despite the hard fall, Kade got her out of the doorway, and they scrambled to the far side of the room.

She glanced around. More windows, all with security bars, and there were two doors, feeding off in both directions. The doors were closed, but that didn't mean someone couldn't be waiting on the other side.

Since she no longer had a gun, Bree grabbed the first thing she could reach—a metal wire wastebasket. It wasn't much of a weapon, but if she got close enough, she could use it to bash someone.

Another shot.

This one also took a chunk out of the doorjamb.

As unnerving at those shots were, it did give Bree some good news. Well, temporary good news, anyway. There likely wasn't about to be another explosion in this area. Not with their assailant so close.

Close enough to gun them down.

"You're like cats with nine lives!" the person shouted, still using the voice scrambler. "You should have been dead by now."

Yes, Bree was painfully aware of that. And so was her body. She was aching and stinging from all the cuts, nicks and bruises. Beside her, Kade was no doubt feeling the same.

"Why don't you come in here and try to finish the job?" Kade shouted back.

Bree prayed the guy would take Kade up on the offer. Because Kade was still armed. But she didn't hear any movement in the hall or outside the building.

Were Nate and the other officers there, waiting to respond?

She hoped so because Bree didn't want this monster to escape. If that happened, the danger would start all over again. The threats to Kade and her would hang over their heads. The heads of their babies, too.

That couldn't happen.

This had to end now, tonight.

"Are you too scared to face us?" Bree yelled. Yeah, it might be a stupid move to goad their assailant, but it could work.

Maybe.

"Not scared. And I'm not stupid, either. This can only end one way—with your deaths."

"Or yours!" Bree fired back.

Kade nodded, motioned for her to keep it up, and while he kept low, he began to inch toward the hall door.

"You know, I think I do remember some things Tim Kirk said," Bree continued, keeping her voice loud to cover Kade's movement. "He wasn't very good at keeping secrets, was he?"

Silence.

Kade stopped. Waited.

"All right," their assailant finally said. "If Kirk told secrets, then who am I?" The person didn't wait for her to answer. "You don't know. You can only guess. And guessing won't help you or Agent Ryland."

Kade moved closer to the door but crouched down so that he was practically on the floor.

"What if it's not a guess?" Bree lied. "What if I've already left a sworn statement with the district attorney? Think about it—I wouldn't have risked coming here if I didn't have an ace in the hole."

She nearly choked on those words, the same ones that Kirk had used to describe her child. Maybe their attacker would recognize them and panic. Mercy, did she want panic. Maybe then the person would make a mistake, and Kade could get off that shot.

"Well?" Bree called out when she didn't get an answer. "Should I call the district attorney and tell him to release my statement?"

She waited, her heart in her throat.

Kade waited, too, his attention fastened on the hall and doorway.

Bree was so focused on what she could say to draw out this monster that she barely heard the sound. Not from the hall or the doorway.

But from behind her.

She turned and saw the shadowy figure in the now-open doorway on the right side of the room.

Oh, God.

The person lifted his arm, ready to fire. Not at her. But at Kade.

Bree didn't think. She dropped the trash can and dived at the person who was about to shoot Kade.

KADE WHIRLED AROUND just in time to see Bree launch herself at the gunman. And there was no mistaking that this was a gunman because Kade spotted the guy's weapon.

He also saw that weapon ram into Bree when she collided with their attacker. But it wasn't just the collision and the gun that latched onto his attention.

Kade's heart went to his knees when the sound of the bullet tore through the room.

"Bree!" Kade heard himself yell.

She had to be all right. If this SOB had shot her... but he couldn't go there. Couldn't bear to think of what might be. He just ran toward her.

And then he had to come to a quick stop.

Their attacker hooked an arm around Bree's throat and snapped her toward him. In the same motion, the person jammed a gun against Bree's head.

Now that Kade's eyes had adjusted to the darkness, he had no trouble seeing the stark fear on her face. Her eyes were wide, and her chest was pumping for air.

"Run!" she told Kade.

But the person ground the barrel of the gun into her temple. "If you run, she dies right now," her captor warned. "Drop your gun and give me the backups."

Kade tried to give Bree a steadying look, and then his gaze went behind her to the figure wearing the dark clothes and black ski mask. Kade also didn't miss the object in the gunman's left hand. But he or she didn't hold on to it for long.

It clattered to the floor.

The voice scrambler, Kade realized.

Their attacker had dropped it, no doubt so that both hands could be used to contain Bree. And it was working. Bree couldn't move without the risk of being either choked or shot.

"I said drop your gun and give me the backups," the man repeated.

And it was a man all right. Kade knew that now that the scrambler was no longer being used. It was a man whose voice Kade recognized.

Anthony.

So, they had the identity of the person who'd made their lives a living hell and had endangered not just them but their newborn daughters.

The anger slammed through Kade, but he tried to tamp it down because he had to figure out a way to get that gun away from Bree's head. He wasn't sure Anthony was capable of cold-blooded, close-contact murder, but considering everything else he'd likely done, it was a risk that Kade couldn't take.

"Why are you doing this, Anthony?" Bree asked, but she kept her attention fastened on Kade. Her left eyebrow was slightly cocked as if asking what she should do.

Kade didn't have an answer to that yet.

"You know why I'm doing this," Anthony assured her.

Kade heard it, but the words hardly registered. That's because he got a better look at the grip Anthony had on the gun. Oh, mercy. Anthony's hand was shaking. Not good. He was probably scared spitless despite the cocky demeanor he'd had earlier, and Kade knew from experience that scared people usually made bad decisions in situations like these.

"Put down the gun." Kade tried to keep calm. Normally, it would be a piece of cake. All those years of training and experience had taught him to disguise the fear he felt crawling through him. But this wasn't normal. Bree was on the other end of that gun.

"You don't want murder added to the list of charges," Kade pressed.

"No." And that's all Anthony said for several moments. "But I'll be charged with murder and other things if the cops see the surveillance backups."

Hell. So, that's what was on them. *Murder*. Kade figured it was bad if Anthony was willing to go through all of this to get the backups, but he'd hoped for some lesser charges. Murder meant Anthony had no way out.

This was not going to end well.

"I didn't know my father and Coop had set up the extra cameras," Anthony said, his voice shaking. "And I did some things."

Bree pulled in a hard breath, and Kade knew she'd come to the same conclusion as he had. Anthony couldn't let them out of there alive, not with those backups that could get him the death penalty.

He was a desperate man.

But Kade was even more desperate.

"I didn't know about the backups at first," Anthony went on. "I thought you and Bree were the only two people who could send me to jail."

"So you kidnapped me," Bree provided. She glanced around as if looking for a way to escape. Kade hoped she wouldn't try until he had a better shot. At the moment, he had no shot at all.

"The kidnapping worked." Anthony paused again. "Until Jamie decided to do something stupid like leaving the baby at the hospital and letting you escape." He said the woman's name like venom. "Jamie's dead now. I don't have to worry about her or her stupidity anymore."

Hell. That was not what Kade wanted to hear. Yet another confession to murder to go along with the ones on the surveillance backups.

"The cops are outside," Kade reminded him just in case Anthony had forgotten that he wasn't just going to shoot and stroll out of here.

"Yes, and so is the gunman I hired."

There was an edge in Anthony's voice. Not the edge of someone who was a hundred percent confident in this plan. So Kade decided to see if he could push a button or two.

"You mean the incompetent gunman who was supposed to kill Jamie in the park?" Kade asked.

Anthony stammered out a few syllables before he managed some full-blown profanity. Clearly the gunman was a button, and Kade had indeed managed to push it. Now he could only hope that it didn't put Bree in more danger. Kade needed Anthony distracted, not just fuming mad.

Anthony ripped off his ski mask. "Yes! That's the idiot. But he won't fail me this time. He knows it'll cost him his life if he doesn't succeed."

Kade made an *I-doubt-that* sound in his throat.

Another button push. Every muscle in Anthony's face tightened. "Give me the backups," he demanded. "And put down that gun. If I have to tell you again, you're a dead man."

Despite the *dead man* warning, Kade didn't move until he saw Antony's hand tense. He was going to pull the trigger if Kade didn't do something fast.

"Here's the gun," Kade said. He stooped down and eased it onto the floor.

Kade looked at Bree, just a split-second glance, so that she'd know he was about to try to get them out of this, and she gave a slight nod.

"Now, I want the backups," Anthony ordered.

When he was still in a crouched position, Kade reached into his shirt. But he didn't get the backups. It was now or never. He said a quick prayer and launched himself at Anthony.

Kade rammed into the man before Anthony could pull the trigger. That was the good news. But the bad news was that Bree was still in danger.

Between them.

Where Anthony could kill her.

Anthony no longer had the gun aimed at her head, but he wasn't ready to surrender. Far from it.

Kade tried to shove Bree to the side, but Anthony held on to her, choking her with the crook of his arm. She clawed at his arm while Kade caught the man's shooting hand and bashed it against the floor.

Anthony cursed, but he still didn't stop fighting.

Neither did Bree or Kade. Bree rammed her elbow against Anthony's stomach, and he sputtered out a cough.

It was the break that Kade needed.

For just that split second, Anthony was distracted while he tried to catch his breath. Kade shoved Bree away from the man, and he brought down his fist into Anthony's jaw. His head flopped back.

And he dropped the gun.

Bree hurried to pick it up, and she put it right to Anthony's head.

"Give me a reason to kill you," she said. "Any reason will do."

Maybe she was bluffing, but after everything Anthony had put her through, maybe not.

Either way, Anthony believed her. He stopped struggling and his hands dropped limply by his sides.

Chapter Eighteen

"Can you drive any faster?" Kade asked his brother Nate.

It was exactly the question Bree had wanted to ask. She was more than grateful that Nate had stepped up to rush them to the Silver Creek hospital, but Bree wanted an emphasis on the *rush* part.

It was torture waiting to see their other daughter.

"I could drive faster," Nate drawled. "But I'd rather get there in one piece. Well, what's left of one piece. You do know you're both bleeding, right?"

Bree swiped at her lip again with the back of her hand. Yep. Still bleeding. She dabbed at the cut on Kade's forehead. She hated seeing the injuries there on his otherwise drop-dead gorgeous face, but the injuries were superficial and could wait. The baby couldn't. Well, she could, but Bree thought she might burst if she couldn't see her and make sure she was all right.

Nate's phone buzzed, and he answered it while he took the final turn to Silver Creek. The seconds and miles were just crawling by, even though it had only been twenty minutes or so since they'd left the Fulbright Clinic. When she'd looked back in the rearview mirror at the place, the SAPD officers had been stuffing a handcuffed Anthony McClendon into a patrol car.

Bree hoped he'd rot in jail.

It wasn't a forgive-and-forget sort of attitude to have, but she never wanted the man near her, Kade or their children again. Anthony was slime and had done everything in his power to destroy them.

Thank God, he hadn't succeeded.

"You're still bleeding," Kade let her know when she made another unsuccessful swipe at her mouth. He caught her chin, turned her head to face him and touched his fingers to her lip. "Does it hurt?"

She shook her head. There was probably pain, but she couldn't feel it right now. In fact, Bree couldn't feel much physically, only the concern she still had for Kade and their daughters.

"Does that hurt?" She glanced up at the bump and cut on his forehead.

"No." He kept his fingers on her mouth and his gaze connected with hers. He replaced his fingers with his lips and kissed her gently.

It stung a little, but Bree didn't care. The kiss warmed her and took away some of the ice that Anthony had put there. In fact, it even took some of the edge off her impatience and reminded her of something very important.

She smiled. "We won." With all the turmoil going on inside her and the hatred she had for Anthony, Bree hadn't had time to put things in perspective. Leave it to Kade's kiss to do exactly that. They'd won, and the prize was huge.

Kade smiled, too. "Yeah. And we're the parents of twin girls."

For just a moment that terrified her as she imagined trying to be a mother to both of them. *Twins.* Before Leah, she'd never even held a baby, and now she had two.

"You look like you're about to panic," Kade whispered.

Bree chuckled and winced as it pinched at her busted lip. "So do you."

He nodded. "Maybe a little. I'm thinking about how we can get through those 2:00 a.m. feedings with both of them."

"And the diapers." But suddenly that didn't seem so bad. It even seemed doable. Maybe because Kade had said *we*.

"You mean that?" Bree asked before she could stop herself.

He flexed his eyebrows and made a face from the tug it no doubt gave that knot on his head. "Mean what?"

Bree froze for a moment and considered, well, everything. Kade and she had known each other such a short time, and most of that time they'd been working undercover or getting shot at. Hardly the foundation for a relationship.

But somehow they'd managed just that—a relationship.

Of sorts.

Bree was still a little hazy on Kade's thoughts and feelings. However, hers were clearer now. Maybe because they'd come so close to dying tonight. That had certainly put things in perspective. So, she decided to go for it. She would question that *we*, and then she would tell him it was what she wanted, too. She wanted them to do this family thing together.

Whatever that entailed.

But before Bree could answer, Nate ended his call and looked back at them.

"They found Jamie's body," he let them know.

And just like that, Bree was pulled back into the

nightmarish memories that Anthony had given Kade and her. Enough nightmares to last a lifetime or two, and now Anthony had another victim—Jamie. Even though Bree didn't care for the woman's criminal activity, Jamie had tried to help her, and now she was dead because of it.

"Anthony confessed that he killed her," Kade explained.

"Yes, he confessed it to my men, too," Nate verified. "He'll be booked on capital murder changes, and he's not just looking at jail time but the death penalty."

Bree remembered something else he'd said. "Anthony murdered someone else. It's on the surveillance backups."

Nate nodded. "Kade gave them back to us, and we'll give them a thorough review. Trust me, we'll add any and all charges to make sure Anthony is never back on the streets again. His father, too, because Anthony said there'd be plenty enough on the backups to bring charges against Hector McClendon."

Good. After everything that had gone on at the clinic, McClendon certainly deserved to be punished.

Kade glanced at her first before looking at his brother. "Did Anthony say anything about Coop?"

"No, and from the sound of it, Anthony is blabbing about anyone who can be arrested for anything. A misery loves company sort of thing."

Bree felt the relief wash over her. So, her former boss and mentor wasn't dirty. That was something, at least, even though Kade's and her lives would never be the same.

And part of that wasn't all bad.

In fact, part of it was nothing short of a miracle. She might never have become a parent by choice, and it broke her heart to think of all the things she would have missed. She couldn't imagine life without Kade and the babies.

Except she might not have Kade.

And she didn't know what she would do if that happened.

Bree saw the Silver Creek hospital just ahead and knew her baby was inside. Just like that, the jitters and impatience returned with a vengeance. Her breath started to pound, her mouth went dry. She felt a little queasy.

And then Kade caught her hand in his and gave it a gentle squeeze. That squeeze was a reminder that she didn't want to do this alone.

No, that wasn't it.

She wanted to do this with Kade.

Bree looked at him to ask him about that *we* remark, but again she lost her chance when Nate stopped directly in front of the hospital doors. A discussion that would have to wait.

Kade and she barreled out, leaving Nate behind to park his SUV, and they rushed through the automatic doors. Her heart was in her throat by the time they made it to the lobby.

And then Bree saw them.

Mason was standing near the reception desk, and he was holding a baby who did indeed look exactly like Leah.

Kade's and her baby.

Bree knew that after just a glimpse.

The baby was crying, and Mason was trying to soothe her by rocking her. It wasn't working, and Mason looked more than a little uncomfortable with his baby-holding duties. Bree went to him, took the little girl and pulled her into her arms.

Yes, this child was theirs. Just holding her warmed every bit of Bree's heart.

Kade came closer, sliding his arm around both her and the baby. Leah's twin looked up at them as if trying to figure out if she was going to start crying again. She didn't. She just studied them.

Bree pulled back her blanket and studied her, too. Ten fingers, ten toes. There didn't appear to be a scratch on her, thank God.

"She's okay?" Bree asked Mason.

He nodded. "She's got a healthy set of lungs. And she peed on me." Mason frowned when he looked down at the wet spot on his shirt.

Bree smiled. Laughed. And then the tears came just as quickly. Her emotions were a mess right now, but the one thing she felt the most was the unconditional love. She pulled the baby closer and held on tight.

"It'll be okay," Kade whispered to her.

"Yes," Bree managed to say. "These are happy tears."

Kade smiled too. Kissed her, and then he kissed their daughter.

"The doc did a DNA test," Mason let them know. "But I don't think it's necessary."

"Neither do I," Kade agreed. "She's ours."

Behind them, the doors swished open, and because of the events of the night, Bree automatically pulled her daughter into a protective stance. Kade moved, too, to position himself in front of them.

But all their posturing wasn't necessary.

Grayson came through the doors, and he was carrying Leah in the crook of his arm. He stopped a moment, looking at the baby Bree was holding, and he smiled.

"Yeah, she's a Ryland all right." Grayson came closer and handed Leah to Kade.

"She's got a healthy set of lungs," Mason repeated in a mumble. He glanced at both babies. "Hope you don't expect me to babysit."

His tone was gruff, but Bree thought she saw the start of a smile. So this was what it felt like to be surrounded by family?

By love.

The *l*-word stopped her for a moment, and she looked up at Kade. No stop this time.

She was in love with him.

Bree wasn't sure why it'd taken her so long to come to that conclusion. It felt as if she'd loved him forever. Just like the babies.

Of course, that didn't mean he felt the same way about her. Yes, they had the twins, but that only meant they were parents. Not a couple in love. And it tore at her heart to realize she wanted it all, but she might not get it.

Kade might not love her.

"Why don't I get all you back to the ranch?" Grayson suggested. He gave the other twin's toes a jiggle. "What are you going to name her?"

"I've been calling her Mia," Mason volunteered and then looked uncomfortable with the admission. "Well, I had to call her something other than *kid,* and it rhymes with Leah."

Bree shrugged and looked up at Kade. He shrugged, too. "It works for me."

It worked for Bree, too.

So, they had Leah and Mia. The girls might hate the rhyming names when they got older, but they fit.

Everything about this moment fit.

Except for the person who came through the hospital doors.

Coop.

Everyone's attention went to him, and judging from Grayson's and Kade's scowls, they weren't any happier to see the man than she was. Bree wanted to spend this time with Kade and the girls. She definitely didn't want to go another round with her former boss.

"We were about to leave," Bree *greeted* him. And she hoped he understood there was nothing he had to say that she wanted to hear. She only wanted to leave.

Coop nodded. Glanced at the babies. There was no smile, only concern on his face. "I heard what happened, and I wanted to say how sorry I am."

There was no anger in his eyes or tone. The apology sounded heartfelt, and Bree was glad they were mending some fences, but her mind could hardly stay on the conversation.

"I came here to give you back your badge," Coop added. "I was wrong to put that kind of pressure on you."

"Yes, you were," Kade agreed.

Coop reached in his pocket and held out her badge.

Bree stared it a moment and then looked at each of her daughters. Then, at Kade. She had a decision to make and was surprised that it wasn't that hard to do.

"No, thanks," Bree said. And there wasn't a shred of doubt about this. "I can't go back to that life. It wouldn't give me much time for the girls."

Or Kade.

Coop's eyes widened. "You're serious?"

"Completely," she verified. "I want a job that'll keep me closer to Silver Creek."

Grayson shrugged. "I've got a deputy position open

in the Silver Creek sheriff's office. It's yours if you want it. After you've taken some maternity leave, that is."

Bree nodded and managed to whisper a thanks around the sudden lump in her throat. Later, she would tell him how much she appreciated that. The deputy position would keep her in law enforcement. And Silver Creek.

"But an FBI agent isn't just your job. It's who you are," Coop argued.

Bree looked him straight in the eye. "Not anymore. Goodbye, Coop."

Keeping a firm grip on the baby, Bree extended her hand for him to shake, but for a moment, she thought he might refuse. Finally, Coop accepted and shook her hand. He also hugged her.

"Have a good life, Bree." And he turned and walked back out.

Bree expected to feel some kind of pangs of… whatever, but she didn't. She looked up at Kade and didn't feel pangs there, either.

She just saw the man she loved.

Mason cleared his throat. "I'll bring the car to the door."

Grayson gave both Kade and her a look, too. "I'll help."

Clearly, Kade's brothers realized that this might become a private discussion. The *we* talk.

But Kade didn't exactly launch into a discussion. He leaned in and kissed her. Not a peck. A real kiss. It lasted so long that a nurse passing by cleared her throat.

Kade broke the intimate contact with a smile on his face. "No regrets about giving up your badge?"

"Not a one." And this was a do-or-die moment. A moment Bree couldn't let slip away again. "The only thing I regret is not telling you that I'm in love with you."

Kade froze in midkiss, and he eased back so they were eye to eye. Between them, both babies were wide-awake and playing footsies with each other. They both had their eyes fastened to their parents.

Then, Kade smiled. Really smiled. "Good." He hooked his left arm around Bree's waist and got as close to her as he could. "Because I'm in love with you, too."

Bree's breath vanished, and the relief she felt nearly brought her to her knees.

Kade was right there to catch her.

And kiss her.

This one melted her.

"Of course, that I-love-you comes with a marriage proposal," Kade said.

The melting turned to heat, and Bree wished they were somewhere private so she could haul him off to bed. Well, after the babies were asleep, anyway. She wasn't sure how they would work such things into their crazy schedule, but with this fierce attraction, they'd find a way.

Kade took Bree by her free hand. "Will you marry me, Bree?"

She didn't even have to think of her answer. "In a heartbeat."

Kade let out a whoop that startled both babies and had several members of the hospital staff staring at them. Bree ignored the stares. Kissed both babies.

And then she kissed Kade.

She didn't stop until the babies' kicking became an issue, but Bree ended the kiss knowing there would be plenty of others in her future.

"Want to go home?" Kade asked.

Another easy answer. "Yes," she whispered.

Going home with Kade and their daughters was exactly what Bree wanted.

* * * * *

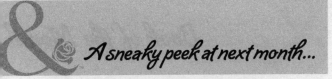

A sneaky peek at next month...

INTRIGUE...

BREATHTAKING ROMANTIC SUSPENSE

My wish list for next month's titles...

In stores from 15th February 2013:

❏ Gage – Delores Fossen

& Mason – Delores Fossen

❏ Alpha One – Cynthia Eden

& Internal Affairs – Alana Matthews

❏ O'Halloran's Lady – Fiona Brand

& Seduction Under Fire – Melissa Cutler

❏ Colton's Deep Cover – Elle Kennedy

Available at WHSmith, Tesco, Asda, Eason, Amazon and Apple

Just can't wait?

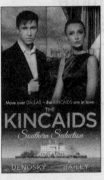

MILLS & BOON® Book Club   *2 Free Books!*

Get your free books now at
www.millsandboon.co.uk/freebookoffer

Or fill in the form below and post it back to us

THE MILLS & BOON® BOOK CLUB™—HERE'S HOW IT WORKS: Accepting your free books places you under no obligation to buy anything. You may keep the books and return the despatch note marked 'Cancel'. If we do not hear from you, about a month later we'll send you 5 brand-new stories from the Intrigue series, including two 2-in-1 books priced at £5.49 each and a single book priced at £3.49*. There is no extra charge for post and packaging. You may cancel at any time, otherwise we will send you 5 stories a month which you may purchase or return to us—the choice is yours. *Terms and prices subject to change without notice. Offer valid in UK only. Applicants must be 18 or over. Offer expires 31st July 2013. **For full terms and conditions, please go to www.millsandboon.co.uk/freebookoffer**

Mrs/Miss/Ms/Mr (please circle)
_____

First Name
_____

Surname
_____

Address
_____

_____

_____ Postcode

E-mail
_____

Send this completed page to: Mills & Boon Book Club, Free Book Offer, FREEPOST NAT 10298, Richmond, Surrey, TW9 1BR

Find out more at
www.millsandboon.co.uk/freebookoffer

Visit us Online

0113/I3XEb

The World of Mills & Boon®

There's a Mills & Boon® series that's perfect for you. We publish ten series and, with new titles every month, you never have to wait long for your favourite to come along.

Blaze®

Scorching hot, sexy reads
4 new stories every month

By Request

Relive the romance with the best of the best
9 new stories every month

Cherish™

Romance to melt the heart every time
12 new stories every month

Desire™

Passionate and dramatic love stories
8 new stories every month